Book Two of The Malloreon

KING OF THE MURGOS

By David Eddings
Published by Ballantine Books

THE BELGARIAD
Book One: *Pawn of Prophecy*
Book Two: *Queen of Sorcery*
Book Three: *Magician's Gambit*
Book Four: *Castle of Wizardry*
Book Five: *Enchanters' End Game*

THE MALLOREON
Book One: *Guardians of the West*
Book Two: *King of the Murgos*
Book Three: *Demon Lord of Karanda**
Book Four: *Sorceress of Darshiva**
Book Five: *The Seeress of Kell**

HIGH HUNT

**Forthcoming*

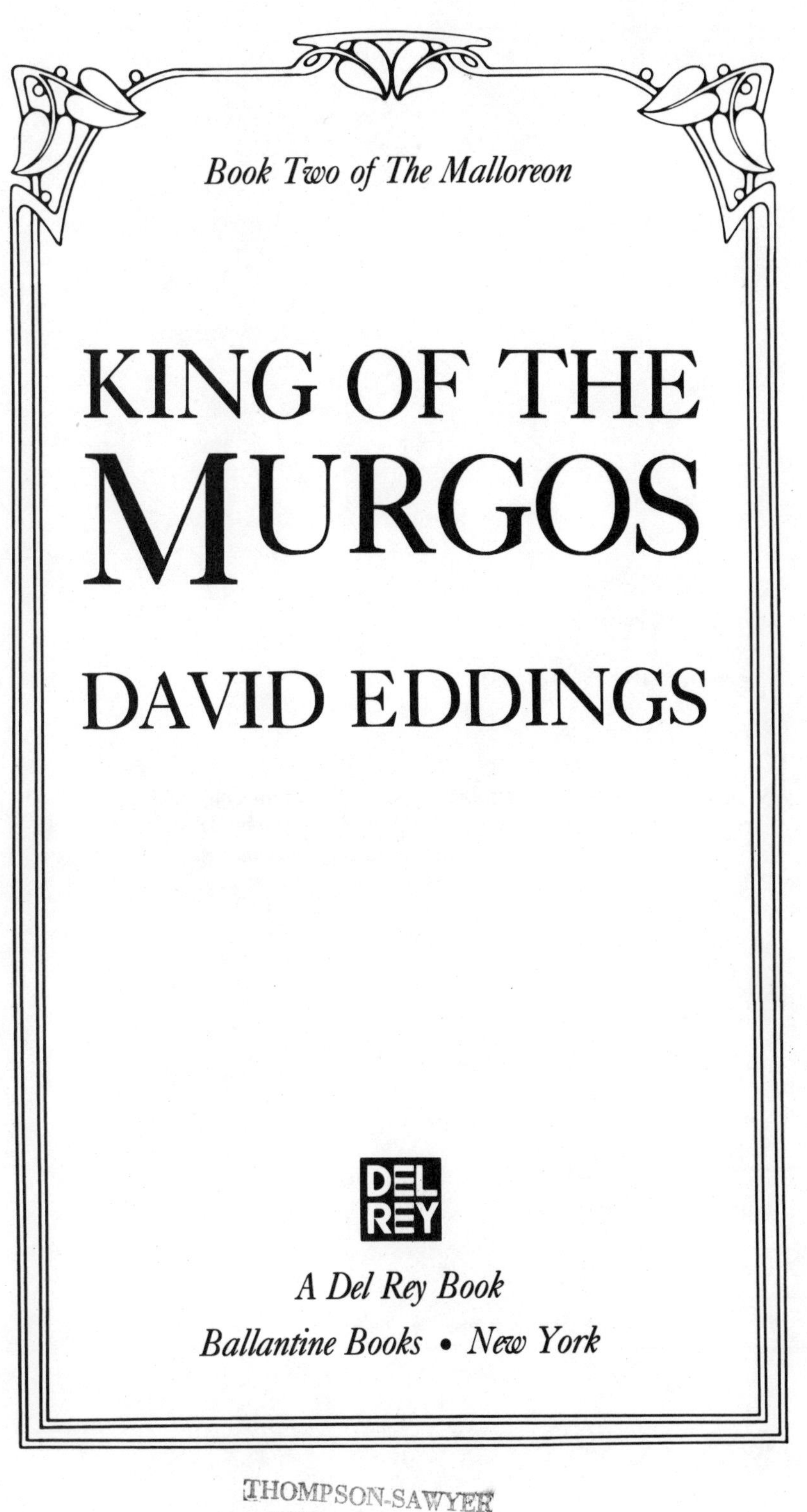

Book Two of The Malloreon

KING OF THE MURGOS

DAVID EDDINGS

DEL REY

A Del Rey Book

Ballantine Books • New York

A Del Rey Book
Published by Ballantine Books

Maps by Shelly Shapiro

 Published in the United States of America by Ballantine Books, a division of Random House, Inc., New York, and simultaneously in Canada by Random House of Canada Limited, Toronto.

Library of Congress Cataloging-in-Publication Data

Eddings, David.
King of the Murgos.

(The Malloreon / David Eddings; bk. 2)
"A Del Rey book."
I. Title. II. Series: Eddings, David.
Malloreon; bk. 1.
PS3555.D38K5 1988 813'.54 87-19473
ISBN 0-345-33002-1

Design by Holly Johnson

Manufactured in the United States of America

10 9 8 7 6 5 4 3 2

For Den, for reasons he will understand—
—and for our dear Janie,
just for being the way she is.

At this time I would like to express my indebtedness to my wife, Leigh Eddings, for her support, her contributions, and her wholehearted collaboration in this ongoing story. Without her help, none of this would have been possible.

I would also like to take this opportunity to thank my editor, Lester del Rey, for his patience and forbearance, as well as for contributions too numerous to mention.

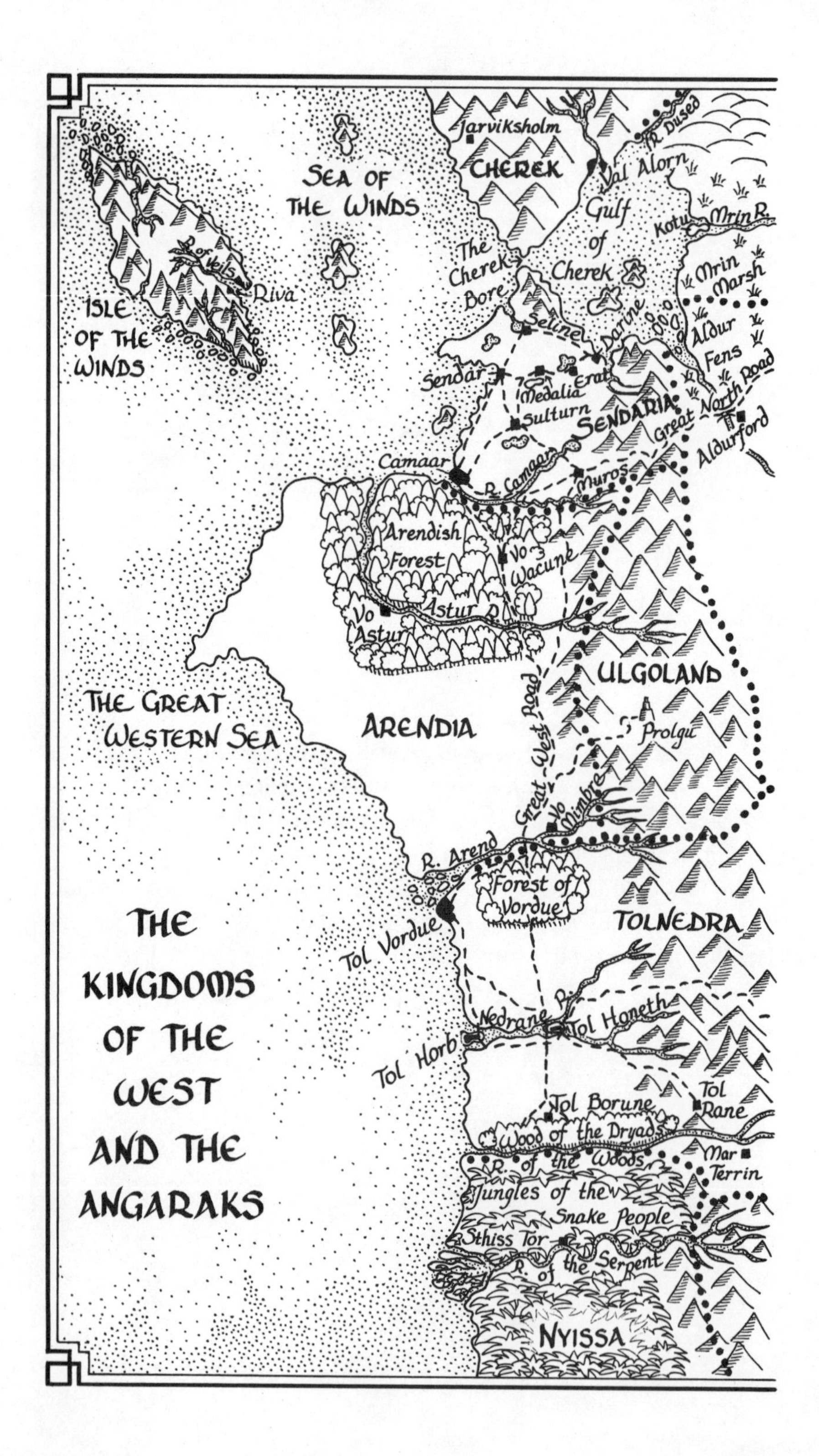

THE KINGDOMS OF THE WEST AND THE ANGARAKS
Sea of the Winds
Isle of the Winds
Riva
Jarviksholm
Cherek
Val Alorn
R. Dused
Gulf of Cherek
Kotu
Mrin R.
Mrin Marsh
Aldur Fens
The Cherek Bore
Seline
Darine
Sendar
Medalia
Erat
Sulturn
Sendaria
Great North Road
Aldurford
Camaar
R. Camaar
Muros
Arendish Forest
Vo Wacune
Vo Astur
Astur R.
Ulgoland
Prolgu
The Great Western Sea
Arendia
Great West Road
Vo Mimbre
R. Arend
Forest of Vordue
Tol Vordue
Tolnedra
Nedrane R.
Tol Honeth
Tol Horb
Tol Borune
Tol Rane
Wood of the Dryads
Mar Terrin
R. of the Woods
Jungles of the Snake People
Sthiss Tor
R. of the Serpent
Nyissa

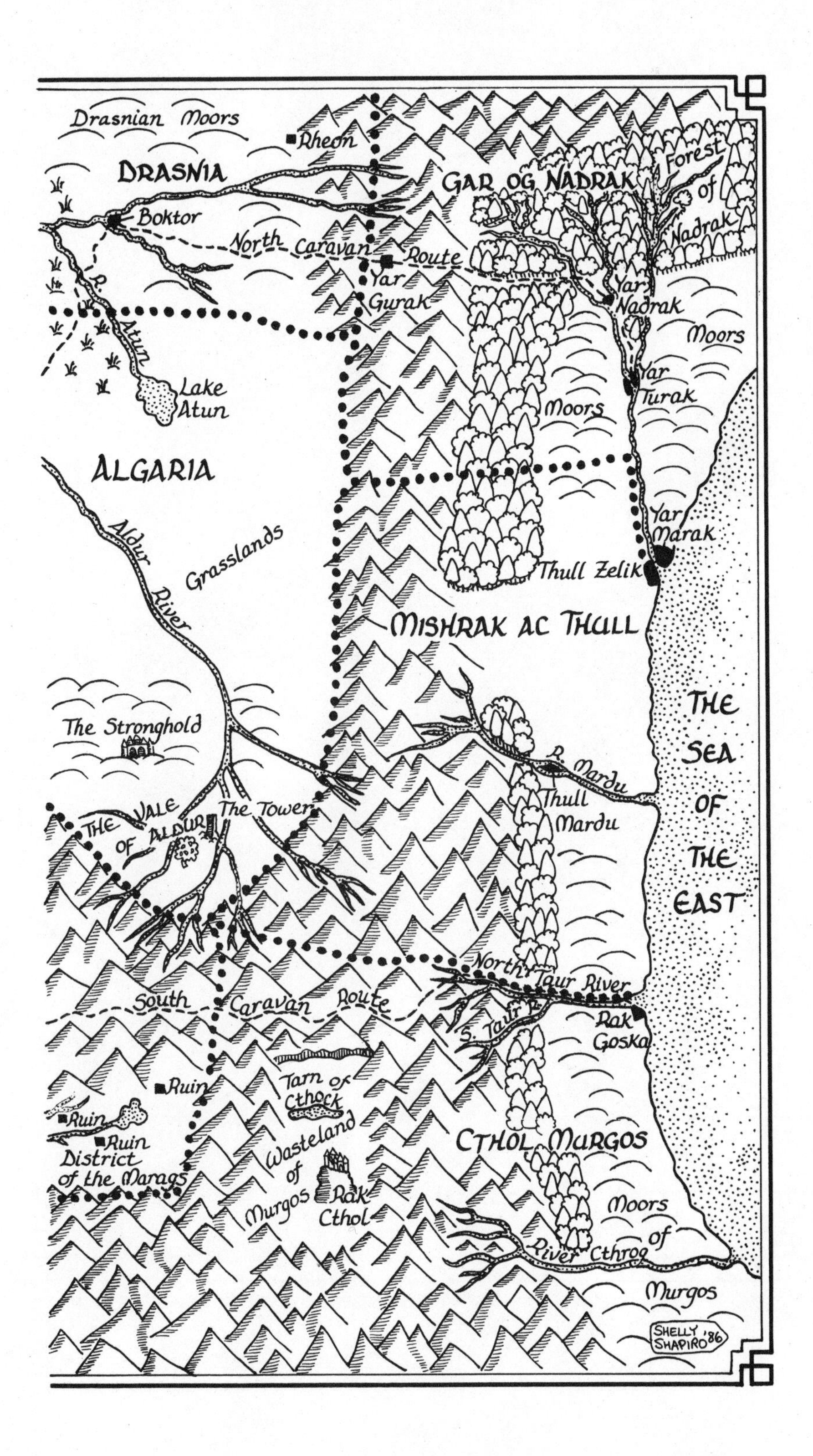
Drasnian Moors
Rheon
DRASNIA
Boktor
North Caravan Route
Yar Gurak
R. Atun
Lake Atun
GAR OG NADRAK
Forest of Nadrak
Yar Nadrak
Moors
Yar Turak
Moors
ALGARIA
Aldur River
Grasslands
Yar Marak
Thull Zelik
MISHRAK AC THULL
THE SEA OF THE EAST
The Stronghold
R. Mardu
Thull Mardu
THE VALE OF ALDUR
The Tower
North Taur River
South Caravan Route
S. Taur R.
Rak Goska
Ruin
Ruin
Ruin
Tarn of Cthock
District of the Marags
Wasteland of Murgos
Rak Cthol
CTHOL MURGOS
Moors of Murgos
River Cthrog
SHELLY SHAPIRO '86

Prologue

Being an account of how Belgarion's Son was stolen and how he learned the Abductor was that Zandramas against whom the puissant Orb of Aldur had warned.
—from *The Lives of Belgarion the Great* (Introduction, Vol. IV)

Now, as has been told, in the earliest of days the Gods created the world and filled it with all manner of beasts and fowls and plants. Men also they created, and each God chose from among the races of men those whom they would guide and over whom they would rule. The God Aldur, however, took none, choosing to live apart in his tower and study the creation which they had made.

But a time came when a hungry child arrived at Aldur's tower, and Aldur took the child in and taught him the Will and the Word, by which all power may be used, in the manner that men call sorcery. And when the boy showed promise, Aldur named him Belgarath and made him a disciple. Then in time others came, and Aldur taught them and made them also his disciples. Among these was a malformed child whom Aldur named Beldin.

There came a day when Aldur took up a stone and shaped it and he called it his Orb, for the stone had fallen from beyond the stars and was a seat of great power, a center for one of the two Destinies which had been in conflict for control of all creation since the beginning of days.

But the God Torak coveted the stone and stole it, for the Dark Destiny had claimed his soul for its agent. Then the men of Aloria, known as Alorns, met with Belgarath, who led Cherek Bear-shoulders and his three sons into the far East where Torak had built Cthol Mishrak, the City of Eternal Night. By stealth, they stole back the Orb and returned with it.

With the counsel of the Gods, Belgarath divided Aloria into the kingdoms of Cherek, Drasnia, Algaria, and Riva, naming each for one who had accompanied him. And to Riva Iron-grip, who was to rule over the Isle of the Winds, he gave the keeping of the Orb, which Riva placed on the pommel of the great sword that he hung upon the wall of the Hall of the Rivan King, behind his throne.

Then Belgarath sought his home, but found tragedy awaiting him. His beloved wife Poledra had passed from the world of the living in giving birth to twin girls. In time, he sent Beldaran, the fairer of these, to be a wife to Riva Iron-grip to found the line of Rivan kings. His other daughter, Polgara, he kept with him, since her dark hair bore a single lock of white, the mark of a sorceress.

Guarded by the power of the Orb, all went well with the West for thousands of years. Then, on an evil day, King Gorek of Riva and his sons and sons' sons were slain by foul treachery. One child escaped, however, to be henceforth guarded in secret by Belgarath and Polgara. On the Isle, the Rivan Warder, Brand, sorrowfully took over the authority of his slain lord, and his sons continued to guard Aldur's Orb and all were known as Brand.

But there came a time when Zedar the Apostate found a child of such innocence that he could touch the Orb without being destroyed by its fire. Thus Zedar stole the Orb and fled with it toward the place where his dread Master, Torak, lay hidden.

When Belgarath learned of this, he went up to the quiet farm in Sendaria where Polgara was rearing a boy named Garion, who was the last descendant of the Rivan line. Taking the boy with them, they set out after the Orb. After many perilous adventures, they found the child, whom they named Errand. And, with Errand bearing the Orb, they returned to set the Orb back upon the sword.

Then Garion, now named Belgarion for the powers of sorcery he had shown, learned of the Prophecy, which revealed that the time was at hand when he, as the Child of Light, must confront the evil God Torak, to kill or to be killed. Fearfully, he departed eastward for the City of Endless Night to meet his fate. But with the aid of the great sword that bore the Orb of Aldur, he prevailed and slew the God.

Thus Belgarion, descendant of Riva Iron-grip, was crowned King of Riva and Overlord of the West. He took to wife the Tolnedran Princess Ce'Nedra, while Polgara took the faithful smith Durnik as her husband, since the Gods had raised him from the dead and had given him the power of sorcery to be her equal. With Belgarath, she and Durnik left for the Vale of Aldur in Algaria, where they planned to rear the strange, gentle child Errand.

The years passed as Belgarion learned to be a husband to his young bride and began mastering his powers of sorcery and the power of his throne. There was peace in the West, but trouble stirred in the South, where Kal Zakath, Emperor of Mallorea, waged war upon the King of the Murgos. And

Belgarath, returning from a trip to Mallorea, reported dark rumors of a stone known as the Sardion. But what it might be, other than an object of fear, he could not say.

Then on a night when young Errand was visiting in the Citadel at Riva, he and Belgarion were awakened by the voice of the Prophecy within their minds and directed to the throne room. And there the blue Orb on the pommel of the sword turned angry red of a sudden and it spoke, saying, "*Beware Zandramas!*" But none could learn who or what Zandramas was.

Now, after years of waiting, Ce'Nedra found herself with child. But the fanatic followers of the Bear-cult were active again, crying that no Tolnedran should be Queen and that she must be set aside for one of the true blood of the Alorns.

When the Queen was great with child, she was set upon by an assassin in her bath and almost drowned. The assassin fled to the tower of the Citadel and from there threw herself to her death. But Prince Kheldar, the Drasnian adventurer who was also known as Silk, saw from her garments that she might be a follower of the cult. Belgarion was wroth, but he did not yet move to war.

Time passed, and Queen Ce'Nedra was delivered of a healthy male heir to the Throne of Riva. And great was the rejoicing from all the lands of the Alorns and beyond, and notables assembled at Riva to rejoice and celebrate this happy birth.

When all had departed and peace again descended upon the Citadel, Belgarion resumed his studies of the ancient Prophecy which men called the Mrin Codex. A strange blot had long troubled him, but now he found that he could read it in the light cast by the Orb. Thus he learned that the Dark Prophecy and his obligations as the Child of Light had not ended with the slaying of Torak. The Child of Dark was now Zandramas, whom he must meet in time to come "in the place which is no more."

His soul was heavy within him as he journeyed hastily to confer with his grandfather Belgarath in the Vale of Aldur.

But even as he was speaking with the old man, new words of ill were brought him by messenger. Assassins had penetrated the Citadel at night, and the faithful Rivan Warder, Brand, had been killed.

With Belgarath and his Aunt Polgara, Belgarion sped to Riva, where one assassin weakly clung to life. Prince Kheldar arrived and was able to identify the comatose assassin as a member of the Bear-cult. New evidence revealed that the cult was massing an army at Rheon in Drasnia and was building a fleet at Jarviksholm on the coast of Cherek.

Now King Belgarion declared war upon the Bear-cult. Upon the advice of the other Alorn monarchs, he moved first against the shipyards at Jarviksholm to prevent the threat of a hostile fleet in the Sea of the Winds. His attack was quick and savage. Jarviksholm was razed to the ground, and the half-built fleet was burned before a single keel touched water.

But victory turned to ashes when a message from Riva reached him. His infant son had been abducted.

Belgarion, Belgarath, and Polgara turned themselves into birds by sorcery and flew back to Riva in a single day. The city of Riva had already been searched house by house. But with the aid of the Orb, Belgarion was able to follow the trail of the abductors to the west coast of the Isle. There they came upon a band of Cherek cultists and fell upon them. One survived, and Polgara forced him to speak. He declared that the child had been stolen on the orders of Ulfgar, leader of the Bear-cult, whose headquarters were at Rheon in eastern Drasnia. Before Polgara could wrest further information from him, however, the cultist leaped from the top of the cliff upon which they stood and dashed himself to death on the rocks below.

Now the war turned to Rheon. Belgarion found his troops badly outnumbered and an ambush awaiting his advance toward the city. He was facing defeat when Prince Kheldar arrived with a force of Nadrak mercenaries to turn the tide of battle. Reinforced by the Nadraks, the Rivans besieged the city of Rheon.

Belgarion and Durnik combined their wills to weaken the walls of the city until the siege engines of Baron Mandorallen could bring them down. The Rivans and Nadraks poured into the city, led by Belgarion. The battle inside was savage, but the cultists were driven back and most of them were slaughtered. Then Belgarion and Durnik captured the cult leader, Ulfgar.

Though Belgarion had already learned that his son was not within the city, he hoped that close questioning might drag the child's whereabouts from Ulfgar. The cult leader stubbornly refused to answer; then, surprisingly, Errand drew the information directly from Ulfgar's mind.

While it became clear that Ulfgar had been responsible for the attempt on Ce'Nedra's life, he had played no part in the theft of the child. Indeed, his chief goal had been the death of Belgarion's son, preferably before its birth. He obviously knew nothing of the abduction, which did not at all suit his purpose.

Then the sorcerer Beldin joined them. He quickly recognized Ulfgar as Harakan, an underling of Torak's last living disciple Urvon. Harakan suddenly vanished, and Beldin sped in pursuit.

Messengers now arrived from Riva. Investigations following Belgarion's departure had discovered a shepherd in the hills who had seen a figure carrying what might have been a baby embark upon a ship of Nyissan design and sail southward.

Then Cyradis, a Seeress of Kell, sent a projection of herself to tell them more. The child, she claimed, had been taken by Zandramas, who had spun such a web of deceit to throw the blame upon Harakan that even the cult members who had been left behind to be discovered had believed what Polgara had extracted from the captive on the cliff of the Isle of the Winds.

Clearly, she said, the Child of Dark had stolen the baby for a purpose. That purpose was connected with the Sardion. Now they must pursue Zandramas. Beyond that she would not speak, except to identify those who must go with Belgarion. Then, leaving her huge, mute guide Toth behind to accompany them, she vanished.

Belgarion's heart sank within him as he realized that his son's abductor was now months ahead and that the trail had grown extremely dim. But he grimly gathered his companions to pursue Zandramas, even to the edge of the world or beyond, if need be.

Part One

THE SERPENT QUEEN

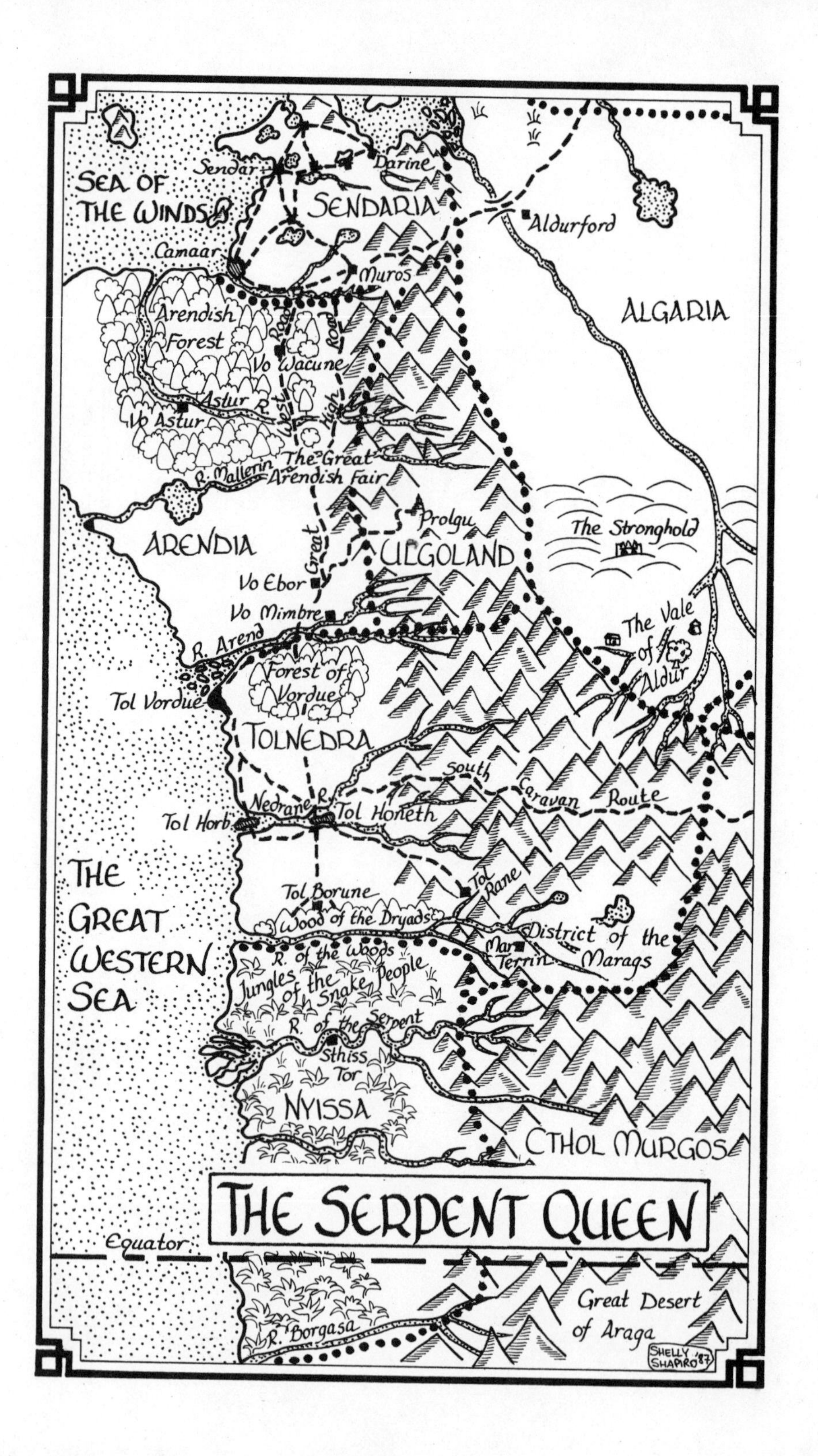
Sea of the Winds
Sendar
Darine
Sendaria
Aldurford
Camaar
Muros
Algaria
Arendish Forest
Vo Wacune
West Road
High Road
Astur R.
Vo Astur
R. Mallerin
The Great Arendish Fair
Prolgu
Great
The Stronghold
Arendia
Ulgoland
Vo Ebor
Vo Mimbre
The Vale of Aldur
R. Arend
Forest of Vordue
Tol Vordue
Tolnedra
South Caravan Route
Nedrane R.
Tol Honeth
Tol Horb
The Great Western Sea
Tol Rane
Tol Borune
Wood of the Dryads
District of the Marags
Mar Terrin
R. of the Woods
Jungles of the Snake People
R. of the Serpent
Sthiss Tor
Nyissa
Cthol Murgos
The Serpent Queen
Equator
Great Desert of Araga
R. Borgasa
Shelly Shapiro '87

CHAPTER ONE

Somewhere in the darkness, Garion could hear the crystalline tap of water dripping with a slow, monotonous regularity. The air around him was cool, smelling of rock and dampness overlaid with the musty odor of pallid white things that grow in the dark and flinch from the light. He found himself straining to catch all the myriad sounds that whispered through the dark caves of Ulgo—the moist trickle of water, the dusty slither of dislodged pebbles slowly running down a shallow incline, and the mournful sighing of air coming down from the surface through minute fissures in the rock.

Belgarath stopped and lifted the smoky torch that filled the passageway with flickering orange light and leaping shadows. "Wait here a moment," he said, and then he moved off down the murky gallery with his scuffed, mismatched boots shuffling along the uneven floor. The rest of them waited with the darkness pressing in all around them.

"I hate this," Silk muttered, half to himself. "I absolutely hate it."

They waited.

The ruddy flicker of Belgarath's torch reappeared at the far end of the gallery. "All right," he called. "It's this way."

Garion put his arm about Ce'Nedra's slender shoulders. A kind of deep silence had fallen over her during their ride south from Rheon as it had grown increasingly evident that their entire campaign against the Bear-cult in eastern Drasnia had done little more than give Zandramas a nearly insurmountable lead with the abducted Geran. The frustration that made Garion want to beat his fists against the rocks around him and howl in impotent fury had plunged Ce'Nedra into a profound depression instead, and now she stumbled through the dark caves of Ulgo, sunk in a kind of numb misery, neither knowing nor caring where the others led her. He turned his head to look back at Polgara, his face mirroring all his deep concern. The look she returned him was grave, but seemingly unperturbed. She parted the front of her blue cloak and moved her hands in the minute gestures of the Drasnian secret language. —*Be sure she stays warm*—she said. —*She's very susceptible to chills just now.*—

A half-dozen desperate questions sprang into Garion's mind; but with Ce'Nedra at his side with his arm about her shoulders, there was no way he could voice them.

—*It's important for you to stay calm, Garion*—Polgara's fingers told him. —*Don't let her know how concerned you are. I'm watching her, and I'll know what to do when the time comes.*—

Belgarath stopped again and stood tugging at one earlobe, looking dubiously down a dark passageway and then down another which branched off to the left.

"You're lost again, aren't you?" Silk accused him. The rat-faced little Drasnian had put aside his pearl-gray doublet and his jewels and gold chains and now wore an old brown tunic, shiny with age, a moth-eaten fur cloak and a shapeless, battered hat, once again submerging himself in one of his innumerable disguises.

"Of course I'm not lost," Belgarath retorted. "I just haven't pinpointed exactly where we are at the moment."

"Belgarath, that's what the word *lost* means."

"Nonsense. I think we go this way." He pointed down the left-hand passageway.

"You *think*?"

"Uh—Silk," Durnik the smith cautioned quietly, "you really ought to keep your voice down. That ceiling up there doesn't look all that stable to me, and sometimes a loud noise is all it takes to bring one of them down."

Silk froze, his eyes rolling apprehensively upward and sweat visibly standing out on his forehead. "Polgara," he whispered in a strangled tone, "make him stop that."

"Leave him alone, Durnik," she said calmly. "You know how he feels about caves."

"I just thought he ought to know, Pol," the smith explained. "Things *do* happen in caves."

"Polgara!" Silk's voice was agonized. "*Please!*"

"I'll go back and see how Errand and Toth are doing with the horses," Durnik said. He looked at the sweating little Drasnian. "Just try not to shout," he advised.

As they rounded a corner in the twisting gallery, the passageway opened out into a large cavern with a broad vein of quartz running across its ceiling. At some point, perhaps even miles away, the vein reached the surface, and refracted sunlight, shattered into its component elements by the facets of the quartz, spilled down into the cavern in dancing rainbows that flared and faded as they shifted across the sparkling surface of the small, shallow lake in the center of the cave. At the far end of the lake, a tiny waterfall tinkled endlessly from rock to rock to fill the cavern with its music.

"Ce'Nedra, look!" Garion urged.

"What?" She raised her head. "Oh, yes," she said indifferently, "very pretty." And she went back to her abstracted silence.

Garion gave Aunt Pol a helpless look.

"Father," Polgara said then, "I think it's just about lunch time. This seems like a good place to rest a bit and have a bite to eat."

"Pol, we're never going to get there if we stop every mile or two."

"Why do you always argue with me, father? Is it out of some obscure principle?"

He glowered at her for a moment, then turned away, muttering to himself.

Errand and Toth led the horses down to the shore of the crystal lake to water them. They were a strangely mismatched pair. Errand was a slight young man with blond, curly hair and he wore a simple brown peasant smock. Toth towered above him like a giant tree looming over a sapling. Although winter was coming on in the Kingdoms of the West, the huge mute still wore only sandals, a short kirtle belted at the waist, and an unbleached wool blanket drawn over one shoulder. His bare arms and legs were like tree trunks, and his muscles knotted and rippled whenever he moved. His nondescript brown hair was drawn straight back and tied at the nape of his neck with a short length of leather thong. Blind Cyradis had told them that this silent giant was to aid them in the search for Zandramas and Garion's stolen son, but so far Toth seemed content merely to follow them impassively, giving no hint that he even cared where they were going.

"Would you like to help me, Ce'Nedra?" Polgara asked pleasantly, unbuckling the straps on one of the packs.

Ce'Nedra, numb-faced and inattentive, walked slowly across the smooth stone floor of the cavern to stand mutely beside the pack horse.

"We'll need bread," Polgara said, rummaging through the pack as if unaware of the young woman's obvious abstraction. She took out several long, dark brown loaves of peasant bread and piled them like sticks of firewood in the little queen's arms. "And cheese, of course," she added, lifting out a wax-covered ball of Sendarian cheddar. She pursed her lips. "And perhaps a bit of the ham as well, wouldn't you say?"

"I suppose so," Ce'Nedra replied in an expressionless tone.

"Garion," Polgara went on, "would you lay this cloth on that flat rock over there?" She looked back at Ce'Nedra. "I hate to eat off an uncovered table, don't you?"

"Umm," Ce'Nedra replied.

The two of them carried the loaves of bread, the wax-coated cheese, and the ham to the improvised table. Polgara snapped her fingers and shook her head. "I forgot the knife. Would you get it for me?"

Ce'Nedra nodded and started back toward the pack horse.

"What's wrong with her, Aunt Pol?" Garion asked in a tense whisper.

"It's a form of melancholia, dear."

"Is it dangerous?"

"It is if it goes on for too long."

"Can you do anything? I mean, could you give her some kind of medicine or something?"

"I'd rather not do that unless I have to, Garion. Sometimes the medicines just mask the symptoms, and other problems start to crop up. Most of the time, it's best to let these things run their natural course."

"Aunt Pol, I can't stand to see her like this."

"You're going to have to endure it for a while, Garion. Just behave as if you weren't aware of the way she's acting. She's not quite ready to come out of it yet." She turned with a warm smile. "Ah, there it is," she said, taking the knife from Ce'Nedra. "Thank you, dear."

They all gathered around Polgara's makeshift table for their simple lunch. As he ate, Durnik the smith gazed thoughtfully at the small crystal lake. "I wonder if there could be any fish in there," he mused.

"No, dear," Polgara said.

"It *is* possible, Pol. If the lake's fed by streams from the surface, the fish could have been washed down here when they were minnows, and—"

"No, Durnik."

He sighed.

After lunch, they re-entered the endless, twisting galleries, once again following Belgarath's flickering torch. The hours limped by as they trudged mile after mile with the darkness pressing palpably in around them.

"How much farther do we have to go, Grandfather?" Garion asked, falling in beside the old man.

"It's hard to say exactly. Distances can be deceptive here in the caves."

"Have you got any idea at all about why we had to come here? I mean, is there anything in the Mrin Codex—or maybe the Darine—that talks about something that's supposed to happen here in Ulgo?"

"Not that I remember, no."

"You don't suppose we might have misunderstood, do you?"

"Our friend was pretty specific, Garion. He said that we have to stop at Prolgu on our way south, because something that has to happen is going to happen here."

"Can't it happen without us?" Garion demanded. "We're just floundering around here in these caves, and all the while Zandramas is getting farther and farther ahead of us with my son."

"What's that?" Errand asked suddenly from somewhere behind them. "I thought I heard something."

They stopped to listen. The guttering sound of Belgarath's torch suddenly sounded very loud as Garion strained his ears, trying to reach out into the darkness to capture any wayward sound. The slow drip of water echoed its soft tapping from somewhere in the dark, and the faint sigh of air coming down through the cracks and crevices in the rock provided a mournful accompaniment. Then, very faintly, Garion heard the sound of singing, of choral voices raised in the peculiarly discordant but deeply reverent hymn to UL that had echoed and re-echoed through these dim caverns for over five millennia.

"Ah, the Ulgos," Belgarath said with satisfaction. "We're almost to Prolgu. Now maybe we'll find out what it is that's supposed to happen here."

They went perhaps another mile along the passageway which rather suddenly became steeper, taking them deeper and deeper into the earth.

"*Yakk!*" a voice from somewhere ahead barked sharply. "*Tacha velk?*"

"*Belgarath, Iyun hak*," the old sorcerer replied calmly in response to the challenge.

"*Belgarath?*" The voice sounded startled. "*Zajek kallig, Belgarath?*"

"*Marekeg Gorim, Iyun zajek.*"

"*Veed mo. Mar ishum Ulgo.*"

Belgarath extinguished his torch as the Ulgo sentry approached with a phosphorescently glowing wooden bowl held aloft.

"*Yad ho, Belgarath. Groja UL.*"

"*Yad ho,*" the old man answered the ritual greeting. "*Groja UL.*"

The short, broad-shouldered Ulgo bowed briefly, then turned and led them on down the gloomy passageway. The greenish, unwavering glow from the wooden bowl he carried spread its eerie light in the dim gallery, painting all their faces with a ghostly pallor. After another mile or so, the gallery opened out into one of those vast caverns where the pale glow of that strange, cold light the Ulgos contrived winked at them from a hundred openings high up in the stone wall. They carefully moved along a narrow ledge to the foot of a stone stairway that had been chipped from the rock wall of the cave. Their guide spoke briefly to Belgarath.

"We'll have to leave the horses here," the old man said.

"I can stay with them," Durnik offered.

"No. The Ulgos will tend to them. Let's go up." And he started up the steep flight of stairs.

They climbed in silence, the sound of their footsteps echoing back hollowly from the far side of the cavern.

"Please don't lean out over the edge like that, Errand," Polgara said when they were about halfway up.

"I just wanted to see how far down it goes," he replied. "Did you know that there's water down there?"

"That's one of the reasons I'd rather you stayed away from the edge."

He flashed her a sudden smile and went on up.

At the top of the stairs, they skirted the edge of the dim subterranean abyss for several hundred yards, then entered one of the galleries where the Ulgos lived and worked in small cubicles carved from the rock. Beyond that gallery lay the Gorim's half-lit cavern with its lake and its island and the peculiarly pyramid-shaped house surrounded by solemn white pillars. At the far end of the marble causeway which crossed the lake, the Gorim of Ulgo, dressed as always in his white robe, stood peering across the water. "Belgarath?" he called in a quavering voice, "is that you?"

"Yes, it's me, Holy One," the old man replied. "You might have guessed that I'd turn up again."

"Welcome, old friend."

Belgarath started toward the causeway, but Ce'Nedra darted past him with her coppery curls flying and ran toward the Gorim with her arms outstretched.

"Ce'Nedra?" he said, blinking as she threw her arms about his neck.

"Oh, Holy Gorim," she sobbed, burying her face in his shoulder, "someone's taken my baby."

"They've done what?" he exclaimed.

Garion had started almost involuntarily to cross the causeway to Ce'Nedra's side, but Polgara put her hand on his arm to stop him. "Not just yet, dear," she murmured.

"But—"

"This may be what she needs, Garion."

"But, Aunt Pol, she's crying."

"Yes, dear. That's what I've been waiting for. We have to

let her grief run its course before she can begin to come out of it."

The Gorim held the sobbing little queen in his arms, murmuring to her in a soft, comforting tone. After the first storm of her weeping had subsided, he raised his lined old face. "When did all this happen?" he asked.

"Late last summer," Belgarath told him. "It's a fairly involved story."

"Come inside then, all of you," the Gorim said. "My servants will prepare food and drink for you, and we can talk while you eat."

They filed into the pyramid-shaped house standing on the Gorim's island and entered the large central room with its stone benches and table, its glowing crystal lamps hanging on chains from the ceiling, and its peculiar, inward-sloping walls. The Gorim spoke briefly with one of his silent servants, then turned with his arm still about Ce'Nedra's shoulders. "Sit, my friends," he said to them.

As they sat at the stone table, one of the Gorim's servants entered, carrying a tray of polished crystal goblets and a couple of flagons of the fiery Ulgo drink.

"Now," the saintly old man said, "what has happened?"

Belgarath filled himself one of the goblets and then quickly sketched in the events of the past several months, telling the Gorim of the murder of Brand, of the attempt to sow dissension in the Alorn ranks and of the campaign against the cult stronghold at Jarviksholm.

"And then," he went on as the Gorim's servants brought in trays of raw fruits and vegetables and a smoking roast hot from the spit, "right about at the same time we captured Jarviksholm, someone crept into the nursery in the Citadel at Riva and took Prince Geran out of his cradle. When we got back to the Isle, we discovered that the Orb will follow the baby's trail—as long as it stays on dry land, anyway. It led us to the west side of the island, and we encountered some Cherek Bear-cultists the abductor had left behind. When we questioned them, they told us that the new cult leader, Ulfgar, had ordered the abduction."

"But what they told you was not true?" the Gorim asked shrewdly.

"Not by half," Silk replied.

"Of course the problem there was that they didn't *know* they were lying," Belgarath continued. "They'd been very carefully prepared, and the story we got from them sounded quite plausible—particularly in view of the fact that we were already at war with the cult. Anyway, we mounted a campaign against the last cult stronghold at Rheon in northeastern Drasnia. After we took the town and captured Ulfgar, the truth started to come out. Ulfgar turned out to be a Mallorean Grolim named Harakan and he had absolutely nothing to do with the abduction. The real culprit was this mysterious Zandramas I told you about several years ago. I'm not sure exactly what part the Sardion plays in all this; but for some reason, Zandramas wants to take the baby to the place mentioned in the Mrin Codex—the place which is no more. Urvon desperately wants to prevent that, so he sent his henchman here to the west to kill the baby to keep it from happening."

"Have you any idea at all about where to begin the search?" the Gorim asked.

Belgarath shrugged. "A couple of clues is all. We're fairly sure that Zandramas left the Isle of the Winds aboard a Nyissan ship, so that's where we're going to start. The Codex says that I'm supposed to find the path to the Sardion in the mysteries, and I'm fairly certain that when we find the Sardion, Zandramas and the baby won't be far away. Maybe I can get some hints in those prophecies—*if* I can ever find any uncorrupted copies."

"It also appears that the Seers of Kell are directly involving themselves," Polgara added.

"The seers?" The Gorim's voice was startled. "They've never done that before."

"I know," she replied. "One of them—a girl named Cyradis—appeared at Rheon and gave us some additional information, and certain instructions."

"That is very unlike them."

"I think that things are moving toward the ultimate climax, Holy One," Belgarath said. "We were all concentrating so much on the meeting between Garion and Torak that we lost sight of the fact that the *real* meetings are the ones between the Child of Light and the Child of Dark. Cyradis told us that this is going to be the last meeting, and that *this* time, everything's going to be decided once and for all. I rather suspect that's the reason that the seers are finally coming out into the open."

The Gorim frowned. "I would not have ever thought to see them concern themselves with the affairs of other men," he said gravely.

"Just who *are* these seers, Holy Gorim?" Ce'Nedra asked in a subdued voice.

"They are our cousins, child," he replied simply.

Her look betrayed her bafflement.

"After the Gods made the races of man, there came the time of the choosing," he explained. "There were seven races of man—even as there are seven Gods. Aldur chose to go his way alone, however, and that meant that one of the races of man remained unchosen and Godless."

"Yes," she nodded, "I've heard that part of the story."

"We were all of the same people," the Gorim continued. "Us, the Morindim, the Karands in the north of Mallorea, the Melcenes far to the east and the Dals. We were closest to the Dals, but when we went forth in search of the God UL, they had already turned their eyes to the skies in their attempt to read the stars. We urged them to come with us, but they would not."

"And you've lost all contact with them, then?" she asked.

"On occasion, some few of their seers have come to us, usually on some quest of which they would not speak. The seers are very wise, for the Vision which comes to them gives them knowledge of the past, the present, and the future—and more importantly, the meaning of it."

"Are they all women, then?"

"No. There are men as well. When the sight comes to them, they always bind their eyes to exclude all common light so that this other light can be seen more clearly. Inevitably, when a seer appears, there also appears a mute to be guide and protector. They are always paired—forever."

"Why are the Grolims so afraid of them?" Silk asked suddenly. "I've been in Mallorea a few times and I've seen Mallorean Grolims go all to pieces at just the mention of Kell."

"I suspect that the Dals have taken steps to keep the Grolims away from Kell. It's the very center of their learning, and Grolims are intolerant of non-Angarak things."

"What is the purpose of these seers, Holy One?" Garion asked.

"It's not only the seers, Belgarion," the Gorim replied. "The Dals are involved in all branches of arcane knowledge—necromancy, wizardry, magic, witchcraft—all of these and more. No one—except the Dals themselves—seems to know exactly what their purpose might be. Whatever it is, though, they are entirely committed to it—both the ones in Mallorea and those here in the west."

"In the west?" Silk blinked. "I didn't know that there were any Dals here."

The Gorim nodded. "They were divided by the Sea of the East when Torak used the Orb to crack the world. The western Dals were enslaved by the Murgos during the third millennium. But wherever they live—east or west—they have labored for eons at some task. Whatever that task may be, they are convinced that the fate of all creation depends on it."

"Does it?" Garion asked.

"We don't know, Belgarion. We don't know what the task is, so we can't even guess at its significance. We *do* know that they follow neither of the Prophecies which dominate the universe. They believe that their task was laid upon them by some higher destiny."

"And *that's* the thing that concerns me," Belgarath said. "Cyradis is manipulating us with these cryptic little announcements of hers; and for all I know, she's manipulating Zandramas as well. I don't like being led around by the nose—particularly by someone whose motives I don't understand. She complicates this whole business, and I don't like complications. I like nice, simple situations and nice, easy, solutions."

"Good and Evil?" Durnik suggested.

"That's a difficult one, Durnik. I prefer 'them and us.' That clears away all the excess baggage and allows you to get right down to cases."

Garion slept restlessly that night and he rose early with his head feeling as if it were stuffed with sand. He sat for a time on one of the stone benches in the central room of the Gorim's house; then, caught in a kind of moody restlessness, he went outside to look across the quiet lake surrounding the island. The faint light from the globes hanging on their chains from the ceiling of the cavern cast a dim glow on the surface of the lake, and that glow filled the cave with a pale luminosity that seemed more like a light seen in a dream than any kind of illumination to be found in the real world. As he stood lost in thought at the water's edge, a movement on the far shore caught his eye.

They came singly and in groups of two and three, pale young women with the large, dark eyes and colorless hair of the Ulgos. They all wore modest white gowns, and they gathered shyly on the shore on the far side of the marble causeway, waiting in the dim light. Garion looked across the lake at them, then raised his voice to call, "Was there something you wanted?"

They whispered together for a moment, then pushed one of their number forward to speak for them. "We—we wanted to see the Princess Ce'Nedra," she blurted bashfully, her face dyed with a rosy blush. "If she's not too busy, that is." Her speech was halting, as if she were talking in a language not wholly familiar to her.

"I'll go see if she's awake," Garion offered.

"Thank you, sir," she replied, shrinking back into the protection of her group of friends.

Garion went back inside and found Ce'Nedra sitting up in bed. Her face had none of that numb indifference that had marked it for the past several weeks, and her eyes seemed alert. "You're up early," she noted.

"I had a little trouble sleeping. Are you all right?"

"I'm fine, Garion. Why do you ask?"

"I was just—" He broke off with a shrug. "There are some young Ulgo women outside. They want to see you."

She frowned. "Who could they possibly be?"

"They seemed to know you. They said that they wanted to see the Princess Ce'Nedra."

"Of course!" she exclaimed, springing from her bed. "I'd almost forgotten them." She quickly pulled on a teal-green dressing gown and dashed from the room.

Curiously, Garion started to follow her, but stopped in the central hall of the house when he saw Polgara, Durnik, and the Gorim sitting quietly at the stone table.

"What was that all about?" Polgara asked, looking after the scurrying little queen.

"There are some Ulgo women outside," Garion replied. "They seem to be friends of hers."

"She was very popular during her visit here," the Gorim said. "Ulgo girls are very shy, but Ce'Nedra befriended them all. They adored her."

"Excuse me, your Worship," Durnik said, "but is Relg anywhere about? I thought I might look in on him, as long as we're here."

"Relg and Taiba have taken their children and moved to Maragor," the Gorim replied.

"Maragor?" Garion blinked. "What about the ghosts there?"

"They are under the protection of the God Mara," the Gorim told him. "There seems to be some kind of understanding between Mara and UL. I'm not sure I entirely understand it, but Mara insists that Taiba's children are Marags and he has vowed to watch over them in Maragor."

Garion frowned. "But isn't their first-born son going to be Gorim someday?"

The old man nodded. "Yes. His eyes are still as blue as sapphires. I was concerned myself at first, Belgarion, but I'm certain that UL will return Relg's son to the caves of Ulgo at the proper time."

"How is Ce'Nedra this morning, Garion?" Polgara asked seriously.

"She seems to be almost back to normal. Does that mean that she's all right?"

"It's a good sign, dear, but it might be a little early to be sure. Why don't you go keep an eye on her?"

"All right."

"Just try not to be obvious. This is a rather critical time, and we don't want her getting the idea that we're spying on her."

"I'll be careful, Aunt Pol." He went outside and began walking around the small island as if he were only stretching his legs. He cast frequent glances at the group on the far shore. The pale, white-gowned Ulgo women were clustered about Ce'Nedra. Her green robe and her flaming red hair stood out in sharp contrast in the midst of the group. A sudden image came into Garion's mind. With her vibrant coloring, Ce'Nedra looked very much like a single crimson rose growing in the midst of a bed of white lilies.

After about a half an hour, Polgara came out of the house. "Garion," she said, "have you seen Errand this morning?"

"No, Aunt Pol."

"He's not in his room." She frowned slightly. "What *is* that boy thinking of? Go see if you can find him."

"Yes, ma'am," he replied automatically. As he started across the causeway, he smiled to himself. In spite of all that had happened, he and Aunt Pol always returned to the same relationship they had shared when he was a boy. He was fairly certain that most of the time she did not even remember that he was a king, and so she often sent him on menial errands with no real awareness that they might be beneath his dignity. Moreover, he found that he did not really mind. To fall back into the pattern of immediately obeying her peremptory commands relieved him of the necessity of making difficult decisions and took him back to those days when he was just a simple farm boy with none of the cares and responsibilities that had come to him with the crown of Riva.

Ce'Nedra and her friends were seated on rocks not far from the dim lake shore. Their conversation was subdued, and Ce'Nedra's face was somber again.

"Are you all right?" he asked her as he approached them.

"Yes," she replied. "We were just talking, that's all."

He looked at her, but decided not to say anything more. "Have you seen Errand?" he asked instead.

"No. Isn't he in the house?"

He shook his head. "I think he's gone exploring. Aunt Pol asked me to find him."

One of the young Ulgo women whispered something to Ce'Nedra.

"Saba says that she saw him in the main gallery when she was coming here," Ce'Nedra told him. "It was about an hour ago."

"Which way is that?" he asked.

"Over there." She pointed toward an opening leading back into the rock.

He nodded. "Are you warm enough?" he asked her.

"I'm fine, Garion."

"I'll be back in a bit," he said and walked toward the gallery she had pointed out. It made him uncomfortable to be forced to step around her this way, but the possibility that a chance remark might push her back into that bleak depression made him wary and half-afraid to speak at all. A purely physical ailment was one thing, but an illness of the mind was something horrifying.

The gallery he entered, like all the caves and passageways in which the Ulgos lived out their lives, was faintly illuminated by the dim glow of phosphorescent rocks. The cubicles on either side of the gallery were scrupulously neat, and he saw entire families gathered about stone tables for their morning meal, apparently oblivious to the fact that the fronts of their quarters were open to scrutiny by anyone who chanced to pass this way.

Since few of the Ulgos could speak his language, it was impossible for Garion to ask anyone if Errand had passed, and he soon found that he was wandering more or less aimlessly, hoping that he might chance across his friend. At the far end of the gallery, he emerged into the vast cavern where that flight of chiseled stairs led downward toward the dim reaches below.

He considered the possibility that Errand might have gone down to visit his horse, but something seemed to tell him that he should turn instead to follow the broad ledge circling the edge of the chasm. He had gone no more than a few hundred yards when he heard the sound of voices issuing from the mouth of a dark passageway angling back into the rock face. The shifting echoes made it impossible to distinguish individual words, but it seemed to Garion that one of the voices was Errand's. He entered the passageway, following the sound alone.

At first there was no light in the unused gallery, and he put his hand to the rough rock wall to grope his way along; but as he rounded a corner, he saw a light coming from somewhere ahead—a peculiar kind of steady white radiance quite unlike the faint greenish glow of phosphorescence that normally illuminated this dark world of the caves. And then the corridor he was following bent sharply to the left, and he rounded that corner to see Errand talking with a tall, white-robed figure. Garion's eyes widened. The light he had seen was emanating from that figure, and he felt the awesome presence of a transcendent being.

The glowing figure did not turn, but spoke in a calm, quiet voice. "Join us, Belgarion, and welcome."

Garion found that he was actually trembling as he wordlessly obeyed. Then the figure in white turned, and he found himself looking directly into the timeless face of UL himself.

"I have been instructing young Eriond here in the task which lies before him," the Father of the Gods said.

"Eriond?"

"It is his true name, Belgarion. It is time for him to put aside the childish name of his boyhood and to assume his true one. Even as thou wert concealed beneath thy simple 'Garion,' so hath he lain hidden under that 'Errand.' There is wisdom in this, for the true name of a man with a great task lying before him can oft times bring danger when its owner hath not yet come into his inheritance."

"It's a good name, don't you think, Belgarion?" Eriond said proudly.

"It's an excellent name, Eriond," Garion agreed.

The Orb, standing on the pommel of the great sword sheathed across Garion's back, glowed its blue response to the incandescently white radiance of UL, and the God nodded his acknowledgement of the stone.

"Tasks have been set for each of you," UL continued, "and for the companions who accompany you. All these tasks must be completed ere the meeting between the Child of Light and the Child of Dark may come again."

"Please, Holy UL," Garion said, "can you tell me—is my son all right?"

"He is well, Belgarion. The one who holds him will see to his needs. For the moment he is in no danger."

"Thank you," Garion said gratefully. Then he squared his shoulders. "And what is my task?" he asked.

"Thy task hath already been revealed to thee by the Seeress of Kell, Belgarion. Thou must bar the path of Zandramas to the Sardion; for should the Child of Dark reach that dread stone with thy son, the Dark shall prevail in this final meeting."

Garion steeled himself and then blurted his next question, afraid of what the answer might be. "In the Oracles of Ashaba it says that the Dark God will come again," he said. "Does that mean that Torak will be reborn and that I'm going to have to fight him again?"

"Nay, Belgarion. My son himself will not return. Thy flaming sword reft him of his life, and he is no more. The enemy in *this* meeting will be more perilous. The spirit which infused Torak hath found another vessel. Torak was maimed and imperfect by reason of his pride. The one who shall rise in his stead—shouldst thou fail in thy task—will be invincible; and not thy sword nor all the swords in all this world will be enough to withstand him."

"Then it's Zandramas that I have to fight," Garion said grimly. "I've got reason enough, that's certain."

"The meeting between the Child of Light and the Child of Dark shall not be a meeting between thee and Zandramas," UL told him.

"But the Codex says that Zandramas is the Child of Dark," Garion protested.

"At this present time, yes—even as at this present time thou art the Child of Light. That burden, however, shall pass from each of you ere the final meeting can take place. Know this, moreover. The event which began with the birth of thy son must be completed in a certain time. The tasks which lie before thee and thy companions are many, and all must be completed ere the time appointed for this meeting. Shouldst thou or any of thy companions fail in the completion of any task, then shall all our striving for uncounted ages come to naught. This final meeting between the Child of Light and the Child of Dark must be complete, and all of the necessary conditions must be met, for it is in *this* meeting that all that was divided shall be made one again. The fate of this world—and of all other worlds—lies in *thy* hands, Belgarion, and the outcome will not depend upon thy sword but upon a choice which thou must make."

The Father of the Gods looked at the two of them fondly. "Be not afraid, my sons," he told them, "for though you are different in many ways, you share the same spirit. Aid and sustain each other and be comforted in the knowledge that I am with you." Then the glowing figure shimmered and was gone, and the caves of Ulgo resounded with an echo like the aftersound of some unimaginably huge bell.

CHAPTER TWO

A kind of unthinking serenity had come over Garion, a calm resolve much akin to that which he had felt when he had faced Torak in the decaying ruins of the City of Endless Night half a world away. As he thought back on that dreadful night, he began to grope his way toward a startling truth. The maimed God had not been striving for a purely physical victory. He had been trying with all the dreadful force of his will to force them to submit to him, and it had been their steadfast refusal to yield, more than Garion's flaming sword, which had defeated him in the end. Slowly, almost like the onset of dawn, the truth came to Garion. Although evil might seem invincible as it stalked the world in darkness, it nonetheless yearned toward the light, and only in the surrender of the light could the darkness prevail. So long as the Child of Light remained firm and unyielding, he was still invincible. As he stood in the dark cave listening to the shimmering aftersound of UL's departure, Garion seemed to see directly into the mind of his enemy. Beneath it all, Torak had been afraid, and even now that same fear gnawed at the heart of Zandramas.

And then Garion perceived yet another truth, a truth at once enormously simple and at the same time so profound that the scope of it shook every fiber of his being. There was no such thing as darkness! What seemed so vast and overwhelming was nothing more than the absence of light. So long as the Child of Light kept that firmly in mind, the Child of Dark could never win. Torak had known this; Zandramas knew it; and now at last Garion himself understood it, and the knowledge brought with it a surging exultation.

"It gets easier once you understand, doesn't it?" the young man they had always called Errand asked quietly.

"You knew what I was thinking, didn't you?"

"Yes. Does that bother you?"

"No. I suppose not." Garion looked around. The gallery in which they stood suddenly seemed very dark now that UL was gone. Garion knew the way back, but the idea which he had just grasped seemed to require some kind of affirmation. He turned his head and spoke directly to the Orb riding on the pommel of his great sword. "Could you give us a bit of light?" he asked it.

The Orb responded by igniting into blue fire and at the same time filling Garion's mind with its crystal song. Garion looked at Eriond. "Shall we go back now? Aunt Pol was sort of worried when she couldn't find you."

As they turned and followed the deserted gallery back along the way they had come, Garion laid his arm affectionately across his young friend's shoulders. For some reason they seemed very close just now.

They emerged from the gallery at the brink of the dim abyss

where pale lights dotted the sheer walls and the murmur of a waterfall far below came whispering up to them.

Garion suddenly remembered something that had happened the day before. "What is it about you and water that concerns Aunt Pol so much?" he asked curiously.

Eriond laughed. "Oh, that. When I was little—just after we moved into Poledra's cottage in the Vale—I used to fall into the river fairly often."

Garion grinned. "That seems like a perfectly natural thing to me."

"It hasn't happened for a long time now, but I think that Polgara feels that maybe I'm saving it up for a special occasion of some sort."

Garion laughed, and they entered the cubicle-lined corridor that led toward the Gorim's cavern. The Ulgos who lived and worked there threw startled glances in their direction as they passed.

"Uh—Belgarion," Eriond said, "the Orb is still glowing."

"Oh," Garion replied, "I'd forgotten about that." He looked back over his shoulder at the cheerfully burning stone. "It's all right now," he told it. "You can stop."

The Orb's final flicker seemed faintly disappointed.

The others were gathered at breakfast in the central room of the Gorim's house. Polgara looked up as the two of them entered. "Where have you—" she began, then stopped as she looked into Eriond's eyes more closely. "Something's happened, hasn't it?" she asked instead.

Eriond nodded. "Yes," he replied. "UL wanted to talk with us. There were some things we needed to know."

Belgarath pushed aside his plate, his face becoming intent. "I think you'd better tell us about this," he said to them. "Take your time and don't skip over anything."

Garion crossed to the table and sat down beside Ce'Nedra. He described the meeting with the Father of the Gods carefully, trying as best he could to repeat UL's exact words. "And then he said that Eriond and I shared the same spirit and that we were supposed to aid and sustain each other," he concluded.

"Was that all he said?" Belgarath asked.

"Pretty much, yes."

"Except that he told us he was with us," Eriond added.

"He didn't say anything more specific about this certain time when everything has to be completed?" the old man demanded with a slightly worried expression.

Garion shook his head. "No. I'm sorry, Grandfather. I'm afraid not."

Belgarath's expression suddenly became exasperated. "I *hate* working to a schedule I haven't seen," he muttered. "I can't tell if I'm ahead or behind."

Ce'Nedra had been clinging to Garion, her face filled with both concern and relief. "Are you really sure he said that our baby is all right?" she demanded.

"He said that he is well," Eriond assured her. "He told us that the one who holds him will see to his needs and that for the moment he's in no danger."

"For the moment?" Ce'Nedra exclaimed. "What's that supposed to mean?"

"He didn't get any more specific, Ce'Nedra," Garion said.

"Why didn't you ask UL where he is?"

"Because I'm sure he wouldn't have told me. Finding Geran and Zandramas is my job, and I don't think they're going to let me evade it by getting somebody else to do it for me."

"They? Who are they?"

"The Prophecies—both of them. They're playing a game, and we all have to follow the rules—even if we don't know what they are."

"That's nonsense."

"Go tell them. It wasn't my idea."

Aunt Pol was looking oddly at Eriond. "Have you known?" she asked him. "About your name, I mean?"

"I knew I had another name. When you called me Errand,

it didn't seem quite right, for some reason. Do you mind very much, Polgara?"

She rose with a smile, came around the table, and embraced him warmly. "No, Eriond," she told him, "I don't mind at all."

"Just exactly what is the task UL set for you?" Belgarath asked.

"He said that I'd recognize it when I came to it."

"Is that all he said about it?"

"He said that it was very important and that it was going to change me."

Belgarath shook his head. "Why does everything always have to be in riddles?" he complained.

"It's another one of those rules Garion mentioned," Silk told him, refilling his goblet from one of the flagons. "Well, what next, old man?"

Belgarath thought about it, tugging at an earlobe and looking up at one of the faintly glowing lamps. "I think it's fairly safe to say that this meeting was the thing that was supposed to happen here at Prolgu," he said, "so I expect that it's time for us to move along. It might not hurt for us to get where we're going a little early, but I'm positive that it's going to be a disaster if we get there late." He rose from his seat and put his hand on the Gorim's frail shoulder. "I'll try to get word to you from time to time," he promised. "Could you ask some of your people to lead us through the caves to Arendia? I want to get out into the open as soon as possible."

"Of course, my old friend," the Gorim replied, "and may UL guide your steps."

"I hope *somebody* does," Silk murmured.

Belgarath gave him a hard look.

"It's all right, Belgarath," Silk said expansively. "The fact that you get lost all the time doesn't diminish our respect for you in the slightest. I'm sure it's just a bad habit you picked up somewhere—probably because your mind was on weightier matters."

Belgarath looked at Garion. "Did we really *have* to bring him along?"

"Yes, Grandfather, we really did."

It was shortly after sunrise two days later when they reached the irregularly shaped cave mouth that opened out into a birch forest. The white trees lifted their bare limbs toward an intensely blue sky, and fallen leaves covered the ground with a carpet of gold. The Ulgos who had guided them through the caves winced visibly and drew back from the sunlight. They murmured a few words to Belgarath, he thanked them, and then they retreated back into the protective darkness.

"You have absolutely no idea how much better I feel now," Silk said with relief as he emerged from the cave and looked around at the frosty morning sunlight. Here and there back among the trees were patches of frozen snow, crusty and sparkling in the slanting rays of the morning sun; somewhere off to the left, they could hear the rush and babble of a mountain brook tumbling over stones.

"Have you any notion of exactly where we are?" Durnik asked Belgarath as they rode out into the birch trees.

The old man squinted back over his shoulder, gauging the angle of the new-risen sun. "My guess is that we're in the foothills above central Arendia," he replied.

"South of the lower end of the Arendish forest?" Silk asked.

"That's hard to say for sure."

The little Drasnian looked around. "I'd better take a look," he said. He pointed at a hill rising out of the forest. "I might be able to see something from up there."

"And I think some breakfast might be in order," Polgara said. "Let's find a clear spot and build a fire."

"I won't be too long," Silk said, turning his horse and riding off through the white trunks of the birches.

The rest of them rode on down the slope, the hooves of their horses rustling the deep-piled carpet of golden leaves. Several hundred yards into the forest, they reached a clearing on the banks of the brook they had heard when they had emerged from the cave. Polgara drew in her horse. "This should do," she decided. "Garion, why don't you and Eriond gather some firewood? I think some bacon and toasted bread might be nice."

"Yes, Aunt Pol," he said automatically, swinging down from his saddle. Eriond joined him, and the two of them went back in among the white trees in search of fallen limbs.

"It's pleasant being back out in the sunlight again," Eriond said as he pulled a large branch out from under a fallen tree. "The caves are nice enough, I suppose, but I like to be able to look at the sky."

Garion felt very close to this open-faced young man. The experience they had shared in the cave had brought them even closer together and had focused an idea that had hovered on the edge of Garion's awareness for several years now. The fact that both he and Eriond had been raised by Aunt Pol and Durnik had made them in many respects very much like brothers. He considered that as he bundled several large limbs together with a length of rope. He realized at the same time that he knew very little about Eriond and what might have happened to him before they had found him at Rak Cthol. "Eriond," he said curiously, "can you remember anything at all about where you lived before Zedar found you?"

The young man looked up toward the sky, his eyes lost in thought. "It was in a city of some kind, I think," he replied. "I seem to remember streets—and shops."

"Do you remember your mother at all?"

"I don't think so. I don't remember living in any place for very long—or staying with the same people. It seems that I just used to go to a door, and people would take me inside and give me something to eat and a place to sleep."

Garion felt a sudden sharp pang of sympathy. Eriond was as much—or even more—an orphan as he was himself. "Do you remember the day when Zedar found you?" he asked.

Eriond nodded. "Yes," he replied, "quite clearly. It was cloudy, and there weren't any shadows, so I couldn't tell exactly what time of day it was. I met him in a very narrow street—an alley of some kind, I think. I remember that his eyes had a sort of injured look in them—as if something terrible had happened to him." He sighed. "Poor Zedar."

"Did he ever talk to you?"

"Not very often. About all he ever said was that he had an errand for me. He used to talk in his sleep once in a while, though. I remember that he used to say 'Master.' Sometimes when he said it, his voice would be full of love. Other times it was full of fear. It was almost as if he had two entirely different Masters."

"He did. At first he was one of the disciples of Aldur. Then later, his Master was Torak."

"Why do you suppose he did that, Belgarion? Changed Masters, I mean?"

"I don't know, Eriond. I really don't know."

Durnik had built a small fire in the center of the clearing, and Polgara, humming softly to herself, was setting out her pots and pans beside it. As Garion and Eriond began breaking the branches they had gathered into manageable lengths, Silk rode back down the hill to rejoin them. "You can see quite a way from up there," he reported as he swung down from his saddle. "We're about ten leagues above the high road from Muros."

"Could you see the River Malerin?" Belgarath asked him.

Silk shook his head. "Not the river itself," he replied, "but there's a fairly good-sized valley off to the south. I'd imagine that it runs through there."

"I was fairly close then. How's the terrain look between here and the high road?"

"We've got some rough going ahead of us," Silk told him. "It's steep, and the woods look pretty dense."

"We'll have to make the best time we can. Once we get to the high road, we'll be all right."

Silk made a sour face. "There's another problem, though," he said. "There's a storm coming in from the west."

Durnik lifted his face to sniff at the frosty air and nodded. "Snow," he confirmed. "You can smell it coming."

Silk gave him a disgusted look. "You had to say it, didn't you, Durnik?" he said almost accusingly.

Durnik's look was slightly puzzled.

"Didn't you know that talking about unpleasant things makes them happen?"

"Silk, that's pure nonsense."

The little man sniffed. "I know—but it's true all the same."

The breakfast of bread, dried fruit, and bacon Aunt Pol prepared for them was simple, but there was more than enough to satisfy them all. When they had finished, they repacked, quenched their fire with water from the icy brook, and rode on down the steep slope, following the course of the tumbling stream through the white-trunked birch forest.

Durnik fell in beside the mute Toth as they rode. "Tell me, Toth," he said tentatively, eyeing the frothy white water pitching down over mossy green boulders, "have you ever done any fishing?"

The huge man smiled shyly.

"Well, I've got lines and hooks in one of the packs. Maybe if we get the chance . . . " Durnik left it hanging.

Toth's smile broadened into a grin.

Silk stood up in his stirrups and peered on ahead. "That storm isn't much more than a half-hour away," he told them.

Belgarath grunted. "I doubt that we'll make very good time once it hits," he replied.

"I *hate* snow." Silk shivered glumly.

"That's a peculiar trait in a Drasnian."

"Why do you think I left Drasnia in the first place?"

The heavy bank of cloud loomed in front of them as they continued on down the hill. The morning sunlight paled and then disappeared as the leading edge of the storm raced high overhead to blot out the crisp blue of the autumn sky. "Here it comes," Eriond said cheerfully as the first few flakes began to dance and swirl in the stiff breeze moving up the ridge toward them.

Silk gave the young man a sour look, crammed his battered

hat down lower over his ears and pulled his shabby cloak tighter about him. He looked at Belgarath. "I don't suppose you'd consider doing something about this?" he asked pointedly.

"It wouldn't be a good idea."

"Sometimes you're a terrible disappointment to me, Belgarath," Silk said, drawing himself even more deeply into his cloak.

It began to snow harder, and the trees about them became hazy and indistinct in the shifting curtain of white that came seething up through the forest.

A mile or so farther down the hill they left the birch trees and entered a dark green forest of towering firs. The thick evergreens broke the force of the wind, and the snow sifted lazily down through the boughs, lightly dusting the needle-strewn floor of the forest. Belgarath shook the snow out of the folds of his cloak and looked around, choosing a route.

"Lost again?" Silk asked.

"No, not really." The old man looked back at Durnik. "How far down this hill do you think we're going to have to go to get below this?" he asked.

Durnik scratched at his chin. "It's sort of hard to say," he replied. He turned to the mute at his side. "What do you think, Toth?" he asked.

The giant lifted his head and sniffed at the air, then made a series of obscure gestures with one hand.

"You're probably right," Durnik agreed. He turned back to Belgarath. "If the slope stays this steep, we ought to be able to get below the snowline sometime this afternoon—if we keep moving."

"Well, I guess we'd better move along then," Belgarath said and led the way on down the hill at a jolting trot.

It continued to snow. The light dusting on the ground beneath the firs became a covering, and the dimness that had hovered among the dark tree trunks faded as the white snow brought its peculiar, sourceless light.

They stopped about noon and took a quick lunch of bread and cheese, then continued to descend through the forest toward Arendia. By midafternoon, as Durnik and Toth had predicted, the snow was mixed with a chill rain. Soon the few large, wet flakes were gone, and they rode through a steady drizzle that wreathed down among the trees.

Late in the afternoon the wind picked up, and the rain driven before it was cold and unpleasant. Durnik looked around. "I think that it's about time for us to find a place to stop for the night," he said. "We'll need shelter from this wind, and finding dry firewood might be a bit of a problem."

The huge Toth, whose feet very nearly dragged on the ground on either side of his horse, looked around and then pointed toward a dense thicket of sapling evergreens standing at the far edge of the broad clearing they had just entered. Once again he began to move his hands in those peculiar gestures. Durnik watched him intently for a few moments, then nodded, and the two of them rode on across to the thicket, dismounted, and went to work.

The campsite they constructed was well back among the slender tree trunks of the thicket where the force of the wind was broken and the dense branches shed the rain like a thatched roof. The two of them bent a half circle of the tall saplings over and tied their tips to the trunks of other trees to form a domelike framework of considerable size. Then they covered the frame with tent canvas and tied it in place securely. The resulting structure was a round-topped, open-fronted pavilion perhaps as big as a fair-sized room. At the front, they dug in a firepit and lined it with rocks.

The rain had soaked down the forest, and collecting dry firewood was difficult, but Garion drew upon the experience he had gained during the quest for the Orb to seek out those sheltered hollows under fallen trees, the spots on the leeward sides of large tree trunks and the brush-choked areas under overhanging rocks where dry twigs and branches could be found. By evening he and Eriond had piled up a considerable supply of wood not far from the fire pit where Polgara and Ce'Nedra were preparing supper.

There was a small spring several hundred yards on down

the slope, and Garion slipped and slid downhill with two leather waterbags slung over his shoulders. The light was fading rapidly under the dark, windswept evergreens, and the ruddy glow of their campfire beckoned cheerfully as he started back up through the trees with the full waterbags hanging pendulously down against his thighs.

Polgara had hung her damp cloak on a tree limb and was humming softly to herself as she and Ce'Nedra worked over the fire.

"Why, thank you, your Majesty," Ce'Nedra said as Garion handed her the waterbags. Her little smile was somehow wistful, as if she were making a conscious effort to be lighthearted.

"It's my pleasure, your Majesty," he replied with a florid bow. "A good scullion can always find water when the cook's helper needs it."

She smiled briefly, kissed his cheek, and then sighed and went back to dicing vegetables for the stew Polgara was stirring.

After they had eaten, they all sat drowsily before the fire, listening to the sound of the wind in the tree tops and the seething hiss of the rain in the forest about them.

"How far did we come today?" Ce'Nedra asked in a voice near sleep as she leaned wearily against Garion's shoulder.

"Seven or eight leagues, I'd guess," Durnik replied. "It's slow going when you don't have a road to follow."

"We'll make better time, once we hit the high road from Muros to the Great Fair," Silk added. His eyes brightened at that thought, and his long, pointed nose started to twitch.

"Never mind," Belgarath told him.

"We *will* need supplies, Belgarath," Silk said, his eyes still bright.

"I think we'll let Durnik take care of that. People who do business with you always seem to develop this sense of outrage once they've had time to think things through."

"But, Belgarath, I thought you said that you were in a hurry."

"I don't quite get the connection."

"People always travel faster when somebody's chasing them—or hadn't you noticed that?"

Belgarath gave him a long, hard look. "Just let it drop, Silk," he said. "Why don't we all get some sleep?" he suggested to the rest of them. "We've got a long day tomorrow."

It was well after midnight when Garion suddenly started into wakefulness. He lay rolled up in his blankets beside Ce'Nedra, listening to her regular breathing and the soft patter of the rain on the tree limbs. The wind had died, and the fire at the front of their snug shelter had burned down to a few ruddy coals. He shook the last remnants of sleep from his mind, trying to remember what it was that had awakened him.

"Don't make any noise," Belgarath said softly from the far side of the shelter.

"Did something wake you, too, Grandfather?"

"I want you to get out of your blankets very slowly," the old man said in a voice so quiet that it scarcely reached Garion's ears, "and get your hands on your sword."

"What is it, Grandfather?"

"Listen!" Belgarath said.

From high overhead in the rainy darkness there came the ponderous flap of vast wings and a sudden flare of sooty red light. The wings flapped again, and then the sound was gone.

"Move, Garion," Belgarath said urgently. "Get your sword—and put something over the Orb so that she can't see the glow from it."

Garion untangled his legs from his blankets and groped in the darkness for Iron-grip's sword.

Again there was the vast flapping sound overhead, and then a strange, hissing cry, accompanied by another flare of that sooty red light.

"What's that?" Ce'Nedra cried out.

"Be still, girl!" Belgarath snapped.

They lay tensely in the darkness as the flapping sound faded off into the rainswept night.

"What's out there, Belgarath?" Silk asked tensely.

"She's a very large beast," the old man replied quietly.

"Her eyes aren't very good, and she's as stupid as a stump, but she's very dangerous. She's hunting. Possibly she smells the horses—or us."

"How do you know it's a she?" Durnik asked.

"Because there's only one of them left in the world. She doesn't come out of her cave very often, but over the centuries enough people have caught glimpses of her to give rise to all those legends."

"I'm starting to get a very uneasy feeling about this," Silk murmured.

"She doesn't really look that much like the dragons in all those drawings," Belgarath continued, "but she *is* big, and she *does* fly."

"Oh, come now, Belgarath," Durnik scoffed. "There's no such thing as a dragon."

"I'm glad to hear it. Now, why don't you go out and explain that to her?"

"Is she the same creature we heard that night in the mountains above Maragor?" Garion asked.

"Yes. Have you got your sword?"

"Right here, Grandfather."

"Good. Now, very slowly, creep out and smother the last of those coals with dirt. Fire attracts her, so let's not take any chances on a sudden flare-up."

Garion inched his way out through the open front of the shelter and hurriedly scooped dirt over the fire pit with his hands.

"Is it really a flying lizard?" Silk whispered hoarsely.

"No," Belgarath replied, "actually she's a species of bird. She has a long, snakelike tail, and what she's covered with looks more like scales than feathers. She also has teeth—lots of very long, sharp teeth."

"Just exactly how big is she?" Durnik asked.

"You remember Faldor's barn?"

"Yes."

"About that big."

From quite some distance off there came another screeching bellow and the murky red flare.

"Her fire isn't really all that serious," Belgarath continued in the same low voice, "particularly since these woods are so wet. It's when she catches you in dry grass that it starts to be a problem. She's big, but she's not very brave—and on the ground she's as clumsy as a pig on a frozen pond. If it gets down to a fight, we probably won't be able to hurt her very much. About the best we can hope for is to frighten her off."

"Fight?" Silk choked. "You're not serious."

"We may not have any choice. If she's hungry and picks up our scent or the scent of the horses, she'll tear these woods apart looking for us. She has a few sensitive spots. Her tail is probably the best. Her wings get in the way, so she can't see behind her too well, and when she's on the ground, she can't turn very fast."

"Let's see if I've got this straight," Silk said. "You want us to sneak up behind this dragon and hit it on the tail, is that it?"

"Approximately, yes."

"Belgarath, have you lost your mind? Why not just use sorcery to drive it away?"

"Because she's immune to sorcery," Polgara explained calmly. "It was one of the little refinements Torak added when he and the other Gods created her species. He was so impressed with the concept of a dragon that he chose it as his totem creature. He tried in every way he could to make it invincible."

"It was one of his character defects," Belgarath added sourly. "All right, the dragon is clumsy and stupid and she's not used to pain. If we're careful, we can probably frighten her away without anyone getting hurt."

"She's coming back," Eriond said.

They listened as the flapping of those huge wings reverberated again through the sodden forest.

"Let's get out into the open," Belgarath said tensely.

"That's a good idea," Silk agreed. "If I have to do this, I want lots of level running room around me."

"Ce'Nedra," Polgara said, "I want you to get as far back into this thicket as you can. Find a place to hide."

"Yes, Lady Polgara," Ce'Nedra replied in a frightened little voice.

They crept out of the shelter into the darkness. The rain had slackened to a kind of misty drizzle wreathing down among the trees. Their horses, picketed not far away, snorted nervously, and Garion could smell the sharp odor of their fear over the resinous scent of wet evergreens.

"All right," Belgarath whispered. "Spread out—and be careful. Don't try to attack her unless you're sure that her attention is someplace else."

They crept out of the thicket into the broad clearing and started across. Garion, sword in hand, moved carefully, feeling for obstructions with his feet. When he reached the far side, he located a large tree trunk and went around behind it.

They waited tensely, straining their eyes toward the rain-swept night sky.

The heavy flapping of great wings reverberated down among the trees, and once again they heard that vast bellow. Even as the sound crashed down on them, Garion saw the huge billow of smoky flame in the sky overhead and, outlined by that flame, the shape of the dragon herself. She was even bigger than he had imagined. Her wings might easily have shaded an acre. Her cruel beak was agape, and he could clearly see her pointed teeth with the flames writhing about them. She had a very long, snakelike neck, huge talons, and a long, reptilian tail that lashed at the air behind her as she plunged down toward the clearing.

Then Eriond stepped out from behind a tree trunk and walked out into the center of the clearing as calmly as if he were merely taking a midmorning stroll.

"Eriond!" Polgara cried as, with a triumphant shriek, the dragon swooped down into the clearing. Talons extended, she struck at the unprotected young man. Her beak gaped, and vast billows of sooty orange flame poured forth to engulf him. With fear for the boy clutching at his heart, Garion ran forward with his sword aloft; but even as he ran at the huge beast, he felt the sudden familiar surge of Aunt Pol's will, and Eriond vanished as she translocated him to safety.

The earth shook as the dragon struck the ground, and her vast roar of frustration filled the clearing with the ruddy light of her fire. She was enormous. Her half-folded, scaly-looking wings reared above her higher than any house. Her lashing tail was thicker than the body of a horse, and her curved, tooth-studded beak was dreadful. A sickening stench filled the clearing each time she belched forth her billows of flame. By the light of her fire, Garion could clearly see her slitted yellow eyes. From what Belgarath had said, he expected a look of dull stupidity, but the burning eyes that searched the clearing were alert and filled with an intense, frightening eagerness.

Then Durnik and Toth were upon her. They dashed from the shelter of the trees, Durnik with his axe and Toth with the smith's sharp-bladed spade, and methodically they began to chop at the dragon's writhing tail. She shrieked, belching flame into the air, and began to claw at the sodden forest loam with her talons.

"Look out!" Silk shouted. "She's turning!"

The dragon whirled awkwardly, her wings beating at the air and her talons throwing up huge clots of earth, but Durnik and Toth had already run back into the shelter of the trees. As she swept the clearing with her burning eyes, Silk nimbly darted out behind her with his short, broad-bladed Drasnian sword in his hand. Again and again he drove it into the base of her huge tail. Then, as she floundered around to meet his attack, he danced clear to regain the safety of the surrounding forest.

And then Eriond stepped into the clearing again. Without any sign of fear but with a grave expression on his face, he walked out of the trees and moved directly toward the raging beast. "Why are you doing this?" he asked her calmly. "You know that this isn't the time or place."

The dragon almost seemed to flinch back at the sound of his voice, and her burning eyes grew wary.

"You can't avoid what's going to happen," he continued seriously. "None of us can—and you can't change it with this kind of foolishness. You'd better go. We really don't want to have to hurt you."

The dragon faltered, and Garion suddenly sensed that she was not only baffled, but that she was also afraid. Then she seemed to clench herself. With an enraged bellow, she sent out a vast sheet of flame from her gaping beak to engulf Eriond, who made no effort to escape.

Every nerve in Garion's body shrieked at him to run to his young friend's aid, but he found that he could not move so much as a muscle. He stood, sword in hand, locked in a kind of helpless stasis.

As the billow of flame subsided, Eriond emerged from it unscathed and with an expression of regretful firmness on his face. "I'd hoped that we wouldn't have to do this," he said to the dragon, "but you aren't giving us too much choice, you know." He sighed. "All right, Belgarion," he said, "make her go away—but please try not to hurt her too much."

With a kind of surging exultation, as if those words had somehow released him from all restraint, Garion ran directly up behind the dragon with his suddenly blazing sword and began to rain blows on her unprotected back and tail. The awful reek of burning flesh filled the clearing, and the dragon shrieked in pain. She flailed her huge tail in agony, and it was more to protect himself from that ponderous lashing than out of any conscious effort to injure the beast that Garion swung a massive blow with Iron-grip's sword. The sharp edge sheared effortlessly through scale and flesh and bone, smoothly lopping off about four feet of the writhing tip of the tail.

The shriek which thundered from the dragon's beak was shattering, and her fire boiled skyward in a huge cloud. A great jet of streaming blood spurted from the wound the sword had left, splashing into Garion's face and momentarily blinding him.

"Garion!" Polgara shouted. "Look out!"

He clawed at his eyes to clear away the hot blood. With terrifying agility, the dragon whirled, her talons tearing at the earth and her wings thundering. The Orb exploded into intense fire, and its blue flame ran anew up the sword, hissing and smoking as it burned away the thick blood which besmeared the blade. In the very act of striking at him with her beak, the dragon flinched back from the incandescence of the burning sword. Garion raised his blade, and once again the dragon flinched, retreating step by step across the wet clearing.

She was afraid! For some reason, the blue fire of the sword frightened her! Shrieking and trying desperately to defend herself with furnacelike gusts of fire, she backed away, her wounded tail still spraying the clearing with blood. There was clearly something about the fire of the Orb which she found unbearable. Once again filled with that wild surge of excitement, Garion raised his sword, and a searing pillar of fire erupted from its tip. He began to lash at the dragon with that whip of flame and heard the crackling sizzle as it seared her wings and shoulders. Fiercely he flogged her with the flame of his sword until, with a howl of agony, she turned and fled, tearing the earth with her talons and desperately flapping the huge sails of her wings.

Ponderously, she hurled herself into the air and clawed at the night with her wings, struggling to lift her vast bulk. She crashed through the upper branches of the firs at the edge of the clearing, fighting in panic to rise above the forest until she was clear. Shrieking, she flew off toward the southwest, filling the murky air with seething clouds of fire and streaming blood behind her as she went.

A stunned silence fell over them all as they looked up at the great beast fleeing through the rainy sky.

Polgara, her face dreadfully pale, came out from under the

trees to confront Eriond. "Just exactly what were you thinking of?" she asked him in a terribly quiet voice.

"I don't quite follow you, Polgara," he replied, looking puzzled.

She controlled herself with an obvious effort. "Doesn't the word 'danger' have any meaning to you at all?"

"You mean the dragon? Oh, she wasn't really all that dangerous."

"She *did* sort of bury you up to the eyebrows in fire, Eriond," Silk pointed out.

"Oh, that," Eriond smiled. "But the fire wasn't real." He looked around at the rest of them. "Didn't you all know that?" he asked, looking slightly surprised. "It was only an illusion. That's all that evil ever really is—an illusion. I'm sorry if any of you were worried, but I didn't have time to explain."

Aunt Pol stared at the unperturbed young man for a moment, then turned her eyes on Garion, who stood still holding his burning sword. "And you—you—" Words somehow failed her. Slowly she sank her face into her trembling hands. "Two of them," she said in a terrible voice. "Two of them! I don't think I can stand this—not two of them."

Durnik looked at her gravely, then handed his axe to the giant Toth. He stepped over and put his arm about her shoulders. "There, there," he said. For a moment she seemed to resist, but then she suddenly buried her face in his shoulder. "Come along now, Pol," he said soothingly and gently turned her around to walk her back to their shelter. "Things won't seem nearly so bad in the morning."

CHAPTER THREE

Garion slept very little during the remainder of that rainy night. His pulse still raced with excitement, and he lay under his blankets beside Ce'Nedra, living and reliving his encounter with the dragon. It was only toward the tag end of the night that he became calm enough to consider an idea that had come to him in the midst of the fight. He had *enjoyed* it. He had actually enjoyed a struggle that should have terrified him; the more he thought about it, the more he realized that this was not the first time that this had happened. As far back as his early childhood, this same wild excitement had filled him each time he had been in danger.

The solid good sense of his Sendarian upbringing told him that this enthusiasm for conflict and peril was probably an unhealthy outgrowth of his Alorn heritage and that he should strive to keep it rigidly controlled, but deep inside he knew that he would not. He had finally found the answer to the plaintive "Why me?" which he had voiced so often in the past. He was inevitably chosen for these dreadful, frightening tasks because he was perfectly suited for them.

"It's what I do," he muttered to himself. "Any time there's something so ridiculously dangerous that no rational human being would even consider trying it, they send for me."

"What was that, Garion?" Ce'Nedra murmured drowsily.

"Nothing, dear," he replied. "I was just thinking out loud. Go back to sleep."

"Ummm," she murmured and snuggled closer to him, filling his nostrils with the warm fragrance of her hair.

Dawn crept slowly under the overspreading limbs of the sodden forest with a kind of growing paleness. The persistent drizzle joined with a morning mist rising from the forest floor to form a kind of damp, gray cloud enveloping the dark trunks of fir and spruce.

Garion awoke from a half doze and saw the shadowy forms of Durnik and Toth standing quietly beside the cold fire pit at the front of the shelter. He slipped out from under the blankets, moving carefully to avoid waking his sleeping wife, and pulled on his clammy boots. Then he stood up, pulled on his cloak, and moved out from under the tent canvas to join them.

He looked up toward the gloomy morning sky. "Still raining, I see," he noted in that quiet tone people use when they rise before the sun.

Durnik nodded. "At this time of year it probably won't blow over for a week or so." He opened the leather pouch at his hip and took out his wad of tinder. "I suppose we'd better get a fire going," he said.

Toth, huge and silent, went over to the side of their shelter, picked up two leather water bags and started down the steep slope toward the spring. Despite his enormous size, he made almost no sound as he moved through the fog-shrouded bushes.

Durnik knelt by the fire pit and carefully heaped dry twigs in the center. Then he laid his ball of tinder beside the twigs and took out his flint and steel.

"Is Aunt Pol still asleep?" Garion asked him.

"Dozing. She says that it's very pleasant to lie in a warm bed while somebody else builds up the fire." Durnik smiled gently.

Garion also smiled. "That's probably because for all those years she was usually the first one up." He paused. "Is she still unhappy about last night?" he asked.

"Oh," Durnik said, bending over the pit and striking at his flint with his steel, "I think she's regained her composure a bit." His flint and steel made a subdued clicking sound; with each click a shower of bright, lingering sparks spilled down into the pit. One of them fell glowing onto the tinder, and the smith gently blew on it until a tiny tongue of orange flame rose from the center. Then he carefully moved the tinder under the twigs, and the flame grew and spread with a dry crackling. "There we are," he said, brushing the fire from the tinder and returning it to his pouch along with his flint and steel.

Garion knelt beside him and began snapping a dry branch into short lengths.

"You were very brave last night, Garion," Durnik said as the two of them fed the small fire.

"I think the word is insane," Garion replied wryly. "Would anybody in his right mind try to do something like that? I think the trouble is that I'm usually right in the middle of those things before I give any thought to how dangerous they are. Sometimes I wonder if Grandfather wasn't right. Maybe Aunt Pol *did* drop me on my head when I was a baby."

Durnik chuckled softly. "I sort of doubt it," he said. "She's very careful with children and other breakable things."

They added more branches to the fire until they had a cheerful blaze going, and then Garion stood up. The firelight reflected back from the fog with a soft, ruddy glow that had about it a kind of hazy unreality, as if, all unaware, they had inadvertently crossed the boundaries of the real world sometime during the night and entered the realms of magic and enchantment.

As Toth came back up from the spring with the two dripping waterbags, Polgara emerged from their shelter, brushing her long, dark hair. For some reason the single white lock above her left brow seemed almost incandescent this morning. "It's a very nice fire, dear," she said, kissing her husband. Then she looked at Garion. "Are you all right?" she asked him.

"What? Oh, yes. I'm fine."

"No cuts or bruises or singes you might have overlooked last night?"

"No. I seem to have gotten through it without a scratch." He hesitated. "Were you really upset last night, Aunt Pol—with Eriond and me, I mean?"

"Yes, Garion, I really was—but that was last night. What would you like for breakfast this morning?"

Some time later, as the pale dawn crept steadily under the trees, Silk stood shivering on one side of the fire pit with his hands stretched out to the flames and his eyes suspiciously fixed on the bubbling pot Aunt Pol had set on a flat rock at the very edge of the fire. "Gruel?" he asked. "Again?"

"Hot porridge," Aunt Pol corrected, stirring the contents of the pot with a long-handled wooden spoon.

"They're the same thing, Polgara."

"Not really. Gruel is thinner."

"Thick or thin, it's all the same."

She looked at him with one raised eyebrow. "Tell me, Prince Kheldar, why are you always so disagreeable in the morning?"

"Because I detest mornings. The only reason there's such a thing as morning in the first place is to keep night and afternoon from bumping into each other."

"Perhaps one of my tonics might sweeten your blood."

His eyes grew wary. "Ah—no. Thanks all the same, Polgara. Now that I'm all the way awake, I feel much better."

"I'm so glad for you. Now, do you suppose you could move away a bit? I'm going to need that side of the fire for the bacon."

"Anything you say." And he turned and went quickly back into the shelter.

Belgarath, who was lounging on top of his blankets, looked at the little man with an amused expression. "For a supposedly intelligent man, you *do* have a tendency to blunder from time to time, don't you?" he asked. "You should have learned by now not to bother Pol when she's cooking."

Silk grunted and picked up his moth-eaten fur cape. "I think I'll go check the horses," he said. "Do you want to come along?"

Belgarath cast an appraising eye at Polgara's dwindling supply of firewood. "That might not be a bad idea," he agreed, rising to his feet.

"I'll go with you," Garion said. "I've got a few kinks I'd like to work out. I think I slept on a stump last night." He slung the loop of his sword belt across one shoulder and followed the other two out of the shelter.

"It's sort of hard to believe that it really happened, isn't it?" Silk murmured when they reached the clearing. "The dragon, I mean. Now that it's daylight, everything looks so prosaic."

"Not quite," Garion said, pointing at the scaly chunk of the dragon's tail lying on the far edge of the clearing. The tip end of it was still twitching slightly.

Silk nodded. "That *is* the sort of thing you wouldn't ordinarily run across on a casual morning stroll." He looked at Belgarath. "Is she likely to bother us again?" he asked. "This is going to be a very nervous journey if we have to keep looking back over our shoulders every step of the way. Is she at all vindictive?"

"How do you mean?" the old man asked him.

"Well, Garion *did* kind of cut her tail off, after all. Do you think she might take it personally?"

"Not usually," Belgarath replied. "She doesn't really have that much in the way of a brain." He frowned thoughtfully. "What bothers me is that there was something about the whole encounter that was all wrong."

"Even the idea of it was wrong," Silk shuddered.

Belgarath shook his head. "That's not what I mean. I can't be sure if I imagined it or not, but she seemed to be looking specifically for one of us."

"Eriond?" Garion suggested.

"It sort of seemed that way, didn't it? But when she found him, she looked almost as if he frightened her. And what did he mean by those peculiar things he said to her?"

"Who knows?" Silk shrugged. "He's always been a strange boy. I don't think he lives in the same world with the rest of us."

"But why was the dragon so afraid of Garion's sword?"

"That sword frightens whole armies, Belgarath. The fire alone is pretty terrifying."

"She *likes* fire, Silk. I've seen her try to be coy and seductive for the benefit of a burning barn, and one time she flew around for a week making calves' eyes at a forest fire. There's something about last night that keeps nagging at me."

Eriond came out of the thicket where the horses were picketed, walking carefully around the dripping bushes.

"Are they all right?" Garion asked.

"The horses? They're fine, Belgarion. Is breakfast almost ready?"

"If that's what you want to call it," Silk replied sourly.

"Polgara's really a very good cook, Kheldar," Eriond assured him earnestly.

"Not even the best cook in the world can do very much with porridge."

Eriond's eyes brightened. "She's making porridge? I love porridge."

Silk gave him a long look, then turned sadly to Garion.

"You see how easily the young are corrupted?" he observed. "Just give them the faintest hint of a wholesome upbringing, and they're lost forever." He squared his shoulders. "All right," he said grimly, "let's go get it over with."

After breakfast, they broke down their night's encampment and set out through the soft drizzle falling from the weeping sky. It was about noon when they reached a wide swath of cleared land, a stretch of bushy, stump-dotted ground perhaps a quarter of a mile wide, and in the center of that swath lay a wide, muddy road.

"The high road from Muros," Silk said with some satisfaction.

"Why did they cut down all the trees?" Eriond asked him.

"They used to have trouble with robbers lying in ambush right beside the road. The cleared space on each side gives travelers a sporting chance to get away."

They rode out from under the dripping trees and across the weed-grown clearing to the muddy road. "Now we should be able to make better time," Belgarath said, nudging his horse into a trot.

They followed the road south for several hours, moving at a steady canter. As they rode down out of the forested foothills, the trees gave way to rolling grasslands. They crested a hilltop and reined in to give their steaming mounts a brief rest. Somewhat to the northwest they saw the dark border of the great Arendish forest, hazy in the misty drizzle, and not far ahead the grim, gray-walled pile of Mimbrate castle brooding down on the grasslands lying below. Ce'Nedra sighed as she stared out over the sodden plain and at the fortress that seemed to hold in its very stones all the stiff-necked, wary suspicion that was at the core of Arendish society.

"Are you all right?" Garion asked her, fearful that her sigh might signify a return to that bleak melancholy which she had so recently shaken off.

"There's something so mournful about Arendia," she replied. "All those thousands of years of hatred and grief, and what did they prove? Even that castle seems to be weeping."

"That's just the rain, Ce'Nedra," he said carefully.

"No," she sighed again. "It's more than that."

The road from Muros was a muddy yellow scar, stretching between fields of browned, drooping grasses as it wound down to the Arendish plain, and for the next several days they rode past great, rearing Mimbrate castles and through dirty thatch and wattle villages where acrid wood smoke hung in the chill air like a miasma and the hopeless expressions on the faces of the ragged serfs bespoke lives lived out in misery and despair. They stopped each night in mean, shabby wayside inns reeking of spoiled food and unwashed bodies.

On the fourth day, they crested a hill and looked down at the garish sprawl of the Great Arendish Fair, standing at the junction of the high road from Muros and the Great West Road. The tents and pavilions spread for a league or more in every direction in a gaudy profusion of blue and red and yellow beneath a weeping gray sky, and pack-trains going to and from that great commercial center crawled across the plain like streams of ants.

Silk pushed his shabby hat back from his face. "Maybe I'd better go down and take a quick look around before we all ride in," he said. "We've been out of touch for a while, and it might not hurt to get the feel of things."

"All right," Belgarath agreed, "but no chicanery."

"Chicanery?"

"You know what I mean, Silk. Keep your instincts under control."

"Trust me, Belgarath."

"Not if I can help it."

Silk laughed and thumped his heels to his horse's flanks.

The rest of them rode at a walk down the long slope as Silk galloped on ahead toward that perpetually temporary tent-city standing in its sea of mud. As they approached the fair, Garion could hear a cacophonous tumult filling the air—a sort of bawling clamor of thousands of voices shouting all at once. There was also a myriad of scents—of spices and cooking food, of rare perfumes, and of horse corrals.

Belgarath drew in his mount. "Let's wait here for Silk," he said. "I don't want to blunder into anything."

They sat their horses to one side of the road in the chill rain, watching the slow crawl of pack trains slipping and sliding up the muddy road toward them.

About three-quarters of an hour later, Silk came pounding back up the hill. "I think we might want to approach carefully," he said, his pointed face serious.

"What's the matter?" Belgarath asked.

"I ran into Delvor," Silk replied, "and he told me that there's an Angarak merchant who's been asking questions about us."

"Maybe we should just bypass the fair, then," Durnik suggested.

Silk shook his head. "I think we ought to find out a little bit more about this curious Angarak. Delvor's offered to put us up in his tents for a day or so, but it might not be a bad idea if we circle the fair and come in from the south. We can join one of the caravans coming up from Tol Honeth. That way we won't be quite so obvious."

Belgarath considered it, squinting up at the rainy sky. "All right," he decided. "I don't want to waste too much time, but I don't like the idea of someone following us, either. Let's go see what Delvor can tell us."

They rode in a wide half circle through the rain-drenched grass and reached the muddy track of the Great West Road a mile or so south of the fair. A half-dozen Tolnedran merchants wrapped in rich fur cloaks rode at the head of a string of creaking wagons, and Garion and his friends unobtrusively fell in at the tail end of their column as the gradual darkening of the sky announced the approach of a dreary, rain-swept evening.

The narrow lanes lying between the tents and pavilions seethed with merchants from all parts of the world. The soupy mud was ankle-deep, churned by the hooves of hundreds of horses and the feet of brightly dressed men of trade, who bawled and shouted and haggled with each other, ignoring the mud and rain. Torches and lanterns hung at the sides of open-fronted booths made of canvas, where treasures of incalculable worth stood in curious proximity to brass pots and cheap tin plates.

"It's this way," Silk said, turning into a side lane. "Delvor's tents are a few hundred yards on up ahead."

"Who's Delvor?" Ce'Nedra asked Garion as they rode past a noisy tavern pavilion.

"A friend of Silk's. We met him the last time we were here. I think he's a member of Drasnian Intelligence."

She sniffed. "Aren't all Drasnians members of the intelligence service?"

He grinned. "Probably," he agreed.

Delvor was waiting for them in front of his blue and white striped pavilion. Silk's friend had changed very little in the years since Garion had last seen him. He was as bald as an egg, and his expression was still as shrewd and cynical as it had been before. He wore a fur-trimmed cloak pulled tightly about his shoulders, and his bald head gleamed wetly in the rain. "My servants will care for your horses," he told them as they dismounted. "Let's get in out of sight before too many people see you."

They followed him into his warm, well-lighted pavilion, and he carefully tied down the tent flap behind them. The pavilion was very nearly as comfortable-looking as a well-appointed house. There were chairs and divans and a large, polished table set with a splendid supper. The floors and walls were carpeted in blue, oil lamps hung on chains from the ceiling, and in each corner there was an iron brazier filled with glowing coals. Delvor's servants all wore sober livery and they wordlessly took the dripping cloaks from Garion and his friends and carried them through a canvas partition to an adjoining tent.

"Please," Delvor said politely, "seat yourselves. I took the liberty of having a bit of supper prepared."

Silk looked around as they all sat down at the table. "Opulent," he noted.

Delvor shrugged. "A little planning—and quite a bit of money. A tent doesn't *have* to be uncomfortable."

"And it's portable," Silk added. "If one has to leave someplace in a hurry, a tent can be folded up and taken along. That's hard to do with a house."

"There's that, too," Delvor admitted blandly. "Please eat, my friends. I know the kind of accommodations—and meals—that are offered in the inns here in Arendia."

The supper that had been set for them was as fine as one that might have come to the table of a nobleman. A heap of smoking chops lay on a silver platter, and there were boiled onions and peas and carrots swimming in a delicate cheese sauce. The bread was of the finest white, still steaming hot from the oven, and there was a wide selection of excellent wines.

"Your cook appears to be a man of some talent, Delvor," Polgara noted.

"Thank you, my Lady," he replied. "He costs me a few dozen extra crowns a year and he's got a foul temper, but I think he's worth the expense and aggravation."

"What's this about a curious Angarak merchant?" Belgarath asked, helping himself to a couple of the chops.

"He rode into the fair a few days ago with a half-dozen servants, but no pack horses or wagons. Their horses looked hard-ridden, as if he and his men had come here in a hurry. Since he arrived, he hasn't done any business at all. He and his people have spent all their time asking questions."

"Are they specifically asking for us?"

"Not by name, Ancient One, but the way they've been describing you didn't leave much doubt. He's been offering money for information—quite a bit of money."

"What kind of Angarak is he?"

"He claims to be a Nadrak, but if he's a Nadrak, I'm a Thull. I think he's a Mallorean. He's about medium height and build, clean-shaven and soberly dressed. About the only thing unusual about him is his eyes. They seem to be completely white—except for the pupils. There's no color to them at all."

Aunt Pol raised her head quickly. "Blind?" she asked.

"Blind? No, I don't think so. He seems to be able to see where he's going. Why do you ask, my Lady?"

"What you just described is the result of a very rare condition," she replied. "Most of the people who suffer from it are blind."

"If we're going to ride out of here without having him about ten minutes behind us, we're going to need some kind of distraction to delay him," Silk said, toying with a crystal goblet. He looked at his friend. "I don't suppose you still have any of those lead coins you hid in that Murgo tent the last time we were here, do you?"

"I'm afraid not, Silk. I had to go through customs at the Tolnedran border a few months ago. I didn't think it would be wise to have the customs people find that kind of thing in my packs, so I buried them under a tree."

"Lead coins?" Ce'Nedra said with a puzzled look. "What could you possibly buy with coins made of lead?"

"They're gilded, your Majesty," Delvor told her. "They look exactly like Tolnedran gold crowns."

Ce'Nedra's face suddenly went pale. "That's horrible!" she gasped.

Delvor's face mirrored his puzzlement at the vehemence of her reaction.

"Her Majesty is a Tolnedran, Delvor," Silk reminded him, "and counterfeit money strikes at the very core of a Tolnedran's being. I think it has something to do with their religion."

"I don't find that particularly amusing, Prince Kheldar," Ce'Nedra said tartly.

After supper they talked for a while longer, the comfortable talk of people who are warm and well-fed, and then Delvor led them into an adjoining tent that had been partitioned off into sleeping chambers. Garion fell asleep almost as soon as his head touched the pillow and he awoke the following morning feeling more refreshed than he had in weeks. He dressed quietly to avoid waking Ce'Nedra and went out into the main pavilion.

Silk and Delvor sat at the table talking quietly. "There's a great deal of ferment going on here in Arendia," Delvor was saying. "The news of the campaign against the Bear-cult in the Alorn kingdoms has stirred the blood of all the young hotheads—both Mimbrate and Asturian. The thought of a fight someplace that they weren't invited to attend fills young Arends with anguish."

"There's nothing new about that," Silk said. "Good morning, Garion."

"Gentlemen," Garion said politely, pulling up a chair.

"Your Majesty," Delvor greeted him. Then he turned back to Silk. "The thing that concerns everybody more than the casual belligerence of the young nobles, though, is the unrest that's arisen among the serfs."

Garion remembered the miserable hovels in the villages they had passed in the last few days and the hopeless looks on the faces of their inhabitants. "They have reason enough for discontent, don't you think?" he said.

"I'd be the first to agree, your Majesty," Delvor said, "and it's not the first time it's happened. This time, though, it's a little more serious. The authorities have been finding caches of weapons—fairly sophisticated ones. A serf with a pitchfork isn't much of a match for an armored Mimbrate knight. A serf with a crossbow, however, is an altogether different matter. There have been several incidents—and some reprisals."

"How could serfs get those kinds of weapons?" Garion asked him. "Most of the time they don't even have enough to eat. How could they possibly afford to buy crossbows?"

"They're coming in from outside the country," Delvor told him. "We haven't been able to pinpoint the source yet, but it's fairly obvious that *somebody* wants to make sure that the Arendish nobility is too busy at home to get involved in anything anyplace else."

"Kal Zakath, perhaps?" Silk suggested.

"It's entirely possible," Delvor agreed. "There's no question that the emperor of Mallorea has global ambitions, and turmoil in the Kingdoms of the West would be his best ally if he decides to turn his armies northward after he finally kills King Urgit."

Garion groaned. "That's all I need," he said, "one *more* thing to worry about."

When the others joined them in the main pavilion, Delvor's servants brought in a huge breakfast. There were whole platters of eggs, heaps of bacon and sausage, and plate after plate of fruit and rich pastries.

"Now *this* is what I call a breakfast," Silk said enthusiastically.

Polgara gave him a cool look. "Go ahead and say it, Prince Kheldar," she said. "I'm sure that you have all sorts of interesting observations to make."

"Would *I* say anything about that excellent gruel you offer us every morning, dear lady?" he asked with exaggerated innocence.

"Not if you're at all concerned about your health, you wouldn't," Ce'Nedra said sweetly.

One of the servants entered the tent with an offended expression on his face. "There's an obnoxious, filthy hunchback outside, Delvor," he reported. "He has the foulest mouth I've ever run across and he's demanding to be let in. Do you want us to chase him off?"

"Oh, that would be Uncle Beldin," Polgara said.

"You know him?" Delvor seemed surprised.

"I've known him since I was a baby," she replied. "He's not really as bad as he seems—once you get used to him." She frowned slightly. "You probably ought to let him come in," she advised. "He can be *terribly* unpleasant when people irritate him."

"Belgarath," Beldin growled, roughly pushing his way past the protesting servant, "is this all the farther you've come? I thought you'd be in Tol Honeth by now."

"We had to stop at Prolgu to see the Gorim," Belgarath replied mildly.

"This isn't a grand tour, you blockhead," Beldin snapped irritably. The little hunchback was as filthy as ever. The wet rags he wore for clothes were tied to his body here and there with lengths of rotten twine. His hair was matted and had twigs and bits of straw clinging to it. His hideous face was as black as a thundercloud as he stumped to the table on his short, gnarled legs and helped himself to a bit of sausage.

"Please try to be civil, uncle," Aunt Pol said.

"Why?" He pointed at a small pot standing on the table. "What's in that?"

"Jam," Delvor replied, looking slightly intimidated.

"Interesting," Beldin said. He dipped one dirty hand into the pot and began feeding gobs of jam into his mouth. "Not bad," he said, licking his fingers.

"There's bread right there, uncle," Aunt Pol said pointedly.

"I don't like bread," he grunted, wiping his hand on his clothes.

"Did you manage to catch up with Harakan?" Belgarath asked him.

Beldin retorted with a number of expletives that made Ce'Nedra's face blanch. "He gave me the slip again. I don't have the time to waste chasing him, so I'll have to forgo the pleasure of splitting him up the middle." He dipped his hand into the jam pot again.

"If we run across him, we'll take care of it for you," Silk offered.

"He's a sorcerer, Kheldar. If you get in his way, he'll hang your guts on a fence."

"I was going to let Garion do it."

Beldin set down the empty jam pot and belched.

"Can I offer you anything else?" Delvor asked him.

"No, thanks all the same, but I'm full now." He turned back to Belgarath. "Were you planning to get as far as Tol Honeth before summer?"

"We're not really *that* far behind, Beldin," Belgarath protested.

Beldin made an indelicate sound. "Keep your eyes open on the way south," he advised. "There's a Mallorean who's been asking questions about you and the others. He's been hiring people all up and down the Great West Road."

Belgarath looked at him sharply. "Could you get any kind of name?"

"He uses several. The one that crops up most often is Naradas."

"Have you got any idea of what he looks like?" Silk asked.

"About all I've been able to pick up is the fact that he's got funny eyes. From what I've been told, they're all white."

"Well," Delvor said, "well, well, well."

"What's that supposed to mean?" Beldin asked him.

"The man with white eyes is right here in the fair. He's been asking questions here, too."

"That makes it fairly easy, then. Have somebody go run a knife into his back."

Belgarath shook his head. "The legionnaires who police the fair get excited when unexplained bodies start showing up," he said.

Beldin shrugged. "Rap him on the head with something, then drag him a few miles out onto the plain. Cut his throat and dump him in a hole. He probably won't sprout until spring." He looked over at Polgara with a sly grin creasing his ugly face. "If you keep nibbling on that pastry, girl, you're going to spread. You're chubby enough already."

"*Chubby?*"

"That's all right, Pol. Some men like girls with fat bottoms."

"Why don't you wipe the jam out of your beard, uncle?"

"I'm saving it for lunch." He scratched one armpit.

"Lice again?" she asked coolly.

"It's always possible. I don't mind a few lice, though. They're better company than most people I know."

"Where are you going now?" Belgarath asked him.

"Back to Mallorea. I want to root around in Darshiva for a while and see what I can dig up about Zandramas."

Delvor had been looking at the grimy little man with a speculative squint. "Were you planning to leave immediately, Master Beldin?" he asked.

"Why?"

"I'd like a word with you in private, if you've got a few moments."

"Secrets, Delvor?" Silk asked.

"Not really, old boy. I've got a sort of an idea, but I'd like to get it a bit more developed before I tell you about it." He turned back to the hunchback. "Why don't we take a little stroll, Master Beldin? I have a notion that might appeal to you, and it really won't take very long."

Beldin's look was curious. "All right," he agreed, and the two of them went outside into the drizzling morning.

"What was that all about?" Garion asked Silk.

"It's an irritating habit Delvor picked up at the Academy. He likes to pull off clever ploys without any advance warning. That way he can sit around afterward and bask in everyone's stunned admiration." The little man looked at the table. "I believe I'll have just a bit more of that sausage," he said, "and maybe a few more eggs. It's a long way to Tol Honeth, and I'd like to put in a buffer against all that gruel."

Polgara looked at Ce'Nedra. "Have you ever noticed that when some people find a notion they think is funny, they tend to keep playing with it long past the point where it bores everyone else to tears?"

Ce'Nedra looked at Silk with a sly little twinkle in her eyes. "I've noticed that, Lady Polgara. Do you suppose it might be the result of a limited imagination?"

"I'm sure that has something to do with it, dear." Aunt Polgara looked at Silk with a serene smile. "Now, did you want to play some more, Kheldar?"

"Ah—no, Polgara. I don't really think so."

It was shortly before noon when Delvor and Beldin returned, each with a self-satisfied smirk on his face. "It was a truly masterful performance, Master Beldin," Delvor congratulated the little hunchback as they entered.

"Child's play." Beldin shrugged deprecatingly. "People inevitably believe that a deformed body houses a defective brain. I've used that to my advantage many times."

"I'm sure they'll tell us what this is all about eventually," Silk said.

"It wasn't too complicated, Silk," Delvor told him. "You'll be able to leave now without any worries about that curious Mallorean."

"Oh?"

"He was trying to buy information," Delvor shrugged, "so we sold him some, and he left—at a full gallop."

"What sort of information did you sell him?"

"It went sort of like this," Beldin said. He stooped a bit more, deliberately exaggerating his deformity, and his face took on an expression of vapid imbecility. "An' it please yer honor," he said in a squeaky voice dripping with servile stupidity, "I hears that you wants to find some people an' that you says you'll pay to know where they be. I seed the people yer lookin fer, an' I kin tell you where they was—if you gimme enough money. How much was you willin' to pay?"

Delvor laughed delightedly. "Naradas swallowed it whole. I took Master Beldin to him and told him that I'd found someone who knew about the people he was looking for. We agreed to a price, and then your friend here gulled him completely."

"Which way did you send him?" Belgarath asked.

"North." Beldin shrugged. "I told him that I'd seen you camped by the roadside up in the Arendish forest—that one of the members of your party had fallen sick and that you'd stopped to nurse him back to health."

"Wasn't he at all suspicious?" Silk asked.

Delvor shook his head. "The thing that makes people suspicious is help that comes for no particular reason. I gave Naradas every reason to believe that I was sincere. I cheated Master Beldin—outrageously. Naradas gave him a few silver coins for his information. *My* price, however, was much higher."

"Brilliant," Silk murmured admiringly.

"There's something you ought to know about White Eyes, though," Beldin told Belgarath. "He's a Mallorean Grolim. I didn't probe into him too hard, because I didn't want him to catch what I was doing, but I *was* able to get that much. He's got a great deal of power, so watch out for him."

"Did you find out whom he's working for?"

Beldin shook his head. "I pulled back as soon as I found out what he was." The hunchback's face grew bleak. "Be careful about this one, Belgarath. He's very dangerous."

Belgarath's face grew grim. "So am I, Beldin," he said.

"I know, but there are some things you *won't* do. Naradas doesn't feel that kind of restraint."

CHAPTER FOUR

They rode south under clearing skies for the next six days. A cold wind bent the winter-browned grass at the sides of the road, and the rolling plain of southern Arendia lay dead and sere beneath a chill blue sky. They passed an occasional mud-and-wattle village where ragged serfs clenched themselves to endure yet another winter and more infrequently a rearing stone keep where a proud Mimbrate baron kept a watchful eye on his neighbors.

The Great West Road, like all roads that formed a part of the Tolnedran highway system, was patrolled by scarlet-cloaked Imperial Legionnaires. Garion and his friends also encountered an occasional merchant traveling northward with wary eyes and accompanied by burly hirelings whose hands never strayed far from their weapons.

They reached the River Arend on a frosty midmorning and looked across the sparkling ford at the Forest of Vordue in northern Tolnedra. "Did you want to stop at Vo Mimbre?" Silk asked Belgarath.

The old man shook his head. "Mandorallen and Lelldorin have probably already advised Korodullin about what happened in Drasnia, and I'm not really in the mood for three or four days of speeches filled with thee's and thou's and forasmuches. Besides, I want to get to Tol Honeth as soon as possible."

As they splashed through the swallow waters of the ford, Garion remembered something. "Will we have to stop at that customs station?" he asked.

"Naturally," Silk replied. "Everybody has to go through customs—except for licensed smugglers, of course." He looked over at Belgarath. "Do you want me to handle things when we get there?"

"Just don't get too creative."

"Nothing could have been further from my mind, Belgarath. All I want is a chance to try these out." He indicated the seedy clothing he wore.

"I've been sort of wondering what you had in mind when you picked out your wardrobe," Durnik said.

Silk gave him a sly wink.

They rode up out of the ford and on into the Forest of Vordue with its neatly spaced trees and groomed undergrowth. They had gone no more than a league when they came to the whitewashed building that housed the customs station. One corner of the long, shedlike structure showed signs of a recent fire, and the red-tile roof was badly soot-darkened at that end. A half-dozen slovenly soldiers of the customs service were huddled in the muddy yard about a small open fire, drinking cheap wine to ward off the chill. One of them, a stubble-faced man in a patched cloak and rusty breastplate, indolently rose, stepped into the middle of the road, and held up one beefy hand. "That's as far as you go," he declared. "Take your horses over there beside the building and open your packs for inspection."

Silk pushed forward. "Of course, sergeant," he replied in an obsequious, fawning tone. "We have nothing to hide."

"*We'll* decide that," the unshaven soldier said, swaying slightly as he barred their path.

The customs agent emerged from the station with a blanket wrapped about his shoulders. It was the same stout man whom they had encountered years before when they had passed this way during their pursuit of Zedar and the stolen Orb. On their previous meeting, however, there had been a certain smug self-satisfaction about him. Now his florid face bore the discontented expression of a man who lives with the conviction that life has somehow cheated him. "What do you have to declare?" he demanded brusquely.

"Nothing on this trip, I'm afraid, your Excellency," Silk answered in a whining voice. "We're just poor travelers on our way to Tol Honeth."

The paunchy agent peered at the little man. "I think we've met before, haven't we? Aren't you Radek of Boktor?"

"The same, your Excellency. You have an extremely good memory."

"In my business, you have to. How did you do with your Sendarian woolens that time?"

Silk's face grew melancholy. "Not nearly as well as I'd hoped. The weather broke before I got to Tol Honeth, so the price was less than half of what it should have been."

"I'm sorry to hear that," the agent said perfunctorily. "Would you mind opening your packs?"

"All we have is food and spare clothing." The little Drasnian was actually sniveling.

"It's been my experience that people sometimes forget that they're carrying things of value. Open the packs, Radek."

"Anything you say, Excellency." Silk clambered down from his horse and began unbuckling the straps on the packs.

"I wish I *did* have things of value in here," he sighed tragically, "but that unfortunate venture in the wool market started a long decline for me, I'm afraid. I'm virtually out of business."

The agent grunted and rummaged through their packs for several minutes, shivering all the while. Finally he turned back to Silk with a sour look. "It seems that you're telling the truth, Radek. I'm sorry I doubted you." He blew on his hands trying to warm them. "Times have been hard of late. Nothing's come through here in the last six months that was even worth a decent bribe."

"I've heard that there's been some trouble down here in Vordue," Silk whined as he buckled the packs shut again. "Something about a secession from the rest of Tolnedra."

"The most idiotic thing in the history of the Empire," the agent exploded. "All the brains went out of the Vordue family after the Grand Duke Kador died. They should have known that fellow was an agent for a foreign power."

"Which fellow was that?"

"The one who claimed that he was an eastern merchant. He wormed his way into the confidence of the Vordues and puffed them up with flattery. By the time he was done, they actually believed that they were competent enough to run their own kingdom, independent of the rest of Tolnedra. But that Varana's a sly one, let me tell you. He struck a bargain with King Korodullin, and before long all of Vordue was crawling with Mimbrate knights stealing everything in sight." He pointed at the scorched corner of his station. "You see that? A platoon or so of them came by here and sacked the building. Then they set fire to the place."

"Tragic," Silk commiserated with him. "Did anyone ever find out just who that so-called merchant was working for?"

"Those idiots in Tol Vordue didn't, that's for certain, but I knew who he was the minute I laid eyes on him."

"Oh?"

"The man was a Rivan, and that puts the whole thing right in the lap of King Belgarion. He's always hated the Vordues anyway, so he came up with this scheme to break their power in northern Tolnedra." He smiled bleakly. "He's getting exactly what he's got coming to him, though. They forced him to marry the Princess Ce'Nedra, and she's making his life miserable."

"How were you able to tell that the agent was Rivan?" Silk asked curiously.

"That's easy, Radek. The Rivans have been isolated on that island of theirs for thousands of years. They're so inbred that all kinds of defects and deformities crop up in them."

"He was deformed?"

The agent shook his head. "It was his eyes," he said. "They didn't have any color to them at all—absolutely white." He shuddered. "It was a chilling thing to see." He pulled his blanket tighter about his shoulders. "I'm sorry, Radek, but I'm freezing out here. I'm going back inside where it's warm. You and your friends are free to go." And with that he hurried back into the station and the warmth of his fireside.

"Isn't *that* interesting?" Silk said as they rode away.

Belgarath was frowning. "The next question is who this busy man with the white eyes is working for," he said.

"Urvon?" Durnik suggested. "Maybe he put Harakan to work in the north and Naradas here in the south—both of them trying to stir up as much turmoil as possible."

"Maybe," Belgarath grunted, "but then again maybe not."

"My dear Prince Kheldar," Ce'Nedra said, pushing back the hood of her cloak with one mittened hand, "what exactly was the purpose of all that cringing and sniveling?"

"Characterization, Ce'Nedra," he replied airily. "Radek of Boktor was a pompous, arrogant ass—as long as he was rich. Now that he's poor, he's gone the other way entirely. It's the nature of the man."

"But, there *isn't* any such person as Radek of Boktor."

"Of course there is. You just saw him. Radek of Boktor exists in the memories of people all over this part of the world. In many ways he's even more real than that bloated time-server back there."

"But he's *you*. You just made him up."

"Certainly I did, and I'm really rather proud of him. His existence, his background, and his entire life history are a matter of public record. He's as real as you are."

"That doesn't make sense at all, Silk," she protested.

"That's because you aren't Drasnian, Ce'Nedra."

They reached Tol Honeth several days later. The white marble Imperial City gleamed in the frosty winter sunshine, and the legionnaires standing guard at the carved bronze gates were as crisp and burnished as always. As Garion and his friends clattered across the marble-paved bridge to the gate, the officer in charge of the guard detachment took one look at Ce'Nedra and banged his clenched fist on his polished breastplate in salute. "Your Imperial Highness," he greeted her. "If we had known you were approaching, we would have sent out an escort."

"That's all right, Captain," she replied in a tired little voice. "Do you suppose you could send one of your men on ahead of us to the palace to advise the Emperor that we're here?"

"At once, your Imperial Highness," he said, saluting again and standing aside to let them pass.

"I just wish that someday somebody in Tolnedra would remember that you're married," Garion muttered, feeling a bit surly about it.

"What was that, dear?" Ce'Nedra asked.

"Can't they get it through their heads that you're the Queen of Riva now? Every time one of them calls you 'Your Imperial Highness,' it makes me feel like some kind of hanger-on—or a servant of some sort."

"Aren't you being a little oversensitive, Garion?"

He grunted sourly, still feeling just a bit offended.

The avenues of Tol Honeth were broad and faced with the proud, lofty houses of the Tolnedran elite. Columns and statuary abounded on the fronts of those residences in vast, ostentatious display, and the richly garbed merchant princes in the streets were bedecked with jewels beyond price. Silk looked at them as he rode past and then ruefully down at his own shabby, threadbare garments. He sighed bitterly.

"More characterization, Radek?" Aunt Polgara asked him.

"Only in part," he replied. "Of course Radek *would* be envious, but I have to admit that I do sort of miss my own finery."

"How on earth do you keep all these fictitious people straight?"

"Concentration, Polgara," he said, "concentration. You can't succeed at any game if you don't concentrate."

The Imperial Compound was a cluster of sculptured marble buildings enclosed within a high wall and situated atop a hill in the western quarter of the city. Warned in advance of their approach, the legionnaires at the gate admitted the party immediately with crisp military salutes. Beyond the gate lay a paved courtyard, and standing at the foot of the marble stairs leading up to a column-fronted building stood the Emperor Varana. "Welcome to Tol Honeth," he said to them as they dismounted. Ce'Nedra hurried toward him, but stopped at the last moment and curtsied formally. "Your Imperial Majesty," she said.

"Why so ceremonial, Ce'Nedra?" he asked, holding out his arms to her.

"Please, Uncle," she said, glancing at the palace functionaries lining the top of the stairs, "not here. If you kiss me here, I'll break down and cry, and a Borune never cries in public."

"Ah," he said with an understanding look. Then he turned to the rest of them. "Come inside, all of you. Let's get in out of the cold." He turned, offered Ce'Nedra his arm and limped up the stairs.

Just inside the doors, there was a large circular rotunda, lined along its walls with marble busts of the last thousand years or so of Tolnedran Emperors. "Look like a gang of pickpockets, don't they?" Varana said to Garion with a wry smile.

"I don't see yours anywhere," Garion replied.

"The royal sculptor is having trouble with my nose. The Anadiles descended from peasant stock, and my nose isn't suitably imperial for his taste." He led them down a broad hallway to a large, candle-lit room with a crimson carpet and drapes and deeply upholstered furniture of the same hue. In each corner stood a glowing iron brazier, and the room was pleasantly warm. "Please," the Emperor said, "make yourselves comfortable. I'll send for something hot to drink and have the kitchen prepare a dinner for us." He spoke briefly with the legionnaire at the door as Garion and his friends removed their cloaks and seated themselves.

"Now," Varana said, closing the door, "what brings you to Tol Honeth?"

"You've heard about our campaign against the Bear-cult?" Belgarath asked him, "and the reason for it?"

The Emperor nodded.

"As it turned out, the campaign was misdirected. The cult was not involved in the abduction of Prince Geran, although there was an effort to implicate them. The person we're looking for is named Zandramas. Does that name mean anything to you?"

Varana frowned. "No," he replied, "I can't say that it does."

Belgarath rapidly sketched in the situation, telling Varana what they had learned about Zandramas, Harakan, and the Sardion. When he had finished, the Emperor's expression was slightly dubious.

"I can accept most of what you say, Belgarath," he said, "but some of it—" He shrugged, holding up both hands.

"What's the problem?"

"Varana's a sceptic, father," Polgara said. "There are certain things he prefers not to think about."

"Even after everything that happened at Thull Mardu?" Belgarath looked surprised.

"It's a matter of principle, Belgarath." Varana laughed. "It has to do with being a Tolnedran—and a soldier."

Belgarath gave him an amused look. "All right, then, can you accept the fact that the abduction might have been *politically* motivated?"

"Of course. I understand politics."

"Good. There have always been two major centers of power in Mallorea—the throne and the church. Now it looks as if this Zandramas is raising a third. We can't tell if Kal Zakath is directly involved in any way, but there's some kind of power struggle going on between Urvon and Zandramas. For some reason Garion's son is central to that struggle."

"We've also picked up some hints along the way that for one reason or another the Malloreans don't want us to become involved," Silk added. "There are agents stirring up trouble in Arendia, and it may have been a Mallorean who was behind the Vordue secession."

Varana looked at him sharply.

"A man named Naradas."

"Now that's a name I *have* heard," the Emperor said. "Supposedly he's an Angarak merchant here to negotiate some very sweeping trade agreements. He travels a great deal and spends a lot of money. My commercial advisors think that he's an agent for King Urgit. Now that Zakath controls the mining regions in eastern Cthol Murgos, Urgit desperately needs money to finance the war he's got going on down there."

Silk shook his head. "I don't think so," he said. "Naradas is a Mallorean Grolim. It's not likely that he'd be working for the King of the Murgos."

There was a respectful tap at the door.

"Yes?" Varana said.

The door opened and Lord Morin, the Imperial Chamberlain, entered. He was an old man now and very thin. His hair had gone completely white and it stood out in wisps. His skin had that waxy transparency one sees in the very old, and he moved slowly. "The Drasnian Ambassador, your Majesty," he announced in a quavering voice. "He says that he has some information of great urgency for you—and for your guests."

"You'd better show him in then, Morin."

"There's a young lady with him, your Majesty," Morin added. "A Drasnian noblewoman, I believe."

"We'll see them both," Varana said.

"As you wish, your Majesty," Morin replied with a creaky bow.

When the aged Chamberlain escorted the ambassador and his companion into the room, Garion blinked in surprise. "His Excellency, Prince Khaldon, Ambassador of the Royal Court of Drasnia," Morin announced, "and her Ladyship, the Margravine Liselle, a—uh—" He faltered.

"Spy, your Excellency," Liselle supplied with aplomb.

"Is that an official designation, your Ladyship?"

"It saves a great deal of time, Excellency."

"My," Morin sighed, "how the world changes. Should I introduce your Ladyship to the Emperor as an official spy?"

"I think he's gathered that already, Lord Morin," she said, touching his thin hand affectionately.

Morin bowed and tottered slowly from the room.

"What a dear old man," she murmured.

"Well, hello, cousin," Silk said to the ambassador.

"Cousin," Prince Khaldon replied coolly.

"Are you two somehow related?" Varana asked.

"Distantly, your Majesty," Silk told him. "Our mothers were second cousins—or was it third?"

"Fourth, I think," Khaldon said. He eyed his rat-faced relative. "You're looking a bit seedy, old man," he noted. "The last time I saw you, you were dripping gold and jewels."

"I'm in disguise, cousin," Silk said blandly. "You're not supposed to be able to recognize me."

"Ah," Khaldon said. He turned to the Emperor. "Please excuse our banter, your Majesty. Kheldar here and I have loathed each other since childhood."

Silk grinned. "It was hate at first sight," he agreed. "We absolutely detest each other."

Khaldon smiled briefly. "When we were children, they used to hide all the knives every time our families visited each other."

Silk looked curiously at Liselle. "What are you doing in Tol Honeth?" he asked her.

"It's a secret."

"Velvet brought several dispatches from Boktor," Khaldon explained, "and certain instructions."

"Velvet?"

"Silly, isn't it?" Liselle laughed. "But then, I suppose they could have chosen a worse nickname for me."

"It's better than some that spring to mind," Silk agreed.

"Be nice, Kheldar."

"There was something you thought we ought to know, Prince Khaldon?" Varana asked.

Khaldon sighed. "It saddens me to report that the courtesan Bethra has been murdered, your Majesty."

"*What?*"

"She was set upon by assassins in a deserted street last night when she was returning from a business engagement. She was left for dead, but she managed to drag herself to our gate, and she was able to pass on some information before she died."

Silk's face had gone quite white. "Who was responsible for it?" he demanded.

"We're still working on that, Kheldar," his cousin replied. "We have some suspicions, of course, but nothing concrete enough to take before a magistrate."

The Emperor's face was bleak, and he rose from the chair in which he had been sitting. "There are some people who will need to know about this," he said grimly. "Would you come with me, Prince Khaldon?"

"Of course, your Majesty."

"Please excuse us," Varana said to the rest of them. "This is a matter that needs my immediate attention." He led the Drasnian Ambassador from the room.

"Did she suffer greatly?" Silk asked the girl known as Velvet in a voice filled with pain.

"They used knives, Kheldar," she replied simply. "That's never pleasant."

"I see." His ferretlike face hardened. "Could she give you any kind of idea what might have been behind it?"

"I gather that it had to do with several things. She mentioned the fact that she once informed Emperor Varana of a plot against the life of his son."

"The Honeths!" Ce'Nedra grated.

"What makes you say that?" Silk asked quickly.

"Garion and I were here when she told Varana. It was at the time of my father's funeral. Bethra came secretly to the palace and said that two Honethite nobles—Count Elgon and Baron Kelbor—were hatching a scheme to murder Varana's son."

Silk's face was stony. "Thank you, Ce'Nedra," he said grimly.

"There's something else you should know, Kheldar," Velvet said quietly. She looked at the rest of them. "We all *will* be discreet about this, won't we?"

"Of course," Belgarath assured her.

Velvet turned back to Silk. "Bethra was Hunter," she told him.

"Hunter? *Bethra?*"

"She has been for several years now. When the struggle over the succession started heating up here in Tolnedra, King Rhodar instructed Javelin to take steps to make sure that the man who followed Ran Borune to the throne would be someone the Alorns could live with. Javelin came to Tol Honeth and recruited Bethra to see to it."

"Excuse me," Belgarath interrupted, his eyes alight with curiosity, "but exactly what is this 'Hunter'?"

"Our most secret spy," Velvet replied. "Hunter's identity is known only to Javelin, and Hunter deals with only the most sensitive situations—things that the Drasnian crown simply cannot openly become involved in. Anyway, when it appeared that the Grand Duke Noragon of the House of Honeth was almost certain to be the next Emperor, King Rhodar made a certain suggestion to Javelin, and a few months later, Noragon accidentally ate some bad shellfish—some *very* bad shellfish."

"Bethra did that?" Silk's tone was amazed.

"She was extraordinarily resourceful."

"Margravine Liselle?" Ce'Nedra said, her eyes narrowed thoughtfully.

"Yes, your Majesty?"

"If the identity of Hunter is the deepest state secret in Drasnia, how is it that *you* were aware of it?"

"I was sent from Boktor with certain instructions for her. My uncle knows that I can be trusted."

"But you're revealing it now, aren't you?"

"It's after the fact, your Majesty. Bethra's dead. Someone else will be Hunter now. Anyway, before she died, Bethra told us that someone had found out about her involvement in the death of Grand Duke Noragon and had passed the information on. She believed that it was that information that triggered the attack on her."

"It's definitely narrowing down to the Honeths then, isn't it?" Silk said.

"It's not definite proof, Kheldar," Velvet warned him.

"It's definite enough to satisfy me."

"You're not going to do anything precipitous, are you?" she asked him. "Javelin wouldn't like that, you know."

"That's Javelin's problem."

"We don't have time to get involved in Tolnedran politics, Silk," Belgarath added firmly. "We're not going to be here that long."

"It's not going to *take* me all that long."

"I'll have to report what you're planning to Javelin," Velvet warned.

"Of course. But I'll be finished with it by the time your report reaches Boktor."

"It's important that you don't embarrass us, Kheldar."

"Trust me," he said and quietly left the room.

"It always makes me nervous when he says that," Durnik murmured.

Early the following morning, Belgarath and Garion left the Imperial Palace to visit the library at the university. It was chilly in the broad streets of Tol Honeth, and a raw wind was blowing in off the Nedrane River. The few merchants abroad at that hour walked briskly along the marble thoroughfares with fur cloaks pulled tightly about them, and gangs of roughly dressed laborers thronged up out of the poorer sections of the city with their heads bent into the wind and their chapped hands burrowed deep into their clothing.

Garion and his grandfather passed through the deserted central marketplace and soon reached a large cluster of buildings enclosed by a marble wall and entered through a gate stamped with the Imperial Seal. The grounds inside the compound were as neatly trimmed as those surrounding the palace, and there were broad marble walks stretching from building to building across the lawns. As they moved along one of those walks, they encountered a portly, black-robed scholar pacing along with his hands clasped behind his back and his face lost in thought.

"Excuse me," Belgarath said to him, "but could you direct us to the library?"

"What?" The man looked up, blinking.

"The library, good sir," Belgarath repeated. "Which way is it?"

"Oh," the scholar said. "It's over there someplace." He gestured vaguely.

"Do you suppose you could be a bit more precise?"

The scholar gave the shabbily dressed old man an offended look. "Ask one of the porters," he said brusquely. "I'm busy. I've been working on a problem for twenty years now and I've almost found the solution."

"Oh? Which problem is that?"

"I doubt that it would be of much interest to an uneducated mendicant," the scholar replied loftily, "but if you really must know, I've been trying to calculate the exact weight of the world."

"Is that all? And it's taken you twenty years?" Belgarath's face was astonished. "I solved *that* problem a long time ago—in about a week."

The scholar stared at him, his face going dead white. "That's impossible!" he exclaimed. "I'm the only man in the world who's looking into it. No one has ever asked the question before."

Belgarath laughed. "I'm sorry, learned scholar, but it's been asked several times already. The best solution I ever saw was by a man named Talgin—at the University of Melcena, I think. It was during the second millennium. There should be a copy of his calculations in your library."

The scholar began to tremble violently, and his eyes bulged. Without a word he spun on his heel and dashed across the lawn with the skirts of his robe flapping behind him.

"Keep an eye on him, Garion," Belgarath said calmly. "The building he runs to should be the library."

"Just how much *does* the world weigh?" Garion asked curiously.

"How should I know?" Belgarath replied. "No sane man would even be curious about it."

"But what about this Talgin you mentioned—the one who wrote the solution?"

"Talgin? Oh, there's no such person. I just made him up."

Garion stared at him. "That's a dreadful thing to do, Grandfather," he accused. "You've just destroyed a man's entire life work with a lie."

"But it *did* get him to lead us to the library," the old man said slyly. "Besides, maybe now he'll turn his attention to something a bit more meaningful. The library's in that building with the tower. He just ran up the steps. Shall we go?"

There was a marble rotunda just inside the main entrance to the library, and in the precise center of that rotunda stood a high, ornately carved desk. A bald, skinny man sat behind the desk laboriously copying from a huge book. For some reason the man looked familiar to Garion, and he frowned as they approached the desk, trying to remember where he had seen him before.

"May I help you?" the skinny man asked, looking up from his copying as Belgarath stopped in front of his desk.

"Possibly so. I'm looking for a copy of the Prophecies of the Western Grolims."

The skinny man frowned, scratching at one ear. "That

would be in the comparative theology section," he mused. "Could you hazard a guess as to the date of composition?"

Belgarath also frowned, staring up into the vault of the rotunda as he considered it. "My guess would be early third millennium," he said finally.

"That would put it at the time of either the second Honethite Dynasty or the second Vorduvian," the scholar said. "We shouldn't have too much trouble finding it." He rose to his feet. "It's this way," he said, pointing toward one of the hallways fanning out from the rotunda. "If you'll follow me, please."

Garion still felt the nagging certainty that he knew this polite, helpful scholar. The man certainly had better manners than the pompous, self-important world-weighter they had met outside, and—Then it came to him. "Master Jeebers?" he said incredulously, "is that you?"

"Have we met before, sir?" Jeebers asked politely, looking at Garion with a puzzled squint.

Garion grinned broadly. "We have indeed, Master Jeebers. You introduced me to my wife."

"I don't seem to recall—"

"Oh, I think you do. You crept out of the palace with her one night and rode south toward Tol Borune. Along the way, you joined a party of merchants. You left rather suddenly when my wife told you that leaving Tol Honeth was *her* idea instead of Ran Borune's."

Jeebers blinked and then his eyes widened. "Your Majesty," he said with a bow. "Forgive me for not recognizing you at once. My eyes aren't what they once were."

Garion laughed, clapping him on the shoulder in delight. "That's quite all right, Jeebers," he said. "I'm not going about announcing who I am on this trip."

"And how is little Ce'Nedra—Uh, her Majesty, that is?"

Garion was about to tell his wife's former tutor about the abduction of their son, but Belgarath gave him a discreet nudge. "Uh—fine, just fine," he said instead.

"I'm so glad to hear it," Jeebers said with a fond smile.

"She was an absolutely impossible student, but strangely I find that much of the fun went out of my life after she and I parted company. I was delighted to hear of her fortuitous marriage and not nearly as surprised as my colleagues here when we heard that she had raised an army and marched on Thull Mardu. She always was a fiery little thing—and brilliant." He gave Garion a rather apologetic look. "To be honest, though, I have to tell you that she was an erratic and undisciplined student."

"I've noticed those qualities in her from time to time."

Jeebers laughed. "I'm sure you have, your Majesty," he said. "Please convey my regards to her—" He hesitated. "And if you don't think it's presumptuous—my affection as well."

"I will, Jeebers," Garion promised. "I will."

"This is the comparative theology section of our library," the bald scholar said, pushing open a heavy door. "All the items are catalogued and stored by Dynasty. The antiquity sections are back this way." He led them along a narrow aisle between tall book racks filled with leather-bound volumes and tightly rolled scrolls. The skinny man paused once and rubbed his finger along one of the shelves. "Dust," he sniffed disapprovingly. "I expect I'd better speak sharply to the custodians about that."

"It's the nature of books to collect dust," Belgarath said.

"And it's the nature of custodians to avoid doing anything about it," Jeebers added with a wry smile. "Ah, here we are." He stopped in the center of a somewhat broader aisle where the books showed marked signs of extreme age. "Please be gentle with them," he said, touching the backs of the volumes with an odd kind of affection. "They're old and brittle. The works written during the Second Honethite Dynasty are on this side, and those dating back to the Second Vordue Dynasty are over here. They're further broken down into kingdom of origin, so it shouldn't be hard for you to locate the one you want. Now, if you'll excuse me, I shouldn't stay away from my desk for too long. Some of my colleagues get impatient and start rooting through the shelves on their own. It takes weeks sometimes to get things put right again."

"I'm sure we can manage from here, Master Jeebers," Belgarath assured him, "and thank you for your assistance."

"It's my pleasure," Jeebers replied with a slight bow. He looked back at Garion. "You *will* remember to give little Ce'Nedra my greetings, won't you?"

"You have my word on it, Master Jeebers."

"Thank you, your Majesty." And the skinny man turned and went on out of the book-lined room.

"An enormous change there," Belgarath noted. "Probably the little fright Ce'Nedra gave him at Tol Borune that time knocked all the pomposity out of him." The old man was peering intently at the shelves. "I'll have to admit that he's a very competent scholar."

"Isn't he just a librarian?" Garion asked, "somebody who looks after books?"

"That's where all the rest of scholarship starts, Garion. All the books in the world won't help you if they're just piled up in a heap." He bent slightly and pulled a black-wrapped scroll from a lower shelf. "Here we are," he said triumphantly. "Jeebers led us right to it." He moved to the end of the aisle where a table and bench sat before a tall, narrow window and where the pale winter sunlight fell golden on the stone floor. He sat and carefully undid the ties that held the scroll tightly rolled inside its black velvet cover. As he pulled the scroll out, he muttered a number of fairly sulfurous oaths.

"What's the matter?" Garion asked.

"Grolim stupidity," Belgarath growled. "Look at this." He held out the scroll. "Look at the parchment."

Garion peered at it. "It looks like other parchment to me."

"It's human skin," the old man snorted disgustedly.

Garion drew back in revulsion. "That's ghastly."

"That's not the point. Whoever provided the skin was finished with it anyway. The problem is that human skin won't hold ink." He unrolled a foot or so of the scroll. "Look at that. It's so faded that you can't even make out the words."

"Could you use something to bring them out again—the way you did with Anheg's letter that time?"

"Garion, this scroll's about three thousand years old. The solution of salts I used on Anheg's letter would probably dissolve it entirely."

"Sorcery then?"

Belgarath shook his head. "It's just too fragile." He started to swear again even as he carefully unrolled the scroll inch by inch, moving it this way and that to catch the sunlight. "Here's something," he grunted with some surprise.

"What does it say?"

"'. . . seek the path of the Child of Dark in the land of the serpents . . . ' The old man looked up. "That's something, anyway."

"What does it mean?"

"Just what it says. Zandramas went to Nyissa. We'll pick up the trail there."

"Grandfather, we already knew that."

"We *suspected* it, Garion. There's a difference. Zandramas has tricked us into following false trails before. Now we know for certain that we're on the right track."

"It isn't very much, Grandfather."

"I know, but it's better than nothing."

CHAPTER FIVE

"Would you just look at that?" Ce'Nedra said indignantly the following morning. She had just arisen and stood at the window, wrapped in a warm robe.

"Hmmm?" Garion murmured drowsily. "Look at what, dear?" He was burrowed deeply under the warm quilts and was giving some serious thought to going back to sleep.

"You can't see it from there, Garion. Come over here."

He sighed, slipped out of bed, and padded barefoot over to the window.

"Isn't that disgusting?" she demanded.

The grounds of the Imperial Compound were blanketed in white, and large snowflakes were settling lazily through the dead-calm air.

"Isn't it sort of peculiar for it to snow in Tol Honeth?" he asked.

"Garion, it *never* snows in Tol Honeth. The last time I saw snow here was when I was five years old."

"It's been an unusual winter."

"Well, I'm going back to bed, and I'm not going to get up until every bit of it melts."

"You don't really have to go out in it, you know."

"I don't even want to *look* at it." She flounced back to their canopied bed, let her robe drop to the floor, and climbed back under the quilts. Garion shrugged and started back toward the bed. Another hour or two of sleep seemed definitely in order.

"Please pull the curtains on the bed shut," she told him, "and don't make too much noise when you leave."

He stared at her for a moment, then sighed. He closed the heavy curtains around the bed and sleepily began to dress.

"Do be a dear, Garion," she said sweetly. "Stop by the kitchen and tell them that I'll want my breakfast in here."

Now that, he felt, was *distinctly* unfair. He pulled on the rest of his clothes, feeling surly.

"Oh, Garion?"

"Yes, dear?" He kept it neutral with some effort.

"Don't forget to comb your hair. You always look like a straw stack in the morning." Her voice already sounded drowsy and on the edge of sleep.

He found Belgarath sitting moodily before the window in an unlighted dining room. Although it was quite early, the old man had a tankard on the table beside him. "Can you believe this?" he said disgustedly, looking out at the softly falling snow.

"I don't imagine that it's going to last very long, Grandfather."

"It *never* snows in Tol Honeth."

"That's what Ce'Nedra was just saying." Garion held out his hands to a glowing iron brazier.

"Where is she?"

"She went back to bed."

"That's probably not such a bad idea. Why didn't you join her?"

"She decided that it was time for me to get up."

"That hardly seems fair."

"The same thought occurred to me."

Belgarath scratched absently at his ear, still looking out at the snow. "We're too far south for this to last for more than a day or so. Besides, the day after tomorrow is Erastide. A lot of people will be traveling after the holiday, so we won't be quite so conspicuous."

"You think we should wait?"

"It's sort of logical. We wouldn't make very good time slogging through all that, anyway."

"What do you plan to do today, then?"

Belgarath picked up his tankard. "I think I'll finish this and then go back to bed."

Garion pulled up one of the red velvet upholstered chairs and sat down. Something had been bothering him for several days now, and he decided that this might be a good time to bring it out into the open. "Grandfather?"

"Yes?"

"Why is it that all of this seems to have happened before?"

"All of what?"

"Everything. There are Angaraks in Arendia trying to stir up trouble—just as they were when we were following Zedar. There are intrigues and assassinations in Tolnedra—the same as last time. We ran into a monster—a dragon this time instead of the Algroths—but it's still pretty close to the same sort of thing. It seems almost as if we were repeating everything that happened when we were trying to find the Orb. We've even been running into the same people—Delvor, that customs man, even Jeebers."

"You know, that's a very interesting question, Garion." Belgarath pondered for a moment, absently taking a drink from his tankard. "If you think about it in a certain way, though, it does sort of make sense."

"I don't quite follow you."

"We're on our way to another meeting between the Child of Light and the Child of Dark," Belgarath explained. "That meeting is going to be a repetition of an event that's been happening over and over again since the beginning of time. Since it's the same event, it stands to reason that the circumstances leading up to it should also be similar." He thought about it a moment longer. "Actually," he continued, "they'd almost have to be, wouldn't they?"

"That's a little deep for me, I'm afraid."

"There are two Prophecies—two sides of the same thing. Something happened an unimaginably long time ago to separate them."

"Yes. I understand that."

"When they got separated, things sort of stopped."

"What things?"

"It's kind of hard to put into words. Let's call it the course of things that were supposed to happen—the future, I suppose. As long as those two forces are separate—and equal—the future can't happen. We all just keep going through the same series of events over and over again.

"When will it end?"

"When one of the Prophecies finally overcomes the other. When the Child of Light finally defeats the Child of Dark—or the other way around."

"I thought I already did that."

"I don't think it was conclusive enough, Garion."

"I killed Torak, Grandfather. You can't get much more conclusive than that, can you?"

"You killed *Torak*, Garion. You didn't kill the Dark Prophecy. I think it's going to take something more significant than a sword fight in the City of Night to settle this."

"Such as what?"

Belgarath spread his hands. "I don't know. I really don't. This idea of yours could be very useful, though."

"Oh?"

"If we're going to go through a series of events that are similar to what happened last time, it could give us a notion of what to expect, couldn't it? You might want to think about that—maybe spend a little time this morning remembering exactly what happened last time."

"What are you going to do?"

Belgarath drained his tankard and stood up. "As I said—I'm going back to bed."

That afternoon, a polite official in a brown mantle tapped on the door of the room where Garion sat reading and advised him that the Emperor Varana wanted to see him. Garion set aside his book and followed the official through the echoing marble halls to Varana's study.

"Ah, Belgarion," Varana said as he entered. "A bit of news has just reached me that you might find interesting. Please, have a seat."

"Information?" Garion asked, sitting in the leather-upholstered chair beside the Emperor's desk.

"That man you mentioned the other day—Naradas—has been seen here in Tol Honeth."

"Naradas? How did he manage to get down here that fast? The last I heard, he was riding north from the Great Fair in Arendia."

"Has he been following you?"

"He's been asking a lot of questions and spreading money around."

"I can have him picked up, if you want. I have a few questions I'd like to ask him myself, and I could hold him for several months if need be."

Garion thought about it. Finally he shook his head rather regretfully. "He's a Mallorean Grolim, and he could be out of any kind of prison cell you could put him in within a matter of minutes."

"The Imperial Dungeon is quite secure, Belgarion," Varana said a bit stiffly.

"Not that secure, Varana." Then Garion smiled briefly, remembering the Emperor's stubborn convictions about such things. "Let's just say that Naradas has some out-of-the-ordinary resources available to him. It's one of those things that makes you uncomfortable to talk about."

"Oh," Varana said distastefully, "that."

Garion nodded. "It might be better in the long run just to have your people keep an eye on him. If he doesn't know that we're aware that he's here, he might lead us to others—or at least to certain information. Harakan's been seen here in Tolnedra, too, I understand, and I'd like to find out if there's some kind of connection between the two of them."

Varana smiled. "Your life is a great deal more complicated than mine, Belgarion," he said. "I only have one reality to deal with."

Garion gave a wry shrug. "It helps to fill up my spare time," he replied.

There was a light tap on the door, and Lord Morin slowly shuffled into the room. "I'm sorry to disturb your Majesties, but there's some unsettling news from the city."

"Oh?" Varana said. "What's been happening, Morin?"

"Someone's been killing members of the Honeth family—very quietly, but very efficiently. Quite a few have died in the last two nights."

"Poison?"

"No, your Majesty. This assassin is more direct. He smothered a few with their own pillows night before last, and there was one nasty fall. At first the deaths appeared to be of natural causes. Last night, though, he started using a knife." Morin shook his head disapprovingly. "Messy," he sniffed. "Very messy."

Varana frowned. "I thought that all the old feuds had settled down. Do you think it might be the Horbites? They hold grudges forever sometimes."

"No one seems to know, your Majesty. The Honeths are terrified. They're either fleeing the city or turning their houses into forts."

Varana smiled. "I think I can live with the discomfort of the Honeth family. Did this fellow leave any kind of trademark? Can we identify him as a known assassin?"

"We haven't a clue, your Majesty. Should I put guards around the houses of the Honeths—the ones who are left?"

"They have their own soldiers." Varana shrugged. "But put out some inquiries and let this fellow know that I'd like to have a little talk with him."

"Are you going to arrest him?" Garion asked.

"Oh, I don't know that I want to go *that* far. I just want to find out who he is and suggest to him that he ought to follow the rules a little more closely, that's all. I wonder who he could possibly be."

Garion, however, had a few private suspicions about the matter.

The Erastide festivities were in full swing in Tol Honeth, and the revelers, many far gone in drink, lurched and staggered from party to party as the great families vied with one another in a vulgar display of ostentatious wealth. The huge mansions of the rich and powerful were festooned with gaily hued buntings and hung with colored lanterns. Fortunes were spent on lavish banquets, and the entertainments provided often exceeded the bounds of good taste. Although the celebrations at the palace were more restrained, Emperor Varana nonetheless felt obliged to extend his hospitality to many people he privately loathed.

The event which had been long in the planning for that particular evening was a state banquet to be followed by a grand ball. "And you two will be my guests of honor," Varana firmly told Garion and Ce'Nedra. "If *I* have to endure this, then so do you."

"I'd really rather not, uncle," Ce'Nedra told him with a sad little smile. "I'm not much in the mood for festivities just now."

"You can't just turn off your life, Ce'Nedra," he said gently. "A party—even one of the stuffy ones here in the palace—might help to divert your mind from your tragic circumstances." He gave her a shrewd look. "Besides," he added, "if you don't attend, the Honeths, Horbites, and Vordues will all be smirking up their sleeves about your absence."

Ce'Nedra's head came up quickly, and her eyes took on a flinty look. "That's true, isn't it?" she replied. "Of course, I really don't have a thing to wear."

"There are whole closets filled with your gowns in the imperial apartments, Ce'Nedra," he reminded her.

"Oh, yes. I'd forgotten those. All right, uncle, I'll be happy to attend."

And so it was that Ce'Nedra, dressed in a creamy white velvet gown and with a jeweled coronet nestling among her flaming curls, entered the ballroom that evening on the arm of her husband, the King of Riva. Garion, dressed in a borrowed blue doublet that was noticeably tight across the shoulders, approached the entire affair with a great lack of enthusiasm. As a visiting head of state, he was obliged to stand for an hour or so in the reception line in the grand ballroom, murmuring empty responses to the pleasantries offered by assorted Horbites, Vordues, Ranites, and Borunes—and their often giddy wives. The Honeths, however, were conspicuous by their absence.

Toward the end of that interminable ceremony, Javelin's honey-blond niece, the Margravine Liselle, dressed in a spectacular gown of lavender brocade, came past on the arm of Prince Khaldon. "Courage, your Majesty," she murmured as she curtsied to Garion. "Not even this can last forever—though it might seem like it."

"Thanks, Liselle," he replied drily.

After the reception line had wound to its tedious conclusion, Garion circulated politely among the other guests, enduring the endlessly repeated comment: "'It *never* snows in Tol Honeth."

At the far end of the candlelit ballroom, a group of Arendish musicians sawed and plucked and tootled their way through a repertoire of holiday songs that were common to all the Kingdoms of the West. Their lutes, violas, harps, flutes, and oboes provided a largely unheard background to the chattering of the Emperor's guests.

"I had engaged Madame Aldima to entertain us this evening," Varana was saying to a small cluster of Horbites. "Her singing was to have been the high point of the festivities. Unfortunately, the change in the weather has made her fearful of coming out of her house. She's most protective of her voice, I understand."

"And well she should be," a Ranite lady standing just behind Garion murmured to her companion. "It wasn't much of a voice to begin with, and time hasn't been kind to it—all those years Aldima spent singing in taverns, no doubt."

"It hardly seems like Erastide without singing," Varana continued. "Perhaps we might persuade one of these lovely ladies to grace us with a song or two."

A stout Borune lady of middle years quickly responded to the Emperor's suggestion, joining with the orchestra in a rendition of an old favorite delivered in a warbling soprano voice that struggled painfully to reach the higher registers. When she had finished and stood red-faced and gasping, the Emperor's guests responded to her screeching with polite applause which lasted for almost five seconds. Then they returned to their inane chatter.

And then the musicians struck up an Arendish air so old that its origins were lost in the mists of antiquity. Like most Arendish songs, it was of a melancholy turn, beginning in a minor key with an intricate waterfall of notes from the lute. As the deep-toned viola entered with the main theme, a rich contralto voice joined in. Gradually, the conversations died out as that voice poignantly touched the guests into silence. Garion was startled. Standing not far from the orchestra, the Margravine Liselle had lifted her head in song. Her voice was marvelous. It had a dark, thrilling timbre and was as smooth as honey. The other guests drew back from her in profound respect for that glorious voice, leaving her standing quite alone in a golden circle of candlelight. And then, to Garion's astonishment, Ce'Nedra stepped into that candlelight to join the lavender-gowned Drasnian girl. As the flute picked up the counterharmony, the tiny Rivan Queen raised her sad little face and joined her voice with that of the Margravine. Effortlessly, her clear voice rose with that of the flute, so perfectly matching its tone and color that one could not separate exactly the voice of the instrument from hers. And yet, there was a sadness bordering on heartbreak in her singing, a sorrow that brought a lump to Garion's throat and tears to his eyes. Despite the festivities around her, it was clearly evident that Ce'Nedra still nursed her abiding anguish deep in her heart, and no gaiety nor entertainment could lessen her suffering.

As the song drew to its conclusion, the applause was thunderous. "More!" they shouted. "More!"

Encouraged by the ovation, the musicians returned to the beginning of that same ancient air. Once again the lute spilled out its heart in that rippling cascade, but this time as the viola led Liselle into the main theme, yet a third voice joined in—a voice Garion knew so well that he did not even have to look to see who was singing.

Polgara, dressed in a deep blue velvet gown trimmed in silver, joined Liselle and Ce'Nedra in the candlelit circle. Her voice was as rich and smooth as the Margravine's, and yet there was in it a sorrow that went even beyond Ce'Nedra's—a sorrow for a place that had been lost and could never return again. Then, as the flute accompanied Ce'Nedra into the rising counterpoint, Polgara's rose to join hers as well. The harmony thus created was not the traditional one which was so familiar in all the Kingdoms of the West. The Arendish musicians, their eyes filled with tears, took up those strange antique chords to recreate a melody that had not been heard in thousands of years.

As the last notes of that glorious song faded, there was an awed silence. And then, many of them weeping openly, the guests burst into applause as Polgara silently led the two young women out of that golden circle of light.

Belgarath, looking somewhat unusually regal in a snowy Tolnedran mantle, but holding nonetheless a full silver goblet, stood in her path, his eyes a mystery.

"Well, father?" she asked.

Wordlessly he kissed her forehead and handed her the goblet. "Lovely, Pol, but why revive something that's been dead and gone for all these centuries?"

Her chin lifted proudly. "The memory of Vo Wacune will never die so long as I live, father. I carry it forever in my heart, and every so often I like to remind people that there was once a shining city filled with grace and courage and beauty and that this mundane world in which we now live allowed it to slip away."

"It's very painful for you, isn't it, Polgara?" he asked gravely.

"Yes, father, it is—more painful than I can say—but I've endured pain before, so . . . " She left it hanging with a slight shrug and moved with regal step from the hall.

After the banquet, Garion and Ce'Nedra took a few turns about the ballroom floor, more for the sake of appearances than out of any real desire for it.

"Why does Lady Polgara feel so strongly about the Wacite Arends?" Ce'Nedra asked as they danced.

"She lived in Vo Wacune for quite some time when she was young," Garion replied. "I think she loved the city—and the people—very much."

"I thought my heart would break when she sang that song."

"Mine nearly did," Garion said quietly. "She's suffered so very much, but I think that the destruction of Vo Wacune hurt her more than anything else that's ever happened. She's never forgiven Grandfather for not coming to the aid of the city when the Asturians destroyed it."

Ce'Nedra sighed. "There's so much sorrow in the world."

"There's hope, too," he reminded her.

"But only such a little." She sighed again. Then a sudden impish smile crossed her lips. "That song absolutely destroyed all the ladies who are here," she smirked. "Absolutely *destroyed* them."

"Try not to gloat in public, love," he gently chided her. "It's really not very becoming."

"Didn't Uncle Varana say that I was one of the guests of honor?"

"Well—yes."

"It's my party then," she said with a toss of her head, "so I'll gloat if I want to."

When they all returned to the set of rooms Varana had provided for their use, Silk was waiting for them, standing by the fire and warming his hands. The little man had a furtive, slightly worried look on his face, and he was covered from top to toe with reeking debris. "Where's Varana?" he asked tensely as they entered the candlelit sitting room.

"He's down in the ballroom entertaining his guests," Garion said.

"What *have* you been doing, Prince Kheldar?" Ce'Nedra asked, wrinkling her nose at the offensive odors emanating from his clothes.

"Hiding," he replied, "under a garbage heap. I think we might want to leave Tol Honeth—fairly soon."

Belgarath's eyes narrowed. "Exactly what have you been up to, Silk?" he demanded, "and where have you been for the past couple of days?"

"Here and there," Silk said evasively. "I really should go get cleaned up."

"I don't suppose you know anything about what's been happening to the Honeth family, do you?" Garion asked.

"What's this?" Belgarath said.

"I was with Varana this afternoon when Lord Morin brought the report. The Honeths have been dying at a surprising rate. Eight or ten at last count."

"Twelve, actually," Silk corrected meticulously.

Belgarath turned on the rat-faced man. "I think I'd like an explanation."

"People die," Silk shrugged. "It happens all the time."

"Did they have help?"

"A little, maybe."

"And were *you* the one who provided this assistance?"

"Would I do that?"

Belgarath's face grew bleak. "I want the truth, Prince Kheldar."

Silk spread his hands extravagantly. "What is truth, old friend? Can any man ever really know what the truth is?"

"This isn't a philosophical discussion, Silk. Have you been out butchering Honeths?"

"I don't know that I'd say 'butchering' exactly. That word smacks of a certain crudity. I pride myself on my refinement."

"Have you been killing people?"

"Well," Silk's face took on a slightly offended expression, "if you're going to put it *that* way—"

"Twelve people?" Durnik's tone was incredulous.

"And another that isn't very likely to survive," Silk noted. "I was interrupted before I had time to make sure of him, but I probably did enough to get the job done."

"I'm still waiting, Silk," Belgarath said darkly.

Silk sniffed at one rancid sleeve and made a face. "Bethra and I were very good friends." He shrugged as if that explained everything.

"But—" Durnik objected. "Didn't she try to have you killed once?"

"Oh, that. That wasn't anything important. It was business—nothing personal."

"Isn't trying to kill somebody about as personal as you can get?"

"Of course not. I was interfering with something she was working on. You see, she had this arrangement with the Thullish ambassador, and—"

"Quit trying to change the subject, Silk," Belgarath said.

Silk's eyes grew hard. "Bethra was a special woman," he replied. "Beautiful, gifted, and totally honest. I admired her very much. You could almost say that I loved her—in a rather special kind of way. The idea that someone saw fit to have her cut down in the street greatly offended me. I did what I thought was appropriate."

"Despite the importance of what we're doing?" Belgarath's face was like a thundercloud. "You just dropped everything and ran out to do a little private killing?"

"There are some things you just don't let slide, Belgarath.

There's also a principle involved. We do *not* allow the killing of a member of Drasnian intelligence to go unpunished. It's bad for business if people get the idea that they can get away with that sort of thing. Anyway, the first night I went to some pains to make things look sort of natural."

"Natural?" Durnik asked. "How can you make a murder look natural?"

"Please, Durnik. Murder is such an ugly word."

"He smothered them in their beds with their own pillows," Garion explained.

"And one fellow sort of accidentally fell out of a window," Silk added. "Rather a high one as I recall. He came down on an iron fence."

Durnik shuddered.

"I managed to visit five of them night before last, but the methods were taking entirely too long, so last night I was a bit more direct. I *did* sort of linger for a time with the Baron Kelbor, though. He was the one who actually gave the order to have Bethra killed. We had a very nice chat before he left us."

"Kelbor's house is the most closely guarded in Tol Honeth," Ce'Nedra said. "How did you manage to get in?"

"People seldom look up at night—particularly when it's snowing. I went in over the rooftops. Anyway, Kelbor gave me some very useful information. It seems that the man who told the Honeths about Bethra's activities was a Mallorean."

"Naradas?" Garion asked quickly.

"No. This one had a black beard."

"Harakan, then?"

"Lots of people have beards, Garion. I'd like a little bit more confirmation—not that I'd object to cutting Harakan up into little pieces, but I'd hate to let the real culprit get away because I was concentrating too much on our old friend." His face went bleak again. "That's particularly true in view of the fact that, from what Kelbor said, this helpful Mallorean arranged and participated in Bethra's murder—sort of as a favor to the Honeth family."

"I *do* wish that you'd go take a bath, Prince Kheldar," Ce'Nedra said. "What on earth possessed you to take up residence in a garbage heap?"

He shrugged. "I was interrupted during my last visit, and a number of people were chasing me. This snow complicated things a bit. My tracks were fairly easy for them to follow. I needed a place to hide, and the garbage heap was handy." His look became disgusted. "It *never* snows in Tol Honeth."

"You'd be amazed at how many people have told me the same thing today," Garion murmured.

"I really think we should leave almost immediately," Silk said.

"What for?" Durnik asked. "You got away, didn't you?"

"You forget the tracks, Durnik." Silk held up one foot. "Rivan boots—an affectation, perhaps. They're very comfortable, but they do leave distinctive tracks. I expect that it's only going to be a matter of time before somebody puts a few things together and I'm not really in the mood for dodging Honethite assassins. They're fairly inept, but they can be an inconvenience."

The door opened rather quietly, and Silk instantly went into a crouch, his hands diving inside his smeared doublet for his daggers.

"My goodness," the lavender-gowned Velvet said mildly, entering and closing the door behind her, "aren't we jumpy this evening?"

"What are you doing in here?" Silk demanded.

"I was attending the Imperial Ball. You have no idea how much gossip one can pick up at such affairs. The whole ballroom is buzzing with the accidents that have been befalling the Honeths in the past couple nights. Under the circumstances, I thought it might have occurred to you that it was time for us to leave."

"Us?"

"Oh, didn't I tell you? How forgetful of me. I'll be joining you."

"You most certainly will *not!*" Belgarath said.

"I hate to contradict you, Ancient One," she said regretfully, "but I'm acting on orders." She turned to Silk. "My uncle has been a little nervous about some of your activities during the past few years. He *trusts* you, my dear Kheldar—you must never think that he doesn't trust you—but he *does* sort of want somebody to keep an eye on you." She frowned. "I think that he's going to be quite cross when he hears about your midnight visits to the Honeth family."

"You know the rules, Liselle," Silk replied. "Bethra was one of our people. We don't let those things go."

"Naturally not. But Javelin prefers to order that sort of retaliation personally. Your somewhat hasty vengeance has robbed him of that opportunity. You're just too independent, Silk. He's right, you know. You *do* need to be watched." She pursed her lips slightly. "I must admit, though, that it *was* a very nice job."

"Now you listen to me, young lady," Belgarath said hotly. "I am *not* conducting a guided tour for the benefit of the Drasnian spy network."

She gave him a disarming little smile and fondly patted his bearded cheek. "Oh, come now, Belgarath," she said, her soft brown eyes appealing, "do be reasonable. Wouldn't it be more civilized—and convenient—to have me in your party rather than trailing along behind you? I *am* going to follow my orders, Revered One, whether you like it or not."

"Why is it that I have to be surrounded by women who won't do as they're told?"

Her eyes went very wide. "Because we love you, Immortal One," she explained outrageously. "You're the answer to every maiden's dreams, and we follow you out of blind devotion."

"That's about enough of that, Miss," he said ominously. "You're not going with us, and that's final."

"*You know,*" the dry voice in Garion's mind mused, "*I think I've finally isolated the difficulty I've always had with Belgarath. It's his pure, pigheaded contrariness. He doesn't really have any reason for these arbitrary decisions of his. He just does it to irritate me.*"

"Do you mean that she's *supposed* to go along?" Garion blurted, so startled that he said it aloud.

"*Of course she is. Why do you think I went to all the trouble to get her to Tol Honeth before you all left. Go ahead and tell him.*"

Belgarath's expression, however, clearly showed that Garion's inadvertent exclamation had already told him that he had just been overruled. "Another visitation, I take it?" he said in a slightly sick tone of voice.

"Yes, Grandfather," Garion said. "I'm afraid so."

"She goes along then?"

Garion nodded.

"*I love to watch his expression when he loses one of these arguments,*" the dry voice said smugly.

Polgara began to laugh.

"What's so funny, Pol?" Belgarath demanded.

"Nothing, father," she replied innocently.

He suddenly threw his hands into the air. "Go ahead," he said in exasperation. "Invite all of Tol Honeth to come along. I don't care."

"Oh, father," Polgara said to him, "stop trying to be such a curmudgeon."

"Curmudgeon? Pol, you watch your tongue."

"That's really very difficult, father, and it makes one look ridiculous. Now, I think we should make a few plans. While the rest of us are changing clothes and packing, why don't you and Garion go explain to Varana that we're going to have to leave. Think up some suitable excuse. I don't know that we necessarily want him to know about Silk's nocturnal activities." She looked at the ceiling thoughtfully. "Durnik and Eriond and Toth will see to the horses, of course," she mused, "and I have a rather special little job for you, Prince Kheldar."

"Oh?"

"Go wash—thoroughly."

"I suppose I should have my clothes laundered as well,"

he noted, looking down at his garbage-saturated doublet and hose.

"No, Silk. Not laundered—burned."

"We can't leave tonight, Lady Polgara," Ce'Nedra said. "All the gates of the city are locked, and the legionnaires won't open them for anybody—except on the Emperor's direct orders."

"I can get us out of the city," Velvet said confidently.

"How are you going to manage that?" Belgarath asked her.

"Trust me."

"I *wish* people wouldn't keep saying that to me."

"Oh, by the way," she continued, "I saw an old friend of ours today. A large group of Honeths were riding toward the south gate." She looked over at Silk. "You really must have frightened them, Kheldar. They had whole battalions of their soldiers drawn up around them to keep you at a distance. Anyway, riding right in the middle of them and looking every inch a Tolnedran gentleman was the Mallorean, Harakan."

"Well, well," Silk said. "Isn't *that* interesting?"

"Prince Kheldar," Velvet said pleasantly, "please *do* go visit the baths—or at the very least, don't stand quite so close."

CHAPTER SIX

A chill gray fog had risen from the river to shroud the broad avenues of Tol Honeth. The snow had turned to rain—a cold drizzle that sifted down through the fog, and, although the roofs and courtyards were still mantled in white, the thoroughfares and avenues were clogged with seeping brown slush, crossed and crisscrossed with the tracks of wagons and carriages. It was nearly midnight when Garion and the others quietly left the grounds of the Imperial Compound, and the few bands of holiday revelers they encountered in the streets were much the worse for drink.

Velvet, riding a chestnut mare and wrapped and cowled in a heavy gray cloak, led them down past the marble-fronted houses of the merchant barons of Tol Honeth, through the empty central market place and into the poorer quarters of the city lying to the south. As they turned the corner of a side street, an authoritative voice came out of the fog. "Halt!"

Velvet reined in her horse and sat waiting as a squad of helmeted and red-cloaked legionnaires armed with lances marched out of the rainy mist. "State your business, please," the sergeant in charge of the patrol said brusquely.

"It's not really business, dear fellow," Velvet replied brightly. "We're on our way to an amusement. Count Norain is giving a party at his house. You *do* know the count, don't you?"

Some of the suspicion faded from the sergeant's face. "No, your Ladyship," he answered. "I'm afraid not."

"You don't know Norry?" Velvet exclaimed. "What an extraordinary thing! I thought everyone in Tol Honeth knew him—at least he always says so. Poor Norry's going to be absolutely crushed. I'll tell you what. Why don't you and your men come along with us so that you can meet him? You'll adore it. His parties are always so amusing." She gave the sergeant a wide-eyed, vapid smile.

"I'm sorry, your Ladyship, but we're on duty. Are you certain that you're following the right street, though? You're entering one of the meaner sections of the city, and I don't recall any noblemen's houses hereabouts."

"It's a short cut," Velvet told him. "You see, we go down through here, and then we turn left." She hesitated, "Or was it right? I forget exactly, but I'm sure one of my friends knows the way."

"You must be careful in this part of town, your Ladyship. There are footpads and cutpurses about."

"My goodness!"

"You really ought to be carrying torches."

"Torches? Great Nedra, no! The smell of the smoke from a torch lingers in my hair for weeks. Are you sure you can't join us? Norry's parties are *so* delightful."

"Give the count our regrets, your Ladyship."

"Come along, then," Velvet said to the others. "We really must hurry. We're terribly late as it is. Good-bye, Captain."

"Sergeant, your Ladyship."

"Oh? Is there a difference?"

"Never mind, your Ladyship. Hurry along now. You wouldn't want to miss any of the fun."

Velvet laughed gaily and moved her horse out at a steady trot.

"Who is Count Norain?" Durnik asked her curiously when they were out of earshot of the patrol.

"A figment of my imagination, Goodman Durnik," Velvet laughed.

"She's a Drasnian, all right," Belgarath murmured.

"Did you have any doubts, Eternal One?"

"Exactly where are you taking us, Liselle?" Polgara asked as they rode on down the foggy street.

"There's a house I know, Lady Polgara. It's not a very nice house, but it's built up against the south wall of the city, and it has a very useful back door."

"How can it have a back door if it's up against the city wall?" Ce'Nedra asked, pulling the hood of her green cloak forward to shield her face from the rainy mist.

Velvet winked at her. "You'll see," she said.

The street down which they rode grew shabbier and shabbier. The buildings looming out of the fog were built of plain stone instead of marble, and many of them were windowless warehouses, presenting blank faces to the street.

They passed a rank-smelling tavern from which came shouts and laughter and snatches of bawdy songs. Several drunken men burst from the door of the tavern and began pummeling each other with fists and clubs. One burly, unshaven ruffian lurched into the street and stood swaying in their path.

"Stand aside," Velvet said coolly to him.

"Who says so?"

The impassive Toth moved his horse up beside Velvet's

mount, reached out with one huge arm, set the tip of the staff he carried against the man's chest, and gave him a light push.

"Just watch out who you're shoving!" The drunken man said, knocking the staff aside.

Without changing expression, Toth flicked his wrist, and the tip of the staff cracked sharply against the side of the fellow's head, sending him reeling, vacant-eyed and twitching, into the gutter.

"Why, thank you," Velvet said pleasantly to the mute giant, and Toth inclined his head politely as they rode on down the shabby street.

"What in the world were they fighting about?" Ce'Nedra asked curiously.

"It's a way to keep warm," Silk replied. "Firewood's expensive in Tol Honeth, and a nice friendly fight stirs up the blood. I thought that everybody knew that."

"Are you making fun of me?"

"Would I do that?"

"He's always had a certain streak of flippancy in his nature, your Majesty," Velvet said.

"Liselle," Ce'Nedra told her quite firmly, "since we're going to be traveling together, let's drop the formalities. My name is Ce'Nedra."

"If your Majesty prefers it that way."

"My Majesty does."

"All right then, Ce'Nedra," the blond girl said with a warm smile.

They rode on through the unlighted streets of the Imperial City until they reached the looming mass of the south wall. "We go this way," Velvet told them, turning down a rainy street lying between the wall and a long string of warehouses. The house to which she led them was a stout, two-storey building, its stones black and shiny from the rain and fog, and it was set about a central courtyard and had a heavy front gate. Its narrow windows were all tightly shuttered, and a single small lantern gleamed over its gate.

Velvet dismounted carefully, holding her skirt up to keep

its hem out of the slush. She stepped to the gate and tugged at a rope. Inside the courtyard a small bell tinkled. A voice from inside answered, and she spoke quietly for a moment to the gatekeeper. Then there was the sound of a clanking chain, and the gate swung open. Velvet led her horse into the courtyard, and the rest followed her. Inside, Garion looked around curiously. The courtyard had been cleared of snow, and the cobblestones gleamed wetly in the still-falling drizzle. Several saddled horses stood under an overhanging roof, and a couple of well-appointed carriages were drawn up to a solid-looking door.

"Are we going inside?" Ce'Nedra asked, looking about curiously.

Velvet gave her a speculative look, then turned to look at Eriond. "Perhaps that might not be such a good idea," she said.

The muffled sound of laughter came from somewhere inside, followed by a woman's shrill squeal.

One of Polgara's eyebrows went up. "I think Liselle is right," she said firmly. "We'll wait out here."

"I'm a grown woman, Lady Polgara," Ce'Nedra objected.

"Not *that* grown, dear."

"Will you accompany me, Prince Kheldar?" Velvet asked the little man. "The presence of an unescorted woman in this house is sometimes misunderstood."

"Of course," he replied.

"We won't be long," Velvet assured the rest of them. With Silk at her side, she went to the door, rapped on its panels, and was immediately admitted.

"I still don't see why we can't wait inside where it's warm and dry," Ce'Nedra complained, shivering and pulling her cloak more tightly about her.

"I'm sure you would if you went in there," Polgara told her. "A little rain won't hurt you."

"What could possibly be *that* bad about this house?"

There was another squeal from inside followed by more raucous laughter.

"That, for one thing," Polgara replied.

Ce'Nedra's eyes grew wide. "You mean that it's one of *those* places?" Her face suddenly went bright red.

"It's got all the earmarks of it."

After about a quarter of an hour, a slanting cellar door at the rear of the rain-drenched courtyard creaked open, and Silk came up from below carrying a gleaming lantern. "We're going to have to lead the horses down," he told them.

"Where are we going?" Garion asked.

"Down to the cellars. This place is full of surprises."

In single file, leading their skittish horses, they followed Silk down a slanting stone ramp. From somewhere below, Garion could hear the gurgle and wash of running water; when they reached the foot of the ramp, he saw that the narrow passageway opened out into a large, cavelike chamber, roofed over with massive stone arches and dimly lighted by smoky torches. The center of the chamber was filled with dark, oily-looking water, and a narrow walkway ran around three sides of the pool. Moored to the walkway was a fair-sized barge, painted black and with a dozen dark-cloaked oarsmen on each side.

Velvet stood on the walkway beside the barge. "We can only cross two at a time," she said to them, her voice echoing hollowly in the vaulted chamber, "because of the horses."

"Cross?" Ce'Nedra said. "Cross where?"

"To the south bank of the Nedrane," Velvet replied.

"But we're still inside the city walls."

"Actually, we're *under* the city wall, Ce'Nedra. The only thing between us and the river are two of the marble slabs that form the exterior facing."

There came then the clanking of a heavy windlass somewhere in the dimness, and the front wall of the subterranean harbor creaked slowly open, dividing in the middle and swinging ponderously on great, well-greased iron hinges. Through the opening between the two slowly moving stone slabs, Garion could see the rain-dimpled surface of the river moving slowly by with its far shore lost in the dripping fog.

"Very clever," Belgarath said. "How long has this house been here?"

"Centuries," Velvet replied. "It was built to provide just about anything anyone could desire. Occasionally, one of the customers wants to leave—or enter—the city unobserved. That's what this place is for."

"How did you find out about it?" Garion asked her.

She shrugged. "Bethra owned the house. She told Javelin about its secrets."

Silk sighed. "She even reaches out from the grave to help us."

They were ferried in pairs across the foggy, rain-swept expanse of the Nedrane to land on a narrow, mist-shrouded sand beach backed by a thicket of willows. When Velvet finally joined them, it was perhaps three hours past midnight. "The oarsmen will brush our tracks out of the sand," she told them. "It's part of the service."

"Did this cost very much?" Silk asked her.

"A great deal, actually, but it comes out of the budget of the Drasnian Embassy. Your cousin didn't like that too much, but I persuaded him to pay—finally."

Silk grinned viciously.

"We have a few hours left until daylight," Velvet continued. "There's a wagon road on the other side of these willows, and it joins the Imperial Highway about a mile or so downriver. We should probably travel at a walk until we're out of earshot of the city. The legionnaires at the south gate might become curious if they hear galloping."

They mounted their horses in the soggy darkness and rode through the willows, down onto the muddy wagon track. Garion pulled his horse in beside Silk's. "What was going on in that place?" he asked curiously.

"Almost anything you could imagine." Silk laughed. "And probably a number of things you couldn't. It's a very interesting house with all sorts of diversions for people with enough money to be able to afford them."

"Did you recognize anybody there?"

"Several, actually—some highly respected members of the noble houses of the Empire."

Ce'Nedra, who rode directly behind them, sniffed disdainfully. "I cannot understand why any man would choose to frequent that sort of place."

"The customers are not exclusively male, Ce'Nedra," Silk told her.

"You can't be serious."

"A fair number of the highborn ladies of Tol Honeth have found all kinds of interesting ways to relieve their boredom. They wear masks, of course—although very little else. I recognized one countess, however—one of the pillars of the Horbite family."

"If she was wearing a mask, how could you recognize her?"

"She has a distinctive birthmark—in a place where it's seldom seen. Some years back, she and I were quite friendly, and she showed it to me."

There was a long silence. "I don't know that I really want to discuss this any more," Ce'Nedra said primly and nudged her horse past them to join Polgara and Velvet.

"She *did* ask," Silk protested innocently to Garion. "You heard her, didn't you?"

They rode south for several days in clearing weather. Erastide had passed virtually unnoticed while they were on the road, and Garion felt a strange kind of regret about that. Since his earliest childhood, the midwinter holiday had been one of the high points of the year. To allow it to pass unobserved seemed somehow to violate something very sacred. He wished that there might have been time to buy something special for Ce'Nedra, but about the best he could manage in the way of a gift was a tender kiss.

Some leagues above Tol Borune, they met a richly dressed couple riding north toward the Imperial Capital, accompanied by a dozen or so liveried servants. "You there, fellow," the velvet-clad nobleman called condescendingly to Silk, who happened to be riding in the lead, "what news from Tol Honeth?"

"The usual, your Lordship," Silk replied obsequiously. "Assassinations, plots, and intrigues—the normal amusements of the highborn."

"I don't care much for your tone, fellow," the nobleman said.

"And I don't care much for being called 'fellow,' either."

"We've heard such amazing stories," the giddy-looking lady in a fur-lined red velvet cape said breathlessly. "Is it true that someone is actually trying to kill all the Honeths? We heard that whole families have been murdered in their beds."

"Balera," her husband said in disgust, "you're just repeating wild rumors. What could a seedy-looking commoner like this know about what's really happening in the capital? I'm sure that if there were any substance to those wild stories, Naradas would have told us."

"Naradas?" Silk's eyes suddenly filled with interest. "An Angarak merchant with colorless eyes?"

"You know him?" the nobleman asked with some surprise.

"I know *of* him, your Lordship," Silk replied carefully. "It's not wise to go around announcing that you're acquainted with that one. You *did* know that the Emperor has put a price on his head, didn't you?"

"Naradas? Impossible!"

"I'm sorry, your Honor, but it's common knowledge all over Tol Honeth. If you know where to put your hands on him, you can earn yourself a thousand gold crowns without much effort."

"A thousand crowns!"

Silk looked around conspiratorially. "I wouldn't really want this to go any further," he said in a half whisper, "but it's widely rumored in Tol Honeth that those gold coins he's so free with are false."

"False?" the noble exclaimed, his eyes suddenly bulging.

"Very clever imitations," Silk continued. "Just enough gold is mixed with baser metals to make the coins look authentic, but they aren't worth a tenth of their face value."

The noble's face turned pasty white, and he clutched involuntarily at the purse attached to his belt.

"It's all part of a plot to destroy the Tolnedran economy by debasing the coinage," Silk added. "The Honeths were involved in it in some way, and that's why they're all being murdered. Of course, anyone caught with any of those coins in his possession is immediately hanged."

"*What?*"

"Naturally." Silk shrugged. "The Emperor intends to root out this monstrous business immediately. Stern measures are absolutely essential."

"I'm ruined!" the nobleman groaned. "Quickly, Balera!" he said, wheeling his horse, "we must return to Tol Borune at once!" And he led his frightened wife back southward at a dead run.

"Don't you want to hear about which kingdom was behind it all?" Silk called after them. Then he doubled over in his saddle, convulsed with laughter.

"Brilliant, Prince Kheldar," Velvet murmured admiringly.

"This Naradas moves around quite a bit, doesn't he?" Durnik said.

"I think I just put a bit of an anchor on him," Silk smirked. "Once that rumor spreads, I expect that he's going to have a little trouble spending his money—not to mention the interest that reward I mentioned is going to generate in certain quarters."

"That was a dreadful thing you did to that poor nobleman, though," Velvet said disapprovingly. "He's on his way back to Tol Borune to empty out all his strongboxes and bury the money."

Silk shrugged. "That's what he gets for consorting with Angaraks. Shall we press on?"

They passed Tol Borune without stopping and rode on south toward the Wood of the Dryads. When the ancient forest came into view on the southern horizon, Polgara pulled her horse in beside the mount of the dozing Belgarath. "I think we should stop by and pay our respects to Xantha, father," she said.

The old man roused himself and squinted in the direction of the Wood. "Maybe," he grunted doubtfully.

"We owe her the courtesy, father, and it's not really out of our way."

"All right, Pol," he said, "but just a brief stop. We're months behind Zandramas already."

They crossed the last band of open fields and rode in under the ancient, mossy oaks. The leaves had fallen to the chill winds of winter, and the bare limbs of the huge trees were starkly etched against the sky.

A peculiar change came over Ce'Nedra as they entered the Wood. Although it was still not really warm, she pushed back the hood of her cloak and shook out her coppery curls, causing her tiny, acorn-shaped gold earrings to tinkle musically. Her face became strangely calm, no longer mirroring the sorrow that had marked it since the abduction of her son. Her eyes became soft, almost unfocused. "I have returned," she murmured into the quiet air beneath the spreading trees.

Garion felt, rather than heard, the soft, murmuring response. From all around him he seemed to hear a sibilant sighing, although there was no trace of a breeze. The sighing was almost like a chorus, joining just below the level of hearing into a quiet, mournful song, a song filled with a gentle regret and at the same time an abiding hope.

"Why are they sad?" Eriond quietly asked Ce'Nedra.

"Because it's winter," she replied. "They mourn the falling of their leaves and regret the fact that the birds have all flown south."

"But spring will come again," he said.

"They know, but winter always saddens them."

Velvet was looking curiously at the little queen.

"Ce'Nedra's background makes her peculiarly sensitive to trees," Polgara explained.

"I didn't know that Tolnedrans were that interested in the out-of-doors."

"She's only half Tolnedran, Liselle. Her love of trees comes from the other side of her heritage."

"I'm a Dryad," Ce'Nedra said simply, her eyes still dreamy.

"I didn't know that."

"We didn't exactly make an issue of it," Belgarath told her. "We were having trouble enough getting the Alorns to accept a Tolnedran as the Rivan Queen without complicating matters by telling them that she was a nonhuman as well."

They made a simple camp not far from the place where they had been set upon by the hideous mud-men Queen Salmissra had dispatched to attack them so many years before. Because they could not hew limbs from live trees in this sacred wood, they were obliged to make shelters as best they could with what they found lying on the leaf-strewn forest floor, and their fire was of necessity very small. As twilight settled slowly over the silent Wood, Silk looked dubiously at the tiny, flickering flame and then out at the vast darkness moving almost visibly out from among the trees. "I think we're in for a cold night," he predicted.

Garion slept badly. Although he had piled fallen leaves deeply in the makeshift bed he shared with Ce'Nedra, their damp cold seemed to seep through to chill his very bones. He awoke from a fitful doze just as the first pale, misty light seeped in among the trees. He sat up stiffly and was about to throw off his blanket, but stopped. Eriond was sitting on a fallen log on the other side of their long-dead campfire, and sitting beside him was a tawny-haired Dryad.

"The trees say that you are a friend," the Dryad was saying as she absently toyed with a sharp-tipped arrow.

"I'm fond of trees," Eriond replied.

"That's not exactly the way they meant it."

"I know."

Garion carefully pushed his blankets aside and stood up.

The Dryad's hand moved swiftly toward the bow lying at her side, then she stopped. "Oh," she said, "it's you." She looked at him critically. Her eyes were as grey as glass. "You've gotten older, haven't you?"

"It's been quite a few years," he said, trying to remember just exactly where he had seen her before.

A faint hint of a smile touched her lips. "You don't remember me, do you?"

"Well, sort of."

She laughed, then picked up her bow. She set the arrow she was holding to the string and pointed it at him. "Does this help your memory at all?"

He blinked. "Weren't you the one who wanted to kill me?"

"It was only fair, after all. I was the one who caught you, so I should have been the one who got to kill you."

"Do you kill every human you catch?" Eriond asked her.

She lowered her bow. "Well, not *every* one of them. Sometimes I find other uses for them."

Garion looked at her a bit more closely. "You haven't changed a bit. You still look the same as before."

"I know." Her eyes grew challenging. "And pretty?" she prompted.

"Very pretty."

"What a nice thing for you to say. Maybe I'm glad that I didn't kill you after all. Why don't you and I go someplace, and you can say some more nice things to me?"

"That's enough, Xbel," Ce'Nedra said tartly from her bed of leaves. "He's mine, so don't get any ideas."

"Hello, Ce'Nedra," the tawny-haired Dryad said as calmly as if they had talked together within the past week. "Wouldn't you be willing to share him with one of your own sisters?"

"You wouldn't lend me your comb, would you?"

"Certainly not—but that's entirely different."

"There's no way that I could ever make you understand," Ce'Nedra said, pushing back her blankets and rising to her feet.

"Humans." Xbel sighed. "You all have such funny ideas." She looked speculatively at Eriond, her slim little hand softly touching his cheek. "How about this one? Does it belong to you, too?"

Polgara came out of another one of their makeshift shelters. Her face was calm, although one of her eyebrows was raised. "Good morning, Xbel," she said. "You're up early."

"I was hunting," the Dryad replied. "Does this blond one belong to you, Polgara? Ce'Nedra won't share that one of hers with me, but maybe—" Her hand lingeringly touched Eriond's soft curls.

"No, Xbel," Polgara said firmly.

Xbel sighed again. "None of you are any fun at all," she pouted. Then she stood up. She was as tiny as Ce'Nedra and as slender as a willow. "Oh," she said, "I almost forgot. Xantha says that I'm supposed to take you to her."

"But you got sidetracked, didn't you?" Ce'Nedra added drily.

"The day hasn't even got started yet." the Dryad shrugged.

Then Belgarath and Silk came out into the open area around the cold fire pit; a moment later, Durnik and Toth joined them.

"You have such a *lot* of them," Xbel murmured warmly. "Surely you can spare me one for just a little while."

"What's this?" Silk asked curiously.

"Never mind, Silk," Polgara told him. "Xantha wants to see us. Right after breakfast, Xbel here will show us the way—won't you, Xbel?"

"I suppose so." Xbel sighed a bit petulantly.

After their simple breakfast, the tawny-haired Dryad led them through the ancient Wood. Belgarath, leading his horse, walked beside her, and the two of them seemed deep in a conversation of some kind. Garion noticed that his grandfather furtively reached into his pocket from time to time and offered something to the slim Dryad—something she greedily snatched and popped into her mouth.

"What's he giving her?" Velvet asked.

"Sweets," Polgara said, sounding disgusted. "They're not

good for her, but he always brings sweets with him when he comes into this Wood."

"Oh," Velvet said. "I see." She pursed her lips. "Isn't she a bit young to be so—well—"

Ce'Nedra laughed. "Appearances can be deceiving, Liselle. Xbel is quite a bit older than she looks."

"How old would you say?"

"Two or three hundred years at least. She's the same age as her tree, and oak trees live for a very long time."

Back in the forest, Garion heard giggles, whispers, and the faint tinkle of little golden bells; once in a while he caught a glimpse of a flitting patch of color as a Dryad scampered through the trees, her earrings jingling.

Queen Xantha's tree was even more vast than Garion remembered it, its branches as broad as highways and the hollows in its bole opening like the mouths of caves. The Dryads in their brightly colored tunics bedecked the huge limbs like flowers, giggling and whispering and pointing at the visitors. Xbel led them into the broad, moss-covered clearing beneath the tree, put her fingers to her lips, and made a curiously birdlike whistle.

Queen Xantha, with her red-haired daughter Xera at her side, emerged from one of the hollows in the vast trunk and greeted them as they dismounted. Ce'Nedra and Xera flew into each others' arms even as the queen and Polgara warmly embraced. Xantha's golden hair was touched with gray at the temples, and her gray-green eyes were tired.

"Are you unwell, Xantha?" Polgara asked her.

The queen sighed. "The time is growing close, that's all." She looked up affectionately at her enormous oak. "He's growing very tired, and his weight presses down upon his roots. He finds it harder and harder each spring to revive himself and put forth leaves."

"Can I do anything?"

"No, dearest Polgara. There's no pain—just a great weariness. I won't mind sleeping. Now, what brings you into our Wood?"

"Someone has taken my baby," Ce'Nedra cried, flying into her aunt's arms.

"What are you saying, child?"

"It happened last summer, Xantha," Belgarath told her. "We're trying to find the trail of the one who stole him—a Mallorean named Zandramas. We think that the abductor sailed south aboard a Nyissan ship."

Xbel was standing not far from the giant Toth, eyeing his awesomely muscled arms speculatively. "I saw one of the boats of the snake-people late last summer," she mentioned, not taking her eyes off the huge mute, "down where our river empties out into the big lake."

"You never mentioned it Xbel," Xantha said.

"I forgot. Is anybody really interested in what the snake-people do?"

"Big lake?" Durnik said with a puzzled frown. "I don't remember any big lakes here in this Wood."

"It's the one that tastes funny," Xbel told him. "And you can't see the other side."

"You must mean the Great Western Sea, then."

"Whatever you want to call it," she replied indifferently. She continued to look Toth up and down.

"Did this Nyissan ship just sail on by?" Belgarath asked her.

"No," she said. "It got burned up. But that was after somebody got off."

"Xbel," Polgara said, stepping between the tawny-haired little Dryad and the object of her scrutiny, "do you think you can remember exactly what you saw?"

"I suppose so. It wasn't really very much, though. I was hunting, and I saw a boat go up to the beach on the south side of the river. This human in a black cloak with the hood pulled up got off with something in its arms. Then the black boat went back out into the water, and the human on the beach waved one hand at it. That's when the ship caught on fire—all over. All at once."

"What happened to the crew?" Durnik asked her.

"You know those big fish with all the teeth?"

"Sharks?"

"I guess so. Anyway, the water around the boat was full of them. When the humans jumped off the boat to get away from the fire, the fish ate them all up." She sighed. "It was a terrible waste. I was hoping that maybe one or two might have gotten away—or maybe even three." She sighed again.

"What did the human on the beach do then?" Polgara asked.

Xbel shrugged. "It waited until the ship burned all up and then it went into the woods on the south side of the river." She stepped around Polgara, her eyes still fixed on the huge mute. "If you're not using this one, Polgara, do you suppose I could borrow it for a little while? I've never seen one quite as big."

Garion spun and ran toward his horse, but Eriond was already there. He held out the reins of his own chestnut stallion. "He's faster, Belgarion," he said. "Take him."

Garion nodded shortly and swung into the saddle.

"Garion!" Ce'Nedra cried, "where are you going?"

But he was already plunging into the forest at a gallop. He was not really thinking as the stallion thundered through the leafless Wood. The only semblance of a thought in his mind was the image the indifferent Xbel had implanted there—a dark figure on the beach with something in its arms. Slowly, however, something else intruded itself on his awareness. There was something strange about the stallion's gait. About every fourth or fifth stride, the horse gave a peculiar lurch, and the wood seemed to blur for an instant. Then the gallop would continue until the next lurch and blurring.

The distance from Xantha's tree to the beach where the River of the Woods emptied into the Great Western Sea was considerable, he knew. At even the fastest gallop, it would take the better part of a day and a half to cover it. But wasn't that the glint of winter sunlight on a huge body of water coming through the trees just ahead?

There was another lurch and that odd blurring; quite suddenly the stallion set his forelegs stiffly, sliding through the sand at the very edge of the rolling surf.

"How did you do that?"

The horse looked back over one shoulder inquiringly.

Then Garion looked around in dismay. "We're on the wrong side of the river," he cried. "We're supposed to be over there." He drew on his will, preparing to translocate himself to the south beach, but the horse wheeled, took two steps, and lurched again.

They were suddenly on the sandy south beach, and Garion was clinging to the saddle to keep from falling off. For an irrational moment, he wanted to scold the animal for not warning him, but there was something much more important to attend to. He slid down from his saddle and ran along the damp sand at the edge of the water, drawing Iron-grip's sword as he went. The Orb glowed eagerly as he held up the blade. "Geran!" he shouted to it. "Find my son."

Between two strides, the Orb tugged at him, almost jerking him off-balance. He slid to a stop on the hard-packed sand, feeling the powerful pull of the sword in his hands. The tip lowered, touched the sand once, and then the Orb flared triumphantly as the blade pointed unerringly up the driftwood-littered beach toward the scrubby forest at its upper end.

It was true! Although he had secretly feared that the hints they had received might have been just another clever ruse, the trail of Zandramas and of his infant son was here after all. A sudden wave of exultation surged through him.

"Run, Zandramas!" he called out. "Run as fast as you can! I have your trail now, and the world isn't big enough for you to find any place to hide from me!"

CHAPTER SEVEN

A chill dampness hung in the air beneath the tangled limbs overhead, and the smell of stagnant water and decay filled their nostrils. The trees twisted upward from the dark floor of the jungle, seeking the light. Gray-green moss hung in streamers from the trees, and ropy vines crawled up their trunks like thick-bodied serpents. A pale, wispy fog hovered back among the trees, rising foul-smelling and dank from black ponds and sluggishly moving streams.

The road they followed was ancient, and it was overgrown with tangled brush. Garion rode now at the head of the party with his sword resting on the pommel of his saddle and the Orb eagerly tugging him on. It was late afternoon, and the day that had been gray and overcast to begin with settled slowly, almost sadly toward evening.

"I didn't know that the Nyissans had ever built roads," Ce'Nedra said, looking at the weed-choked track lying ahead of them.

"They were all abandoned after the Marag invasion at the end of the second millennium," Belgarath told her. "The Nyissans discovered that their highway system provided too easy a route for a hostile army, so Salmissra ordered that all the roads be allowed to go back to the jungle."

The sword in Garion's hands swung slightly, pointing toward the thick undergrowth at the side of the road. He frowned slightly, reining in. "Grandfather," he said, "the trail goes off into the woods."

The rest of them pulled up, peering into the obscuring bushes. "I'll go take a look," Silk said, sliding down from his horse and walking toward the side of the road.

"Watch out for snakes," Durnik called after him.

Silk stopped abruptly. "Thanks," he said in a voice dripping with sarcasm. Then he pushed into the brush, moving carefully and with his eyes fixed on the ground.

They waited, listening to the rustling crackle as Silk moved around back in the undergrowth. "There's a campsite back here," he called to them, "an old fire pit and several lean-tos."

"Let's have a look," Belgarath said, swinging down out of his saddle.

They left Toth with the horses and pushed back into the stiffly rustling brush. Some yards back from the road they came to a clearing and found Silk standing over a cold fire pit with a number of charred sticks lying at the bottom. "Was Zandramas here?" he asked Garion.

Garion moved forward, holding out his sword. It moved erratically in his hands, pointing first this way and then that. Then it tugged him toward one of the partially collapsed shelters. When he reached it, the sword dipped, touched the ground inside the rude lean-to, and the Orb flared.

"I guess that answers that question," Silk said with a certain satisfaction.

Durnik had knelt by the fire pit and was carefully turning over the charred sticks and peering into the ashes beneath. "It's been several months," he said.

Silk looked around. "From the number of shelters I'd say that at least four people made camp here."

Belgarath grunted. "Zandramas isn't alone any more, then."

Eriond had been curiously poking into the crude shelters and he reached down, picked something up from the ground inside one of them, and came back to join the rest. Wordlessly, he held out the object in his hand to Ce'Nedra.

"Oh," she cried, taking it quickly and clutching it tightly against her.

"What is it, Ce'Nedra?" Velvet asked.

The little queen, her eyes brimming, mutely held out the object Eriond had just given her. It was a small, wool-knit cap, lying damp and sad-looking in her hand. "It's my baby's," she said in a choked voice. "He was wearing it the night he was stolen."

Durnik cleared his throat uncomfortably. "It's getting late," he said quietly. "Did we want to set up for the night here?"

Garion looked at Ce'Nedra's agonized face. "I don't think so," he replied. "Let's go on just a little farther."

Durnik also looked at the grieving queen. "Right," he agreed.

About a half mile farther down the road, they reached the ruins of a long-abandoned city, half buried in the rank jungle growth. Trees buckled up the once-broad streets, and climbing vines wreathed their way upward about the empty towers.

"It seems like a good location," Durnik said, looking around the ruins. "Why did the people just go away and leave it empty?"

"There could be half-dozen reasons, Durnik," Polgara said. "A pestilence, politics, war—even a whim."

"A whim?" He looked startled.

"This is Nyissa," she reminded him. "Salmissra rules here, and her authority over her people is the most absolute in all the world. If she came here at some time in the past and told the people to leave, they'd have left."

He shook his head disapprovingly. "That's wrong," he said.

"Yes, dear," she agreed. "I know."

They made camp in the abandoned ruins, and the next morning they continued to ride in a generally southeasterly direction. As they pushed deeper and deeper into the Nyissan jungle, there was a gradual change in the vegetation. The trees loomed higher, and their trunks grew thicker. The underbrush became more dense, and the all-pervading reek of stagnant water grew stronger. Then, shortly before noon, a slight, vagrant breeze suddenly brought another scent to Garion's nostrils. It was an odor of such overpowering sweetness that it almost made him giddy.

"What is that lovely fragrance?" Velvet asked, her brown eyes softening.

Just then they rounded a bend, and there, standing in glory at the side of the road, rose the most beautiful tree Garion had ever seen. Its leaves were a shimmering gold, and long crimson vines hung in profusion from its limbs. It was covered with enormous blossoms of red, blue, and vivid lavender, and among those blossoms hung rich-looking clusters of shiny purple fruit that seemed almost ready to burst. An overwhelming sense of longing seemed to come over him as the sight and smell of that glorious tree touched his very heart.

Velvet, however, had already pushed past him, her face fixed in a dreamy smile as she rode toward the tree.

"Liselle!" Polgara's voice cracked like a whip. "Stop!"

"But—" Velvet's voice was vibrant with longing.

"Don't move," Polgara commanded. "You're in dreadful danger."

"Danger?" Garion said. "It's only a tree, Aunt Pol."

"Come with me, all of you," she commanded. "Keep a

tight rein on your horses, and don't go anywhere near that tree." She rode slowly forward at a walk, holding her horse's reins firmly in both hands.

"What's the matter, Pol?" Durnik asked.

"I thought that all of those had been destroyed," she muttered, looking at the gorgeous tree with an expression of flinty hatred.

"But—" Velvet objected, "why would anyone want to destroy something so lovely?"

"Of course it's lovely. That's how it hunts."

"Hunts?" Silk said in a startled voice. "Polgara, it's only a tree. Trees don't hunt."

"This one does. One taste of its fruit is instant death, and the touch of its blossoms paralyzes every muscle in the body. Look there." She pointed at something in the high grass beneath the tree. Garion peered into the grass and saw the skeleton of a large-sized animal. A half dozen of the crimson tendrils hanging from one of the flower-decked branches had poked their way down into the animal's rib cage and interwoven themselves into the mossy bones.

"Do not look at the tree," Polgara told them all in a deadly tone. "Do not think about the fruit, and try not to inhale the fragrance of its flowers too deeply. The tree is trying to lure you to within range of its tendrils. Ride on and don't look back." She reined in her horse.

"Aren't you coming, too?" Durnik asked with a worried look.

"I'll catch up," she replied. "I have to attend to this monstrosity first."

"Do as she says," Belgarath told them. "Let's go."

As they rode on past that beautiful, deadly tree, Garion felt a wrench of bitter disappointment; as they moved farther down the road away from it, he seemed to hear a silent snarl of frustration. Startled, he glanced back once and was amazed to see the crimson tendrils hanging from the branches writhing and lashing at the air in a kind of vegetative fury. Then he turned back quickly as Ce'Nedra made a violent retching sound.

"What's the matter?" he cried.

"The tree!" she gasped. "It's horrible! It feeds on the agony of its victims as much as upon their flesh!"

As they rounded another bend in the road, Garion felt a violent surge, and there was a huge concussion behind them, followed by the sizzling crackle of a fire surging up through living wood. In his mind he heard an awful scream filled with pain, anger, and a malevolent hatred. A pall of greasy black smoke drifted low to the ground, bringing with it a dreadful stench.

It was perhaps a quarter of an hour later when Polgara rejoined them. "It will not feed again," she said with a note of satisfaction in her voice. She smiled almost wryly. "That's one of the few things Salmissra and I have ever agreed upon," she added. "There's no place in the world for that particular tree."

They rode on down into Nyissa, following the weed-choked track of the long-abandoned highway. About noon of the following day, Eriond's chestnut stallion grew restive, and the blond young man pulled up beside Garion, who still rode in the lead with his sword on the pommel of his saddle. "He wants to run." Eriond laughed gently. "He always wants to run."

Garion looked over at him. "Eriond," he said, "there's something I've been meaning to ask you."

"Yes, Belgarion?"

"When I was riding your horse to the beach back up there in the Wood of the Dryads, he did something that was sort of odd."

"Odd? How do you mean?"

"It should have taken nearly two days to reach the sea, but he did it in about a half an hour."

"Oh," Eriond said, "that."

"Can you explain how he does it?"

"It's something he does sometimes when he knows that

I'm in a hurry to get someplace. He kind of goes to another place, and when he comes back, you're much farther along than you were when he started."

"Where is this other place?"

"Right here—all around us—but at the same time, it's not. Does that make any sense?"

"No. Not really."

Eriond frowned in concentration. "You told me one time that you could change yourself into a wolf—the same way Belgarath does."

"Yes."

"And you said that when you do that, your sword is still with you, but at the same time it's not."

"That's what Grandfather told me."

"I think that's where this other place is—the same place where your sword goes. Distance doesn't seem to mean the same thing there as it does here. Does that explain it at all?"

Garion laughed. "It doesn't even come close, Eriond, but I'll take your word for it."

About midafternoon the next day, they reached the marshy banks of the River of the Serpent where the highway turned toward the east, following the winding course of that sluggish stream. The sky had cleared, though the pale sunlight had little warmth to it.

"Maybe I'd better scout on ahead," Silk said. "The road looks a bit more well traveled along this stretch, and we didn't exactly make a lot of friends the last time we were here." He spurred his horse into a brisk canter; in a few minutes he was out of sight around a bend in the weed-choked road.

"We won't have to go through Sthiss Tor, will we?" Ce'Nedra asked.

"No," Belgarath replied. "It's on the other side of the river." He looked at the screen of trees and brush lying between the ancient highway and the mossy riverbank. "We should be able to slip past it without too much trouble."

An hour or so later, they rounded a bend in the road and caught a glimpse of the strange, alien-looking towers of the capital of the snake-people rising into the air on the far side of the river. There seemed to be no coherent pattern to Nyissan architecture. Some of the towers rose in slender spires, and others were bulky, with bulblike tops. Some even twisted in spirals toward the sky. They were, moreover, painted every possible hue—green, red, yellow, and even some in a garish purple. Silk was waiting for them a few hundred yards farther along the road. "There won't be any trouble getting past here without being seen from the other side," he reported, "but there's someone on up ahead who wants to talk to us."

"Who?" Belgarath asked sharply.

"He didn't say, but he seemed to know we were coming."

"I don't like that very much. Did he say what he wants?"

"Only that he's got a message of some kind for us."

"Let's go find out about this." The old man looked at Garion. "You'd better cover the Orb," he suggested. "Let's keep it out of sight—just to be on the safe side."

Garion nodded, took out a soft, tight-fitting leather sleeve and pulled it down over the hilt of Iron-grip's sword.

The shaven-headed Nyissan who awaited them was dressed in shabby, stained clothing and he had a long scar running from forehead to chin across an empty eye socket. "We thought you'd get here earlier," he said laconically as they all reined in. "What kept you?"

Garion looked at the one-eyed man closely. "Don't I know you?" he asked. "Isn't your name Issus?"

Issus grunted. "I'm surprised you remember. Your head wasn't too clear the last time we met."

"It wasn't the sort of thing I'd be likely to forget."

"Somebody in the city wants to see you," Issus said.

"I'm sorry, friend," Belgarath told him, "but we're pressed for time. I don't think there's anybody in Sthiss Tor that we need to talk with."

Issus shrugged. "That's up to you. I was paid to meet you and give you the message." He turned and started back through the slanting, late-afternoon sunlight toward the rank growth along the river bank. Then he stopped. "Oh. I almost forgot. The man who sent me said to tell you that he has some information about somebody named Zandramas, if that means anything to you."

"Zandramas?" Ce'Nedra said sharply.

"Whoever that is," Issus replied. "If you're interested, I've got a boat. I can take some of you across to the city if you want."

"Give us a minute or two to talk it over," Belgarath said to him.

"Take as long as you want. We can't cross until after dark anyway. I'll wait in the boat while you decide." He went on down through the bushes toward the river bank.

"Who is he?" Silk asked Garion.

"His name is Issus. He's for hire. Last time I saw him, he was working for Sadi—the Chief Eunuch in Salmissra's palace—but I get the feeling that he'll work for anybody as long as he gets paid." He turned to Belgarath. "What do you think, Grandfather?"

The old man tugged at one ear lobe. "It could be some kind of ruse," he said, "but somebody over there knows enough about what we're doing to realize that we're interested in Zandramas. I think I'd like to find out who this well-informed citizen is."

"You won't get anything out of Issus," Silk told him. "I've already tried."

Belgarath pondered a moment. "Go see how big this boat of his is."

Silk went over to the edge of the road and peered down through the bushes. "We can't all go," he reported. "Maybe four of us."

Belgarath scratched his chin. "You, me, Pol, and Garion," he decided. He turned to Durnik. "Take the others—and the horses—and go back into the jungle a ways. This might take us a while. Don't build up any fires that can be seen from the city."

"I'll take care of things, Belgarath."

The boat Issus had rowed across from the city was painted

a dull black, and it was moored to a half-sunken log, and screened by overhanging tree limbs. The one-eyed man looked critically at Garion. "Do you have to take that big sword?" he asked.

"Yes," Garion replied.

Issus shrugged. "Suit yourself."

As twilight settled on the river, a mist of tiny gnats rose from the surrounding bushes and swarmed about them as they sat in the boat waiting for darkness. Silk absently slapped at his neck.

"Don't jiggle the boat," Issus warned. "The leeches are hungry this time of year, so it's not a good time for swimming."

They sat huddled in the small boat enduring the biting of the gnats as the light gradually faded. After about a half-hour of discomfort, Issus peered out through the concealing branches. "It's dark enough," he said shortly. He untied the boat and pushed it out from the bank with one oar. Then he settled himself and started to row toward the lights of Sthiss Tor on the far side. After about twenty minutes, he swung his boat into the deep shadows beneath the wharf jutting out into the water from the Drasnian enclave, that commercial zone on the river front where northern merchants were permitted to conduct business. A tar-smeared rope was slung under the wharf, and Issus pulled them hand over hand beneath the protecting structure until they reached a ladder. "We go up here," he said, tying his boat to a piling beside the ladder. "Try not to make too much noise."

"Exactly where are you taking us?" Polgara asked him.

"It's not far," he replied and quietly went up the ladder.

"Keep your eyes open," Belgarath muttered. "I don't altogether trust that fellow."

The streets of Sthiss Tor were dark, since all the ground-level windows were thickly shuttered. Issus moved on catlike feet, keeping to the shadows, although Garion could not be sure if his stealth was out of necessity or merely from habit. As they passed a narrow alleyway, Garion heard a skittering noise coming from somewhere in the darkness, and his hand flew to his sword hilt. "What's that?" he asked.

"Rats." Issus shrugged. "They come up from the river at night to feed on garbage—and then the snakes crawl in out of the jungle to eat the rats." He held up one hand. "Wait here a moment." He moved on ahead to peer cautiously up and down a broad street lying just ahead of them. "It's clear," he said. "Come ahead. The house we want is just across the street."

"That's Droblek's house, isn't it?" Polgara asked as they joined the furtive Nyissan, "the Drasnian Port Authority?"

"You've been here before, I see. Let's go. They're expecting us."

Droblek himself opened the door of his house in response to Issus' light tap. The Drasnian port official wore a loose-fitting brown robe and was, if anything, more grossly fat than he had been when Garion had last seen him. As he opened the door, he looked nervously out into the street, peering this way and then that in the gloom. "Quickly," he whispered, "Inside—all of you." Once he had closed the door behind them and secured it with a stout lock, he seemed to relax a bit. "My Lady," he wheezed to Polgara with a portly bow, "my house is honored."

"Thank you, Droblek. Are you the one who sent for us?"

"No, my Lady. I helped to make the arrangements, though."

"You seem a bit nervous, Droblek," Silk said to him.

"I'm concealing something in my house that I'd rather not have here, Prince Kheldar. I could get into a lot of trouble if anyone found out about it. The Tolnedran Ambassador always has people watching my house, and he'd delight in embarrassing me."

"Where's the man we're supposed to meet?" Belgarath asked brusquely.

Droblek's face was awed as he replied. "I have a hidden chamber at the back of the house, Ancient One. He's waiting there."

"Let's go see him, then."

"At once, Eternal Belgarath." Waddling and puffing noticeably, the Drasnian official led them down a dimly lighted hallway. At its far end, he ran his hand down the wall and touched one of its stones. With a loud click, an irregularly shaped section of the wall came unlatched to protrude slightly from the rest.

"Exotic," Silk murmured.

"Who's there?" a shrill voice came from the other side of that hidden door.

"It's me—Droblek," the fat man answered. "The people you wanted to see have arrived." He pulled the stone-slab covered door open. "I'll go keep watch," he said to them.

Beyond the door was a small, dank, hidden chamber lit by a single candle. Sadi the eunuch stood fearfully beside a battered wooden table. His shaven head was stubbled and his scarlet silk robe tattered. There was a hunted look about his eyes. "At last," he said with relief.

"What on earth are you doing here, Sadi?" Polgara asked him.

"Hiding," he said. "Come in, please, all of you, and close the door. I don't want anybody to find out accidentally where I am."

They stepped into the small room, and Droblek pushed the door shut behind them.

"Why is the Chief Eunuch of Salmissra's palace hiding in the house of the Drasnian Port Authority?" Silk asked curiously.

"There's been a slight misunderstanding at the palace, Prince Kheldar," Sadi replied, sinking into a chair by the wooden table. "I'm not Chief Eunuch any more. As a matter of fact, there's a price on my head—a fairly large one, I'm told. Droblek owed me a favor, so he let me hide here—not very willingly, but—" He shrugged.

"Since we're talking about prices, I'll take my money now," Issus said.

"I have one more little job for you, Issus," the eunuch said in his oddly contralto voice. "Do you think that you could get into the palace?"

"If I need to."

"There's a red leather case in my quarters—under the bed. It has brass hinges. I need it."

"Did you want to discuss the price?"

"I'll pay you whatever you think is fair."

"All right. Let's say double what you already owe me."

"*Double?*"

"The palace is very dangerous right now."

"You're taking advantage of the situation, Issus."

"Go fetch it yourself then."

Sadi looked at him helplessly. "All right," he surrendered, "double."

"It's always a pleasure doing business with you, Sadi," Issus said flatly. Then he went to the door and slipped out.

"What happened here?" Silk asked the nervous eunuch.

Sadi sighed. "Certain accusations were made against me," he said in a pained voice. "I wasn't entirely prepared to defend myself against them, so I thought it might be wiser to take an extended leave from my duties. I've been working too hard lately anyway."

"Were the accusations unfounded?"

Sadi ran one long-fingered hand over his stubbled scalp. "Well—not entirely," he admitted, "but the matter was blown all out of proportion."

"Who took your place at the palace?"

"Sariss." Sadi almost spat the name. "He's a third-rate schemer with no real sense of style at all. Someday I'm going to take a great deal of pleasure in cutting out several things he needs rather badly—with a dull knife."

"Issus told us that you had some information about someone called Zandramas," Belgarath said.

"I do indeed," Sadi replied. He rose from his chair and went to the narrow, unmade bed standing against one wall. He rummaged around under the dirty brown blanket, took out a small silver flask, and opened it. "Excuse me," he said, taking a small sip. He grimaced. "I wish it didn't taste so bad."

Polgara gave him a cool look. "Do you suppose you could tell us what you know about Zandramas—*before* you start seeing the butterflies?"

Sadi looked at her innocently. "Oh, no. This isn't one of those, Lady Polgara," he assured her, shaking the flask. "It just has a certain calming effect. My nerves have been absolutely destroyed by what's happening in the past few months."

"Why don't we get down to business?" Belgarath suggested.

"Very well. I have something you want, and you have something I want. I think a trade is in order."

"Why don't we discuss that?" Silk said, his eyes suddenly brightening and his long nose twitching.

"I'm very much aware of your reputation, Prince Kheldar." Sadi smiled. "I'm not foolish enough to try to bargain with *you*."

"All right, just what *is* this thing you want from us, Sadi?" Belgarath asked the dead-eyed eunuch.

"You're on your way out of Nyissa. I want you to take me with you. In exchange, I'll tell you everything I've learned about Zandramas."

"Totally out of the question."

"I think you're speaking in haste, Ancient One. Hear me out first."

"I don't trust you, Sadi," Belgarath said bluntly.

"That's quite understandable. I'm not the sort of man who *should* be trusted."

"Then why should I saddle myself with you?"

"Because I know why you're following Zandramas—and more importantly, I know where Zandramas is going. It's a very dangerous place for *you*, but I can arrange a way for us to move around freely once we get there. Now, why don't we put aside all this childishness about trusting each other and get down to business?"

"We're just wasting time here," Belgarath said to the rest of them.

"I can be very useful to you, Ancient One," Sadi told him.

"Or to anyone who might want to know where we are," Silk added.

"That wouldn't be in my own best interests, Kheldar."

"Which brings up an interesting point," Silk said. "I have a splendid opportunity here to turn a quick profit. You mentioned the fact that there's a large price on your head. If you don't want to be co-operative, I might just decide to collect that price. How much did you say it was?"

"You won't do that, Kheldar," Sadi replied placidly. "You're in a hurry to catch up with Zandramas, and there are always a hundred administrative details involved in collecting a reward. It would probably be a month before you saw any of the money, and Zandramas would be that much farther ahead of you by then."

"That's probably true," Silk admitted. He reached for one of his daggers with a regretful expression. "There's this other alternative, however—messy, but usually fairly effective."

Sadi backed away from him. "Belgarath," he said in a faintly alarmed voice.

"That won't be necessary, Silk," the old man said. He turned to Polgara. "See what you can do, Pol," he suggested.

"All right, father." She turned to the eunuch. "Sit down, Sadi," she told him. "I want you to look at something."

"Of course, Lady Polgara," he agreed amiably, seating himself in a chair by the table.

"Look closely," she said, making a curious gesture in front of his eyes.

The eunuch continued to smile. "How charming," he murmured, looking at something which seemed to have appeared before his eyes. "Can you make it do any other tricks, too?"

She bent forward and looked closely into his eyes. "I see. You're more clever than I thought, Sadi." She turned back to the rest of them. "He's drugged," she said. "Probably what he drank out of that flask. Right now there's absolutely nothing I can do with him."

"That takes us back to the other alternative, doesn't it?" Silk said, reaching for his dagger again.

Polgara shook her head. "Right now, he wouldn't even feel it."

"Oh," Sadi said in a disappointed voice, "you made it go away—and I rather liked it."

"The drug won't last forever." Silk shrugged. "And by the time it wears off, we should be far enough from the city to be able to carve some answers out of him without the screams attracting any attention." His hand strayed again to the hilt of his dagger.

"*Alorns,*" the dry voice in Garion's mind said disgustedly. "*Why is it that your solution to every problem comes out of a scabbard?*"

"*What?*"

"*Tell the little thief to put away his knife.*"

"*But—*"

"*Don't argue with me, Garion. You have to have Sadi's information about Zandramas, and I can't give it to you.*"

"*You're not suggesting that we take him along?*" Garion was profoundly shocked at the idea.

"*I'm not suggesting anything, Garion. I'm telling you. Sadi goes along. You can't do what you have to do without him. Now tell your grandfather.*"

"*He's not going to like it.*"

"*I can face that prospect with enormous fortitude.*" Then the voice was gone.

"Grandfather," Garion said in a sick tone.

"What?" The old man's tone was testy.

"This isn't my idea, Grandfather, but—" Garion looked at the dreamy-faced eunuch with distaste and then lifted his hands helplessly.

"You're not serious!" Belgarath exclaimed after a moment.

"I'm afraid so."

"Am I missing something?" Sadi asked curiously.

"Shut up!" Belgarath snapped. Then he turned back to Garion. "Are you absolutely sure?"

Garion nodded dejectedly.

"This is sheer idiocy!" The old man turned and glared at Sadi. Then he reached across the table and took the front of the eunuch's iridescent robe in his fist. "Listen to me very carefully, Sadi," he said from between clenched teeth. "You're going with us, but keep your nose out of that flask. Do you understand me?"

"Of course, Ancient One," the eunuch replied in that same dreamy voice.

"I don't think you fully grasp what I'm talking about," Belgarath continued in a dreadfully quiet voice. "If I catch you with your brains full of dandelion fluff just once, I'll make you wish that Kheldar had gotten to you with his knife first. Do you follow me?"

Sadi's eyes grew wide, and his face blanched. "Y—yes, Belgarath," he stammered fearfully.

"Good. Now start talking. Just exactly what do you know about Zandramas?"

CHAPTER EIGHT

"It all started last year," Sadi began, still eyeing Belgarath apprehensively. "A Mallorean posing as a jewel merchant came to Sthiss Tor and sought out my chief rival at the palace—a petty schemer named Sariss. It was rather general knowledge that Sariss had long coveted my position, but I hadn't gotten around to having him killed yet." He made a face. "A grave oversight, as it turned out. Anyway, Sariss and the Mallorean negotiated for a bit, and the bargain they struck had nothing to do with gem stones. This so-called jeweler needed something that only someone in a position of authority could provide, so he gave Sariss certain information that Sariss was able to use to discredit me and usurp my position."

"I just love politics, don't you?" Silk said to no one in particular.

Sadi grimaced again. "The details of my fall from the queen's favor are tedious," he continued, "and I really don't want to bore you with them. At any rate, Sariss supplanted me as Chief Eunuch, and I barely escaped from the palace with my life. Once Sariss had consolidated his position, he was able to keep his part of the bargain he had reached with his Mallorean friend."

"And what exactly did the Mallorean want?" Silk asked.

"This, Prince Kheldar," Sadi said, rising and going to his rumpled cot. He drew a carefully folded parchment from beneath the mattress and handed it to the little man.

Silk read it quickly and then whistled.

"Well?" Belgarath said.

"It's an official document," Silk replied. "At least, it's over the queen's seal. Early last spring, Salmissra dispatched a diplomatic mission to Sendaria."

"That's fairly routine, Silk."

"I know, but there are also some secret instructions to the diplomats. She tells them that they will be met at the mouth of the River of the Serpent by a foreigner, and that they are to render this stranger every possible aid. The gist of the whole thing is that these diplomats were to make arrangements to get the foreigner to the port of Halberg on the west coast of Cherek *and* to have a Nyissan ship standing off the Rivan coast on a certain date about the middle of last summer."

"Coincidence, perhaps?" Belgarath suggested.

Silk shook his head and held up the parchment. "It identifies the foreigner by name. The diplomats were supposed to identify their passenger by the name 'Zandramas.'"

"That explains a few things, doesn't it?" Garion said.

"May I see that?" Polgara asked.

Silk handed her the parchment.

She looked at it briefly and then held it out to Sadi. "Are you positive that this is Salmissra's seal?" she asked him.

"There's no question about it, Polgara," he replied, "and no one dares to touch that seal without her consent."

"I see."

"How did you come by the document, Sadi?" Silk asked curiously.

"Four copies of all official documents are routinely made, Prince Kheldar. It's one of the resources of those with access to the queen's favor. The purchase price of the extra copies has been established for centuries."

"All right," Garion said, "so Zandramas came to Nyissa posing as a merchant, arranged to have Sariss replace you as Chief Eunuch, and somehow managed to get Salmissra to issue that order. Is that it?"

"It's not quite that simple, Belgarion," Sadi told him. "The Mallorean merchant was *not* Zandramas. No one here in Sthiss Tor ever saw Zandramas. The 'stranger' the document talks about joined the diplomats on their way to Sendaria. So far as I've been able to determine, Zandramas never passed through Sthiss Tor. Not only that, but after the arrangements for the ship to Halberg had been made, all the diplomats conveniently died. They were stopping over at an inn in Camaar on their way to the capital, and there was a fire in the middle of the night. No one escaped the fire."

"That's got a familiar ring to it," Silk said.

"All right then," Garion said, "who *was* the Mallorean jeweler?"

Sadi spread his hands helplessly. "I was never able to find out," he confessed.

"Did you ever see him?"

"Once. He was a strange-looking fellow. His eyes were absolutely colorless."

There was a long pause, and then Silk said, "That clears up a few other things, doesn't it?"

"Maybe so," Garion said, "but it still doesn't answer my main question. We know who Naradas is working for now. We know how Zandramas got to Cherek and escaped from the Isle of the Winds with my son, but what I need to know is where the trail we're following is going to lead."

Sadi shrugged. "Rak Verkat."

"How did you arrive at that conclusion?" Silk asked him.

"Sariss hasn't been in power long enough to weed out the more untrustworthy of his underlings. I found one who was open to the notion of private enterprise. Zandramas has to be in Mallorea with Prince Geran by this coming spring, and the route must be by way of Rak Verkat."

"Wouldn't it be shorter to sail from Rak Cthan?" Silk asked.

Sadi looked at him with a faintly surprised expression. "I thought you knew," he said. "Kal Zakath has put a very handsome price on the head of Zandramas, and the Mallorean reserves are concentrated at Rak Hagga. If Zandramas tried to go through Hagga to reach Cthan, all those troops would drop whatever they were doing to go head-hunting. The only safe port for Zandramas to sail from is Rak Verkat."

"Was this underling you bribed reliable?" Silk demanded.

"Of course not. As soon as he had finished telling me all this, he had planned to turn me in for the reward—dead, naturally, so he didn't really have any reason to lie to me, and he was too stupid to make up a coherent lie anyway." The eunuch smiled bleakly. "I know of a certain plant, though. It's a *very* reliable plant. The man was telling me the absolute truth. As a matter of fact, he kept telling me the truth long after it had begun to bore me. Sariss provided Zandramas with an escort across Nyissa and detailed maps of the shortest route to the Isle of Verkat."

"Was that all the fellow said?" Garion asked.

"Oh, no," Sadi replied. "He was busy confessing to me that he had cheated on an examination in school when I finally had Issus cut his throat. I can only deal with so much truth in one day."

"All right," Garion said, ignoring that, "Zandramas is going to the Isle of Verkat. How does that help us?"

"The route Zandramas will have to follow will be roundabout—because of that reward I mentioned. We, on the other hand, can go straight across southern Cthol Murgos to the Isle. It will save us months."

"That route goes right through the war zone," Silk protested.

"That's no particular problem. I can take you directly through to Verkat without any hindrance from either the Murgos or the Malloreans."

"How do you propose to manage that?"

"When I was younger, I was engaged in the slave trade in Cthol Murgos. I know all the routes and I know whom to bribe and whom to avoid. Slavers are useful to both sides in the war between the Murgos and Malloreans, so they're allowed to move around freely. All we have to do is dress as slave traders, and no one will interfere with us."

"What's to keep you from selling us to the Grolims as soon as we cross the border?" Silk asked bluntly.

"Self-interest." Sadi shrugged. "Grolims are an ungrateful lot. If I sell you to them, it's quite likely that they'll turn around and sell me to Salmissra. I don't think I'd like that at all."

"Is she really that angry with you?" Garion asked.

"Irritated," Sadi said. "A snake doesn't really get angry. I've heard, however, that she wants to bite me personally. That's a great honor, of course, but one I'd prefer to forgo."

The door to the hidden room clicked open, and Droblek looked in. "Issus is back," he said.

"Good," Belgarath replied. "I want to get back across the river before morning."

The one-eyed man came in carrying the case Sadi had described. It was a flat, square box a couple of feet across and several inches thick. "What's in this, Sadi?" he asked. "It gurgles." He took the case.

"Be careful man!" Sadi exclaimed. "Some of those bottles are fragile."

"What's this?" Belgarath demanded.

"A bit of this, a bit of that," Sadi replied evasively.

"Drugs?"

"And poisons and antidotes—a few aphrodisiacs, an anesthetic or two, a fairly effective truth drug—and Zith."

"What is Zith?"

"Zith is a who, Ancient One, not a what. I never go anywhere without her." He opened the case and lovingly took out a small earthenware bottle, securely corked and with a series of small holes encircling its neck. "Would you hold this, please?" he said, handing the bottle to Silk. "I want to make sure Issus didn't break anything." He began to carefully examine the row after row of little vials nested in velvet-lined pockets inside the case.

Silk looked curiously at the bottle, then took hold of the cork.

"I really wouldn't do that, Prince Kheldar," Sadi advised. "You might get a nasty surprise."

"What's in here?" Silk asked, shaking the bottle.

"Please, Kheldar. Zith becomes vexed when people shake her." Sadi closed the case, set it aside, and took the bottle from Silk. "There, there," he said to it in a crooning voice. "It's nothing to be alarmed about, dear. I'm right here and I won't let him disturb you any more."

From inside the bottle came a peculiar purring sound.

"How did you get a cat in there?" Garion asked.

"Oh, Zith isn't a cat, Belgarion," Sadi assured him. "Here, I'll show you." Carefully he worked the cork out and laid the bottle on its side on the table. "You can come out now, dear," he crooned to it.

Nothing happened.

"Come along now, Zith. Don't be shy."

Then a small, bright-green snake slithered obediently from the mouth of the bottle. She had gleaming yellow eyes and a vibrant red stripe running down her back from nose to tail. Her forked tongue flickered out, touching Sadi's outstretched hand.

Silk recoiled with a sharp intake of breath.

"Isn't she beautiful?" Sadi said, gently stroking the little snake's head with one finger. The snake began to purr contentedly, then raised her head, fixed Silk with a cold, reptilian eye, and hissed spitefully at him.

"I do believe that you offended her, Prince Kheldar," Sadi said. "Maybe you should stay away from her for a while."

"Don't worry," Silk said fervently, backing away. "Is she venomous?"

"She's the deadliest little snake in the world, aren't you, dear?" Sadi stroked the snake's head again. "Also the rarest. Her species is highly prized in Nyissa because they're the most intelligent of all reptiles. They're friendly—even affectionate—and, of course, the purr is absolutely delightful."

"But she *does* bite," Silk added.

"Only people who irritate her—and never a friend. All you have to do is feed her and keep her warm and show her a little affection now and then, and she'll follow you around like a puppy."

"Not *me*, she won't."

"Sadi," Belgarath said, pointing at the case, "what's the idea of all this? I don't need a walking apothecary shop trailing along behind me."

Sadi held up one hand. "Murgos aren't really very interested in money, Ancient One, but there are people I'll have to bribe when we go across Cthol Murgos. Some of them have picked up certain habits. That case is going to be worth more to us than a pack horse loaded down with gold."

Belgarath grunted. "Just keep *your* face out of it. I don't want your head full of smoke at a crucial moment—and keep your snake under control."

"Of course, Belgarath."

The old sorcerer turned to Issus. "Can you get a bigger boat? We need to get back across the river, and that one of yours won't hold all of us."

Issus nodded.

"Not just yet, father," Polgara said. "I'm going to need him for a while."

"Pol, we need to get back on the other side of the river before dawn."

"I won't be too long, father, but I have to go to the palace."

"The palace?"

"Zandramas went to Cherek—where no Angarak has been allowed since the days of Bear-shoulders. Salmissra arranged that and she also engineered the escape from the Isle of the Winds after the abduction of Ce'Nedra's baby. I want to know why."

"We're a bit pressed for time, Polgara. Can't this wait?"

"I don't think so, father. I think we need to know if there were any *other* arrangements. I'd rather not be surprised by a battalion or so of Nyissan troops lurking in the jungle along the trail we're following."

He frowned. "You might be right."

"You're going to the palace?" Garion asked her.

"I must, dear."

"All right," he said, squaring his shoulders. "Then I'm going with you."

She gave him a long, steady look. "You're going to insist, I take it?"

He nodded. "Yes, Aunt Pol, I think I am." He said it quite decisively.

She sighed. "How quickly they grow up," she said. Then she turned to Issus. "Do you know a back way to the palace?" she asked him.

The one-eyed man nodded.

"Will you show us?"

"Of course," he replied. He paused. "We can discuss the price later."

"Price?"

"Nothing for nothing, Lady," he shrugged. "Shall we go?"

It was nearly midnight when Issus led Polgara and Garion out the rear door of Droblek's house into a narrow alleyway that smelled strongly of rotting garbage. They made their way furtively through a twisting series of similar alleys, sometimes passing through the lower corridors of houses to move from one alley to another.

"How do you know which houses have unlocked doors?"

Garion whispered as they emerged from a tall, narrow house in a run-down quarter of the city.

"It's my business to know," Issus replied. He straightened and looked around. "We're getting close to the palace," he told them. "The streets and alleys in this part of the city are patrolled. Wait here a minute." He stealthily crossed the alley, opened a recessed door, and slipped inside. A couple of moments later he emerged, carrying two silk robes, a pair of lances, and a couple of brass helmets. "We'll wear these," he said to Garion, "and if you don't mind, Lady, pull your hood farther over your face. If anybody stops us, let me do the talking."

Garion pulled on the robe and helmet and took one of the lances from the assassin.

"Tuck your hair up under the helmet," Issus instructed. Then he stepped out boldly, trusting to their disguises rather than to stealth.

They had no sooner entered the next street than they were stopped by a half-dozen armed men.

"What's your business?" the man in charge of the patrol demanded.

"We're escorting a visitor to the palace," Issus replied.

"What kind of visitor?"

Issus gave him a disgusted look. "You don't really want to interfere, corporal," he said. "The one she's visiting wouldn't like it."

"And who is that?"

"Now, that's a very stupid question, man. If this woman's friend finds out that I told you, we'll probably *both* wind up in the river."

"How do I know that you're telling me the truth?"

"You don't—but do you really want to take a chance on it?"

The corporal's expression grew faintly nervous as he thought about it. "You'd better move along," he said finally.

"I was sure you'd see it my way," Issus observed. He

roughly took hold of Polgara's arm. "Move, you," he commanded.

When they reached the end of the street, Garion glanced back. The soldiers were still watching them, but made no move to follow.

"I hope you aren't offended, Lady," Issus apologized.

"No," Polgara replied. "You're a very resourceful fellow, Issus."

"That's what I get paid for. We go this way."

The wall of Salmissra's palace was very high, constructed of great roughhewn stone blocks that had stood for eons in this dank city by the river. Issus led them into the dense shadows under the wall and to a small, iron-barred gate. He fumbled with the lock for a moment, then carefully swung the gate open. "Let's go," he muttered.

The palace was a maze of dimly lighted corridors, but Issus led them confidently, moving along as if he were on an important mission. As they approached the broader, somewhat more brightly lighted hallways near the center of the palace, a grotesquely made-up eunuch lurched by, his legs stiff and his eyes unfocused. His mouth was fixed in a stupefied grin, and his body twitched spasmodically as he stumbled past them. They passed an open doorway and heard someone inside giggling uncontrollably. Garion could not be sure if that unseen person was a man or a woman.

The one-eyed man stopped and opened a door. "We have to go through here," he said, taking a smoky lamp from the niche beside the door. "Be careful. It's dark, and there are snakes on the floor."

The room was cool and had a musty smell. Garion could clearly hear the dry, dusty hiss of scales rubbing against each other in the corners. "It's fairly safe," Issus said. "They were fed today, and that always makes them sluggish." He stopped at the door, opened it a crack and peered out. "Wait," he whispered.

Garion heard a couple of men talking and the sound of their

footsteps in the corridor outside. Then a door opened and closed.

"It's clear," Issus said quietly. "Let's go." He led them out into the corridor and along its dimly lighted length to a polished door. He looked at Polgara. "Are you sure you want to see the queen?" he asked her.

She nodded.

"All right," he said. "Sariss is in here. He'll take us to the throneroom."

"Are you sure?" Garion whispered.

Issus reached under the robe he had donned in the alley and drew out a long, saw-edged dagger. "I can practically guarantee it," he said. "Give me a moment. Then come in and close the door." He shoved the door open and jumped into the room like a great, soft-footed cat.

"What—" someone inside the room cried out in a high-pitched voice. Then there was a terrified silence.

Garion and Polgara entered quickly, closing the door behind them. A man sat at the table, his eyes bulging with fright and with the needlepoint of Issus' dagger pushed against his throat. He wore a crimson silk robe, and his shaven head was pasty white. Rolls of greasy, unhealthy-looking fat drooped from his jowls, and his frightened eyes were small and piglike.

Issus was talking to him in a dreadfully quiet voice, emphasizing what he was saying by pressing the point of his knife into the skin of the fat man's throat. "This is an Ulgo knife, Sariss. It causes almost no damage when it goes in, but when you pull it out, it jerks out all kinds of things along with it. Now, we aren't going to make any kind of outcry, are we?"

"N-no," Sariss stammered in a squeaky voice.

"I was sure you'd see it my way. This is what we're going to do. This lady and her young friend want to have a word with the queen, so you're going to take us to the throne room."

"The queen?" Sariss gasped. "No one goes into her presence without permission. I-I can't do it."

"This conversation has suddenly taken a definite turn for the worse." Issus looked over at Polgara. "Would you like to turn your head, Lady?" he asked politely. "The sight of a man with his brains oozing out of his ears makes some people queasy."

"Please," Sariss begged him. "I can't. The queen will kill me if I take you into the throne room without being summoned."

"And I'll kill you if you don't. Somehow, I've got the feeling that this isn't going to be one of your good days, Sariss. Now get on your feet." The assassin jerked the trembling fat man from his chair.

They stepped out into the corridor with the eunuch leading the way. Sweat was streaming down his face, and there was a wild look in his eyes.

"No blunders, Sariss," Issus warned. "Remember that I'm right behind you."

The two burly guards at the entrance to the throne room bowed respectfully to the Chief Eunuch and swung the heavy doors open for him.

Salmissra's throne room was unchanged. The enormous stone statue of Issa, the Serpent God, still loomed behind the dais at the far end of the room. The crystal lamps still glowed dimly on their silver chains, and the two dozen bald and crimson-robed eunuchs still knelt on the polished floor, ready to murmur in unison their phrases of adoration. Even the gold-framed mirror still stood on its pedestal at the side of the divanlike throne.

Salmissra herself, however, was dreadfully changed. She was no longer the beautiful, sensuous woman Garion had seen when, drugged and bemused, he had first been led into her presence. She lay on her throne with her mottled coils undulating restlessly. Her polished scales gleamed in the lamplight, and her flat reptile's head rose on its long, thin neck, with the golden crown of the serpent queen resting lightly above her dead, incurious eyes.

She glanced briefly at them as they entered, then turned back to regard her reflection in the mirror. "I do not recall having summoned you, Sariss," she said in a dry, dusty whisper.

"The queen questions the Chief Eunuch," the two dozen shaven-headed men kneeling near the dais intoned in unison.

"Forgive me, Eternal Salmissra," the eunuch pleaded, prostrating himself on the floor before the throne. "I was forced to bring these strangers into your presence. They threatened to kill me if I refused."

"Then you should have died, Sariss," the serpent whispered. "You know that I do not like to be disturbed."

"The queen is displeased," half of the kneeling eunuchs murmured.

"Ah," the other half responded with a certain spiteful satisfaction.

Salmissra swung her swaying head slightly to fix her eyes on Issus. "I seem to know you," she said.

The one-eyed man bowed. "Issus, your Majesty," he replied. "The assassin."

"I do not wish to be disturbed just now," the Serpent Queen told him in her emotionless whisper. "If that means that you're going to kill Sariss, please take him out into the corridor to do it."

"We will not disturb you for long, Salmissra," Polgara said, pushing back the hood of her cloak.

The snake's head turned slowly, her forked tongue tasting the air. "Ah, Polgara," she hissed without any evident surprise. "It has been some time since your last visit."

"Several years," Polgara agreed.

"I no longer take note of the years." Salmissra's dead gaze turned to Garion. "And Belgarion," she said. "I see that you're not a boy any more."

"No," he replied, fighting down an involuntary shudder.

"Come closer," she whispered. "Once you thought that I was beautiful and yearned for my kiss. Would you like to kiss me now?"

Garion felt a strange compulsion to obey and found that he could not take his eyes from those of the Serpent Queen. Not even aware that he did it, he took a hesitant step toward the dais.

"The fortunate one approaches the throne," the eunuchs murmured.

"Garion!" Polgara said sharply.

"I will not hurt him, Polgara. I never intended to hurt him."

"I have a few questions for you, Salmissra," Polgara said coldly. "Once you answer them, we'll leave you to your entertainments."

"What manner of questions, Polgara? What could I possibly know that your sorcery could not ferret out?"

"You recently met a Mallorean named Naradas," Polgara said. "A man with colorless eyes."

"Is that his name? Sariss never told me."

"You made an arrangement with him."

"Did I?"

"At his request, you sent diplomats to Sendaria. Among them was a foreigner named Zandramas. Your diplomats were instructed to give the foreigner every possible assistance in getting to Halberg on the west coast of Cherek. You also ordered a ship to the Isle of the Winds to bring Zandramas back to Nyissa."

"I gave no such orders, Polgara. I have no interest in the affairs of Zandramas."

"The name is familiar to you?"

"Of course. I told you once that the priests of Angarak and the sorcerers of Aloria are not the only ones who can find a truth that lies hidden. I know of your desperate pursuit of the one who took Belgarion's son from the Citadel at Riva."

"But you say that you were in no way involved in the arrangements?"

"The one you call Naradas came to me with gifts," Salmissra whispered, "but said nothing more than that he wished my permission to trade here in Nyissa."

"Then how do you explain this?" Aunt Pol took the parchment sheet Sadi had given her from under her cloak.

Salmissra flicked her tongue at one of the kneeling eunuchs. "Bring it to me," she ordered.

The eunuch leaped to his feet, took the parchment from Aunt Pol, and then knelt on the edge of the dais, holding the sheet open and extended toward his queen.

"This is not the order I gave," Salmissra said flatly after the briefest of glances. "I ordered the diplomats to Sendaria—nothing more. Your copy is not accurate, Polgara."

"Would the original be about anywhere?" Garion asked her.

"Sariss should have it."

Garion looked at the fat eunuch groveling on the floor. "Where is it?" he demanded.

Sariss stared at him, then his gaze went in terror to the enthroned serpent.

Garion considered several alternatives but discarded most of them in favor of simplicity. "Make him talk, Issus," he said shortly.

The one-eyed man stepped over, straddled the trembling eunuch, and grasped his chin firmly from behind. Then he pulled up sharply until Sariss was arched backward. The saw-edged dagger made a steely grating sound as it came out of its sheath.

"Wait!" Sariss begged in a choked voice. "It—it's in the drawer at the bottom of my wardrobe in my room."

"Your methods are direct, assassin," the queen observed.

"I'm a simple man, your Majesty," Issus replied. "I do not have the temperament for subtlety nor intricacy. I've found that directness saves time in the long run." He released the terrified Sariss and pushed his Ulgo dagger back into his sheath. He looked at Garion. "Do you want me to go get the parchment?" he asked.

"I think we're going to need it."

"All right." Issus turned and left the room.

"An interesting man," Salmissra noted. She bent and caressingly touched her mottled coils with her blunt nose. "My life is much changed since you were last here, Polgara," she whispered in her dusty voice. "I am no longer driven by those hungers I had before, but pass my days instead in restless doze. I lull myself into slumber with the sweet sound of my own scales caressing each other. As I sleep, I dream. I dream of mossy caves in deep, cool forests, and I dream of the days when I was still a woman. But sometimes in my dreams, I am a bodiless spirit, seeking out the truths that others would hide. I know of the fear which lies in your heart, Polgara, and the desperate need that drives Zandramas. I even know of the terrible task which lies upon Cyradis."

"But you still say that you are not involved in this matter?"

"I have no interest in it. You and Zandramas can pursue each other across all the kingdoms of the world, but I am incurious as to the outcome."

Aunt Pol's eyes narrowed as she looked at her.

"I have no reason to lie to you, Polgara," Salmissra said, sensing the suspicion in that look. "What could Zandramas possibly offer me that would buy my aid? All of my needs are satisfied, and I no longer have desires." Her blunt head came up and her tongue flickered. "I rejoice, however, that your quest has brought you again into my presence so that I may gaze once more upon the perfection of your face."

Polgara's chin lifted. "Look quickly then, Salmissra. I have little patience for the involuted amusements of a snake."

"The centuries have made you waspish, Polgara. Let us be civil to one another. Would you like to have me tell you what I know of Zandramas? She is no longer what she once was."

"*She!*" Garion exclaimed.

"You did not even know that?" the serpent hissed maliciously. "Your sorcery is a sham, then, Polgara. Could you not sense your enemy is a woman? And did you perhaps not even realize that you have already met her?"

"What are you talking about, Salmissra?"

"Poor, dear Polgara. The long, long centuries have filled your wits with cobwebs. Did you really think that you and Belgarath are the only ones in the world who can change their shapes? The dragon who visited you in the mountains above

Arendia appears quite different when she resumes her natural form."

The door to the throne room opened and Issus came back in, holding a parchment sheet with a red wax seal on the bottom of it.

"Bring it to me," Salmissra commanded.

Issus looked at her, his single eye narrowing as he gauged the distance between the serpent's throne and his own unprotected skin. Then he went over to the prostrate eunuch who had presented Polgara's document to the queen. Without changing expression, he kicked the man solidly in the ribs. "Here," he said, thrusting out the parchment. "Take this to her Majesty."

"Are you afraid of me, Issus?" Salmissra asked, sounding faintly amused.

"I am unworthy to approach you too closely, my Queen."

Salmissra bent her head to examine the parchment the trembling eunuch held out for her to read. "There appears to be some discrepancy," she hissed. "This document is the same as the one you showed me, Polgara, but it is *not* the document to which I ordered my seal affixed. How is this possible?"

"May I speak, my Queen?" the eunuch who held the parchment asked in a quavering voice.

"Of course, Adiss," she replied almost pleasantly, "so long as you realize that if your words displease me, the kiss I will give you in payment will bring you death." Her forked tongue flickered out toward him.

The eunuch's face went a ghastly gray color, and his trembling became so violent that he very nearly collapsed.

"Speak, Adiss," she whispered. "It is my command that you disclose your mind to me. We will determine then whether you live or die. Speak. Now."

"My Queen," he quavered, "the Chief Eunuch is the only person in the palace permitted to touch your Majesty's royal seal. If the document in question is false, must we not look to him for an explanation?"

The serpent considered that, her head swaying rhythmically back and forth and her forked tongue flickering. At last she stopped her reptilian dance and leaned slowly forward until her tongue brushed the cringing eunuch's cheek. "Live, Adiss," she murmured. "Your words have not displeased me, and so my kiss grants the gift of life." Then she reared her mottled form again and regarded Sariss with her dead eyes. "Do you have an explanation, Sariss? As our most excellent servant Adiss has pointed out, you are my Chief Eunuch. You affixed my seal. How did this discrepancy come to pass?"

"My Queen—" His mouth gaped open, and his dead-white face froze in an expression of stark terror.

The still-shaken Adiss half rose, his eyes filled with a sudden wild hope. He held up the parchment in his hand and turned to his crimson-robed companions kneeling to one side of the dais. "Behold," he cried in a triumphant voice. "Behold the proof of the Chief Eunuch's misconduct!"

The other eunuchs looked first at Adiss and then at the groveling and terrified Chief Eunuch. Their eyes also furtively tried to read the enigmatic expression on Salmissra's face. "Ah," they said in unison at last.

"I'm still waiting, Sariss," the Serpent Queen whispered.

Sariss, however, quite suddenly scrambled to his feet and bolted toward the throne room door, squealing in mindless, animal panic. As fast as his sudden flight was, though, Issus was even faster. The shabby, one-eyed assassin bounded after the fleeing fat man, his horrid dagger leaping into his hand. With the other he caught the back of the Chief Eunuch's crimson robe and jerked him up short. He raised his knife and looked inquiringly at Salmissra.

"Not yet, Issus," she decided. "Bring him to me."

Issus grunted and dragged his struggling captive toward the throne. Sariss, squealing and gibbering in terror, scrambled his feet ineffectually on the polished floor.

"I will have an answer from you, Sariss," Salmissra whispered.

"Talk," Issus said in a flat voice, setting his dagger point against the eunuch's lower eyelid. He pushed slightly, and a sudden trickle of bright-red blood ran down the fat man's cheek.

Sariss squealed and began to blubber. "Forgive me, your Majesty," he begged. "The Mallorean Nadaras compelled it of me."

"How did you do it, Sariss?" the serpent demanded implacably.

"I-I put your seal at the very bottom of the page, Divine Salmissra," he blurted. "Then when I was alone, I added the other orders."

"And were there other orders as well?" Aunt Pol asked him. "Will we encounter hindrances and traps on the trail of Zandramas?"

"No. Nothing. I gave no orders other than that Zandramas be escorted to the Murgo border and provided the maps she required. I pray you, your Majesty. Forgive me."

"That is quite impossible, Sariss," she hissed. "It had been my intention to hold myself aloof in the dispute between Polgara and Zandramas, but now I am involved because you have abused my trust in you."

"Shall I kill him?" Issus asked calmly.

"No, Issus," she replied. "Sariss and I will share a kiss, as is the custom in this place." She looked oddly at him. "You are an interesting man, assassin," she said. "Would you like to enter my service? I am certain that a position can be found for one of your talents."

Adiss the eunuch gasped, his face suddenly going pale. "But your Majesty," he protested, leaping to his feet, "your servants have always been eunuchs, and this man is—" He faltered, suddenly realizing the temerity of his rash outburst.

Salmissra's dead eyes locked on his, and he sank white-faced to the floor again. "You disappoint me, Adiss," she said in that dusty whisper. She turned back to the one-eyed assassin. "Well, Issus?" she said. "A man of your talents could rise to great eminence, and the procedure, I'm told, is a minor one. You would soon recover and enter the service of your queen."

"Ah—I'm honored, your Majesty," he replied carefully, "but I'd really prefer to remain more or less intact. There's a certain edge my profession requires, and I'd rather not endanger that by tampering with things."

"I see." She swung her head briefly to look at the cowering Adiss and then back to the assassin. "You have made an enemy today, however, I think—and one that may some day grow quite powerful."

Issus shrugged. "I've had many enemies," he replied. "A few of them are even still alive." He gave the cowering eunuch a flinty look. "If Adiss wants to pursue the matter, he and I can discuss it privately some day—or perhaps late some night when our discussions won't disturb anyone."

"We must leave now," Polgara said. "You have been most helpful, Salmissra. Thank you."

"I am indifferent to your gratitude," Salmissra replied. "I do not think that I will see you again, Polgara. I think that Zandramas is more powerful than you and that she will destroy you."

"Only time can reveal that."

"Indeed. Farewell, Polgara."

"Good-bye, Salmissra." Polgara deliberately turned her back on the dais. "Come along, Garion—Issus," she said.

"Sariss," Salmissra said in a peculiar, almost singing tone, "come to me." Garion glanced back over his shoulder and saw that she had reared her mottled body until it rose high above the dais and her velvet-covered throne. She swayed rhythmically back and forth. Her dead eyes had come alight with a kind of dreadful hunger and they burned irresistably beneath her scaly brows.

Sariss, his mouth agape and with his piglike eyes frozen and devoid of all thought, lurched toward the dais with jerky, stiff-legged steps.

"Come, Sariss," Salmissra crooned. "I long to embrace you and give you my kiss."

Aunt Pol, Garion, and Issus reached the ornately carved door and went quietly into the corridor outside. They had gone no more than a few yards when there came from the throne room a sudden shrill scream of horror, dying hideously into a gurgling, strangled squeal.

"I think that the position of Chief Eunuch just became vacant," Issus observed drily. Then, as they continued on down the dimly lighted hallway he turned to Polgara. "Now, my Lady," he said, ticking the items off on his fingers, "first of all there was the fee for getting you and the young man into the palace. Then there was the business of persuading Sariss to take us to the throne room, and then . . . "

Part Two

RAK URGA

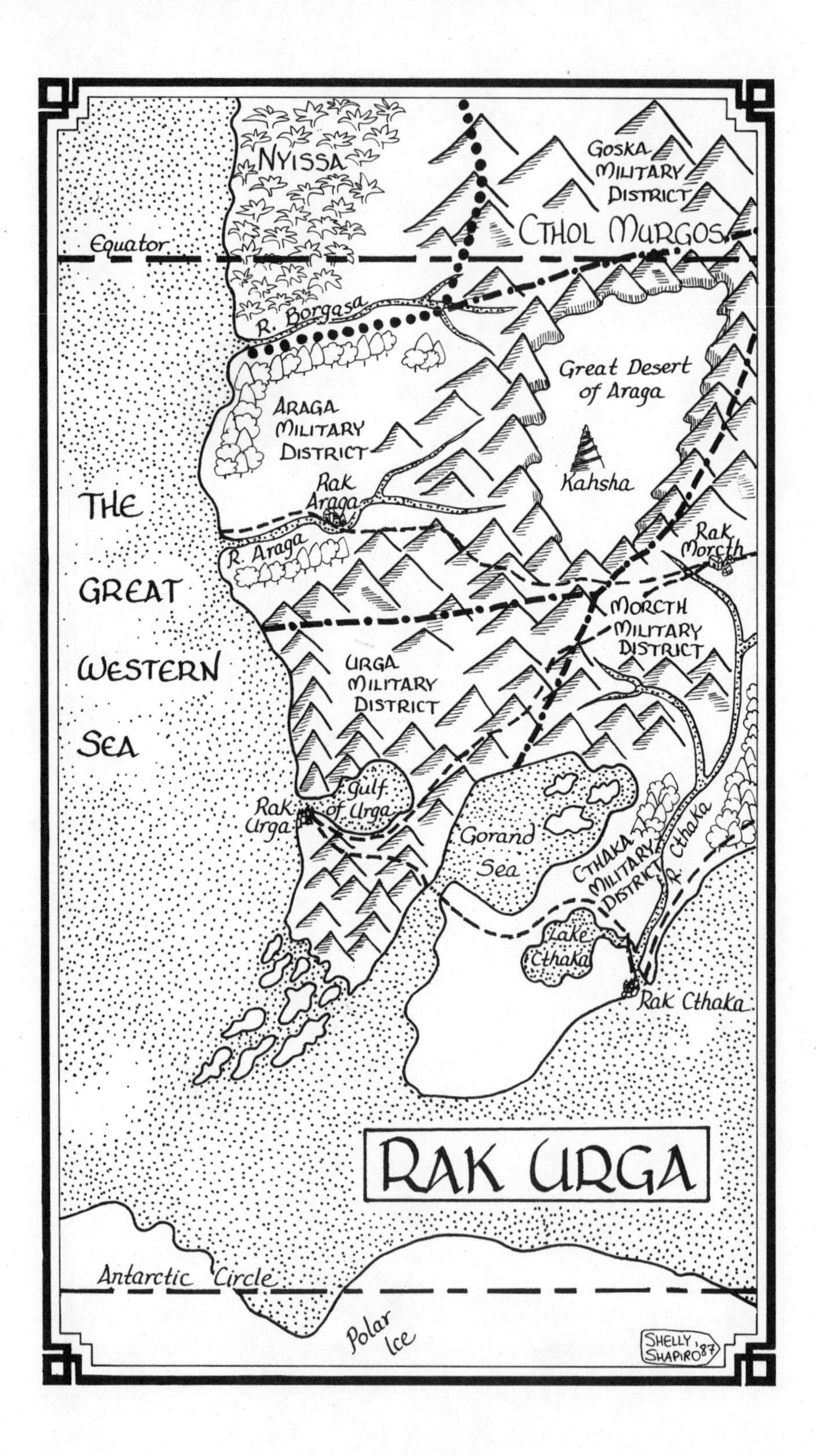

NYISSA
GOSKA MILITARY DISTRICT
CTHOL MURGOS
Equator
R. Borgasa
Great Desert of Araga
ARAGA MILITARY DISTRICT
Kahsha
Rak Araga
THE GREAT WESTERN SEA
R. Araga
Rak Morcth
MORCTH MILITARY DISTRICT
URGA MILITARY DISTRICT
Gulf of Urga
Rak Urga
Gorand Sea
CTHAKA MILITARY DISTRICT
R. Cthaka
Lake Cthaka
Rak Cthaka
RAK URGA
Antarctic Circle
Polar Ice
SHELLY SHAPIRO '87

CHAPTER NINE

It was almost dawn when they crept quietly out of Droblek's house. A thick gray fog shrouded the narrow, twisting streets of Sthiss Tor as they followed Issus through the shabby quarter near the docks. The smell of the river and the reek of the surrounding swamps lay heavy in the foggy darkness, filling Garion's nostrils with the odors of decay and stagnant water.

They emerged from a narrow alleyway, and Issus motioned them to a halt as he peered into the mist. Then he nodded. "Let's go," he whispered. "Try not to make any noise." They hurried across a glistening cobblestone street, ill-lit by torches, each surrounded by a nimbus of hazy red light, and entered the deeper shadows of another garbage-strewn alley. At the far end of that alley, Garion could see the slow-moving surface of the river sliding ponderously by, pale in the fog.

The one-eyed assassin led them along another cobblestone street to the foot of a rickety wharf jutting out into the fog. He stopped in the shadows beside a dilapidated shack that stood partially out over the water and fumbled briefly at the door. He opened it slowly, muffling the protesting creak of a rusty hinge with a tattered piece of rag. "In here," he muttered, and they followed him into the dank-smelling shack. "There's a boat tied at the end of this wharf," he told them in a half whisper. "Wait here while I go get it." He went to the front of the shack, and Garion heard the creak of hinges as a trapdoor opened.

They waited, listening nervously to the skittering and squeaking of the rats that infested this part of town. The moments seemed to creep by as Garion stood watch beside the door, peering out through a crack between two rotting boards at the foggy street running along the edge of the river.

"All right," he heard Issus say from below after what seemed like hours. "Be careful on the ladder. The rungs are slippery."

One by one, they climbed down the ladder into the boat the one-eyed man had pulled into place under the wharf. "We have to be quiet," he cautioned them after they had seated themselves. "There's another boat out there on the river somewhere."

"A boat?" Sadi asked in alarm. "What are they doing?"

Issus shrugged. "Probably something illegal." Then he pushed his craft out into the shadows at the side of the wharf, settled himself on the center seat, and began to row, dipping his oars carefully into the oily surface of the river so that they made almost no sound.

The fog rose from the dark water in little tendrils, and the few lighted windows high in the towers of Sthiss Tor had a hazy unreality, like tiny golden candles seen in a dream. Issus rowed steadily, his oars making only the faintest of sounds.

Then from somewhere not far upsteam, there was a sudden

muffled outcry, followed by a splash and the gurgling sound of bubbles rising to the surface.

"What was that?" Sadi hissed nervously as Issus stopped rowing to listen.

"Be still," the one-eyed man whispered.

From somewhere in the fog, there came the thumping sound of someone moving around in a boat, followed by the splash of an awkwardly pulled oar. A man swore, his voice harsh and loud.

"Keep quiet," another voice said.

"What for?"

"Let's not tell everybody in Sthiss Tor that we're out here."

"You worry too much. That rock I tied to his ankles will keep him down for a long time." The creaking oarlocks faded off into the fog.

"Amateurs," Issus muttered derisively.

"An assassination, perhaps?" Silk asked with a certain professional curiosity. "Or a private killing?"

"What difference does it make?" Issus started to row again, his oars dipping slowly into the water. Behind them Sthiss Tor had disappeared in the fog. Without the reference point of its dim lights, it seemed to Garion that they were not moving at all, but sat motionless on the surface of the dark river. Then, at last, a shadowy shore appeared ahead in the clinging fog; after a few more minutes, he was able to make out the hazy shape of individual tree tops outlined by the pale mist.

A low whistle came to them from the bank, and Issus angled their boat slightly, making for that signal. "Garion, is that you?" Durnik's whispered voice came out of the shadows.

"Yes."

Issus pulled their boat under the overhanging branches, and Durnik caught the bow. "The others are waiting on the far side of the road," he said quietly as he helped Polgara from the boat.

"You've been most helpful, Issus," Sadi said to his hireling.

The one-eyed man shrugged. "Isn't that what you paid me for?"

Silk looked at him. "If you decide to consider my offer, talk to Droblek."

"I'll think about it," Issus replied. He paused, then looked at Polgara. "Good luck on your journey, Lady," he said quietly. "I get the feeling that you're going to need it."

"Thank you, Issus."

Then he pushed his boat back out into the fog and disappeared.

"What was that all about?" Sadi asked Silk.

"Oh, nothing much. Drasnian Intelligence is always looking for a few good men, is all."

Durnik was looking curiously at the shaven-headed eunuch.

"We'll explain when we get back to the others, dear," Polgara assured him.

"Yes, Pol," he agreed. "We go this way." He led them up the brushy bank to the broken stones of the road and then pushed his way into the tangled undergrowth on the far side, with the rest of them close behind him.

Ce'Nedra, Eriond, Toth, and Velvet sat in a little hollow behind the moss-covered trunk of a fallen tree. A single, well-shielded lantern gave forth a dim glow, illuminating the hollow with faint light. "Garion," Ce'Nedra exclaimed with relief, coming quickly to her feet. "What took you so long?"

"We had to make a side trip," he replied, taking her into his arms. As he nestled his face into her hair, he found that it still had that warm, sweet fragrance that had always touched his heart.

"All right," Belgarath said, looking out into the tag end of the foggy night, "I want to get moving, so I'll keep this short." He sat down on the spongy moss beside the lantern. "This is Sadi." He pointed at the shaven-headed eunuch. "Most of you know him already. He'll be going with us."

"Is that altogether wise, Belgarath?" Durnik asked dubiously.

"Probably not," the old man replied, "but it wasn't my idea. He seems to feel that Zandramas has gone down into southern Cthol Murgos and plans to cross the continent to the Isle of Verkat off the southeast coast."

"That's a very dangerous part of the world just now, Ancient One," Velvet murmured.

"We'll have no trouble, dear lady," Sadi assured her in his contralto voice. "If we pose as slavers, no one will interfere with us."

"So you say," Belgarath said somewhat sceptically. "That might have been true before the war started down there, but we still don't know for sure how the Malloreans view the slave trade."

"There's one other thing you should all know," Polgara added quietly. "Garion and I went to the palace to find out if Salmissra was involved in this in any way. She told us that Zandramas is a woman."

"A woman?" Ce'Nedra exclaimed.

"That's what she said, and she had no reason to lie to us."

Durnik scratched at his head. "That's a bit of a surprise, isn't it? Are you sure Salmissra knew what she was talking about?"

She nodded. "She was very certain—and quite smug about the fact that she knew something that I didn't."

"It *does* sort of fit," Velvet said thoughtfully. "Most of the things Zandramas has done were done the way a woman would do them."

"I can't quite follow that," Durnik admitted.

"A man does things one way, Goodman. A woman does them differently. The fact that Zandramas is a woman explains a great deal."

"She's also going to great lengths to conceal the fact," Silk added. "She's made sure that just about everybody who's seen her isn't alive to tell anybody about it."

"We can talk about all this some more later," Belgarath said, standing up and looking around at the gradually lightening fog. "I want to get away from this place before the people on the other side of the river start moving around. Let's saddle the horses."

It took a bit of readjustment of their equipment to free one of the pack horses for Sadi's use, but a short time later they rode out from their sheltered place of concealment and on along the weedy track that followed the winding course of the River of the Serpent. They moved at first at a cautious walk, but once they had passed the outskirts of Sthiss Tor, lying hidden in the fog across the river, they picked up their pace to a canter, clattering along the abandoned road that stretched through the rank jungle and reeking swamps of the land of the snake-people.

As the sun rose, it gave the fog surrounding them a kind of mystical glow, and the droplets hanging along the edges of individual leaves drooping from the undergrowth at the side of the road took on a jewellike sparkle. Garion, sandy-eyed and tired from a night without sleep, looked bemused at the jeweled green leaves, marveling that such beauty could exist in this stinking swamp.

"The whole world is beautiful, Belgarion," Eriond assured him in response to that unspoken thought. "You just have to know how to look at it."

Once the fog had burned off, they were able to move at a much more rapid pace. They encountered no other travelers that day. By the time the sun began to sink into the heavy banks of purple cloud that seemed to hover perpetually over the western horizon, they were well upriver.

"How far is it to the Murgo border?" Garion asked Sadi as the two of them gathered firewood while Durnik and Toth set up the tents for their night's encampment.

"Several more days," the eunuch replied. "The highway fords the river up near the headwaters and then angles down toward Araga. There's a village on the other side of the ford. I'll need to stop there for a few things—suitable garments and the like."

Velvet and Ce'Nedra were unpacking Polgara's cooking utensils not far away, and the blond Drasnian girl looked over at Sadi. "Excuse me," she said, "but I think I've discovered a flaw in your plan."

"Oh?"

"How can we pose as slavers when some of us are obviously women?"

"But there are always women in any party of slave traders, my dear lady," he answered, dropping an armload of firewood beside the stone-lined cooking pit. "I'm sure that if you think about it, you'll understand why."

"I certainly don't," Ce'Nedra declared.

Sadi coughed rather delicately. "We trade in female slaves as well as males, your Majesty," he explained, "and a female who's been guarded by women brings a higher price."

A slow flush crept up her face. "That's revolting."

Sadi shrugged. "I didn't make the world, your Majesty," he replied. "I only try to live in it."

After they had eaten, Sadi took an earthenware bowl, filled it with hot water and began to lather his stubbled scalp.

"There's something I've been meaning to ask you, Sadi," Silk said from the other side of the fire. "Exactly what was it that you did to make Salmissra so discontented with you?"

Sadi gave him a wry look. "Those of us in the queen's service are an extraordinarily corrupt lot, Kheldar," he replied. "We're all knaves and scoundrels and worse. A number of years ago Salmissra laid down certain guidelines to keep our plotting and deceit within reasonable limits—just to keep the government from falling apart. I overstepped a few of those limits—most of them, actually. Sariss found out about it and ran to the Queen to tattle." He sighed. "I do so wish that I'd been able to see his reaction when she kissed him." He picked up his razor.

"Why do all Nyissan men shave their heads?" Ce'Nedra asked him curiously.

"There are all manner of nasty little insects in Nyissa, your Majesty, and hair provides them with a perfect nesting place."

She gave him a startled look, her hand going unconsciously to her coppery curls.

"I shouldn't worry too much," he smiled. "*Most* of the time, they're dormant in winter."

About noon several days later, the road they were following began to climb up out of the jungles into the foothills. The damp chill that had lain over the normally steaming swamps of Nyissa moderated as they climbed, and it was pleasantly warm as they moved up into the hardwood forest lying along the eastern frontier. The river began to tumble over stones beside the road, and its murky waters grew clear as they rode deeper into the hills.

"The ford is just up ahead," Sadi told them as he led them around a broad curve in the road. A stone bridge had once crossed the river there, but time and the turbulent water had eaten away its foundations and tumbled it into the riverbed. The green water rushed over the fallen stones, swift and foaming. Upstream from the fallen bridge, there was a wide stretch of gravel-bottomed shallows that rippled, sparkling in the sun. A well-traveled trail led down to the ford.

"What about the leeches?" Silk asked, eyeing the water with suspicion.

"The water's a little too fast for them, Prince Kheldar," Sadi replied. "Their bodies are too soft to take much bouncing around on rocks." He rode confidently down into the rippling stream and led them on across.

"That village I mentioned is just up ahead," he told them as they emerged from the stream. "It should only take me an hour or so to pick up what we'll need."

"The rest of us can wait here, then," Belgarath said, swinging down from his saddle. "You go with him, Silk."

"I can manage," Sadi protested.

"I'm sure you can. Let's just call it a precaution."

"How am I going to explain to the shopkeeper what a Drasnian is doing with me?"

"Lie to him. I'm sure you'll be very convincing."

Garion dismounted and walked up the slope of the river bank. These were the people he loved most in the world, but sometimes their idle banter set his teeth on edge. Even though he knew that they really meant nothing by it, it seemed somehow to reflect an indifferent frivolity, a callous lack of concern for his personal tragedy—and more importantly, for Ce'Nedra's. He stood atop the river bank, looking with unseeing eyes down the descending gorge of the River of the Serpent and out over the dense green canopy of the jungles of the snake-people. He would be glad to get out of Nyissa. It was not so much the clinging mud, the stink of the swamps, nor even the clouds of insects that hovered perpetually in the air. The real problem with Nyissa was the fact that one could seldom see for more than a few feet in any direction. For some reason, Garion felt an overpowering need to see for long distances, and the obscuring trees and undergrowth that had blocked his vision since they had been in Nyissa had increasingly irritated him. A number of times he had caught himself just on the verge of clenching his will and blasting out long, clear avenues through the jungle.

When Silk and Sadi returned, the little Drasnian's face was angry.

"They're only for show, Prince Kheldar," Sadi protested mildly. "We're not actually going to have any slaves with us anyway, so there won't really be anyone to wear them, will there?"

"It's the idea of them that offends me."

"What's this?" Belgarath asked.

Sadi shrugged. "I purchased a few shackles and slave bells. Kheldar doesn't approve."

"I didn't like the whips either," Silk added.

"I explained that to you, Kheldar."

"I know. It's still disgusting."

"Of course it is. Nyissans are a disgusting people. I thought you knew that."

"We can sort out comparative moralities later on," Belgarath said. "Let's move along."

The road they followed rose steeply up from the river, taking them deeper and deeper into the foothills. The hardwoods gave way to gnarled evergreens and low-lying heather. Great, rounded white boulders lay in scattered profusion among the dark green trees, and the sky overhead was an intense blue.

They camped that night in a grove of low, twisted junipers, building their fire against a boulder so that its white surface could reflect back both light and heat. Above them rose a steep ridge that stood jaggedly outlined against the starry eastern sky.

"Once we cross that ridge, we'll be in Cthol Murgos," Sadi told them as they sat around the fire after supper. "The Murgos watch their borders very carefully, so it's probably time to start wearing our disguises." He opened the large bundle he had brought from the village near the ford and took out a number of dark green silk robes. He looked speculatively at Ce'Nedra and the gigantic Toth. "There may be a slight problem here," he murmured. "The shopkeeper didn't have a wide variety of sizes."

"I'll fix it, Sadi," Polgara said, taking the rolled-up robes from him and opening one of the packs in search of her sewing kit.

Belgarath had been staring thoughtfully at a large map. "There's something that's been bothering me," he said. He turned to Sadi. "Is there any way Zandramas might have taken a ship from one of these ports on the west coast and sailed around the southern end of the continent to Verkat?"

Sadi shook his head, his shaven scalp gleaming in the orange firelight. "Impossible, Ancient One. A Mallorean fleet slipped up behind the Murgos a few years back, and King Urgit still has nightmares about it. He's closed all the west coast ports and has ships patrolling the sea lanes all the way around the tip of the Urga peninsula. No one sails along that coast without his specific permission."

"How far is it to Verkat?" Durnik asked.

Sadi squinted up at the stars. "Three or four months at this time of the year, Goodman."

Polgara had been humming quietly to herself as her needle flashed in the firelight. "Come here, Ce'Nedra," she said.

The little queen rose and went over to where she sat. Polgara held up the green silk robe, measuring it against her tiny frame, then nodded in satisfaction.

Ce'Nedra wrinkled her nose. "Do they have to smell so bad?" she asked Sadi.

"I don't suppose they have to, but they always do, for some reason. Slaves have a certain odor about them, and it seems to rub off."

Aunt Pol was looking at Toth as she held another of the slaver's robes in her hands. "This could be a bit more challenging," she murmured.

The giant gave her a brief, almost shy smile and rose to put more wood on the fire. As he poked the coals with a stick, a column of winking red sparks rose to greet the stars hanging low in the night sky. From somewhere down the ridge, as if in response to those sparks, there came a deep, coughing roar.

"What's that?" Ce'Nedra cried.

"Lion." Sadi shrugged. "Sometimes they hunt along the slave route—the old and crippled ones at any rate."

"Why would they do that?"

"Sometimes slaves get too sick to walk any farther and they have to be left behind. An old lion can't chase anything that's very nimble, and . . ." He left it hanging in the air.

She stared at him in horror.

"You did ask, after all, your Majesty," he reminded her. "As a matter of fact, I don't like the idea very much myself. That's one of the reasons I left the slave trade to go into politics." He stood up and brushed off the back of his robe. "Now, if you dear people will excuse me, I have to go feed Zith. Please be careful when you go to your beds tonight. Sometimes she sneaks away after she's been fed. I think it amuses her to hide from me, and one never knows where she might turn up." He walked out of the circle of golden firelight toward the place where he had spread his blankets.

Silk stared after him, then turned back to the fire. "I don't know about the rest of you," he declared, "but I'm sleeping right here tonight."

The next morning after breakfast, they donned the evil-smelling robes of Nyissan slavers. At Belgarath's instruction, Garion once again covered the hilt of Iron-grip's sword. "I think we'd better keep the Orb well wrapped as long as we're in Cthol Murgos," the old man said. "It tends to get excited when there are Angaraks about."

They mounted their horses and followed the ancient highway up a ravine toward the jagged ridge top. As they rounded a bend, Polgara suddenly reined in her horse with a sharp hiss.

"What's the matter, Pol?" Durnik asked her.

She did not reply immediately, but her face grew pale. Her eyes flashed, and the white lock at her brow suddenly flamed. "Monstrous!" she said.

"What is it, Aunt Pol?" Garion asked.

"Look over there," she answered, pointing with a trembling hand. There were white bones scattered about on the rocky ground several yards from the road; lying among them was a vacant-eyed human skull.

"One of the slaves Sadi mentioned last night?" Silk suggested.

Polgara shook her head. "A part of the arrangement between Sariss and Naradas involved several men to escort Zandramas to the Murgo border," she reminded him. "When she got this far, she didn't need them any more."

Silk's face grew grim. "That seems to be in character. Every time she finishes with somebody, she kills him."

"She didn't just kill them," Polgara said with a look of revulsion. "She broke their legs and left them for the lions. They waited all day for nightfall, and then the lions came."

Ce'Nedra's face blanched. "How horrible!"

"Are you sure, Pol?" Durnik asked, his face slightly sick.

"Some things are so dreadful that they leave their traces in the very rocks."

Belgarath had been staring bleakly at the gnawed bones. "This isn't the first time she's done this. She's not satisfied with just killing people to cover her tracks. She has to commit atrocities."

"She's a monster," Ce'Nedra declared. "She feeds on horror."

"It's a bit more than that," Belgarath replied. "I think she's trying to leave messages for us." He jerked his head toward the scattered bones. "That wasn't really necessary. I think she's trying to scare us off."

"It won't work," Garion said very quietly. "All she's doing is adding to the final reckoning. When the time finally comes for her to pay it, I think she's going to find that all of this is more than she can afford."

At the top of the ridge, the ancient road they had been following ended abruptly, sharply marking the invisible line where Nyissa ended and Cthol Murgos began. From the ridge top they looked out over an endless, unbroken expanse of shattered black rock and miles-wide beds of dark brown gravel, shimmering under a broiling sun.

"Which way did Zandramas go from here?" Durnik asked Garion.

"She turned south," Garion replied, feeling the Orb pulling in a new direction.

"We could gain time if we cut straight across that out there, couldn't we?"

"Absolutely out of the question, Goodman Durnik," Sadi declared. "That's the Great Desert of Araga. It's as big as Algaria. The only water there is in the wells of the Dagashi, and you wouldn't want to get caught dipping into a Dagashi well."

"The Dagashi live out there?" Durnik asked, shading his eyes with one hand to look out at the fiery wasteland.

"They're the only ones who can," Sadi replied. "Perhaps that explains why they're so fearsome. We're going to have to follow this ridge line south for a hundred leagues or so to get around that waste. Then we'll strike out due southeast across Morcth and on down into the Great Southern Forest in Gorut."

Belgarath nodded. "Let's get started then."

They rode south, skirting the western edge of the Desert of Araga and staying well up in the hills, which sloped steeply down to the desert floor. As they rode, Garion noticed that the trees on this side of the ridge were stunted and sparsely distributed. There was no grass growing in the rock-strewn ground, and the heather had given way to scrubby thorn bushes. The sharp ridge line appeared to be an abrupt demarcation between two entirely different climates. What had been only pleasantly warm on the west side became oppressively hot here on the east. There were almost no streams, and the few springs they found were tiny and seeped their water grudgingly into tepid little puddles hidden among the rust-colored boulders.

On the morning of the third day after they had entered Cthol Murgos, Toth belted his blanket across one shoulder, took up his staff, and walked down to the mouth of the ravine where they had spent the night, to look out over the rocky desert lying below. The sun had not yet risen, and the light from the dawn sky was steely and shadowless, etching each rock and crag of the sun-blasted wasteland in sharp detail. After a moment, the giant returned and touched Durnik's shoulder.

"What is it, Toth?" the smith asked.

The mute pointed to the mouth of the ravine.

"All right," Durnik said, rising from the spot where he had been kindling their morning fire. The two of them went on down the ravine in the pale light and stood looking out. After a few moments, Durnik called back over his shoulder. "Belgarath, I think you'd better come here and look at this."

The old sorcerer finished pulling on his scuffed and mismatched boots and went down to join them, with his green silk robe flapping about his ankles. He stared out for a while, then muttered a curse. "We've got a problem," he announced without turning.

The problem became apparent as soon as the rest of them reached the entrance to the ravine. Some distance out on the desert, a large cloud of dust was rising to hang motionless in the still morning air.

"How many men do you think it would take to raise that much dust?" Garion asked quietly.

"At least several hundred," Silk told him.

"Murgos?"

"Not unless the Murgos have changed their habits," Velvet murmured. "Those men are dressed in red."

Silk peered intently out at the dust cloud. "You've got good eyes," he said finally to the blond girl.

"One of the advantages of youth," she replied sweetly.

He gave her a quick, irritable look.

"I thought this was Murgo territory," Durnik objected.

"It is," Sadi said, "but the Malloreans send patrols out every so often. Zakath's been trying to find a way to come at Urgit from behind for a number of years now."

"How did they find water out there?"

"I'm sure they brought it with them."

Toth turned toward the south side of the ravine and scrambled up the steep, rocky bank, sending long streams of dusty brown gravel slithering down behind him.

"Do you think we can outrun them?" Silk asked Belgarath.

"That probably wouldn't be a very good idea. I think we'd better stay here until they're out of the area."

Toth gave a low whistle from the top of the bank he had just climbed.

"Go see what he wants, Durnik," Belgarath said.

The smith nodded and started up the steep slope.

"Do you think they'll find us up here?" Ce'Nedra asked tensely.

"It's not too likely, your Majesty," Sadi replied. "I doubt that they're going to take the time to search every ravine and gully in these mountains."

Belgarath squinted out at the dust cloud. "They're moving toward the southwest," he noted. "If we sit tight for a day or so, they'll move on out of our vicinity."

"I hate to lose the time," Garion fretted.

"So do I, but I don't think we've got much choice."

Durnik came sliding back down the bank of the ravine. "There's another group of men up ahead," he reported tersely. "Murgos, I think."

Belgarath uttered a fairly rancid curse. "I really don't want to get caught in the middle of a skirmish," he said. "Go up there and keep an eye on things," he told Silk. "Let's not have any more surprises."

Silk started up the steep bank of the ravine. On an impulse, Garion followed him. When they reached the top, they took cover behind a scrubby thorn bush.

The fiery ball of the sun slid up out of the desert lying to the east, and the obscuring cloud of dust raised by the advancing Mallorean column turned it to an ominous red. The figures of the men below, both the mounted Malloreans and the concealed Murgos, were tiny in the distance, like toy figures on a miniature landscape.

"As closely as I can tell, they're about evenly matched," Silk noted, looking down at the two parties of troops.

Garion considered it. "The Murgos are going to have the advantage, though. They're on higher ground and they'll have the element of surprise."

Silk grinned. "You're turning into quite a tactician."

Garion let that pass.

"Sadi was right," Silk said. "The Malloreans brought water with them." He pointed at two dozen or so cumbersome-looking wagons loaded with large casks, trailing along at the rear of the column advancing across the desert.

The Malloreans reached the first of the shallow ravines stretching up into the foothills, then halted, while their scouts fanned out to search the rocky terrain. It was only a short time before alarmed shouts announced that at least some of the Murgos had been seen.

"That doesn't make any sense," Garion said. "They didn't even try to keep from being found."

"Murgos aren't notorious for intelligence," Silk replied. As the red-clad Malloreans massed up for a charge, the concealed Murgos rose from their hiding places and began to shower their foes with arrows, but after only a few volleys, they began to pull back.

"Why are they retreating?" Garion demanded in disgust.

"What's the point of setting up an ambush and then turning around and running away from it?"

"Nobody's *that* stupid," Silk muttered his agreement. "They're up to something else."

The retreating Murgos kept up a steady rain of arrows, littering the ravines stretching up into the hills with windrows of red-garbed dead as the Malloreans doggedly charged up into the foothills. Once again, the toylike quality of all those men so far below became apparent. At closer range, the carnage at the edge of that vast desert would have sickened Garion, but from up here he could watch with little more than curiosity.

And then, when the great majority of the charging Malloreans were far up the ravines and gullies, a force of axe-wielding Murgo cavalry came pounding around the tip of a long, rocky ridge that protruded out into the wasteland.

"That's what they were up to," Garion said. "They lured the Malloreans into a charge so that they could attack from the rear."

"I don't think so," Silk disagreed. "I think they're after the supply wagons."

The galloping Murgo cavalry swept across the intervening space and then thundered along the sides of the poorly guarded Mallorean supply column, their axes rising and falling as they chopped open the water casks. With each stroke, sparkling water gushed out to soak into the arid floor of the desert. The sun, obscured by the dust of the charge, glowed red through the choking clouds to dye the gushing streams of water. From their vantage point high above the battle, it looked almost to Garion that the fluid spurting from the ruptured barrels was not water, but blood.

With a great outcry of chagrin, the Mallorean charge faltered. Then the red-clad figures far below turned and desperately ran back toward the desert to protect their precious water supply. But it was too late. With brutal efficiency, the Murgo cavalry had already axed open every barrel and cask and were riding back the way they had come with triumphant jeers.

The Murgos, whose feigned retreat had drawn the Mallorean troops into their fatal charge, ran back down the ridges to resume their former positions. From their vantage points above the now-demoralized Malloreans, they sent great sheets of arrows arching up into the morning sky to rain down upon their enemies. In the midst of that deadly rain, the Malloreans desperately tried to salvage what little water was left in the bottoms of their shattered barrels, but their losses from the arrow storm soon grew unacceptable. The men in red tunics broke and ran out into the waiting desert, leaving their wagons behind.

"That's a brutal way to make war," Silk said.

"The battle's pretty much over then, isn't it?" Garion said as the black-robed Murgos moved down into the ravines to butcher the wounded.

"Oh, yes," Silk replied, sounding almost sick. "The fighting's all done. The dying isn't, though."

"Maybe the ones who are left can make it back across the desert."

"Not a chance."

"All right, then," a lean man in a black robe said, stepping out from behind a nearby rocky outcrop with a half-drawn bow in his hands. "Now that you've seen it all, why don't we go back down to your camp and join the others?"

CHAPTER TEN

Silk rose to his feet slowly, keeping both hands in plain sight. "You're very quiet on your feet, friend," he observed.

"I'm trained to be so," the man with the bow replied. "Move. Your friends are waiting."

Silk gave Garion a quick warning look.—*Let's go along until we can size up the situation*—his fingers cautioned.—*I'm sure this one isn't alone.*—

They turned and slid down the bank to the floor of the ravine, with the stranger following watchfully behind them, his bow at the ready. At the upper end of the gully where they had pitched their tents the previous night, a score of black-robed men armed with bows guarded the others. They all had the scarred cheeks and angular eyes of Murgos, but there were certain subtle differences. The Murgos Garion had seen before had always been heavy-shouldered, and their stance had been marked by a stiff arrogance. These men were leaner, and their bearing was at once wary and peculiarly relaxed.

"You see, noble Tajak," Sadi said obsequiously to the lean-faced man who seemed to be in charge, "it is exactly as I told you. I have only these two other servants."

"We know your numbers, slaver," the lean-faced man replied in a harshly accented voice. "We've been watching you since you entered Cthol Murgos."

"We made no effort to hide," Sadi protested mildly. "The only reason we remained concealed here was to avoid becoming involved in that unpleasantness down at the edge of the desert." He paused. "One is curious, however, to know why the noble Dagashi would choose to concern themselves with the activities of a party of Nyissan slavers. Surely we are not the first to come this way."

Tajak ignored that, looking carefully at Garion and his friends with his slate-hard black eyes. "What's your name, slaver?" he asked Sadi finally.

"I am Ussa of Sthiss Tor, good master, a duly registered slave trader. I have all the proper documents, if you'd care to examine them."

"How is it that none of your servants are Nyissan?"

Sadi spread his hands innocently. "The war here in the south makes most of my countrymen a bit reluctant to venture into Cthol Murgos just now," he explained, "so I was forced to hire foreign adventurers instead."

"Perhaps," the Dagashi said in a flat, unemotional voice. He gave Sadi a penetrating look. "Are you interested in money, Ussa of Sthiss Tor?" he asked suddenly.

Sadi's dead eyes brightened, and he rubbed his hands together eagerly. "Well, now," he said, "why don't we talk about that? Just exactly how may I serve you? And how much would you be willing to pay me?"

"You will need to discuss that with my master," Tajak replied. "My orders were to find a party of slavers and tell them that I could put them in touch with someone who could see that they were well-paid for a fairly minor service. Are you interested in such a proposition?"

Sadi hesitated, glancing surreptitiously at Belgarath for some kind of instruction.

"Well?" Tajak said impatiently. "Are you interested?"

"Of course," Sadi answered carefully. "Who is your master, Tajak? Just who is this benefactor who wants to make me rich?"

"He will tell you his name and what you must do for him when you meet him—at Kahsha."

"Kahsha?" Sadi exclaimed. "You didn't say that I'd have to go there."

"There are many things I didn't say. Well? Do you agree to go with us to Kahsha?"

"Do I have any choice?"

"No."

Sadi spread his arms helplessly.

*—What's Kahsha?—*Garion's fingers asked Silk.

—The headquarters of the Dagashi. It's got an unsavory reputation.—

"All right," Tajak said decisively, "let's break down these tents and get ready to leave. It's many hours to Kahsha, and midafternoon is not a good time to be out in the desert."

The sun was well up when they rode out of the mouth of the ravine with Tajak's Dagashi formed watchfully around them. Out in the wasteland, the defeated Malloreans had begun their hopeless trek.

"Will they not attempt to use your wells, noble Tajak?" Sadi asked.

"Probably—but they won't be able to find them. We cover our wells with piles of rock, and all piles of rock in the desert look the same."

There were Murgo troops at the base of the foothills, watching the dispirited retreat of the Malloreans. As Tajak approached them, he made a quick, imperious gesture to them, and they grudgingly stood aside.

As they rode through a narrow defile that opened out into the desert, Garion took the opportunity to pull his horse in beside Belgarath's. "Grandfather," he whispered urgently, "what should we do?"

"We wait and see what this is all about," the old man replied. "Let's not do anything to give away our disguise—not yet, anyway."

As they rode out into the furnace heat of the desert, Sadi looked back at the Murgo soldiers lining the tops of the last low line of hills. "Your countrymen are most accommodating," he said to Tajak. "I'm surprised, though, that they didn't stop us to ask one or two questions."

"They know who we are," Tajak said shortly, "and they know better than to interfere with us." He looked at the already-sweating eunuch. "It would be wise of you to keep your mouth closed now, Ussa. The sun draws the moisture out of a man's body very quickly in this desert, and an open mouth is the first thing it attacks. It's quite possible to talk yourself to death out here."

Sadi gave him a startled look and then clamped his lips tightly together.

The heat was unbelievable. The desert floor was for the most part a vast, flat bed of reddish-brown gravel, broken only by occasional heaps of dark boulders and widely scattered stretches of gleaming white sand. The world seemed to shimmer and undulate as heat waves rose from the blistering gravel. The sun was like a club beating down on Garion's head and neck; though he was sweating profusely, the moisture evaporated from his body so quickly that his clothing remained totally dry.

They rode into that furnace for an hour, and then Tajak signaled for a halt. With a quick gesture, he sent five of his men off across a low rock ridge lying to the northeast. A short while later they returned, carrying lukewarm water in bags made of whole goatskins.

"Water the horses first," Tajak said tersely. Then he strode to the base of the ridge, bent, and scooped up a handful of what appeared to be white sand. He came back. "Hold out your right hands," he said, then spilled perhaps a spoonful into each outstretched palm. "Eat it," he ordered.

Sadi cautiously licked at the white stuff in his palm and then immediately spat. "Issa!" he swore. "Salt!"

"Eat it all," Tajak told him. "If you don't, you'll die."

Sadi stared at him.

"The sun is baking the salt out of your body. Without salt in your blood, you die."

They all reluctantly ate the salt. When they had finished, the Dagashi allowed each of them to drink sparingly; then they remounted and rode on into the inferno.

Ce'Nedra began to droop in her saddle like a wilted flower. The heat seemed to crush her. Garion pulled his horse in beside hers. "Are you all right?" he asked through parched lips.

"No talking!" a Dagashi snapped.

The little queen lifted her face and gave Garion a wan smile and then rode on.

Time lost all meaning in that dreadful place, and even thought became impossible. Garion rode dumbly, his head bent beneath the hammerlike blows of the sun. Hours—or years—later, he raised his head, squinting against the brilliant light around him. He stared stupidly ahead, and only slowly did the realization come to him that what he was seeing was utterly impossible. There, looming in the air before them, floated a vast black island. It hovered above the shimmering, sun-blasted gravel, defying all reason. What manner of sorcery could perform such a feat? How could anyone have that much power?

But it was not sorcery. As they rode nearer, the undulating heat waves began to thin, dispelling the mirage and revealing the fact that what they approached was not an island in the air, but instead a single rock peak rising precipitously from the desert floor. Encircling it was a narrow trail, hacked out of the solid rock and spiraling upward around the mountain.

"Kahsha," Tajak said shortly. "Dismount and lead your horses."

The trail was very steep. After the second spiral around the mountain the shimmering gravel floor of the desert lay far below. Up and up they went, round and round the blisteringly hot peak. And then the trail went directly into the mountain through a large, square opening.

"More caves?" Silk whispered bitterly. "Why is it always caves?"

Garion, however, moved eagerly. He would gladly have entered a tomb to get away from the intolerable sun.

"Take the horses," Tajak instructed some of his men, "and see to them at once. The rest of you, come with me." He led them into a long corridor chopped out of the rock itself. Garion groped along blindly until his eyes became adjusted to the dimness. Though by no means cold, the air in the corridor was infinitely cooler than it had been outside. He breathed deeply, straightened, and looked around. The brutal amount of physical labor it had taken to hack this long corridor out of solid rock was clearly evident.

Sadi, noticing that as well, looked at the grim-faced man striding beside him. "I didn't know that Dagashi were such expert stonecutters," he observed.

"We aren't. The corridor was cut by slaves."

"I didn't know that the Dagashi kept slaves."

"We don't. Once our fortress was finished, we turned them loose."

"Out there?" Sadi's voice was aghast.

"Most of them preferred to jump off the mountain instead."

The corridor ended abruptly in a cavern quite nearly as vast as some Garion had seen in the land of the Ulgos. Here, however, narrow windows high in the wall admitted light. As he looked up, he saw that this was not a natural cave, but rather was a large hollow that had been roofed over with stone slabs supported by vaults and buttresses. On the floor of the cave stood a city of low stone houses, and rising in the center of that city stood a bleak, square fortress.

"The house of Jaharb," their guide said shortly. "He waits. We must hurry."

Silk drew in his breath with a sharp hiss.

"What's the matter?" Garion whispered.

"We're going to have to be very careful here," Silk murmured. "Jaharb is the chief elder of the Dagashi and he has a very nasty reputation."

The houses in the city of the Dagashi all had flat roofs and narrow windows. Garion noticed that there was none of the bustle in the streets which one might see in a western city. The black-robed, unsmiling Dagashi went about their business in silence, and each man he saw moving through that strange, half-lit town seemed to carry a kind of vacant space about him, a circle into which none of his fellow townsmen would intrude.

The fortress of Jaharb was solidly built of huge basalt blocks, and the guards at the heavy front door were formidably armed. Tajak spoke briefly to them, and the door swung open.

The room to which Tajak took them was large and was illuminated by costly oil lamps, swinging on chains from the ceiling. The only furnishings were heaps of yellow cushions scattered on the floor and a row of stout, iron-bound chests standing along the rear wall. Seated in the midst of one of the heaps of cushions was an ancient man with white hair and a dark face that was incredibly wrinkled. He wore a yellow robe and he was eating grapes as they entered, carefully selecting them one by one and then languidly raising them to his lips.

"The Nyissan slavers, Revered Elder," Tajak announced in tones of profoundest respect.

Jaharb set aside his bowl of grapes and leaned forward, resting his elbows on his knees and looking at them intently with his smoky, penetrating eyes. There was something infinitely chilling about that steady gaze. "How are you called?" he asked Sadi finally. His voice was as cold as his eyes, very quiet and with a kind of dusty dryness to it.

"I am Ussa, Revered One," Sadi replied with a sinuous bow.

"So? And what is your business in the lands of the Murgos?" The ancient man spoke slowly, drawing out his words almost as if he were singing them.

"The slave trade, Great Elder," Sadi answered quickly.

"Buying or selling?"

"A bit of each. The present turmoil offers certain opportunities."

"I'm sure it does. You are here for gain, then?"

"A reasonable profit is all, Revered Jaharb."

The Elder's expression did not change, but his eyes bored into the face of the suddenly sweating eunuch. "You seem uncomfortable, Ussa," the dusty voice crooned softly. "Why is that?"

"The heat, Revered Jaharb," Sadi said nervously. "Your desert is very hot."

"Perhaps." The smoky eyes continued their unrelenting gaze. "Is it your purpose to enter the lands controlled by the Malloreans?"

"Why, yes," Sadi replied, "as a matter of fact it is. I am told that many slaves took advantage of the chaos that accompanied the Mallorean invasions to hide themselves in the Forest of Gorut. They are free for the taking, and the fields and vineyards of Hagga and Cthan lie untended for lack of slaves to work them. There is profit in such a situation."

"You will have little time for pursuing runaway slaves, Ussa. You must be in Rak Hagga before two months have passed."

"But—"

Jaharb held up one hand. "You will proceed from this place to Rak Urga, where you are expected. A new servant will join you there. His name is Kabach, and you will find him in the Temple of Torak under the protection of Agachak, the Grolim Hierarch of that place. Agachak and King Urgit will place you and your servants on board a ship which will take you around the southern end of the Urga peninsula to Rak Cthaka. From there you will go directly overland to Rak Hagga. Do you understand all that I have said?"

"Most certainly, Revered Jaharb—and what is it that you want me to do in Rak Hagga?"

"When you reach Rak Hagga, Kabach will leave you, and your task will be complete. Your entire service to me consists of concealing him within your party as you journey to Rak Hagga—a small thing, but your reward will be great."

"The ship will certainly save me months of difficult travel on horseback, Revered Elder, but will I not have difficulty explaining my presence to the Malloreans if I have no slaves to sell in the mart at Rak Hagga?"

"You will buy slaves in Cthaka or Gorut. The Malloreans will have no reason to question you."

"Forgive me, Revered Elder," Sadi said with a slightly embarrassed cough, "but my purse is slender. That's why my plan was to capture runaway slaves. They cost no more than the effort of running them down."

Jaharb did not reply, and his probing eyes remained flat and emotionless. He turned his gaze to Tajak. "Open that chest at the end," he said.

Tajak moved quickly to obey. When he lifted the lid of the chest, Garion heard Ce'Nedra gasp involuntarily. The chest was filled to its very brim with bright red gold coins.

"Take what you need, Ussa," Jaharb said indifferently. Then a faintly amused look flickered in his smoldering eyes. "*But* no more than you can hold in both your hands."

Sadi gaped at the gold-filled chest, his eyes filled with greed and his face and shaven scalp sweating profusely. He looked at the red gold, then down at his own two rather delicately shaped hands. A sudden look of undisguised cunning came over his face. "Gold is heavy, most Revered Jaharb, and my hands are quite weak as a result of a recent illness. Might I have one of my servants gather up your most generous payment?"

"That's not an unreasonable request, Ussa," Jaharb replied, his eyes openly amused now. "But mind, no more than he can hold in his two hands."

"Naturally," Sadi said. "I certainly wouldn't want you to overpay me." He turned. "You there," he said to Toth, "go to that chest and remove a double handful of coins—and be certain that you take no more."

Impassively Toth went to the chest and scooped out perhaps a half pailful of the gleaming red coins in his huge hands.

Jaharb regarded the nervously sweating eunuch for a long moment, his wrinkled face expressionless. Then quite suddenly he threw back his head and laughed a dusty laugh. "Excellent, Ussa," he crooned softly. "Your mind is agile. I like that quality in those who serve me. It may be that you will even live long enough to spend some of the gold you have just so cleverly obtained."

"It was merely a demonstration of my intelligence, Revered Jaharb," Sadi answered quickly, "to prove to you that you made no mistake in selecting me. I'll have him put the coins back if you wish—some of them, anyway."

"No, Ussa. Keep them all. You will earn every one of them by the time you reach Rak Hagga, I think."

"I am much honored to be of service to the Dagashi. Even if it were not for your open-handed generosity, I would be no poorer for having befriended you." He hesitated, glancing quickly at Belgarath. "I have been told, Revered Elder, that the Dagashi know many things."

"Few secrets are hidden from us in this part of the world."

"Might I be so bold as to ask a question? A small thing, but one of some interest to me?"

"You may ask, Ussa. I will decide whether or not to answer after I hear the question."

"I have an extremely wealthy customer in Tol Honeth, Revered Jaharb," Sadi said. "He has an absolute passion for rare books, and he would pay me a fortune for a copy of the Grolim Prophecies of Rak Cthol. Do you possibly know where I might find such a book?"

Jaharb frowned slightly, rubbing at his wrinkled cheek.

"The Dagashi have little interest in books," he said. "The volume you seek would certainly have been in the library of Ctuchik at Rak Cthol, but I'm sure it was lost when Belgarath the Sorcerer destroyed the city." He thought a moment longer. "You might ask Agachak when you get to Rak Urga, however. The Temple library there is most extensive; since the prophecies deal with religion, Agachak is certain to have a copy—if one still exists."

"I am profoundly grateful for the information, Revered Elder," Sadi said, bowing again.

Jaharb straightened. "And now you and your servants will need to rest. You depart for Rak Urga at first light tomorrow morning. A room has been prepared for you." He turned back to his bowl of grapes.

The room to which they were taken was quite large. The stone walls had been whitewashed to enhance the dim light which lay over the city of the assassins, but the furnishings were rudimentary at best, consisting only of a low stone table and heaps of cushions.

As soon as the black-robed Tajak left them alone, Garion pulled off his green slaver's robe. "Grandfather," he said, "what are we going to do? We can't go to Rak Urga. If we're ever going to catch Zandramas, we're going to have to get to Verkat as soon as we can."

The old man sprawled in a pile of cushions. "Actually, Garion, things couldn't have worked out better for us. Once we have the ship that Agachak and Urgit have waiting for us, we can sail directly on to Verkat. That's going to save us months of difficult travel."

"But won't the Dagashi—this Kabach who's waiting at Rak Urga—object if we don't land where Jaharb said we were going to?"

Sadi unlatched his leather case. "Set your mind at ease, Belgarion." He took out a small vial containing a thick blue liquid and held it up. "Two drops of this in his food and he'll be so happy that he won't care *where* we're going."

"You're a very versatile fellow, Sadi," Belgarath said. "How did you know that I was looking for the Prophecies of the Western Grolims?"

Sadi shrugged. "It wasn't hard to deduce, Ancient One. A part of the arrangement between Sariss and Naradas involved the burning of the only copy of that book in the palace library at Sthiss Tor. If Zandramas wanted it destroyed, it was fairly obvious that she didn't want you to get your hands on it."

"I'm starting to revise my opinion of you, Sadi. I still don't entirely trust you, but you certainly can be useful when you set your mind to it."

"Why, thank you, Ancient Belgarath." The eunuch took out the small earthenware bottle.

"Are you going to feed that snake?" Silk asked.

"She *does* get hungry, Kheldar."

"I'll wait outside, then."

"Tell me, Prince Kheldar," Velvet said curiously, "what is the source of this peculiar aversion of yours toward reptiles?"

"Most normal people don't like snakes."

"Oh, they aren't that bad."

"Are you trying to be funny?"

She opened her brown eyes very wide in an expression of exaggerated innocence. "Would I do that?"

He went out into the hallway muttering to himself.

Velvet laughed and then went over to join Ce'Nedra on the pile of cushions near the window. Garion had noticed that the two of them had grown quite close during the weeks since they had left Tol Honeth. Because Polgara had always seemed so totally self-sufficient, he had not fully realized the deep-seated need that most women had for the companionship of other women. As Sadi fed his little green snake, the two of them sat side by side on the cushions and brushed the dust of their journey out of their hair.

"Why do you tease him so much, Liselle?" Ce'Nedra asked, pulling her brush through her flaming locks.

"I'm getting even with him," Velvet replied with an impish smile. "When I was a little girl, he used to tease me outrageously. Now it's my turn."

"You always seem to know just exactly what to say to offend him the most."

"I know him very well, Ce'Nedra. I've been watching him for years now. I know every single one of his weaknesses and I know exactly where he's the most sensitive." The blond girl's eyes grew soft. "He's a legend in Drasnia, you know. At the Academy, whole seminars are devoted to his exploits. We all try to emulate him, but none of us has his outrageous flair."

Ce'Nedra stopped brushing and gave her friend a long, speculative look.

"Yes?" Velvet said, returning the look.

"Oh, nothing," Ce'Nedra said and went back to brushing her hair.

The desert night was surprisingly chill. The air was so totally devoid of moisture that each day's heat evaporated almost as soon as the sun went down. As they set out from Kahsha in the steely dawn light, Garion found that he was actually shivering. By midmorning, however, the burning sun had once again turned the barren waste of Araga into an inferno. It was nearly noon by the time they reached the foothills along the western rim of the desert and began the climb that took them up out of that hideous furnace.

"How long until we get to Rak Urga, good Master?" Sadi asked Tajak, who once again escorted them.

"A week or so."

"Distances are very great in this part of Cthol Murgos, aren't they?"

"It's a very large country."

"And very empty."

"Only if you don't look around you."

Sadi looked at him inquiringly.

"Along that ridge, for example." Tajak pointed toward the ragged stretch of rock outlined against the western sky where a single black-robed Murgo sat astride his horse, watching them.

"How long has he been there?" Sadi asked.

"For the past hour. Don't you ever look up?"

"In Nyissa, we always watch the ground. Snakes, you know."

"That explains it, I suppose."

"What's he doing up there?"

"Watching us. King Urgit likes to keep track of strangers."

"Is he likely to cause trouble?"

"We are Dagashi, Nyissan. Other Murgos do not cause us trouble."

"It's a great comfort to have so formidable an escort, good Tajak."

The country through which they rode for the next week was rocky and only sparsely vegetated. Garion had some difficulty adjusting to the notion that it was late summer here in the southern latitudes. The turn of the seasons had always been so immutable that emotionally and perhaps in his very blood, he found that he could not actually accept the idea that they were reversed here at the bottom of the world.

At a certain point in their journey southward, he felt the well-covered Orb on the pommel of the sword that rode across his back tug strongly off toward the left. He nudged his horse up beside Belgarath's. "Zandramas turned east here," he reported quietly.

The old man nodded.

"I hate to lose the trail," Garion said. "If Sadi's wrong about where she's going, it could take months to find it again."

"We wasted a lot of time on the Bear-cult, Garion," the old man replied. "We have to make that up, and that means taking a few gambles."

"I suppose you're right, Grandfather, but I still don't like it."

"I don't much either, but I don't think we have any choice, do we?"

A series of squalls blew in off the Great Western Sea as they proceeded down the rocky spine of the Urga peninsula, an indication that autumn was rapidly approaching. Although the squalls were blustery, they carried only fitful spates of rain, and the journey continued without interruption. They more frequently saw mounted Murgo patrols now, ranging along the ridge tops and outlined against the dirty gray sky. The Murgos, however, prudently gave the Dagashi a wide berth.

And then, about noon on a windy day when heavy clouds rolled in off the vast ocean, they topped a hill and looked down at a large body of water embraced by steep rock cliffs.

"The Gulf of Urga," Tajak said tersely, pointing at that leaden sea.

A peninsula jutted out from the far shore, sheltering the entrance to the gulf with a rocky headland. Embraced by the curve of that headland was a harbor dotted with black-hulled ships, and rising from that harbor was a fair-sized town.

"Is that it?" Sadi asked.

Tajak nodded. "Rak Urga," he said.

A ferry awaited them on the narrow beach, bobbing in the sullen waves rolling in from the open sea. It was a large, wide-beamed barge manned by two score wretched-looking slaves under the watchful eye of a Murgo boatman armed with a long whip. Tajak and his men led the way down to the gravel strand, then turned without a word and rode back up the trail.

The channel running from the Great Western Sea into the Gulf of Urga was not wide, and Garion could clearly make out the low stone buildings of Rak Urga squatting under a murky sky on the far side. Sadi spoke briefly with the Murgo, a few coins changed hands, and then they led their horses aboard. The Murgo barked a short command to his slaves, cracking his whip over their heads by way of emphasis. Desperately, the slaves pushed the barge off the gravel beach with their oars, casting fearful glances at their cruel-faced master and his whip. Once they were clear of the beach, they quickly took their places and began to row, pulling hard for the city across the narrow channel. The Murgo paced up and down the length of the barge, his face alert, and his eyes intently on his slaves, watching for any hint of flagging effort. Once, when they were about halfway across, he partially raised his whip, apparently for no other reason than out of a desire to use it.

"Excuse me, noble ferryman," Silk said, stepping in front of him, "but did you know that your boat is leaking?"

"Leaking?" the Murgo replied sharply, lowering his whip. "Where?"

"I can't really be sure, but there's quite a bit of water down in the bottom."

The Murgo called to his steersman in the stern and then quickly raised a wooden grating so that the two of them could peer down into the shallow bottom of his boat. "That's bilgewater," he said in disgust, motioning his steersman back to his post. "Don't you know anything about boats?"

"Not much," Silk admitted. "I saw the water and thought you ought to know about it. Sorry to have bothered you." He walked forward to rejoin the others.

"What was that all about?" Belgarath asked.

"Durnik's face was getting a bit bleak." Silk shrugged. "I didn't want his passion for justice to get the better of him."

Belgarath looked at the smith.

"I'm not going to stand around idly, if he starts flogging those poor men," Durnik declared, his face stiff. "The minute he raises that whip, he's going to find himself swimming."

"You see what I mean?" Silk said.

Belgarath looked as if he were about to say something, but Polgara stepped in front of him. "Leave him alone, father," she said. "It's the way he is, and I wouldn't change him for the world."

The harbor of Rak Urga was even more congested with ships than it had appeared to be from the other side. The steersman of the barge picked his way carefully through all those anchored vessels toward the stone quays jutting out into the lead-gray chop of the channel. A dozen or more of the wide-beamed Murgo ships were moored to the quays, bumping against woven rope fenders as gangs of slaves unloaded them.

The barge drew in close to the sheltered side of one of the

quays, and the horses were carefully led up a slanting stone ramp, made slippery by clinging seaweed. Ce'Nedra looked down at the garbage-strewn water sloshing below and sniffed disdainfully. "Why do seaports always look—and smell—the same?" she murmured.

"Probably because the people who live in them find all that water irresistible," Velvet replied.

Ce'Nedra looked puzzled.

"It's just too convenient," the Drasnian girl explained. "They always seem to forget that the garbage they throw into the harbor this morning will come back to haunt them with the afternoon tide."

When they reached the top of the ramp, a self-important Murgo stood waiting for them, his heavy black robe flapping in the stiff breeze. "You there," he said arrogantly. "State your business."

Sadi stepped forward and gave the Murgo an oily bow. "I am Ussa," he replied, "registered slave trader from Sthiss Tor. I have all the necessary documents."

"There's no slave market in Rak Urga," the Murgo declared suspiciously. "Hand over your documents."

"Of course." Sadi dipped his hand inside his green robe and brought out a packet of folded parchment.

"If you're not dealing in slaves, what are you doing here?" the Murgo demanded, taking the packet from him.

"I'm merely doing a favor for my good friend Jaharb, Chief Elder of the Dagashi," Sadi told him.

The Murgo paused in the very act of opening the packet. "Jaharb?" he said a bit apprehensively.

Sadi nodded. "Since I was passing this way anyhow, he asked me to stop by and deliver a message to Agachak, the Hierarch of Rak Urga."

The Murgo swallowed hard and thrust the documents back into Sadi's hands as if they had suddenly grown hot. "On your way, then," he said shortly.

"My thanks, noble sir," Sadi said with another bow. "Excuse me, but could you direct me to the Temple of Torak? This is my first visit to Rak Urga."

"It lies at the head of the street running up from this quay," the Murgo answered.

"Again my thanks. If you'll give me your name, I'll tell Agachak how helpful you were."

The Murgo's face took on a pasty hue. "That won't be necessary," he said quickly, then turned and walked away.

"The names Jaharb and Agachak appear to have a certain impact here," Silk suggested.

Sadi smiled. "I imagine that if you were to mention them in the same breath, every door in town would open for you," he agreed.

Rak Urga was not an attractive city. The streets were narrow, and the buildings were built of roughly squared-off stones and topped by gray slate roofs that overhung the streets, putting the thoroughfares into a perpetually gloomy twilight. It was not merely that gray bleakness, however, that made the city so dreary. There was about it an air of cold unconcern for normal human feelings, coupled with a sense of lingering fear. Grim-faced Murgos in their black robes moved through the streets, neither speaking nor even acknowledging the presence of their fellow townsmen.

"Why are these people all so unfriendly toward each other?" Eriond asked Polgara.

"It's a cultural trait," she told him. "Murgos were the aristocracy at Cthol Mishrak before Torak ordered them to migrate to this continent. They are absolutely convinced that Murgos are the supreme creation of the universe—and every one of them is convinced that he's superior to all the rest. It doesn't leave them very much to talk about."

There was a pall of greasy black smoke hanging over the city, bringing with it a sickening stench.

"What is that dreadful smell?" Velvet asked, wrinkling her nose.

"I don't think you really want to know," Silk told her with a bleak look on his face.

"Surely they aren't still—" Garion left it hanging.

"It seems so," the little man replied.

"But Torak's dead. What's the sense of it?"

"Grolims have never really been all that much concerned about the fact that what they do doesn't make sense, Garion," Belgarath said. "The source of their power has always been terror. If they want to keep the power, they have to continue the terror."

They rounded a corner and saw a huge black building ahead of them. A column of dense smoke rose from a large chimney jutting up from the slate roof, blowing first this way and then that in the gusty wind coming up from the harbor.

"Is that the Temple?" Durnik asked.

"Yes," Polgara replied. She pointed at the two massive, nail-studded doors forming the only break in the blank, featureless wall. Directly above those doors there hung the polished steel replica of the face of Torak. Garion felt the familiar chill in his blood as he looked at the brooding face of his enemy. Even now, after all that had happened in the City of Endless Night, the face of Torak filled him with dread, and he was not particularly surprised to find that he was actually trembling as he approached the entrance to the Temple of the maimed God of Angarak.

CHAPTER ELEVEN

Sadi slid down from his saddle, went up to the nail-studded doors, and clanged the rusty iron knocker, sending hollow echoes reverberating back into the Temple.

"Who comes to the House of Torak?" a muffled voice demanded from inside.

"I bear a message from Jaharb, Chief Elder at Mount Kahsha, for the ears of Agachak, Hierarch of Rak Urga."

There was a momentary pause inside, and then one of the doors creaked open and a pock-marked Grolim looked cautiously out at them. "You are not of the Dagashi," he said accusingly to Sadi.

"No, as a matter of fact, I'm not. There's an arrangement between Jaharb and Agachak, and I'm part of it."

"I have not heard of such an arrangement."

Sadi looked pointedly at the unadorned hood of the Grolim's robe, an obvious indication that the priest was of low rank. "Forgive me, servant of Torak," he said coolly, "but is your Hierarch in the habit of confiding in his doorman?"

The Grolim's face darkened as he glared at the eunuch. "Cover your head, Nyissan," he said after a long moment. "This is a holy place."

"Of course." Sadi pulled the hood of his green robe up over his shaven scalp. "Will you have someone see to our horses?"

"They will be taken care of. Are these your servants?" The Grolim looked past Sadi's shoulder at the others, who still sat their horses in the cobbled street.

"They are, noble priest."

"Tell them to come with us. I will take you all to Chabat."

"Excuse me, priest of the Dragon God. My message is for Agachak."

"No one sees Agachak without first seeing Chabat. Bring your servants and follow me."

The rest of them dismounted and passed through the grim doors into the torchlit corridor beyond. The sickening odor of burning flesh which had pervaded the city was even stronger here in the Temple. A sense of dread came over Garion as he followed the Grolim and Sadi along the smoky hallway into the Temple. The place reeked of an ancient evil, and the hollow-faced priests they passed in the corridor all looked at them with heavy suspicion and undisguised malice.

And then there came from somewhere in the building an agonized shriek, followed by a great iron clang. Garion shuddered, fully aware of the meaning of those sounds.

"Is the ancient rite of sacrifice still performed?" Sadi asked the Grolim in some surprise. "I would have thought that the practice might have fallen into disuse—all things considered."

"Nothing has happened to make us discontinue the performance of our holiest duty, Nyissan," the Grolim replied coldly. "Each hour we offer up a human heart to the God Torak."

"But Torak is no more."

The Grolim stopped, his face angry. "*Never* speak those words again!" he snapped. "It is not the place of a foreigner to utter such blasphemy within the walls of the Temple. The spirit of Torak lives on, and one day he will be reborn to rule the world. He himself will wield the knife when his enemy, Belgarion of Riva, lies screaming on the altar."

"Now there's a cheery thought," Silk murmured to Belgarath. "We get to do it all over again."

"Just shut up, Silk," Belgarath muttered.

The chamber to which the Grolim underpriest led them was large and dimly lighted by several oil lamps. The walls were lined with black drapes, and the air was thick with incense. A slim, hooded figure sat behind a large table with a guttering black candle at its elbow and a heavy, black-bound book before it. A kind of warning tingle prickled Garion's scalp as he sensed the power emanating from that figure. He glanced quickly at Polgara, and she nodded gravely.

"Forgive me, Holy Chabat," the pock-marked Grolim said in a slightly trembling voice as he genuflected before the table, "but I bring a messenger from Jaharb the assassin."

The figure at the table looked up, and Garion suppressed a start of surprise. It was a woman. There was about her face a kind of luminous beauty, but it was not that which struck his eye. Cruelly inscribed into each of her pale cheeks were deep red scars that ran down from her temples to her chin in an ornate design, a design which appeared to represent flames. Her eyes were dark and smoldering, and her full-lipped mouth was drawn into a contemptuous sneer. A deep purple piping marked the edge of her black hood. "So?' she said in a harshly rasping voice. "And how is it that the Dagashi now entrust their messages to foreigners?"

"I—I thought not to ask, Holy Chabat," the Grolim faltered. "This one claims to be a friend of Jaharb."

"And you chose not to question him further?" Her harsh voice sank into a menacing whisper, and her eyes bored into the suddenly trembling underpriest. Then her gaze slowly shifted to Sadi. "Say your name," she commanded.

"I am Ussa of Sthiss Tor, Holy Priestess," he replied. "Jaharb instructed me to present myself to your Hierarch and to give him a message."

"And what is that message?"

"Ah—forgive me, Holy Priestess, but I was told that it was for Agachak's ears alone."

"I *am* Agachak's ears," she told him, her voice dreadfully quiet. "Nothing reaches his ears that I have not heard first." It was the tone of her voice that made Garion suddenly understand. Although this cruelly scarred woman had somehow risen to a position of power here in the temple, she was still uncertain about that power. She bore her uncertainty like an open wound, and the slightest questioning of her authority roused in her an abiding hatred for whomever doubted her. Fervently he hoped that Sadi realized how extremely dangerous she was.

"Ah," Sadi said with polished aplomb. "I was not fully aware of the situation here. I was told that Jaharb, Agachak, and King Urgit have reason to want one Kabach transported safely to Rak Hagga. I am the one who is to provide that transportation."

Her eyes narrowed suspiciously. "That is certainly not the entire message," she accused.

"I'm afraid it is, Noble Priestess. I presume that Agachak will understand its meaning."

"Jaharb said nothing else to you?"

"Only that this Kabach is here in the Temple under Agachak's protection."

"Impossible," she snapped. "I would have known about it if he were. Agachak conceals nothing from me."

Sadi spread his hands in a mollifying gesture. "I can only repeat what Jaharb told me, Holy Priestess."

She gnawed at one knuckle, her eyes suddenly filled with doubt. "If you're lying to me, Ussa—or trying to conceal something—I will have your heart ripped out," she threatened.

"That is the entire message, Holy Priestess. May I now deliver it to your Hierarch?"

"The Hierarch is at the Drojim Palace, consulting with the High King. He is not likely to return until midnight."

"Is there someplace where my servants and I could await his return, then?"

"I have not yet finished with you, Ussa of Sthiss Tor. What is it that this Kabach is to do in Rak Hagga?"

"Jaharb did not think I needed to know that."

"I think you're lying to me, Ussa," she said, her fingernails rapping a nervous staccato on the table top.

"I have no reason to lie to you, Holy Chabat," he protested.

"Agachak would have told me of this matter. He conceals nothing from me—nothing."

"Perhaps he overlooked it. It may not be anything of much importance."

She looked at each of the others in turn then, her eyes hooded beneath her dark brows. She turned a cold gaze on the still-trembling Grolim. "Tell me," she said in a voice scarcely more than a whisper, "how is it that the one over there was permitted to come into my presence bearing a sword?" She pointed at Garion.

The Priest's face grew stricken. "Forgive me, Chabat," he stammered, "I—I failed to notice the sword."

"Failed? How can one fail to see so large a weapon? Can you possibly explain that to me?"

The Grolim began to tremble even more violently.

"Is the sword perhaps invisible? Or is it, perhaps, that my safety is of no concern to you?" Her scarred face grew even more cruel. "Or might it be that you bear me some malice and hoped that this foreigner might decide to slay me?"

The Grolim's face grew ashen.

"I think perhaps that I should bring this matter to the attention of Agachak upon his return. He will doubtless wish to speak with you about this invisible sword—at some length."

The door to the chamber opened and an emaciated Grolim, black-robed, but with his green-lined hood pushed back, entered the chamber. His black hair was greasy and hung in lank tangles about his shoulders. He had the bulging eyes of a fanatic and there was the acrid odor of a long-unwashed body about him. "It's nearly time, Chabat," he announced in a strident voice.

Chabat's smoldering eyes softened as she looked at him. "Thank you, Sorchak," she replied, lowering her eyelashes in an oddly coquettish fashion. She rose, opened a drawer in the table, and took out a black leather case. She opened the case and lovingly lifted out a long, gleaming knife. Then she looked coldly at the Grolim priest she had just chastised. "I go now to the Sanctum to perform the rite of sacrifice," she told him, absently testing the edge of her heavy-bladed knife. "If one single word of anything that has happened here escapes your lips, you yourself will die at the next sounding of the bell. Now take these slavers to suitable quarters where they can await the return of the Hierarch." She turned back to the greasy-haired Sorchak, her eyes alight with a sudden, dreadful eagerness. "Will you escort me to the Sanctum so that you can witness my performance of the rite?"

"I would be honored, Chabat," he replied with a jerky bow; but as the priestess turned from him, his lip curled into a sneer of contempt.

"I will leave you in the care of this bungler," she told Sadi as she passed him. "You and I have not yet finished our discussion, but I must go prepare myself for the sacrifice." With Sorchak at her side, she left the room.

When the door closed, the pock-marked underpriest spat on the floor where she had just stood.

"I had not known that a priestess could rise to the Purple in one of the Temples of Torak," Sadi said to him.

"She is the favorite of Agachak," the Grolim muttered darkly. "Her ability at sorcery is very limited, so her elevation came at his insistence. The Hierarch has a peculiar preference for ugly things. It is only his power that keeps her from getting her throat cut."

"Politics." Sadi sighed. "It's the same the world over. She seems most zealous about the performance of her religious duties, however."

"Her eagerness to perform the rite of sacrifice has little to do with religion. She delights in blood. I myself have seen her drink it as it gushes from the chest of the sacrifice and bathe her face and arms in it." The priest glanced around quickly as if afraid of being overheard. "One day, however, Agachak will discover that she practices witchcraft in the House of Torak and that she and Sorchak celebrate their black sabbaths with obscene rites when all the others in the Temple have gone to their beds. When our Hierarch discovers their corruption, she herself will go screaming under the knife, and every Grolim in the Temple will volunteer to slit her open as she lies on the altar." He straightened. "Come with me," he ordered them.

The rooms to which he led them were little more than a series of narrow, dim cells. In each cell stood a low cot, and, hanging on a peg protruding from the wall in each, was a black Grolim robe. The priest nodded briefly, then silently left. Silk looked around the somewhat larger central room with its single lamp and the rough table and benches in its center. "Hardly what I'd call luxurious," he sniffed.

"We can lodge a complaint, if you'd like," Velvet suggested.

"What happened to her face?" Ce'Nedra asked in a horrified voice. "She's hideous."

"It was a custom in certain Grolim temples in parts of Hagga," Polgara replied. "Priestesses with some ability at sorcery carved their faces in that fashion to seal themselves to Torak forever. The practice has largely been abandoned."

"But she could have been so beautiful. Why did she disfigure herself that way?"

"People sometimes do strange things in the grip of religious hysteria."

"How did that Grolim miss seeing Garion's sword?" Silk asked Belgarath.

"The Orb is taking steps to make itself inconspicuous."

"Did you tell it to do that?"

"No. Sometimes it gets certain ideas on its own."

"Well, things seem to be going rather well, don't you think?" Sadi said, rubbing his hands together in a self-congratulatory manner. "I told you I could be very useful down here."

"Very useful, Sadi," Silk replied sardonically. "So far you've led us into the middle of a battle, directly into the headquarters of the Dagashi, and now to the very center of Grolim power in Cthol Murgos. What did you have planned for us next—assuming that the lady with the interesting face doesn't gut you before morning?"

"We *are* going to get the ship, Kheldar," Sadi assured him. "Not even Chabat would dare to counter the wishes of Agachak—no matter how injured her pride may be. And the ship will save us months."

"There's something else Garion and I need to attend to," Belgarath said. "Durnik, take a look out in that hallway and see if they posted any guards to watch us."

"Where are you going?" Silk asked him.

"I need to find the library. I want to see if Jaharb was right about that book being here."

"Wouldn't it be better to wait until tonight—after everybody's gone to bed?"

The old man shook his head. "It might take us a while to find what we need. Agachak's going to be at the palace until midnight, so this is probably the best time to paw through his library." He gave the little Drasnian a brief smile. "Besides," he added, "although it might upset your notion of order, sometimes you can move around in the daytime more easily than you can by sneaking around corners after midnight."

"That's a terribly unnatural thing to suggest, Belgarath."

"The hallway looks clear," Durnik reported from the doorway.

"Good." Belgarath stepped back into the cells and emerged with a couple of the Grolim robes. "Here," he said, extending one of them to Garion, "put this on." As the two of them pulled off their green robes and replaced them with the black ones, Durnik kept watch at the door. "It's still clear, Belgarath," he said, "but you'd better hurry. I can hear people moving around down at the far end."

The old man nodded, pulling up the hood of his robe. "Let's go," he said to Garion.

The corridors were dim, lighted only by smoky torches set in iron rings protruding from the stone walls. They encountered but few of the black-robed Grolim priests in the hallways. The Grolims walked with an odd, swaying gait, their arms folded in their sleeves, their heads down, and the cowls of their robes covering their faces. Garion guessed that there was some obscure significance to that stiff-legged walk and tried to emulate it as he followed his grandfather along the half-lit halls.

Belgarath moved with feigned confidence, as if he knew precisely where they were going. They reached a broader corridor, and the old man glanced once toward its far end where a pair of heavy doors stood open. Beyond those doors lay a room filled with the flickering light of seething flames. "Not that way," he whispered to Garion.

"What is it?"

"The Sanctum. That's where the altar is." He quickly led the way across the corridor and entered an intersecting hallway.

"This could take hours, Grandfather," Garion said in a low voice.

Belgarath shook his head. "Grolim architecture is fairly predictable," he disagreed. "We're in the right part of the Temple. You check the doors on that side, and I'll take these over here."

They moved along the hall, cautiously opening each door as they came to it.

"Garion," the old man whispered, "it's over here."

The room they entered was quite large and smelled of old parchment and moldy leather bindings. It was filled with row upon row of tall, cluttered bookshelves. Solitary tables, each with a pair of wooden benches and with a single dimly glowing oil lamp hanging over it on a long chain, stood in little alcoves along the walls.

"Take a book—any book," Belgarath said. "Sit at that table over there and try to look as if you're studying. Keep your hood up and your eye on the door. I'm going to have a look around. Cough if anybody comes in."

Garion nodded, took a heavy volume from one of the shelves, and seated himself at the table. The minutes dragged by as he looked unseeing at the pages of his book with his ears straining for the slightest sound. Then, shockingly, there came the now-familiar shriek, a long drawn-out cry of despairing agony, followed by the sullen iron clang of the huge gong in the Sanctum where the Grolims conducted their unspeakable rites. Unbidden, an image rose in his mind—the image of the scar-faced Chabat gleefully butchering a victim. He clenched his teeth together, forcing himself not to leap to his feet to stop that abomination.

Then Belgarath whistled softly to him from a narrow aisle leading back between two of the high-standing bookshelves. "I've got it," he said. "Keep watch on the door. I'll be back here."

Garion sat nervously at the table, his eyes and ears alert. He was not good at this sort of thing. His nerves seemed to wind tighter and tighter as he waited, listening and watching for someone to open that door. What would he do if some black-robed priest entered? Should he speak or just remain silent with his head down over his book? What was customary here? He formulated a half-dozen different strategies, but when the latch of the door clicked loudly, he followed one that he had not even considered—he bolted. He swung his legs over the bench upon which he sat and noiselessly dodged back among the high, dark shelves looking for Belgarath.

"Is it safe to talk in here?" he heard someone say.

Another man grunted. "Nobody comes in here anymore. What was it you wanted to talk about?"

"Have you endured enough of her yet? Are you ready to do something about her?"

"Keep your voice down, you fool. If someone hears you and carries your words back to her, your heart will fry in the coals at the next sounding of the bell."

"I loathe that scar-faced wench," the first Grolim spat.

"We all do, but our lives depend on not letting her know that. As long as she's Agachak's favorite, her power is absolute."

"She won't be his favorite if he finds out that she's practicing magic here in the Temple."

"How will he find out? Will *you* denounce her? She would deny it, and then Agachak would let her have you to do with as she chose."

There was a long, fearful silence.

"Besides," the second Grolim continued, "I don't think Agachak would even care about her petty amusements. The only thing that concerns him at the moment is his search for Cthrag Sardius. He and the other Hierarchs are bending all their thought to locating it. If she wants to dally with Sorchak and try to raise demons in the middle of the night, that's her affair and no business of ours."

"It's an abomination!" The first priest's voice was choked with outrage. "She defiles our Temple."

"I won't listen to such talk. I want to keep my heart inside my chest."

"Very well." The first Grolim's tone grew sly. "It may be as you say. You and I are both of the Green, however, and our elevation to the Purple will be more genuine than hers was. If we came upon her when no one else was around, you could use your power to lock her muscles, and I could sink my knife into her heart. Then she could stand before Torak and listen to *his* judgment upon her for violating his commandment forbidding magic."

"I refuse to listen to this any more." There was the sound of rapid footsteps, and the door slammed.

"Coward," the first priest muttered; then he too went out and closed the door behind him.

"Grandfather," Garion whispered hoarsely, "where are you?"

"Back here. Did they leave?"

"They're gone."

"Interesting conversation, wasn't it?"

Garion joined the old man at the back of the library. "Do you think Chabat could really be trying to raise demons—the way the Morindim do?"

"A fair number of Grolims here seem to think so. If she is, she's walking on very dangerous ground. Torak absolutely forbade the practice of magic. Favorite or no, Agachak would have to condemn her if he found out about it."

"Did you find anything?" Garion looked at the book the old man had on the table in front of him.

"I think this might help. Listen: 'The path that has been lost will be found again on the Southern Isle.'"

"Verkat?"

"It almost has to be. Verkat is the only island of any size in southern Cthol Murgos. It confirms what Sadi told us, and I always like to get confirmation whenever I can."

"But it still means that we're only trailing after Zandramas. Did you find anything that tells us how to get ahead of her?"

"Not yet," Belgarath admitted. He turned a page. "What's this?" he said in a startled voice.

"What is it?"

"Listen." The old man lifted the book so that the lamp light fell upon the page. "'Behold:'" he read, "'In the days which shall follow the ascension of the Dark God into the heavens shall the King of the East and the King of the South do war upon each other, and this shall be a sign unto ye that the day of the meeting is at hand. Hasten therefore unto the

Place which is No More when battles do rage upon the plains of the south. Take with thee the chosen sacrifice and a King of Angarak to bear witness to what shall come to pass. For lo, whichever of ye cometh into the presence of Cthrag Sardius with the sacrifice and an Angarak King shall be exalted above all the rest and shall have dominion over them. And know further that in the moment of the sacrifice shall the Dark God be reborn, and he shall triumph over the Child of Light in the instant of his rebirth.'"

Garion stared at him, feeling the blood drain from his face. "Sacrifice?" he exclaimed. "Is that what Zandramas plans to do with my son?"

"So it would seem," Belgarath grunted. He thought about it for a moment. "This explains a few things, but I still don't quite follow this business about needing an Angarak King present at the meeting. Cyradis didn't say anything about that, and neither did the Prophecy."

"That's a Grolim book you've got there, Grandfather," Garion pointed out. "Maybe it's wrong."

"That's possible, too, but it does help to explain why Zandramas is moving around so stealthily. If Urvon knows about this the way Agachak obviously does, they'll both be doing everything in their power to get your son away from her. Whichever one of them gets to the Sardion with Geran and one of the Kings of Angarak is going to gain absolute control of the Grolim Church."

"Why my son?" Garion demanded. "Why would he be the one chosen for sacrifice?"

"I'm not sure, Garion. We haven't found an explanation for that yet."

"I don't think we'd better tell Ce'Nedra about this," Garion said. "She has problems enough as it is."

The door opened again, and Garion spun, his hand going over his shoulder to the hilt of his sword.

"Belgarath? Are you in here?" It was Silk's voice.

"Back here," Belgarath answered. "Keep your voice down."

"We've got trouble," the little man said, coming to the back of the library to join them. "Eriond is missing."

"What?" Garion exclaimed.

"He slipped out when none of us was watching."

Belgarath slammed his fist down on the table and swore. "What's the matter with that boy?" he burst out.

Silk pushed back the hood of the Grolim robe he wore. "Polgara was going to go looking for him, but Durnik and I talked her out of it. I said I'd come and find you instead."

"We'd better find him," the old man said, rising to his feet. "Pol will only wait for so long before she starts acting on her own. We'd better split up. We can cover more ground that way." He led them to the door of the library, glanced out quickly, and then went out into the hall. "Don't do anything unusual," he cautioned Garion in a whisper. "There are Grolims in this place with enough talent to hear you if you start making any noise."

Garion nodded.

"And check back with the others from time to time. We won't accomplish much if one of us finds Eriond and then has to go looking for the other two. Let's go." He moved quickly off down the dimly lighted hallway.

"How did he manage to slip past Aunt Pol?" Garion whispered to Silk as the two of them went side by side back the way they had come.

"Ce'Nedra had a bout of hysterics," Silk replied. "The sacrifices upset her. Polgara had her in one of the cells trying to calm her down. That's when Eriond slipped out."

"Is she all right?" Garion demanded, the sinking fear that had been with him since Prolgu returning with sudden force.

"I think so. Polgara gave her something, and she's sleeping." Silk carefully looked around a corner. "I'll go this way," he whispered. "Be careful." He moved off on silent feet.

Garion stood waiting for his friend to get well out of sight, then cautiously stepped out into the next corridor, folding his hands on his chest and lowering his cowled head in an imitation of Grolim piety. What could Eriond possibly be thinking of? The sheer irresponsibility of the boy's act made Garion want to pound his fist against the wall. He moved down the corridor, trying his best not to do anything that might look suspicious and carefully cracking open each door he came to.

"What is it?" a harshly accented voice demanded from inside a dark room when he opened the door.

"Sorry, brother," Garion muttered, trying to imitate the thickly accented Angarak speech, "wrong door." He quickly closed it again and went on down the corridor, moving as fast as he dared.

The door behind him was suddenly yanked open, and a half-dressed Grolim stepped out, his face angry. "You there," he shouted after Garion, "stop!"

Garion threw a quick look over his shoulder and was around the corner into the broad central corridor of the Temple in two steps.

"Come back here!" the Grolim shouted, and Garion heard his bare feet slapping on the flagstone floor as he ran in pursuit. Garion swore and then took a gamble. He yanked open the first door that presented itself and darted inside. A quick glance told him that the room was empty, and he closed the door and set his ear against its panel to listen.

"What's the trouble?" he heard someone demand from the corridor outside.

"Someone just tried to come into my cell." Garion recognized the outraged voice of the Grolim upon whom he had just intruded.

There was a sly chuckle. "Perhaps you should have waited to see what she wanted."

"It was a man."

There was a pause. "Well," the first voice said. "Well, well, well."

"What's that supposed to mean?"

"Nothing. Nothing at all. You'd better go put on some clothes. If Chabat catches you in the hall in your undergarments, she might get some peculiar ideas."

"I'm going to look for this intruder. There's something very strange going on here. Will you help me?"

"Why not? I haven't got anything better to do."

From far up the corridor Garion heard a slow, groaning chant and the sound of many shuffling feet.

"Quick," one of the voices outside the door warned, "back down this side passage. If they see us, they'll insist that we join them."

Garion heard their scurrying feet as they dodged back out of sight. Carefully, he opened the door a crack and peered out. The slow shuffling march and the deep-toned chanting came nearer. A line of Grolims, the cowls of their hoods raised and with their hands clasped in front of them, came into view, moving at a ceremonial pace along the torchlit corridor toward the very heart of the Temple. He waited in the dark room for them to pass, and then, on a sudden impulse so strong that he moved without even thinking, he boldly opened the door, stepped out into the corridor, and fell in at the end of the column.

The slow, rhythmic march continued on down the broad hallway, and the reek of burning flesh grew stronger in Garion's nostrils as the file which he had joined approached the Sanctum. Then, chanting even louder, they passed through the arched doorway into the vaulted Sanctum itself.

The ceiling was very high, lost in smoky shadows. On the wall facing the door hung that polished steel mask—the calm, beautiful replica of the unblemished face of the God Torak. Under that uncaring mask stood the black altar with bright rivulets of fresh blood streaking its sides. There stood the glowing brazier, awaiting the next quivering heart to be offered up to the long-dead God; and there the fire pit yawned for the body of the next butchered victim.

Shaking himself, Garion dodged quickly out of sight behind a column standing to one side of the doorway and stood sweating and trembling for several moments, struggling to control his emotions. Better perhaps than any man alive, he knew the full meaning of this awful place. Torak was dead. He himself had felt the faltering beat of the stricken God's heart thrilling down the blazing length of Iron-grip's sword, sunk deep in his enemy's chest. The slaughter that had drenched this foul place with blood in the years since that awful night was senseless, empty—homage paid to a maimed and demented God who had died weeping fire and crying piteously to the indifferent stars. A slow burning rage began to build up in his chest, filling his mouth with a fiery taste as bitter as gall. Unbidden, his will began to clench itself as he envisioned the shattering of the mask and the altar and the sudden destruction of this filthy place.

"*That's not why you're here, Belgarion!*" the voice in his mind cracked.

Slowly, as if, were he to release it all at once, it might destroy the entire city, Garion relaxed his will. Time enough to crush this horror later. Right now, he had to find Eriond. Cautiously, he poked his head around the column which concealed him. A priest with the purple-lined hood of his robe pushed back had just entered from the far side of the Sanctum. In his hands he carried a dark red cushion, and gleaming on that cushion lay a long, cruel knife. He faced the image of his dead God and reverently lifted the cushion and the knife in supplication. "Behold the instrument of thy will, Dragon God of Angarak," he intoned, "and behold him whose heart is to be offered unto thee."

Four Grolims dragged a naked, screaming slave into the Sanctum, ignoring his helpless struggles and panic-sticken pleas for mercy. Without thinking, Garion reached over his shoulder for his sword.

"*Stop that!*" the voice commanded.

"*No! I'm not going to let it happen!*"

"*It won't happen. Now get your hand off your sword!*"

"No chance!" Garion said aloud, drawing his blade and lunging around the pillar. And then as if he had suddenly been turned to stone, he found that he could not move so much as an eyelash. "*Let go of me!*" he grated.

"No! You're here to watch this time, not to act. Now stand there and keep your eyes open."

Garion stared in sudden disbelief as Eriond, his pale blond curls gleaming in the cruel light of the Temple, entered by way of the same door through which the slave had just been dragged. The young man's face bore an expression of almost regretful determination as he entered and walked directly toward the astonished priest. "I'm sorry," he said quite firmly, "but you can't do this any more."

"Seize this desecrator," the priest at the altar shouted. "It shall be *his* heart which shall sizzle in the coals!"

A dozen Grolims leaped to their feet, but suddenly froze, caught in that same stasis which locked Garion's muscles.

"This can't continue," Eriond said in that same determined voice. "I know how much it means to all of you, but it just can't go on. Someday—very soon, I think—you'll all understand."

There was no sound, no rushing surge such as Garion had come to expect, but the yawning fire pit before the altar suddenly roared to a furnace note, sending leaping flames and glowing sparks shooting upward to lick at the very vaults of the ceiling. The suffocatingly hot Sanctum suddenly cooled as if a cleansing breeze had just swept through it. Then the seething fire guttered briefly like a dying candle—and went out. The glowing brazier at the side of the altar also flared into blinding incandescence, and its steel body grew suddenly soft, drooping and sagging as it began to collapse under its own weight. With a flicker, it also went out.

The priest dropped his knife in horror and leaped to the still-glowing brazier. Irrationally, he put forth his hands as if he would force the softened metal back into its original shape, but he howled in pain as the red-hot steel seared deeply into his flesh.

Eriond regarded the dead fires with a look of satisfaction, then turned to the stunned Grolims still holding the naked slave. "Let that man go," he told them.

They stared at him.

"You might as well," Eriond said almost conversationally. "You can't sacrifice him without the fires, and the fires won't burn any more. No matter what you do, you won't ever be able to start them again."

"Done!" the voice in Garion's mind said in a tone of such exultation that it buckled his knees.

The burned priest, still moaning and cradling his charred hands at his chest, raised his ashen face. "Seize him!" he shrieked, pointing at Eriond with a blackened hand. "Seize him and take him to Chabat!"

CHAPTER TWELVE

There was no longer any need for stealth. Alarm bells rang in every quarter of the Temple, and frightened Grolims scurried this way and that, shouting contradictory orders to each other. Garion ran among them, desperately looking for Belgarath and Silk.

As he rounded a corner, a wild-faced Grolim caught him by the arm. "Were you there in the Sanctum when it happened?" he demanded.

"No," Garion lied, trying to free his arm.

"They say that he was ten feet tall, and that he blasted a dozen priests into nothingness before he extinguished the fires."

"Oh?" Garion said, still trying to free himself from the Grolim's grasp.

"Some people say that it was Belgarath the Sorcerer himself."

"I find that hard to believe."

"Who else would have that much power?" The Grolim stopped suddenly, his eyes going very wide. "You know what this means, don't you?" he asked in a trembling voice.

"What?"

"The Sanctum will have to be rededicated, and that requires Grolim blood. Dozens of us will have to die before the Sanctum is purified."

"I really have to go," Garion told him, tugging at the arm the man held fast in both hands.

"Chabat will wade to the hips in our blood," the priest moaned hysterically, ignoring Garion's words.

There was really no choice. Things were much too urgent for diplomacy. Garion feigned a frightened expression as he looked past the babbling Grolim's shoulder. "Is that her coming?" he whispered hoarsely.

The Grolim turned his head to look in fright back over his shoulder. Garion carefully measured him and then smashed his fist into the unprotected side of the terrified man's face. The Grolim slammed back against the wall, his eyes glazed and vacant. Then he collapsed in a heap on the floor.

"Neat," Silk said from a dark doorway a few yards up the hall, "but the reason for it escapes me."

"I couldn't get loose from him," Garion explained, bending to take hold of the unconscious man. He dragged him into a shadowy alcove and propped him up in a sitting position. "Have you got any idea where Grandfather is?"

"He's in here," Silk replied, jerking his thumb over his shoulder at the door behind him. "What happened?"

"I'll tell you in a minute. Let's get in out of sight."

They went through the doorway to find Belgarath seated on the edge of a table. "What's going on out there?" he demanded.

"I found Eriond."

"Good."

"No, not really. He went into the Sanctum just as the Grolims were about to sacrifice a slave and put out the fires."

"He did *what*?"

"I think it was him. I was there and I know that it wasn't me. He just walked in and told them that they couldn't sacrifice people any more, and then the fires went out. Grandfather, he didn't make a sound when he did it—no surge, no noise, nothing."

"Are you sure it was him? I mean—it wasn't something natural?"

Garion shook his head. "No. The fires flared up and then went out like blown-out candles. There were other things going on, too. The voice talked to me and I couldn't even move a muscle. The Grolims who were dragging the slave to the altar just let him go when Eriond told them to. Then he told them all that they won't ever be able to relight the fires."

"Where's the boy now?"

"They're taking him to Chabat."

"Couldn't you stop them?"

"I was told not to." Garion tapped his forehead.

"I should have expected that," Belgarath said irritably. "We'd better go warn Pol and the others. We may have to free Eriond and then fight our way out of here." He opened the door, looked out into the hallway, and motioned Garion and Silk to follow him.

Polgara's face was deathly pale when the three of them reentered the room where she and the others were waiting. "You didn't find him," she said. It was not exactly a question.

"Garion did," Belgarath replied.

She turned to Garion. "Why isn't he with you, then?" she demanded.

"I'm afraid the Grolims have him, Aunt Pol."

"We've got a problem here, Pol," Belgarath said gravely. "From what Garion says, Eriond went into the Sanctum and put out the fires."

"*What?*" she exclaimed.

Garion spread his hands helplessly. "He just walked in and made the fires go out. The Grolims seized him and they're taking him to Chabat."

"This is very serious, Belgarath," Sadi said. "Those fires are supposed to burn perpetually. If the Grolims believe that the boy was responsible, he's in very great danger."

"I know," the old man agreed.

"All right, then," Durnik said quietly. "We'll just have to go take him away from them." He stood up, and Toth silently joined him.

"But our ship is almost ready," Sadi protested. "We could be out of here with no one the wiser."

"There's nothing we can do about that now." Belgarath's face was grimly determined.

"Let me see if I can salvage something out of this mess before any of you do anything irreversible," Sadi pleaded. "There'll always be time for more direct action if I can't talk our way out of this."

Garion looked around. "Where's Ce'Nedra?" he asked.

"She's asleep," Polgara replied. "Liselle's with her."

"Is she all right? Silk said that she was upset. She isn't sick again, is she?"

"No, Garion. It was the sounds coming from the Sanctum. She couldn't tolerate them."

A heavy fist suddenly pounded on the bolted door. Garion jumped and instinctively reached for his sword. "Open up in there!" a harsh voice commanded from outside.

"Quickly," Sadi hissed, "all of you get back into your cells and try to look as if you've been sleeping when you come out."

They hurried back into the cells and waited breathlessly while the thin eunuch went to the door and unbolted it. "What's the matter, reverend sirs?" he asked mildly as the Grolims burst into the room with drawn weapons.

"You have been summoned to an audience with the Hierarch, slaver," one of them snarled. "You and all your servants."

"We're honored," Sadi murmured.

"You're not being honored. You're to be interrogated. I'd advise you to speak the truth, because Agachak has the power to pull you very slowly out of your skin if you lie to him."

"What an unpleasant notion. Has the Hierarch returned from the Drojim Palace then?"

"Word has been sent to him of the monstrous crime one of your servants has committed."

"Crime? What crime?"

The Grolim ignored him. "On Chabat's orders, you are all to be confined until Agachak returns to the Temple."

Garion and the others were roughly shaken out of their feigned sleep and marched through the smoky corridors and down a narrow flight of stone steps into the basement. Unlike the rooms above, these cells were secured with barred iron doors, and the narrow halls had about them that peculiar sour odor that permeates prisons and dungeons the world over. One of the Grolims opened a barred door and gestured for them to enter.

"Is this really necessary, good Priest?" Sadi protested.

The Grolim put his hand threateningly on his sword hilt.

"Calm yourself, sir," Sadi said. "I was merely asking."

"Inside! Now!"

They all filed into the cell, and the black-robed priest slammed it behind them. The sound of the key grating in the lock seemed very loud for some reason.

"Garion," Ce'Nedra said in a frightened little voice, "What's happening? Why are they doing this?"

He put his arm comfortingly about her shoulders. "Eriond got into trouble," he explained. "Sadi's going to try to talk us all out of this."

"What if he can't?"

"Then we'll do it the other way."

Silk looked around at the dimly lit cell with a disdainful sniff. "Dungeons always show such a lack of imagination," he remarked, scuffing at the moldy straw littering the floor with one foot.

"Have you had such a wide experience with dungeons, Kheldar?" Velvet asked him.

"I've been in a few from time to time." He shrugged. "I've never found it convenient to stay for more than a few hours." He raised up on his tiptoes to peer out through the small barred window in the door. "Good," he said, "no guards." He looked at Belgarath. "Do you want me to open this?" he asked, tapping on the door with one knuckle. "I don't think we can accomplish very much from in here."

"Please be patient, Prince Kheldar," Sadi said. "If we break out of this cell, I'll never be able to smooth this over."

"I've got to find out what they've done with Eriond," Polgara told the eunuch firmly. "Go ahead and open it, Silk."

"Polgara?" a light, familiar voice came from the next cell. "Is that you?"

"Eriond!" she said with relief. "Are you all right?"

"I'm fine, Polgara. They put chains on me, but they aren't too uncomfortable."

"Why did you do that—what you did in the Sanctum?"

"I didn't like those fires."

"I didn't either, but—"

"I *really* didn't like them, Polgara. That sort of thing has to be stopped, and we have to start somewhere."

"How did you put them out?" Belgarath asked through the barred window in the door. "Garion was there when you did it and he says that he didn't hear or feel anything."

"I'm not sure, Belgarath. I don't think I actually did anything special to make them go out. I just decided that I didn't want them to burn any more, so I sort of let them know how I felt, and they just went out."

"That's all?"

"As closely as I can remember, yes."

Belgarath turned from the door, his face baffled. "When we get out of here, that boy and I are going to have a very long talk about this. I've meant to do that about a half-dozen times, and every time I make up my mind, I get smoothly diverted." He looked at Garion. "The next time you talk to your friend, tell him to stop that. It irritates me."

"He already knows that, Grandfather. I think that's why he does it."

Somewhere down the corridor outside, a heavy iron door clanged open, and there came the sound of marching feet.

"Grolims," Silk said quietly from the barred window.

"Who else?" Belgarath asked sourly.

The approaching group stopped outside, and a key grated in the lock of Eriond's cell. The door creaked open. "You, boy," a harsh voice barked. "Come with us."

"Father," Polgara whispered urgently.

The old man held up one hand. "Wait," he muttered.

Then someone rattled a key in the lock of their cell door, and it also clanged open. "Agachak has returned," the Grolim in the open doorway announced curtly. "You will come out of there now."

"Splendid," Sadi said with relief. "Whatever this is all about, I'm sure it can be cleared up in just a few minutes."

"No talking!" The Grolim turned abruptly and started down the corridor while a dozen of his fellows fell in behind the prisoners with drawn weapons.

Agachak, the Hierarch of Rak Urga, was a cadaverous-looking man with a long beard. He sat upon a thronelike chair in a large room lighted by glaring torches and hung with dark maroon drapes. The Hierarch's hooded robe was blood red, and his sunken eyes burned beneath their shaggy gray brows. Eriond, still in chains, sat calmly on a rough wooden stool before him, and the slim priestess, Chabat, her purple-lined hood pushed back and the red scars on her cheeks seeming to reflect the torchlight, stood at her master's elbow with a look of cruel triumph on her face.

"Which one of you is Ussa of Sthiss Tor?" the Hierarch demanded in a hollow-sounding voice.

Sadi stepped forward with an oily bow. "I am Ussa, Holy One," he said.

"You're in a great deal of trouble, Ussa," Chabat told him, her throaty voice almost purring. Her lips twisted into an ugly smirk.

"But I have done nothing."

"Here in Cthol Murgos, the master is responsible for the misdeeds of the servant."

Agachak's eyes bored into Sadi, though his bony white face remained expressionless. "Let us proceed," he commanded. "Who is to present the evidence in this matter?"

Chabat turned and gestured to a hooded Grolim standing near the wall. "Sorchak will serve as the priest-inquisitor, Master," she replied in the tone of one who feels fully in charge of a situation. "I'm sure you're aware of his zeal."

"Ah, yes," Agachak said in a noncommittal tone. "I might have guessed that it would be Sorchak." The faintest hint of sardonic amusement touched his lips. "Very well, priest-inquisitor, you may present the charges."

The black-robed Grolim stepped forward, pushing his green-lined hood back from his tangled hair. "The matter itself is simple, my Lord," he declared in his strident voice. "There were dozens of witnesses present, so there can be no question of this young villain's guilt. The implications of that guilt, however, must be pursued."

"Pronounce your sentence, Great Hierarch," Chabat urged the dead-looking man on the throne. "I will wring the whole truth from this greasy Nyissan and from his servants."

"I have heard talk of guilt, Chabat," he replied, "but I have still not heard the charges or the evidence."

Chabat looked slightly taken aback by his words. "I but thought to spare you the tedium of a formal inquiry, Master. I am convinced of the truth of Sorchak's words. You have always accepted my judgment in such matters before."

"Perhaps," Agachak said, "but I think that this time I might like to judge for myself." He looked at the greasy-haired priest standing before him. "The charges, Sorchak," he said. "Exactly what is it that the young man is accused of doing?" There was a faint note of dislike in the Hierarch's voice.

Sorchak's bulging eyes grew slightly less certain as he sensed Agachak's unspoken animosity. Then he drew himself up. "Early this evening," he began, "just as the holiest rite of our faith was about to be performed on the altar in the Sanctum, this young man entered and extinguished the altar fires. That is what he did, and it is that of which I accuse him. I swear that he is guilty."

"Absurd," Sadi protested. "Are the fires at the altar not perpetually attended? How could this boy have gotten close enough to them to put them out?"

"How *dare* you question the sworn word of a priest of Torak?" Chabat said angrily, her scarred cheeks writhing. "Sorchak has sworn to his guilt, and therefore he is guilty. To question the word of a priest is death."

Agachak's sunken eyes were veiled as he looked at her. "I think that I might like to hear the evidence that has so persuaded you and the priest-inquisitor for myself, Chabat," he said in a flat voice. "Accusation and guilt are not always the same thing, and the question raised by Ussa is quite relevant."

A faint hope surged through Garion at the Hierarch's words. Agachak *knew*. He was completely aware of Chabat's involvement with Sorchak, and the very eagerness with which she defended the rancid-smelling Grolim's every word affronted her master.

"Well, priest-inquisitor," Agachak continued, "how *did* this boy manage to put out the altar fires? Has there been some laxity in guarding them?"

Sorchak's eyes grew wary as he realized that he was on dangerous ground. "I have many witnesses, my Lord," he declared. "There is universal agreement by all who were present that the Sanctum was desecrated by means of sorcery."

"Ah, sorcery, is it? That would explain everything, of course." Agachak paused, his dreadful eyes fixed on the now-sweating Sorchak. "I have noticed, however, that the cry 'witch' or 'sorcerer' is frequently raised when there is a lack of solid evidence. Is there no other explanation for what happened in the Sanctum? Is the priest-inquisitor's case so weak that he must fall back on so tired and worn-out an accusation?"

Chabat's expression was incredulous, and Sorchak began to tremble.

"Fortunately, the matter is easily resolved," Agachak added. "The gift of sorcery has a slight drawback. Others with the same gift can clearly sense the use of the power." He paused. "You didn't know that, did you, Sorchak? A priest of the Green hoping for elevation to the Purple would have been more diligent in his studies and would have known that—but you have been otherwise occupied, haven't you?" He turned to the priestess at his side. "I am surprised, however, that you did not instruct your protegé here more completely before you let him make this kind of charge, Chabat. You might have prevented his making a fool of himself—and of you."

Her eyes blazed, and the flamelike scars on her face went livid; then suddenly they began to glow as if an inner fire were running beneath her skin.

"Well, Chabat," he said in a calm, deadly voice, "has the moment come then? Will you finally try your will against mine?"

The awful question hung in the air, and Garion found that he was holding his breath. Chabat, however, averted her eyes and turned her face away from the Hierarch, the fires in her cheeks fading.

"A wise decision, Chabat." Agachak turned to Sadi. "Well, Ussa of Sthiss Tor, how say you to the charge that your servant here is a sorcerer?"

"The priest of Torak is in error, my Lord," Sadi replied diplomatically. "Believe me, this young dunce is no sorcerer. He spends ten minutes every morning trying to decide which of his shoes goes on which foot. Look at him. There's not the faintest glimmer of intelligence in those eyes. He doesn't even have sense enough to be afraid."

Chabat's eyes grew angry again, though there was in them

now a faint hint that she was no longer so sure of herself. "What would a Nyissan slaver know of sorcery, Master?" she sneered. "You know of the habits of the snake-people. Doubtless this Ussa's mind is so fuddled with drugs that one of his servants could be Belgarath himself, and he wouldn't know it."

"A very interesting point," Agachak murmured. "Now, let us examine this matter. We know that the altar fires went out. That much is certain. Sorchak declares that this young man extinguished them by means of sorcery—though he has no proof to substantiate that charge. Ussa of Sthiss Tor, who may be drugged to the point of insensibility, maintains that the young man is a simpleton and thus totally incapable of so extraordinary an act. Now, how may we resolve this dilemma?"

"Put them to the torment, Holy One," Chabat suggested eagerly. "I myself will wring the truth from them—one by one."

Garion tensed himself and looked carefully at Belgarath. The old man stood quite calmly with his short, silvery beard gleaming in the ruddy torchlight. He gave no sign that he might be preparing for any kind of direct action.

"Your fondness for the torture chamber is well known, Chabat," Agachak was saying coldly. "Your skill is such that your victims usually say exactly what you want them to say—which is not always the absolute truth."

"I do but serve my God, Master," she declared proudly.

"We *all* serve here, my Holy Priestess," he rebuked her, "and you would be wise not to assert your own excessive piety in order to elevate yourself—or your underling for that matter." He looked at Sorchak with undisguised contempt. "I am still Hierarch here, and *I* will make the final decision in this matter."

The scar-faced priestess shrank back, her eyes suddenly fearful. "Forgive me, Agachak," she stammered. "This monstrous crime has filled me with righteous outrage, but as you say, the final decision is wholly yours."

"I find your acceptance of my authority gratifying, Chabat. I thought you might have forgotten."

Just then there was a stir at the back of the torchlit room. Two burly Murgos with long, polished halberds in their hands rudely pushed aside the Grolims clustered near the door. With their dark faces impassive, they banged the butts of their weapons on the floor in unison. "Make way!" one of them boomed. "Make way for Urgit, High King of Cthol Murgos!"

The man who sauntered into the room surrounded by guards looked like no Murgo Garion had ever seen before. He was short and had a slender but wiry build. His black hair was lank and his features narrow. His robe was carelessly open at the front, revealing the fact that, instead of the customary mail shirt, he wore a western-style doublet and hose of rich purple. His iron crown was perched somewhat rakishly on one side of his head. His expression was sardonic, but his eyes were wary. "Agachak," he greeted the Hierarch perfunctorily, "I gave some thought to the news which was brought to you at the Drojim, and I finally concluded that I might be of some use to you in sorting out the cause of this regrettable incident."

"The Temple is honored by the presence of the High King," Agachak intoned formally.

"And the High King is honored to be so kindly received by the Hierarch of Rak Urga," Urgit replied. He looked around. "Do you have a chair handy?" he asked. "I've had a long, tiring day."

"See to it," Agachak said flatly to the priestess standing beside his throne.

Chabat blinked, then a slow flush mounted her cheeks. "A chair for his Majesty," she commanded harshly, "and be quick about it."

One of the Grolims near the door scurried out and returned a moment later with a heavy chair.

"Thanks awfully," the King said, sinking into the chair. He looked at Agachak. "I have a small confession to make, Holy One," he said with an apologetic cough. "As I was about to enter your presence in this room, I lingered for a time in the hallway outside, hoping to acquaint myself with the details of this affair." He laughed shortly. "Listening at doors is an old habit of mine, I'm afraid. It comes from my anxious childhood. Anyway, I managed to hear the charges presented by the priest-inquisitor. To be perfectly candid, Agachak, he's got a very shaky case." He gave the Hierarch a quick, ingratiating look. "But of course you've already pointed that out, haven't you?"

Agachak nodded briefly, his face unreadable.

"Now," Urgit went on quickly, "I most certainly wouldn't want to interfere in what is clearly a Church matter, but wouldn't you say that there are dozens of possible natural explanations for this incident?" He looked hopefully at Agachak; then reassured by the look of agreement on the Hierarch's face, he continued. "I mean, we've all seen fires go out before, haven't we? Do we really need to go so far afield to come up with a reason for this really unremarkable occurrence? Isn't it more likely that the keepers of the Temple fires grew careless and that the fires just went out on their own—as fires starved for fuel are likely to do?"

"Absolute nonsense!" the greasy-haired Sorchak snapped.

Urgit flinched visibly, his eyes going in appeal to Agachak.

"You forget yourself, priest-inquisitor," the Hierarch said. "Our guest is the High King of Cthol Murgos; if you offend him, I may decide to give him your head by way of apology."

Sorchak swallowed hard. "Please forgive me, your Majesty," he choked. "I spoke before I thought."

"Quite all right, old boy." Urgit forgave him with a magnanimous wave of his hand. "Sometimes we all speak too quickly when we're excited." He turned back to the Hierarch. "I regret this catastrophe as much as anyone, Agachak," he said, "but this Nyissan slaver was sent here by Jaharb, and both you and I know how desperately urgent his mission is to the Church and to the State. Don't you think that as a matter of policy we could let this incident pass?"

"Surely you're not just going to let these charges drop?"

Chabat's voice was shrill as she faced the Hierarch. "Who is to be punished for the desecration of the Sanctum?"

Urgit's face grew unhappy, and he once again appealed to Agachak for support with pleading eyes. Garion clearly saw that this was not a strong king. Even the slightest resistance to his diffidently offered proposals made him instinctively retreat or seek support from someone he perceived to be stronger.

Agachak turned slowly to look the scarred priestess full in the face. "All this shouting is beginning to weary me, Chabat," he told her bluntly. "If you can't modulate your voice, you can leave."

She stared at him in stunned disbelief.

"There is far more at stake here than the fact that some fires went out," he said to her. "As was foretold ages ago, the time for the final meeting between the Child of Light and the Child of Dark is at hand. If *I* am not the one who is present at that meeting, you will find yourself bowing to either Urvon or Zandramas. I doubt that either one of them would find your antics amusing enough to make them decide to let you go on living. As for the charge of sorcery, there's an easy way to settle that once and for all." He rose from his throne, walked across to Eriond, and placed one hand on each side of his head.

Aunt Pol drew in her breath sharply, and Garion carefully began to gather in his will.

Eriond looked up into the face of the dead-looking Hierarch with a gentle smile on his face.

"Faugh!" Agachak said in disgust, pulling his hands quickly back. "This beardless boy is an innocent. There's no evidence in his mind that he has ever tasted power." He turned to look at Sorchak. "I find your charges groundless, priest-inquisitor, and I dismiss them."

Sorchak's face went white, and his eyes bulged.

"Have a care, Sorchak," the Hierarch said ominously. "If you protest my decision too strenuously, I might just decide that this whole incident was *your* fault. Chabat is sick with disappointment that she has no one to torture to death." His look grew sly as he glanced at the priestess. "Would you like to have Sorchak, my dear?" he asked her. "I have always delighted in giving you these little gifts. I'll even watch with some pleasure while you slowly pull out his entrails with red-hot hooks."

Chabat's flame-marked face was filled with chagrin. Garion saw that she had been convinced that the Hierarch, as he apparently had so many times in the past, would meekly accede to her peremptory demands, and she had staked all of her prestige on the punishment of Sadi, for whom she had developed an instantaneous dislike. Agachak's unexpected and almost contemptuous rejection of the accusations she and Sorchak had leveled struck at the very foundations of her puffed-up self-esteem, but more importantly at her position of power here in the Temple. Unless she could somehow salvage something—anything—out of this, her many enemies would inevitably pull her down. Garion fervently hoped that Sadi realized that she was even more dangerous now than she had been when she had thought she held the upper hand.

Her narrowed eyes grew cautious as she assessed the Hierarch's mood, then she drew herself up and addressed King Urgit. "There is also a civil crime here, your Majesty," she told him. "I had believed that the desecration of the Sanctum was more serious, but since our revered Hierarch has discovered in his wisdom that those charges were unfounded, it is now my duty to advise you of a crime against the State."

Urgit exchanged a quick look with Agachak, then slouched lower in his chair, his eyes unhappy. "The Crown is always ready to listen to the words of the priesthood," he replied without much enthusiasm.

Chabat gave Sadi another look of smug triumph and open hatred. "Since the founding of our nation, the vile drugs and poisons of the snake-people have been forbidden in Cthol Murgos by royal decree," she pointed out. "After this Ussa and his servants were confined in the dungeon, I had their belongings searched." She turned. "Bring in that case," she ordered.

A side door opened, and an obsequious underpriest entered, carrying Sadi's red leather case. The fanatic Sorchak took it from him, his face also gleefully triumphant. "Behold the evidence that Ussa of Sthiss Tor has violated our law and that his life is forfeit," he said in his strident voice. He undid the latch, opened the case, and displayed Sadi's many vials and the earthenware bottle where Zith resided.

Urgit's face grew even more unhappy. He looked uncertainly at Sadi. "Is there some explanation for this, Ussa?" he asked hopefully.

Sadi's face took on an exaggerated expression of innocence. "Surely your Majesty could not believe that I ever intended to try to distribute those items here in Cthol Murgos," he protested.

"Well," Urgit said lamely, "you have got them with you."

"Of course, but they're for trade with the Malloreans. There's quite a market for this sort of thing among those people."

"I wouldn't be in the least surprised," Urgit said, straightening in his chair. "Then you had no intention of peddling your drugs to my subjects?"

"Most certainly not, your Majesty," Sadi replied indignantly.

Urgit's expression grew relieved. "Well," he said to the glowering Chabat, "there you have it, then. Certainly none of us could object to the fact that our Nyissan friend here is bent on corrupting the Malloreans—the more the better, I'd say."

"What about this?" Sorchak said, putting Sadi's case on the floor and lifting out the earthenware bottle. "What secret is hidden in here, Ussa of Sthiss Tor?" He shook the bottle.

"Be careful, man!" Sadi exclaimed, leaping forward with his hand outstretched.

"Ah-ha!" Chabat exclaimed triumphantly. "It appears that there is something in that bottle that the slaver considers important. Let us examine the contents. It may yet be that some undiscovered crime lurks here. Open the bottle, Sorchak."

"I beg of you," Sadi pleaded. "If you value your life, do not tamper with that bottle.'"

"Open it, Sorchak," Chabat ordered relentlessly.

The smirking Grolim shook the bottle again and then began to work out the stopper.

"Please, noble Priest!" Sadi's voice was anguished.

"We'll just have a look." Sorchak grinned. "I'm sure that one look won't hurt anything." He drew out the cork and raised the bottle to his eye to peer in.

Zith, of course, took immediate action.

With a strangled shriek, Sorchak arched backward, flinging both arms into the air. The earthenware bottle sailed upward, and Sadi caught it just before it struck the floor. The stricken priest clapped both hands over his eye. There was a look of horror on his face, and blood spurted out from between his fingers. He began to squeal like a pig, all of his limbs convulsing. He suddenly pitched forward, threshing wildly and clawing tatters of skin from his face. He began to bang his head on the floor. His convulsions grew more violent and he began to froth at the mouth. With a shrill shriek, he suddenly leaped high into the air. When he came down, he was dead.

There was a moment of stunned silence, then Chabat suddenly shrieked, "Sorchak!" Her voice was filled with anguish and insupportable loss. She flew to the side of the dead man and fell across his body, sobbing uncontrollably.

Urgit stared in open-mouthed revulsion at Sorchak's corpse. "Torak's teeth!" he swore in a strangled whisper, "what have you got in that bottle, Ussa?"

"Uh—it's a pet, your Majesty," Sadi replied nervously. "I did try to warn him."

"Indeed you did, Ussa," Agachak crooned. "We all heard you. Do you suppose I might see this pet of yours?" A cruel smile crossed his face as he looked gloatingly at the hysterically sobbing Chabat.

"Certainly, Holy One," Sadi answered quickly. He carefully laid the bottle on the floor. "Just a precaution," he apologized. "She's a little excited, and I wouldn't want her to make any mistakes." He leaned over the bottle. "It's all right now, dear," he said soothingly to the vengeful little reptile lurking inside. "The bad man has gone away, and everything is fine now."

Zith sulked in her bottle, still greatly offended.

"Really, dear," Sadi assured her, "it's all right. Don't you trust me?"

There was a snippy little hiss from inside the bottle.

"That's a very naughty thing to say, Zith," Sadi gently reproved her. "I did everything I could to keep him from disturbing you." He looked apologetically at Agachak. "I really don't know where she picks up such language, Holy One," he declared. He turned his attention back to the bottle. "Please, dear, don't be nasty."

Another spiteful little hiss came from the bottle.

"Now that's going entirely too far, Zith. You come out of there at once."

Cautiously the little green snake poked her head out of the bottle, raised herself and looked at the corpse on the floor. Sorchak's face was a ghastly blue color, and the foam was drying on his lips. Chabat, still weeping hysterically, clung to his stiffening body. Zith slithered the rest of the way out of her little house, dismissed the dead man with a contemptuous flick of her tail, and crawled to Sadi, purring with a smug little sound of self-satisfaction. Sadi reached down his hand to her, and she nuzzled affectionately at his fingers. "Isn't she adorable?" he said fondly. "She's always so kittenish after she bites someone."

A slight movement caught Garion's eye. Velvet was leaning forward, looking at the contentedly purring little reptile with an expression of wholly absorbed fascination.

"You've got her under control, haven't you, Ussa?" Urgit asked in a faintly apprehensive voice.

"Oh, yes, your Majesty," Sadi assured him. "She's perfectly content now. In a little bit, I'll give her a light snack and a nice little bath, and she'll sleep like a baby."

Urgit turned back to the Hierarch. "Well, Agachak?" he said, "what's your decision? Personally, I see no reason to continue this investigation. The slaver and his servants appear to be quite blameless."

The Hierarch considered it, his eyes hooded. "I believe you're right, your Majesty." He turned to one of his Grolims. "Free this idiot boy," he said, pointing at Eriond.

Chabat, her scarred face ravaged by grief, slowly raised herself from Sorchak's body. She looked first at Urgit and then at Agachak. "And what of this?" she demanded in a voice vibrant with her emotion. "What of this?" She indicated the stiffening Sorchak at her feet. "Who is to be punished for this? Upon whom shall I wreak my vengeance?"

"The man died through his own act, Chabat," Agachak dismissed her demand. "There was no crime involved."

"No crime?" Her voice was choked. "No crime?" It rose in a crescendo. "Are Grolim lives so cheap that you will now throw them away?" She spun and fixed Sadi with her burning eyes. "You will pay for this, Ussa of Sthiss Tor," she declared. "I swear it upon the body of Sorchak and upon that of Torak. You will never escape me. I will have revenge upon you and all your servants for the death of Sorchak."

"Why are you so upset, Chabat?" Agachak asked with malicious amusement in his hollow voice. "There are scores of Grolims in the Temple. Sorchak was one like all the rest—greedy, ambitious, and deceitful. His death was the result of his own folly—and of yours." A cruel smile touched his thin lips. "Could it be that your interest in this dead Grolim was personal? You have long been my favorite, Chabat. I trusted you entirely. Is it possible that you have been unfaithful to me, seeking entertainment in the arms of another?"

Her face blanched, and she lifted one trembling hand to her lips as she realized that she had gone too far and revealed too much.

Agachak laughed, a chilling sound. "Did you actually believe that I was so engrossed in my search for the Sardion that I was not aware of your private amusements?" He paused. "Tell me, Chabat," he said in an offhand way, "did you and Sorchak ever succeed in raising a demon?"

She drew back, her eyes wide with sudden terror as she faced her master.

"I thought not," he murmured. "What a shame. All that effort wasted. Perhaps you need a new partner in your midnight rites, Chabat. Sorchak's heart was never really in your attempts anyway. He was nothing more than a cheap opportunist, so your loss is not as great as you might think. Do you know what he called you in private?" he asked her, his eyes alight.

She shook her head numbly.

"I have it on the very best authority that he customarily referred to you as 'that scar-faced hag.' Does that in any way mollify your grief?"

Chabat recoiled from him, her face suffused with mortification as she realized that she had just been cruelly humiliated in public. She whirled in rage and kicked the dead man in his unfeeling side. "Scar-faced hag?" she shrieked, kicking the body again. "Scar-faced hag? Rot, Sorchak! And may the worms enjoy your stinking carcass!" Then she spun and fled, sobbing, from the room.

"She seems a trifle distraught," Urgit observed mildly.

Agachak shrugged. "The shattering of illusions is always painful."

Urgit pulled absently at his pointed nose. "Her distraction, however, raises certain risks here, Agachak," he said thoughtfully. "The mission of this slaver is vital to both of us, and an hysterical woman—particularly one with the kind of power Chabat possesses—can be very dangerous. She obviously bears Ussa here a certain enmity, and since he was involved in both her humiliation and the death of Sorchak, I'd say that right now the Temple might not be the safest place in the world for him."

Agachak nodded gravely. "Your Majesty's point is well taken."

Urgit's face brightened as if an idea had just occurred to him. "Agachak," he said, "what would you say to the notion of my keeping Ussa and his servants at the Drojim until we can see him safely on his way? That would put him beyond Chabat's reach in the event that her distraction impels her into any kind of rashness." He paused nervously. "It's entirely up to you, Holy Agachak," he added quickly.

"There is much to what you say, Urgit," Agachak replied. "A small slip here could put you at the mercy of Kal Zakath and me on my knees before either Urvon or Zandramas. Let us by all means avoid those disasters." He turned to Sadi. "You and your servants will accompany his Majesty to the Drojim Palace, Ussa. I'll have your belongings sent along later. You'll be safe there, and your ship will ready in a few days." He smiled ironically. "I hope you appreciate our tender concern for your well-being."

Sadi bowed. "I am overwhelmed with gratitude, Holy One," he said.

"I'll keep the Dagashi Kabach here in the Temple, however," Agachak said to the King. "That way each of us will have in his hands a vital element in the mission to Rak Hagga. It should encourage us to co-operate."

"Of course," Urgit agreed hastily, "I quite understand." He rose to his feet. "The hour grows late," he noted. "I'll return to the Drojim now and leave you to your many religious duties, Dread Hierarch."

"Give my regards to the Lady Tamazin, your noble mother," Agachak responded.

"I will, Agachak. I know that she'll be smothered with joy to know that you remembered her. Come along then, Ussa." He turned and started toward the door.

"May the spirit of Torak go with you, your Majesty," Agachak called after him.

"I certainly *hope* not," Urgit muttered to Sadi as they passed through the doorway.

"Your Majesty's arrival came at a critical moment," Sadi said quietly as the two of them led the way down the hall. "Things were getting a bit tense."

"Don't flatter yourself," Urgit said sourly. "If it weren't for the absolute necessity of getting Kabach to Rak Hagga, I'd never have risked a confrontation with the Grolims. I'm sure you're a nice enough fellow, but I have my own skin to consider."

When they were outside the nail-studded doors of the Temple, the Murgo King straightened and drew in a deep breath of the cool night air. "I'm always glad to get out of that stinking place," he declared. He motioned to one of his guards. "Go get the horses," he commanded.

"At once, your Majesty."

Then Urgit turned back to the shaven-headed Nyissan. "All right, you sly fox," he said in an amused tone, "now perhaps you'd like to tell me what you're doing down here in Cthol Murgos—and why you've assumed this pose. I almost fainted dead away when I discovered that the mysterious Ussa of Sthiss Tor was none other than my old friend Sadi, Chief Eunuch in the palace of Queen Salmissra."

CHAPTER THIRTEEN

They clattered through the deserted midnight streets of Rak Urga with the king's torch-bearing guards drawn up closely around them. "It's all a sham, of course," Urgit was saying to Sadi. "I bow and scrape to Agachak, mouth pious platitudes to make him happy, and keep my real opinions to myself. I need his support, so I have to stay on the good side of him. He knows that, so he takes every possible advantage of the situation."

"The bond between Church and State here in Cthol Murgos is well known," Sadi noted as they entered a broad square where flaring torches painted the sides of nearby buildings a smoky orange.

Urgit made an indelicate sound. "Bond!" he snorted,

"More like a chain, Sadi—and it's around *my* neck." He looked up at the murky sky, his sharp-featured face ruddy in the torchlight. "Agachak and I agree on one thing, though. It's absolutely essential to get the Dagashi Kabach to Rak Hagga before winter sets in. Jaharb's had his people combing all of western Cthol Murgos for months looking for a slaver to slip Kabach through Mallorean lines." He suddenly grinned at Sadi. "As luck had it, the one he found just happened to be an old friend of mine. I don't know that we need to let Agachak know that we're acquainted, though. I like to keep a few secrets from him."

Sadi made a sour face. "It's not too hard to guess why you're sending an assassin to the city where Kal Zakath's headquarters are located."

"I wouldn't advise lingering for any sight-seeing after you get him there," Urgit agreed. "But then, Rak Hagga's not a very attractive town anyway."

Sadi nodded glumly. "That's more or less what I thought." He considered it, running one long-fingered hand over his shaven scalp. "The death of Zakath won't really solve your problem, though, will it? I can't really see the Mallorean generals packing up and going home just because their emperor's been killed."

Urgit sighed. "One thing at a time, Sadi. I can probably bribe the generals, or pay them tribute or something. The first step is to get rid of Zakath. You can't reason with that man." He looked around at the bleak stone buildings, harshly illuminated by flickering torchlight. "I hate this place," he said suddenly. "I absolutely hate it."

"Rak Urga?"

"Cthol Murgos, Sadi. I hate the whole stinking country. Why couldn't I have been born in Tolnedra—or maybe Sendaria? Why did I have to get stuck in Cthol Murgos?"

"But you're the king."

"That wasn't by choice. One of our charming customs is that when a new king is crowned, all other possible contenders for the throne are put to death. For me, it was either the throne or the grave. I had a number of brothers when I became king, but now I'm an only child." He shuddered. "This is a gloomy subject, don't you think? Why don't we talk about something else? Just what are you doing in Cthol Murgos, Sadi? I thought you were Salmissra's right hand."

Sadi coughed. "Her Majesty and I had a slight misunderstanding, so I thought it might be better for me to leave Nyissa for a while."

"Why Cthol Murgos? Why didn't you go to Tol Honeth instead? It's much more civilized and much, much more comfortable." He sighed again. "I'd give anything to be able to live in Tol Honeth."

"I've made some powerful enemies in Tolnedra, your Majesty," Sadi replied. "I know my way around Cthol Murgos, so I hired these Alorn mercenaries to protect me and came here posing as a slaver."

"And then Jaharb picked you up," Urgit guessed. "Poor old Sadi, no matter where you go, you always seem to get mixed up in politics—even when you don't want to."

"It's a curse," Sadi told him mournfully. "It's been following me for all my life."

They rounded a corner and approached a vast, sprawling building surrounded by a high wall. Its domes and towers rose in barbaric, torchlit profusion, and, unlike the rest of Rak Urga, it was garishly painted in a half-dozen conflicting colors. "Behold the Drojim Palace," King Urgit said extravagantly to Sadi, "the hereditary home of the House of Urga."

"A most unusual structure, your Majesty," Sadi murmured.

"That's a diplomatic way to put it." Urgit looked critically at his palace. "It's gaudy, ugly, and in terribly bad taste. It does, however, suit my personality almost perfectly." He turned to one of his guards. "Be a good fellow and ride on ahead," he instructed. "Tell the gatekeepers that the High King approaches and that if I have to wait while they open the gate for me, I'll have their ears cut off."

"At once, your Majesty."

Urgit grinned at Sadi. "One of my few amusements," he

explained. "The only people I'm allowed to bully are servants and common soldiers, and all Murgos have a deep-seated need to bully somebody."

They rode on through the hastily opened gate and dismounted in a ruddily torchlit courtyard. Urgit looked around at the garishly painted walls of the house. "Ghastly, isn't it?" He shuddered. "Let's go inside."

There was a large door at the top of a flight of stone stairs, and Urgit led them inside and down a long, vaulted corridor. He stopped before a pair of polished double doors guarded by two scar-faced soldiers. "Well?" he said to them.

"Yes, your Majesty?" one replied.

"Do you suppose that I could prevail upon you to open the door?" Urgit asked him. "Or would you prefer an immediate transfer to the war zone?"

"At once, your Majesty," the soldier replied, quickly yanking the door open.

"Excellently done, my dear fellow. Just try not to jerk it off its hinges next time." The king strolled through the door and into the room beyond. "My throne room," he said grandiosely. "The product of whole generations of diseased imaginations."

The room was larger than the Hall of the Rivan King in Garion's Citadel. The ceiling was a maze of intersecting vaults, all covered with sheets of the beaten red gold from the mines of Cthol Murgos. The walls and columns were ablaze with inset jewels, and the chairs lined up at the sides of the room were inlaid with more Angarak gold. At the far end of the room stood a bejeweled throne, backed by blood-red drapes. Seated in a simple chair beside that throne was a silver-haired lady, calmly embroidering.

"Hideous, isn't it?" Urgit said. "The Urgas have been pillaging the treasury at Rak Goska for centuries to decorate the Drojim Palace, but would you believe that the roof still leaks?" He sauntered to the far end of the room and stopped before the black-gowned lady, who was still busy at her needlework.

"Mother," he greeted her with a slightly mocking bow, "you're up late, aren't you?"

"I don't need as much sleep as I did when I was younger, Urgit." She set her sewing aside. "Besides," she added, "we usually talk over the day's events before you retire for the night."

"It's the high point of my day, mother," he replied with a faint smile tugging at his lips.

She returned his smile with good-humored affection. She was, Garion saw as that smile lighted her face, a remarkably attractive woman. Despite the silvery hair and the few lines at the corners of her eyes, her face still bore the signs of what had once been an extraordinary beauty. A faint movement caught his eye, and he saw Silk shrinking behind Toth's broad back and drawing up the hood of his green robe to conceal his face.

"Who are your friends, Urgit?" the silver-haired lady asked her son.

"Ah, forgive me, mother. My manners must be slipping. Allow me to present Sadi, Chief Eunuch to Queen Salmissra of the land of the snake-people."

"*Formerly* Chief Eunuch, I'm afraid," Sadi corrected. He bowed deeply. "I'm honored to meet the Queen Mother of the Kingdom of the Murgos."

"Oh," Urgit said, mounting the dais and sprawling on the throne with one leg cocked up over one of its jeweled arms, "I keep forgetting the amenities. Sadi, this is my royal mother, the Lady Tamazin, jewel of the House of Hagga and grieving widow of my royal father, Taur Urgas the Deranged—may blessings rain down on the hand that sent him to the bosom of Torak."

"Can't you ever be serious about anything, Urgit?" his mother chided him.

"But you *do* grieve, don't you mother? I know that in your heart you miss all those wonderful moments you spent with my father—watching him gnaw on the furniture, listening to his insane gibbering, and enjoying all those playful blows to the stomach and kicks to the head with which he demonstrated his affection for his wives."

"That will do, Urgit," she said firmly.

"Yes, mother."

"Welcome to the Drojim, Sadi," Lady Tamazin greeted the eunuch formally. She looked inquiringly at the others.

"My servants, Lady Tamazin," Sadi said quickly. "Alorns for the most part."

"A most unusual turn of circumstances," she murmured. "The age-old war between Murgo and Alorn has denied me the opportunity to meet very many of that race." She looked directly then at Aunt Pol. "Surely this lady is no servant," she said sceptically.

"A temporary arrangement, my Lady Tamazin," Polgara replied with a profoundly graceful curtsy. "I needed some time in another place to avoid some unpleasantness at home."

The Queen Mother smiled. "I do understand," she said. "Men play at politics, and women must pay the price for their folly." She turned back to her son. "And how did your interview with the Hierarch go?" she asked him.

"Not bad." He shrugged. "I groveled enough to keep him happy."

"That's enough, Urgit." Her voice was sharp. "Agachak's in a position to do you a great service, so show him the proper respect."

Urgit flinched slightly at her tone. "Yes, mother," he replied meekly. "Oh, I almost forgot," he went on. "The priestess Chabat had a bit of a setback."

The Queen Mother's expression became one of disgust. "Her behavior is a public scandal," she declared. "I can't understand why Agachak tolerates her."

"I think he finds her amusing, mother. Grolims have a peculiar sense of humor. Anyway, she had this friend—a very *close* friend—who had a bit of an accident. She'll need to find another playmate before she can scandalize the good people of Rak Urga any more."

"Why do you persist in being so frivolous, Urgit?"

"Why don't we just call it a symptom of my incipient madness?"

"You're not going to go mad," she said firmly.

"Of course I'm going to go mad, mother. I'm rather looking forward to it."

"You're impossible to talk with when you're like this," she chided him. "Are you going to stay up much longer?"

"I don't think so. Sadi and I have a few things to discuss, but they can wait until tomorrow."

The Queen Mother turned back to Polgara. "My quarters are most spacious, Lady," she said. "Would you and your attendants care to share them with me during your stay here in the Drojim?"

"We would be honored, my Lady," Polgara said.

"Very well, then," Urgit's mother said. "Prala," she called.

The girl who stepped from the shadows behind the throne was slender and perhaps sixteen years old. She wore a black gown and had long, lustrous black hair. The dark, angular eyes that made most Murgo men look so alien were in her case very large and delicately almond-shaped, giving her features an exotic beauty. Her expression, however, was filled with a resolve uncommon in one so young. She stepped to Lady Tamazin's chair and helped her to her feet.

Urgit's face darkened, and his eyes grew flinty as he watched his mother limp down from the dais, leaning heavily on the girl's shoulder. "A little gift from the inestimable Taur Urgas," he said to Sadi. "One evening when he was feeling playful, he knocked my mother down a flight of stairs and broke her hip. She's had that limp ever since."

"I don't even notice it any more, Urgit."

"It's amazing how all of our minor aches and pains got better right after King Cho-Hag's saber slid through my father's guts." Urgit paused. "I wonder if it's too late to send Cho-Hag some small token of appreciation," he added.

"Oh," the Queen Mother said to Polgara, "this is Lady Prala, a princess of the House of Cthan."

"Princess," Polgara greeted the slender girl supporting Lady Tamazin.

"My Lady," Prala responded in a clear voice.

Lady Tamazin, leaning on Prala's shoulder, slowly limped from the room with Polgara, Ce'Nedra, and Velvet close behind her.

"That girl makes me very nervous for some reason," Urgit muttered to Sadi. "My mother dotes on her, but she has something else on her mind. She never takes her eyes off me." He shook his head as if to dismiss an unwelcome thought. "You and your people have had a very busy day, Sadi. We can talk further tomorrow after we've both had a good night's sleep." He reached out and tugged at a silken bellpull, and there was the heavy note of a large gong somewhere outside the throne room. Urgit rolled his eyes toward the ceiling. "Why does it always have to be those great bongs and clangs?" he complained. "Someday, I'd like to tug on a bellpull and hear a tiny little tinkle."

The door at the far end of the throne room opened, and a heavy-shouldered Murgo of late middle age entered. His hair was gray, and his scarred face was heavily lined. There was no hint that a smile had ever touched that grim face. "Your Majesty rang?" he said in a rasping voice.

"Yes, Oskatat," Urgit replied in an oddly respectful tone. "Do you suppose that you could escort my good friend Sadi and his servants to suitable quarters?" He turned back to Sadi. "Oskatat is Lord High Seneschal here," he said. "He served my father in the same capacity at Rak Goska." There was no hint of his usual mockery as he spoke. "My mother and I were not popular in my father's house, and Oskatat was the closest thing to a friend either of us had there."

"My Lord," Sadi said to the big, gray-haired man with a deep bow.

The seneschal nodded a curt response, then returned his bleak gaze to the king. "Has my Lady Tamazin retired for the night?" he asked.

"Yes, Oskatat."

"Then you should also seek your bed. The hour is late."

"I was just on my way," Urgit answered, getting quickly to his feet. Then he stopped. "Oskatat," he said plaintively, "I'm not a sickly little boy any more. I don't really need to spend twelve hours in bed every night the way I used to."

"The burdens of the crown are many," the seneschal said shortly. "You need your rest." He turned back to Sadi. "Follow me," he said, starting toward the door.

"Until tomorrow then, Sadi," Urgit said. "Sleep well."

"My thanks, your Majesty."

The rooms to which the bleak-faced Oskatat took them were as garish as the rest of the Drojim Palace. The walls were painted an unwholesome mustard yellow and hung with splotchy tapestries. The furnishings were carved from rare, priceless woods, and the blue Mallorean carpet was a deep as the wool on the back of a sheep. Once he had opened the door for them, Oskatat jerked his head in the briefest of nods, then turned and left them alone.

"Charming fellow there," Sadi murmured.

Garion had been looking curiously at Silk, who still had his face covered by his hood. "Why are you trying so hard to hide?" he asked.

The little man pulled back his hood with a rueful expression. "One of the disadvantages of being a world traveler is that one keeps running into old friends."

"I'm not sure I follow you."

"Do you remember that time when we were on our way to Rak Cthol and Taur Urgas caught me and stuck me in that pit?"

"Yes."

"And do you remember why he did that—and why he planned to peel off my skin inch by inch the next day?"

"You said that you'd been in Rak Goska once and accidentally killed his eldest son."

"Right. You have an excellent memory, Garion. Well, as it happened, I'd been engaged in some negotiations with Taur Urgas himself before that unfortunate incident. I visited the palace in Rak Goska frequently and met the Lady Tamazin several times. She's almost certain to remember me—particularly in view of the fact that she said that she knew my father."

"That could cause some problems," Belgarath said.

"Not if I avoid her." Silk shrugged. "Murgo women seldom socialize with men—particularly with strangers—so I don't imagine we'll be bumping into each other very often in the next few days. Oskatat could be a different matter, though. I also met him while I was there."

"I think that, if it's at all possible, you ought to stay here in our rooms," the old man suggested. "It might even keep you out of trouble for a change."

"Why, Belgarath," Silk said mildly, "what a thing to say."

"Has King Urgit always been like this?" Durnik asked Sadi. "He seems awfully—well—humorous, I guess the word is. I didn't think that Murgos even knew how to smile."

"He's a very complex fellow," Sadi replied.

"Have you known him long?"

"He frequently visited Sthiss Tor when he was younger—usually on missions for his father. I think he jumped at any excuse to get out of Rak Goska. He and Salmissra got on rather well together. Of course, that was before Lady Polgara changed her into a snake." The eunuch rubbed his hand absently over his scalp. "He's not a very strong king," he noted. "His childhood in the palace of Taur Urgas made him timid, and he backs away from any sort of confrontation. He's a survivor, though. He's spent his entire life just trying to stay alive, and that tends to make a man very alert."

"You'll be talking with him again tomorrow," Belgarath said. "See if you can get him to give you some definite information about this ship they plan to give us. I want to get to the Isle of Verkat before the onset of winter, and various people in our party have been doing things that might attract attention, if we have to stay here too long." He gave Eriond a reproving look.

"It wasn't really my fault, Belgarath," the young man protested mildly. "I didn't like the fires in the Sanctum, that's all."

"Try to keep a grip on your prejudices, Eriond," the old man said in a faintly sarcastic voice. "Let's not get sidetracked on these moral crusades just now."

"I'll try, Belgarath."

"I'd appreciate it."

The next morning, the seneschal, Oskatat, summoned them all to another audience with the Murgo King in a brightly candlelit chamber that was smaller and less garish than the vast throne room. Garion noticed that Silk remained carefully hooded until the gray-haired functionary had left the room. Urgit and Sadi spoke quietly together while the rest of them sat unobtrusively in the chairs lining the wall.

"It was probably the first hint that anyone really had that my father's brains were starting to come off their hinges," the Murgo King was saying. He was dressed again in his purple doublet and hose and was sprawled in a chair with his feet thrust out in front of him. "He was suddenly seized with the wild ambition to make himself Overking of Angarak. Personally, I think that Ctuchik planted the notion in his head as a means of irritating Urvon. Anyway," he continued, twisting the heavy gold ring on one of his fingers, "it took the combined efforts of all his generals to convince my manic father that Zakath's army was about five times the size of ours and that Zakath could squash him like a bug any time he chose. Once that notion had finally seeped into his head, he went absolutely wild."

"Oh?" Sadi said.

Urgit grinned. "Threw himself on the floor and started chewing on the carpet. After he calmed down, he decided to try subversion instead. He inundated Mallorea with Murgo agents—and Murgos are probably the clumsiest spies in the world. To keep it short—Zakath was about nineteen at the time and desperately in love with a Melcene girl. Her family was deeply in debt, so my father's agents bought up all their obligations and started putting pressure on them. The brilliant plan that emerged from my father's diseased wits was that the girl should encourage the love-struck young Zakath, marry him, and then slip a knife between the imperial ribs at her earliest opportunity. One of the Melcenes these highly intelligent Murgo spies had bought to help them in their scheme ran to Zakath with the whole sordid story, and the girl and her entire family were immediately put to death."

"What a tragic story," Sadi murmured.

"You haven't heard the best part yet. Several of the Murgo spies were persuaded to reveal the whole story—Malloreans tend to be very good persuaders—and Zakath discovered to his horror that the girl had known absolutely nothing about my father's plan. He locked himself in his room in the palace at Mal Zeth for an entire month. When he went in, he was a pleasant, open young man who showed much promise of becoming one of Mallorea's greatest emperors. When he came out, he was the cold-blooded monster we all know and love. He rounded up every Murgo in Mallorea—including a fair number of my father's relatives—and he used to amuse himself by sending bits and pieces of them in ornate containers to Rak Goska, accompanied by highly insulting notes."

"But didn't the two of them join forces at the battle of Thull Mardu?'

Urgit laughed. "That may be the popular perception, Sadi, but in point of fact, the Imperial Princess Ce'Nedra's army was just unlucky enough to get between two opposing Angarak monarchs. They didn't care a thing about her or about that dungheap people call Mishrak ac Thull. All they were trying to do was kill each other. Then my addled father made the mistake of challenging King Cho-Hag of Algaria to single combat, and Cho-Hag gave him a *very* pointed lesson in swordsmanship." He looked thoughtfully into the fire. "I still think I ought to send Cho-Hag some token of appreciation," he mused.

"Excuse me, your Majesty." Sadi frowned. "But I don't altogether understand. Kal Zakath's quarrel was with your father, and Taur Urgas is dead."

"Oh yes, quite dead," Urgit agreed. "I cut his throat before I buried him—just to make sure. I think that Zakath's problem stems from the fact that he didn't get the chance to kill my father personally. Failing that, I guess he's willing to settle for me." He rose and began to pace moodily up and down. "I've sent him a dozen peace overtures, but all he does is send me back the heads of my emissaries. I think he's as crazy as my father was." He stopped his restless pacing. "You know, maybe I was a bit hasty on my way to the throne. I had a dozen brothers—all of the blood of Taur Urgas. If I'd kept a few of them alive, I might have been able to give them to Zakath. Perhaps, if he had drunk enough Urga blood, it might have made him lose his taste for it."

The door opened and a bulky Murgo with an ornate gold chain about his neck entered the room. "I need your signature on this," he said rudely to Urgit, thrusting a sheet of parchment at him.

"What is it, General Kradak?" Urgit asked meekly.

The officer's face darkened.

"All right," Urgit said in a mollifying tone, "don't get yourself excited." He took the parchment to a nearby table where a quill pen lay beside a silver ink-pot. He dipped the pen, scribbled his name on the bottom of the sheet, and handed it back.

'Thank you, your Majesty," General Kradak said in a flat voice. Then he turned on his heel and left the room.

"One of my father's generals," Urgit told Sadi sourly. "They all treat me like that." He began to pace up and down again, scuffing his feet at the carpet. "How much do you know about King Belgarion, Sadi?" he asked suddenly.

The eunuch shrugged. "Well, I've met him once or twice."

"Didn't you say that most of your servants are Alorns?"

"Alorn mercenaries, yes. They're dependable and very good to have around if a fight breaks out."

The Murgo King turned to Belgarath, who sat dozing in a

chair. "You—old man," he said abruptly. "Have you ever met Belgarion of Riva?"

"Several times," Belgarath admitted calmly.

"What kind of man is he?"

"Sincere," Belgarath replied. "He tries very hard to be a good king."

"Just how powerful is he?"

"Well, he has the whole Alorn Alliance to back him up, and technically he's the Overlord of the West—although the Tolnedrans are likely to go their own way, and the Arends would rather fight each other."

"That's not what I meant. How good a sorcerer is he?"

"Why ask me, your Majesty? Do I look like the kind of man who'd know very much about that sort of thing? He managed to kill Torak, though, and I'd imagine that took a bit of doing."

"How about Belgarath? Is there really such a person, or is he just a myth?"

"No, Belgarath is a real person."

"And he's seven thousand years old?"

"Seven thousand or so." Belgarath shrugged. "Give or take a few centuries."

"And his daughter Polgara?"

"She's also a real person."

"And she's thousands of years old?"

"Something like that. I could probably figure it out if I needed to, but a gentleman doesn't ask questions about a lady's age."

Urgit laughed—a short, ugly, barking sound. "The words 'gentleman' and 'Murgo' are mutually exclusive, my friend," he said. "Do you think Belgarion would receive my emissaries, if I sent them to Riva?"

"He's out of the country just now," Belgarath told him blandly.

"I hadn't heard that."

"He does it from time to time. Every so often he gets bored with all the ceremonies and goes away."

"How does he manage that? How can he just pick up and leave?"

"Who's going to argue with him?"

Urgit began to gnaw worriedly on one fingernail. "Even if the Dagashi Kabach succeeds in killing Zakath, I'm still going to have a Mallorean army on my doorstep. I'm going to need an ally if I'm ever going to get rid of them." He began to pace up and down again. "Besides," he added, "if I can reach an agreement with Belgarion, maybe I'll be able to get Agachak's fist off my throat. Do you think he'd listen to a proposal from me?"

"You could ask him and find out, I suppose."

The door opened again and the Queen Mother, assisted by the girl Prala, entered.

"Good morning, mother," Urgit greeted her. "Why are you out roaming the halls of this madhouse?"

"Urgit," she said firmly, "you'd be much more admirable if you stopped trying to make a joke out of everything."

"It keeps me from brooding about my circumstances," he told her flippantly. "I'm losing a war, half of my subjects want to depose me and send my head to Zakath on a plate, I'll be going mad soon, and I think I'm developing a boil on my neck. There are only a few things left for me to laugh about, mother, so please let me enjoy a joke or two while I still can."

"Why do you keep insisting that you're going to go mad?"

"Every male in the Urga family for the past five hundred years has gone mad before he reached fifty," he reminded her. "It's one of the reasons we make such good kings. Nobody in his right mind would want the throne of Cthol Murgos. Was there anything special you wanted, mother? Or did you just want to enjoy my fascinating companionship?"

She looked around the room. "Which of you gentlemen is married to that little red-haired girl?" she asked.

Garion looked up quickly. "Is she all right, my Lady?"

"Pol, the lady with the white lock at her brow, said that you should come at once. The young woman seems to be in some distress."

Garion stood up to follow as the Queen Mother started slowly back toward the door. Just before she reached it, she stopped and glanced at Silk, who had pulled up his hood as soon as she had entered. "Why don't you accompany your friend?" she suggested, "Just for the sake of appearances?"

They went out of the room and on down one of the garish halls of the Drojim to a dark-paneled door guarded by a pair of mail-shirted men-at-arms. One of them opened the door with a respectful bow to Lady Tamazin, and she led them inside. Her quarters were decorated much more tastefully than the rest of the Drojim. The walls were white, and the decor much more subdued. Aunt Pol sat on a low divan, holding the weeping Ce'Nedra in her arms with Velvet standing nearby.

—*Is she all right?*—Garion's fingers asked quickly.

—*I don't think it's too serious*—Polgara's hands replied. —*A bout of nerves most likely, but I don't want any of these fits of depression to go on for too long. She still hasn't fully recovered from her melancholia. See if you can comfort her.*—

Garion went to the divan and enclosed Ce'Nedra gently in his arms. She clung to him, still weeping.

"Is the young lady subject to these crying-spells, Pol?" the Queen Mother asked as the two of them took chairs on opposite sides of the cheery fire that danced on the grate.

"Not all that frequently, Tamazin," Polgara answered. "There's been a recent tragedy in her family, though, and sometimes her nerves get the best of her."

"Ah," Urgit's mother said. "Could I offer you a cup of tea, Pol? I always find tea in the morning so comforting."

"Why, thank you, Tamazin. I think that would be very nice."

Gradually, Ce'Nedra's weeping subsided, though she still clung tightly to Garion. At last she raised her head and wiped at her eyes with her fingertips. "I'm so very sorry," she apologized. "I don't know what came over me."

"It's all right, dear," Garion murmured, his arms still about her shoulders.

She dabbed at her eyes again, using a wispy little handkerchief. "I must look absolutely terrible," she said with a teary little laugh.

"Moderately terrible, yes," he agreed, smiling.

"I told you once, dear, that you should never cry in public," Polgara said to her. "You just don't have the right coloring for it."

Ce'Nedra smiled tremulously and stood up. "Perhaps I should go wash my face," she said. "And then I think I'd like to lie down for a bit." She turned to Garion. "Thank you for coming," she said simply.

"Any time you need me," he replied.

"Why don't you go with the lady, Prala?" Lady Tamazin suggested.

"Of course," the slender Murgo Princess agreed, coming quickly to her feet.

Silk had been standing nervously near the door with the hood of his green robe pulled up and his head down to keep his face concealed.

"Oh, *do* stop that, Prince Kheldar," the Queen Mother told him after Ce'Nedra and Prala had left the room. "I recognized you last night, so it's no good your trying to hide your face."

He sighed and pushed his hood back. "I was afraid you might have," he said.

"That hood doesn't hide your most salient feature anyway," she told him.

"And which feature was that, my Lady?"

"Your nose, Kheldar, that long, sharp, pointed nose that precedes you wherever you go."

"But it's such a noble nose, my Lady," Velvet said with a dimpled smile. "He wouldn't be nearly the man he is without it."

"Do you mind?" Silk asked her.

"You do get around, don't you, Prince Kheldar?" Lady Tamazin said to him. "How long has it been since you left Rak Goska with half of the Murgo army hot on your heels?"

"Fifteen or twenty years, my Lady," he replied, coming closer to the fire.

"I was sorry to hear that you'd left," she said. "You're not a very prepossessing-looking fellow, but your conversation was most entertaining, and there was very little in the way of entertainment in the house of Taur Urgas."

"You don't plan to make a general announcement about my identity then, I take it?" he said carefully.

"It's not my concern, Kheldar." She shrugged. "Murgo women do not involve themselves in the affairs of men. Over the centuries, we've found that it's safer that way."

"You're not upset, then, my Lady?" Garion asked her. "What I mean is, I'd heard that Prince Kheldar here accidentally killed the eldest son of Taur Urgas. Didn't that offend you just a little?"

"It had nothing to do with me," she replied. "The one Kheldar killed was the child of Taur Urgas' first wife—an insufferable, toothless hag of the House of Gorut who used to gloat over the fact that she had given birth to the heir apparent and that, as soon as he ascended the throne, she was going to have the rest of us strangled."

"I'm relieved to hear that you had no particular fondness for the young man," Silk told her.

"Fondness? He was a monster—just like his father. When he was just a little boy, he used to amuse himself by dropping live puppies into boiling water. The world's a better place without him."

Silk assumed a lofty expression. "I always like to perform these little public services," he declared. "I feel that it's a gentleman's civic duty."

"I thought you said that his death was accidental," Garion said.

"Well, sort of. Actually, I was trying to stab him in the belly—painful perhaps, but seldom fatal—but he bumped my arm as I made the thrust, and somehow my knife went straight into his heart."

"What a shame," Tamazin murmured. "I'd be sort of careful here in the Drojim though, Kheldar. I have no intention of revealing your identity, but the seneschal, Oskatat, also knows you by sight and he would probably feel obliged to denounce you."

"I'd already guessed as much, my Lady. I'll try to avoid him."

"Now tell me, Prince Kheldar, how is your father?"

Silk sighed. "He died, I'm afraid," he replied sadly, "quite a few years ago. It was rather sudden."

As chance had it, Garion was looking directly at the Queen Mother's face as Silk spoke and he saw the momentary flicker of anguish touch her beautiful features. She recovered quickly, though her eyes still brimmed with sorrow. "Ah," she said very quietly. "I'm sorry, Kheldar—more sorry than you could possibly know. I liked your father very much. The memories of the months he was in Rak Goska are among the happiest of my life."

To avoid being caught staring, Garion turned his head, and his eyes fell on Velvet, whose expression was faintly speculative. She returned his look, and her eyes conveyed a world of meaning and several unanswered questions.

CHAPTER FOURTEEN

The following morning dawned clear and cold. Garion stood at the window of his room, looking out over the slate roof tops of Rak Urga. The low, squat houses seemed to huddle together fearfully under the twin presence of the garish Drojim Palace at one end of town and the black Temple of Torak at the other. The smoke from hundreds of chimneys rose in straight blue columns toward the windless sky.

"Depressing sort of place, isn't it?" Silk said as he came into the room with his green robe carelessly slung over one shoulder.

Garion nodded. "It looks almost as if they deliberately went out of their way to make it ugly."

"It's a reflection of the Murgo mind. Oh, Urgit wants to

see us again." The little man caught Garion's inquiring look. "I don't think it's anything particularly important," he added. "He's probably just starved for conversation. I imagine that talking with Murgos can get tedious after a while."

They all trooped through the garish halls on the heels of the mail-shirted guard who had brought the king's summons, returning to the room where they had met with Urgit the previous day. They found him lounging in a chair by the fire with one leg cocked up over the arm and a half-eaten chicken leg in his hand. "Good morning, gentlemen," he greeted them. "Please sit down." He waved his breakfast at the chairs lined against one wall. "I'm not much of a one for formality." He looked at Sadi. "Did you sleep well?" he asked.

"It got a bit cold on toward morning, your Majesty."

"It's the slipshod construction of this place. There are cracks in the walls big enough to push a horse through. In the wintertime we have snow storms in the corridors." He sighed. "Do you realize that it's spring in Tol Honeth right now?" He sighed again, then glanced at Belgarath, who stood smiling peculiarly at him. "Was there something amusing, old boy?"

"Not really. Just remembering something I heard once." The old man went to the fire and held out his hands to the crackling flames. "How are your people coming on that ship?"

"I expect that it's going to be tomorrow at the earliest before it's ready," Urgit replied. "Winter's coming on, and the seas around the southern tip of the Urga peninsula are never what you'd call placid, even in the best of seasons, so I ordered the shipwrights to take special pains." He leaned forward and negligently tossed his chicken-leg into the fireplace. "It was burned," he said absently. "Every meal I get in this place is either burned or raw." He looked peculiarly at Belgarath. "You intrigue me, old man. You don't seem like the type to wind up his career hiring himself out to a Nyissan slaver."

"Appearances can be deceiving." Belgarath shrugged. "You don't look much like a king, either, but you *do* have the crown, after all."

Urgit reached up and pulled off his iron circlet. He looked

at it distastefully and then held it out to Belgarath. "You want this thing?" he asked. "I'm sure you'd look more regal than I do, and I'd be very happy to get rid of it—particularly in view of the fact that Kal Zakath so keenly wants to take my head out from under it." He dropped it on the floor beside his chair with a dull clink. "Let's go back to something we were discussing yesterday. You told me that you know Belgarion."

Belgarath nodded.

"How well?"

"How well can any man know another?"

"You're evading my question."

"It seems that way, doesn't it?"

Urgit let that pass. He looked intently at the old man. "How do you think Belgarion would really react if I proposed that he ally himself with me to drive the Malloreans off the continent? I'm sure their presence here worries him almost as much as it does me."

"The chances aren't very good," Belgarath told him. "You might be able to persuade Belgarion that it's a good idea, but the rest of the Alorn monarchs would probably object."

"They reached an accommodation with Drosta, didn't they?"

"That was between Rhodar and Drosta. There's always been a certain wary friendship between the Drasnians and the Nadraks. The one you'd need to get to accept your idea would be Cho-Hag, and Cho-Hag's never been exactly cordial to Murgos."

"I need allies, old man, not platitudes." Urgit paused. "What if I got word to Belgarath?"

"What would you say to him?"

"I'd try to persuade him that Zakath's a much greater danger to the Kingdoms of the West than I am. Maybe he could make the Alorns listen to reason."

"I don't think you'd have much luck there, either." The old man looked into the dancing flames with the firelight gleaming on his short, silvery beard. "You have to understand that Belgarath doesn't live in the same world with ordinary men. He lives in the world of first causes and primal forces. I'd imagine that he looks upon Kal Zakath as little more than a minor irritation."

"Torak's teeth!" Urgit swore. "Where am I going to get the troops I need?"

"Hire mercenaries," Silk suggested without turning from the window where he stood.

"What?"

"Dip into the royal vaults and bring out some of the fabled red gold of Angarak. Send word into the Kingdoms of the West that you need good men and that you're willing to pay them good gold. You'll be swamped with volunteers."

"I prefer men who fight for patriotism—or religion," Urgit declared stiffly.

Silk turned with an amused expression. "I've noticed that preference in many kings," he observed. "It doesn't put such a strain on royal treasuries. But believe me, your Majesty, loyalty to an ideal can vary in its intensity, but loyalty to money never changes. That's why mercenaries are better fighters."

"You're a cynic," Urgit accused.

Silk shook his head. "No, your Majesty. I'm a realist." He stepped over to Sadi and murmured something. The eunuch nodded, and the rat-faced little Drasnian quietly left the room.

Urgit raised one eyebrow inquiringly.

"He's going to go start packing, your Majesty," Sadi explained. "If we're going to sail tomorrow, we need to start getting ready."

Urgit and Sadi talked quietly for about a quarter of an hour, and then the door at the far end of the room opened again. Polgara and the other ladies entered with the Lady Tamazin.

"Good morning, mother," Urgit greeted her. "You slept well, I trust?"

"Quite well, thank you." She looked critically at him. "Urgit, where's your crown?"

"I took it off. It gives me a headache."

"Put it back on at once."

"What for?"

"Urgit, you don't look very much like a king. You're short and thin and you've got a face like a weasel. Murgos are not bright. If you don't wear your crown all the time, it's altogether possible that they'll forget who you are. Now put it back on."

"Yes, mother." He picked up his crown and clapped it on his head. "How's that?"

"It's lopsided, dear," she said in a calm tone so familiar that Garion gave Polgara a quick, startled look. "Now you look like a drunken sailor."

Urgit laughed and straightened his crown.

Garion looked closely at Ce'Nedra to see if there were any traces left of the storm of weeping that had swept over her the previous day, but he saw no evidence that it might immediately return. She was engaged in a murmured conversation with the Cthan Princess, Prala, and the Murgo girl's face clearly showed that she had already fallen under the queen's spell.

"And you, Urgit," Lady Tamazin said, "did you sleep well?"

"I never really sleep, mother. You know that. I decided years ago that sleeping nervously is infinitely preferable to sleeping permanently."

Garion found himself making a difficult readjustment in his thinking. He had never liked Murgos. He had always distrusted and even feared them. King Urgit's personality, however, was as un-Murgoish as his appearance. He was quick and volatile, and his moods swung from sardonic amusement to gloom so rapidly that Garion was quite uncertain what to expect next. He was obviously not a strong king, and Garion had been a king long enough himself to see where Urgit was making his mistakes. In spite of himself, though, Garion found that he actually liked him and felt a peculiar sympathy for him as he struggled with a job for which he was hopelessly unsuited. That, of course, created a problem. Garion did not *want* to like this man, and this unwanted sympathy seemed wildly out of place. He rose from his chair and withdrew to the far end of the room, making some pretense of looking out the window so that he might put himself beyond the range of the Murgo King's urbane wit. With a kind of unbearable urgency, he wanted to be on board ship and away from this ugly Murgo city, huddled on its barren coast, and from the weak, fearful man who was not really such a bad fellow, but whom Garion knew he should regard as an enemy.

"What's the trouble, Garion?" Polgara asked quietly, coming up behind him.

"Impatience, I guess, Aunt Pol. I want to get moving."

"We all do, dear," she told him, "but we have to endure this for one more day."

"Why can't he just leave us alone?"

"Who's that?"

"Urgit. I'm not interested in his problems, so why does he have to sit around telling us about them all the time?"

"Because he's lonely, Garion."

"All kings are lonely. It comes with the crown. Most of us learn how to endure it, though. We don't sit around and snivel about it."

"That's unkind, Garion," she told him firmly, "and it's unworthy of you."

"Why are we all so concerned about a weak king with a clever mouth?"

"Perhaps it's because he's the first Murgo we've met in eons who shows some human qualities. Because he's the way he is, he raises the possibility that Alorns and Murgos might someday find ways to settle their differences without resorting to bloodshed."

He continued to stare out the window, although a slow flush began to creep up his neck. "I'm being childish, aren't I?" he admitted.

"Yes, dear, I'm afraid you are. Your prejudices are running away with you. Ordinary people can afford that. Kings cannot. Go back to where he's sitting, Garion, and watch him very closely. Don't pass up this opportunity to get to know him. The time may come when that knowledge will help you."

"All right, Aunt Pol." Garion sighed, squaring his shoulders resolutely.

It was almost noon when Oskatat entered the room. "Your Majesty," he announced in his rasping voice, "Agachak, Hierarch of Rak Urga, craves audience with you."

"Show him in, Oskatat," Urgit replied wearily. He turned to his mother. "I think I'm going to have to find another place to hide," he muttered. "Too many people know where to find me."

"I have a splended closet, Urgit," she replied, "warm and dry and dark. You could hide in there and cover yourself with a blanket. We'll slip food in to you from time to time."

"Are you making fun of me, mother?"

"No, dear," she said. "But like it or not, you're the king. You can either *be* king or you can be a spoiled child. The choice is entirely up to you."

Garion glanced guiltily at Polgara.

"Yes?" she murmured.

But he decided not to answer.

The cadaverous-looking Agachak entered and bowed perfunctorily to his king. "Your Majesty," he said in his hollow voice.

"Dread Hierarch," Urgit responded, his voice betraying no hint of his true feeling.

"Time is passing, your Majesty."

"It has a way of doing that, I've noticed."

"My point is that the weather is about to turn stormy. Is the ship nearly ready?"

"I expect it to sail tomorrow," Urgit replied.

"Excellent. I shall instruct Kabach to make ready."

"Has the Priestess Chabat regained her composure?" Urgit asked.

"Not really, your Majesty. She still keenly feels the loss of her paramour."

"Even after she found out what his true feelings were about her? Who can ever hope to understand the workings of the female mind?"

"Chabat is not that difficult to fathom, your Majesty." Agachak shrugged. "A disfigured woman has little chance to attract lovers, and the loss of even an insincere one is most painful. Her loss in this particular case goes a bit deeper, however. Sorchak assisted her in the performance of certain rites of magic. Without him, she will not be able to continue her efforts to summon up demons."

Urgit shuddered. "I thought that she was a sorceress. Isn't that enough for her? Why would she want to dabble in magic, too?"

"Chabat is not really that powerful a sorceress," Agachak replied. "She thinks that she will have a greater advantage when she finally confronts me if she has demons to aid her."

"Confront you? Is that what she's planning?"

"Of course. Her occasional dallying is merely an amusement. Her central goal has always been power. In time, she will have to try to wrest mine from me."

"If that's the case, why did you allow her to gain so much authority in the Temple?"

"It amused me," Agachak said with a chill smile. "I am not as repelled by ugliness as others are, and Chabat, despite her ambition—or perhaps because of it—is very efficient."

"You knew about her affair with Sorchak. Didn't that offend you?"

"Not really," the dead-looking Hierarch answered. "That's just a part of the entertainment I'm preparing for myself. Eventually, Chabat will succeed in raising a demon, and then she will challenge me. At the very instant that her triumph seems complete, I shall also raise a demon, and mine will destroy hers. Then I shall have her stripped and dragged to the Sanctum. There she will be bent backward across the altar and I myself will slowly cut out her heart. I look forward to that moment with a great deal of anticipation, and it will be all the sweeter because it will come just when she thinks she has beaten me." His dead face had come alive with a dreadful pleasure. His eyes burned, and there were flecks of spittle in the corners of his mouth.

Urgit, however, looked faintly sick. "Grolims appear to have more exotic amusements than ordinary men."

"Not really, Urgit. The only reason for power is to be able to use it to destroy your enemies, and it's particularly enjoyable to be able to drag them down from a height before you destroy them. Wouldn't you like to be present when the mighty Kal Zakath dies with a Dagashi knife in his heart?"

"Not really. I just want him out of the way. I don't particularly want to watch the procedure."

"You have not yet learned the true meaning of power, then. The understanding may come when you and I stand in the presence of Cthrag Sardius and witness the rebirth of the Dark God and the final triumph of the Child of Dark."

Urgit's expression grew pained.

"Do not flinch from your destiny, Urgit," Agachak said in his hollow voice. "It is foretold that a King of Angarak will be present at the final meeting. You will be that king—just as I will be the one to make the sacrifice and thus become the first disciple of the reborn God. We are bound together by a chain forged of fate. Your destiny is to become Overking of Angarak, and mine is to rule the Church."

Urgit sighed in resignation. "Whatever you say, Agachak," he said disconsolately. "We still have a few problems to overcome, however."

"They are of little concern to me," the Hierarch declared.

"Well, they do concern me," Urgit said with surprising heat. "First we have to deal with Zakath, and then we'll need to get rid of Gethel and Drosta—just to be on the safe side. I've been involved in a race for a throne before and I think I'd feel more confident if I were the only one running. Your problems, however, are a bit more weighty. Urvon and Zandramas are very serious opponents."

"Urvon is a doddering old fool, and Zandramas is only a woman."

"Agachak," Urgit said pointedly, "Polgara is also only a woman. Would you care to face *her*? No, Dread Hierarch, I think that Urvon doesn't dodder as much as you think, and

Zandramas is probably more dangerous than you'd like to believe. She's managed to spirit away Belgarion's son, and that was no mean trick. She's also slipped past you and all the other Hierarchs as if you weren't even here. Let's neither of us take any of this too lightly."

"I know where Zandramas is," Agachak said with a chill smile, "and I will wrest Belgarion's son from her at the proper time. It is foretold that you and I and the babe who is to be sacrificed will come into the presence of the Sardion at the appointed time. There I will perform the sacrifice, and you will witness the rite, and we shall both be exalted. It is so written."

"Depending on how you read it," Urgit added morosely.

Garion moved to Ce'Nedra's side, trying to look casual. As the meaning of what the Grolim Hierarch had just said came to her, the blood slowly drained from her face. "It's not going to happen," he told her in a firm, quiet voice. "Nobody's going to do that to our baby."

"You knew," she accused him in a choked whisper.

"Grandfather and I found it in the Grolim Prophecies in the Temple library."

"Oh, Garion," she said, biting her lip to keep back the tears.

"Don't worry about it," he said. "The same Prophecy said that Torak was going to win at Cthol Mishrak. That didn't happen, and this isn't going to happen, either."

"But what if—"

"There aren't any ifs," he said firmly. "It's *not* going to happen."

After the Hierarch had left, King Urgit's mood changed. He sat in his chair, brooding sourly.

"Perhaps your Majesty might prefer to be left alone," Sadi ventured.

"No, Sadi." Urgit sighed. "No amount of worrying at it is going to change what we've already set in motion." He shook his head and then shrugged as if dismissing the whole matter. "Why don't you tell me the details of the little misdemeanor that made Salmissra so vexed with you? I adore stories of deceit and dishonesty. They always seem to hint that the world's not really such a bad place after all."

It was not long after, as Sadi was elaborating at some length on the involuted scheme that had caused his downfall, when the seneschal entered the room again. "A dispatch has arrived from the military governor at Cthaka, your Majesty," he rasped.

"What does he want now?" Urgit muttered plaintively.

"He reports that the Malloreans are mounting a major campaign in the south. Rak Gorut is under siege and must inevitably fall within a week."

"In the autumn?" Urgit exclaimed, coming up out of his chair in dismay. "They're mounting a campaign when the summer's already over?"

"So it appears," Oskatat replied. "I think that Kal Zakath's hoping to take you by surprise. Once Rak Gorut falls, there won't be anything between his forces and Rak Cthaka."

"And the garrison there is virtually nonexistent, isn't it?"

"I'm afraid so, Urgit. Rak Cthaka will also fall, and then Zakath will have all winter to consolidate his hold on the south."

Urgit began to swear and moved quickly to a map tacked up on the wall. "How many troops do we have up here in Morcth?" he demanded, tapping the map with one finger.

"A few score thousand. But by the time they had received the order to march south, the Malloreans would already be halfway to Rak Cthaka."

Urgit stared in consternation at the map. Then he suddenly smashed his fist against it. "He's outsmarted me again!" he raged. He returned to his chair and collapsed in it.

"I think I'd better go get Kradak," Oskatat said. "The General Staff will need to know about this."

"Whatever you think best, Oskatat," Urgit replied in a defeated tone.

As the seneschal strode from the room, Garion crossed to look at the map. After only the briefest of glances, he saw a solution to Urgit's problem, but he was reluctant to speak. He did not want to become involved in this. There were a dozen good reasons why he should keep his mouth shut—the most important being the fact that should he offer his solution to the Murgo King, he would in a sense be committed, and he firmly desired to avoid any commitment to the man, no matter how slight. An unresolved problem, however, nagged at his sense of responsibility; to turn his back on one—even one that was not his own—violated something deep within him. He muttered a curse under his breath, then turned to the stricken Urgit. "Excuse me, your Majesty," he said, approaching the matter obliquely, "but how well fortified is Rak Cthaka?"

"It's like every Murgo city," Urgit replied abstactedly. "The walls are seventy feet high and thirty feet thick. What difference does it make?"

"The city could withstand a seige, then—if you had enough men there?"

"That's the whole problem—I don't."

"Then you need to get reinforcements there before the Malloreans can reach the city."

"What a brilliant observation. But if I can't get relief columns there in time, how could I possibly get reinforcements there before the streets are filled with Malloreans?"

Garion shrugged. "Send them by sea."

"By sea?" Urgit suddenly looked stunned.

"Your harbor is full of ships, and your city's bulging with troops. Load enough men on the ships to reinforce the garrison at Rak Cthaka and sail them around to the city. Even if Rak Gorut fell tomorrow, it's still going to take the Malloreans ten days to march overland. Your ships could be there in less than a week. Your reinforced garrison will be able to hold until the relief columns arrive."

Urgit shook his head. "Murgo armies do not move by ship," he said. "My generals wouldn't hear of it."

"You're the king, aren't you? *Make* them hear of it."

Urgit's face grew apprehensive. "They never listen to me."

Garion had a sudden urge to shake him. With some effort he got his irritation under control. "There's nothing holy about walking," he said, "particularly if marching your men to Rak Cthaka is going to cost you the city. Tell your generals to load the men on those ships and also tell them that the matter isn't open to discussion."

"They'll refuse."

"Then dismiss them from their posts and promote a few colonels."

Urgit stared at him, aghast. "I couldn't do that."

"You're the king. You can do anything you want to."

Urgit wrestled with it indecisively.

"Do as he says, Urgit," Lady Tamazin commanded abruptly. "It's the only way to save Rak Cthaka."

He looked at her, a lost expression on his face. "Do you really think I should, mother?" he asked in a small voice.

"Just do it. As the young man said, you're the king—and I think it's about time that you started acting like one."

"There's something else we need to consider, your Majesty," Sadi said, his face grave. "If the Malloreans lay seige to Rak Cthaka, I won't be able to land there. I'm going to have to get past that vicinity before any fighting breaks out. Slavers can move around with very little interference, unless there's an actual battle going on, but once the fighting starts, the Malloreans are sure to detain us. If we don't move very quickly, your Dagashi won't reach Rak Hagga until sometime next summer."

Urgit's face grew even more disconsolate. "I hadn't considered that," he admitted. "I think you and your people had better get ready to leave here immediately. I'll send word to the Temple and tell Agachak that the plans have changed."

The door opened. Oskatat entered, and at his side was the Murgo officer who had so rudely demanded Urgit's signature the previous day.

"Ah, General Kradak," Urgit greeted the officer with an obviously feigned joviality, "so good of you to join us. You've heard about what's going on in the south?"

The general nodded shortly. "The situation is grave," he said. "Rak Gorut and Rak Cthaka are in great peril."

"What do you advise, General?" Urgit asked.

"There's nothing to advise," Kradak said. "We'll have to accept the fact that Gorut and Cthaka are lost and concentrate our efforts on holding Urga, Morcth, and Araga."

"General, that only leaves three of the nine military districts of Cthol Murgos under my control. Zakath is eating my kingdom one bite at a time."

The general shrugged. "We cannot reach Rak Cthaka before the Malloreans do. The city will fall. There's nothing we can do about it."

"What if we were to reinforce the garrison there? Would that change things at all?"

"Certainly, but it's impossible."

"Maybe not," Urgit said with a quick look at Garion. "What do you think of moving reinforcements there by ship?"

"By ship?" The general blinked, and then his face hardened. "That's absurd."

"Why absurd?"

"It's never been done in Cthol Murgos before."

"I imagine that there are a lot of things that have never been done in Cthol Murgos before. Is there any specific reason why it won't work?"

"Ships sink, your Majesty," Kradak pointed out acidly, as if speaking to a child. "The troops know that and they'll refuse to go on board."

Oskatat stepped forward. "Not if you crucify the first ten or so who refuse right there on the dock," he said firmly. "That sort of example should lessen the reluctance of the rest."

Kradak gave the gray-haired man a look of undisguised hatred. "What would a house servant know about command?" he demanded. He looked back at Urgit with a barely concealed sneer. "Just stay on your throne, Urgit," he said harshly. "Play with your crown and your scepter and pretend that you're a real king. But keep your nose out of the business of running the war."

Urgit's face blanched, and he shrank back in his chair.

"Shall I send for the headsman, your Majesty?" Oskatat inquired in an icy voice. "It appears that General Kradak has outlived his usefulness."

Kradak stared at him incredulously. "You wouldn't dare!" he gasped.

"Your life hangs on his Majesty's pleasure just now, Kradak. One word from him, and your head will roll in the dust."

"I am a general officer in the armies of Cthol Murgos." Kradak clutched at the gold chain about his neck as if for reassurance. "My appointment comes from Taur Urgas himself. You have no authority over me, Oskatat."

Urgit straightened in his chair, an angry flush moving up into his face. "Oh, really?" he said in a dangerously quiet voice. "Maybe it's time that we got a few things clarified." He took off his crown and held it up. "Do you recognize this, Kradak?"

The general glared at him with a stony face.

"Answer me!"

"It's the crown of Cthol Murgos," Kradak replied sullenly.

"And the man who wears it has absolute authority, right?"

"Taur Urgas did."

"Taur Urgas is dead. I sit upon the throne now, and you will obey me in the same way you obeyed him. Do you understand me?"

"You are not Taur Urgas."

"That's painfully obvious, General Kradak," Urgit replied coldly. "I am your king, however, and I'm also an Urga. When I grow agitated, I feel the madness of the Urgas creeping up on me—and it's creeping very fast just now. If you don't do exactly as I tell you to do, you're going to be a head shorter before the sun sets. Now go give the order to load the troops on those ships."

"And if I refuse?"

Urgit's expression grew hesitant. For some reason he looked appealingly at Garion.

"Kill him," Garion said in the flat unemotional voice he had discovered immediately got people's attention.

Urgit straightened again and firmly yanked his bellpull. The great gong outside in the hallway clanged. Two burly guards responded immediately. "Yes, your Majesty?" one of them asked.

"Well, Kradak?" Urgit asked. "What's it to be? The ships or the block? Speak up, man. I haven't got all day."

Kradak's face went ashen. "The ships, your Majesty," he replied in a shaky voice.

"Splendid. I'm so happy that we were able to settle our little differences without unpleasantness." Urgit turned to his guards. "General Kradak is going directly to the barracks of the Third Cohort now," he told them, "and you will accompany him. He's going to order those men to board the ships in the harbor and to sail to the relief of the garrison at Rak Cthaka." He gave Kradak a narrow, distrustful look. "If he gives them any other order, you will cut off his head immediately and bring it to me—in a bucket."

"As your Majesty commands," the Murgos replied in unison, each banging his fist against his mail shirt.

Kradak turned, trembling and suddenly broken, and went out with the grim Murgo guards flanking him closely.

Urgit retained his imperious expression until the door closed, and then he threw both arms in the air and began beating his feet on the floor, whooping with delight. "Oh, Gods!" he said ecstatically. "I loved that! I've been wanting to do that all my life!"

The Lady Tamazin rose gravely from her chair, limped to where her son sat, and wordlessly embraced him.

"Affection, mother?" he asked lightly, a broad grin still creasing his sharp-featured face. "How terribly un-Murgoish." And then he laughed and caught her in a rough bear hug.

"There may be hope after all," she observed calmly to Oskatat.

A slow smile crept across the big Murgo's lips. "It looks a bit more promising, my Lady," he agreed.

"Thank you for your support, Oskatat," Urgit said to his friend. "I might not have gotten through that without your help." He paused. "I must say, though, that I'm a little surprised that you approved of my scheme."

"I don't. I think it's an absurd idea almost certainly doomed from the start."

Urgit blinked.

"There was another issue at stake, however—one that is much more important." There was a peculiar pride on the big man's face. "Do you realize that this is the very first time you've ever faced down one of your generals? They've been running roughshod over you since the day you took the throne. The loss of a few ships and a few thousand men is a small price to pay for a real king on the throne of Cthol Murgos."

"Thank you for your candor, Oskatat," Urgit said gravely. "It may just be, though, that things may not turn out so disastrously as you think."

"Perhaps, but Taur Urgas would not have done this."

"It might just be that someday we'll all rejoice in the fact that Taur Urgas is no longer with us, Oskatat." A faint ironic smile crossed the king's lips. "As a matter of fact, I seem to feel a small surge of rejoicing coming over me already. I'm losing this war, my old friend, and a man who's losing can't afford to be conservative. I've got to take a few gambles if I want to keep Kal Zakath from parading through the streets of Rak Urga with my head on a pole."

"As your Majesty commands," the seneschal said with a bow. "I'm also going to have to give certain orders. Have I your permission to withdraw?"

"Of course."

Oskatat turned and started toward the door. Before he reached it, however, it opened and Silk came into the room. The seneschal stopped, staring hard at the Drasnian. Silk's hand moved swiftly toward the hood of his robe, but then he let it drop with a rueful grimace.

Garion groaned inwardly. He moved carefully into position not far behind Oskatat, aware that Durnik and the gigantic Toth were also coming up on either side of him, ready to move quickly to prevent any outcry.

"You!" Oskatat exclaimed to Silk. "What are you doing here?"

Silk's expression grew resigned. "Just passing through, Oskatat," he replied casually. "You've been well, I trust?"

Urgit looked up. "What's this?"

"The seneschal and I are old friends, your Majesty," Silk replied. "We met in Rak Goska some years ago."

"Is your Majesty aware of this man's true identity?" Oskatat demanded.

Urgit shrugged. "He's one of Sadi's servants," he said. "Or so I was told."

"Hardly that, Urgit. This is Prince Kheldar of Drasnia, the most notorious spy in the entire world."

"The seneschal is perhaps a bit lavish in his praise," Silk noted modestly.

"Do you deny that you murdered the soldiers Taur Urgas sent to detain you when your scheme in Rak Goska was exposed?" Oskatat said accusingly.

"I don't know that I'd use the word 'murdered,' exactly, my Lord." Silk winced. "Oh, I'll admit that there was a bit of unpleasantness, but that's such an awkward way to sum up."

"Your Majesty," the grim old Murgo said. "This man was responsible for the death of Dorak Urgas, your eldest brother. There is a long-standing warrant for his immediate execution, so I will send for the headsman at once."

CHAPTER FIFTEEN

Urgit's face had grown cold. His eyes were narrowed, and he chewed nervously on a fingernail. "All right, Sadi," he said, "what's this all about?"

"Your Majesty—I—" The eunuch spread his hand.

"Don't try to play the innocent with me," Urgit snapped. "Did you know about this man?" He pointed at Silk.

"Well, yes, but—"

"And you chose not to tell me? What's your game, Sadi?"

The eunuch hesitated, and Garion saw beads of sweat breaking out on his forehead. Durnik and Toth, moving casually as if merely removing themselves from the vicinity of the confrontation, went past Oskatat and leaned idly against the wall, one on each side of the door.

"Well, Sadi?" Urgit pressed. "I've heard about this Prince Kheldar. He's not merely a spy; he's an assassin as well." His eyes suddenly grew wide. "So that's it!" he gasped, staring at Silk. "Belgarion sent you here to kill me, didn't he—you and these other Alorns."

"Don't be absurd, Urgit," Lady Tamazin said from her chair. "You've been alone with these people for hours at a time since they arrived here. If they were here to kill you, you'd already be dead."

He thought about that. "All right, you—Prince Kheldar—speak up. I want to know exactly what you're doing here. Now talk."

Silk shrugged. "It's as I told my Lord Oskatat, your Majesty. I'm merely passing through. My business is in another part of the world."

"Which part?"

"Here and there," Silk said evasively.

"I'm going to get some straight answers here," Urgit declared.

"Shall I send for the headsman, your Majesty?" Oskatat asked ominously.

"Perhaps that might not be a bad idea," Urgit agreed.

The seneschal turned, but found Durnik and the impassive Toth barring his way from the room. Urgit, perceiving the situation at once, reached quickly for the bellpull which would fill the room with armed Murgos.

"Urgit!" Lady Tamazin snapped. "No!"

He hesitated.

"Do as I say!"

"What's this?" he asked.

"Look around you," she told him. "If you even touch that cord, one of these people will have a knife against your throat before you can tug it even once."

His expression grew suddenly frightened, and he slowly lowered his hand.

Sadi cleared his throat. "Ah—your Majesty," he said. "I believe that the Queen Mother has seen directly to the heart of the matter here. We are both in positions to greatly inconvenience each other. Wouldn't it be wiser for us to discuss things rationally before we resort to any unpleasantness?"

"What is it that you want, Sadi?" Urgit asked him in a slightly quavering voice.

"Only what you had intended all along, your Majesty. As Kheldar said, our business is in another part of the world, and it does not directly concern you. Give us the ship that you were going to give us anyway, and in return we'll deliver your Dagashi to Rak Hagga as we promised. After that, we'll proceed with our own affairs. What could be fairer than that?"

"Listen to him, Urgit," Lady Tamazin urged. "He makes a great deal of sense."

Urgit's expression was filled with doubt. "Do you really think so, mother?"

"What harm can they do you, once they've crossed the Mallorean lines?" she asked. "If you're nervous about them, then get them out of Rak Urga as quickly as possible."

"All except this one." Oskatat pointed at Silk.

"We really need him, my Lord," Sadi said politely.

"He killed Dorak Urgas," the seneschal said stubbornly.

"We can give him a medal for that later, Oskatat," Urgit said.

Oskatat stared at him.

"Oh, come now, my friend. You despised Dorak as much as I did."

"He was a Murgo prince, your Majesty. His murder cannot go unpunished."

"You seem to forget that *I* murdered a dozen of my other brothers—also Murgo princes—on my way to the throne. Were you planning to punish me as well?" Urgit looked back at Sadi. "I think, however, that it might not hurt for me to keep Kheldar here in the Drojim. Sort of as a performance bond. As soon as you deliver Kabach to Rak Hagga, I'll release him. He can catch up with you later."

Sadi's expression grew pained.

"You're overlooking something important here, Urgit," Lady Tamazin said, leaning forward intently.

"Oh? What's that, mother?"

"Prince Kheldar of Drasnia is reputed to be one of King Belgarion's closest friends. You have there the perfect envoy to convey a message to the Rivan King."

He looked sharply at Silk. "Is that true?" he asked. "Do you really know Belgarion?"

"Quite well, actually," Silk replied. "I've known him since he was a little boy."

"That old man over there said that Belgarion isn't at Riva just now. Do you have any idea where you might be able to find him?"

"Your Majesty," Silk answered with a perfectly straight face, "I can honestly tell you that I know exactly where Belgarion is at this very moment."

Urgit scratched at one cheek, his eyes suspicious. "I don't think I like this," he said. "Let's say that I give you a message to deliver to Belgarion. What's to prevent you from just throwing it away and then circling around to rejoin your friends?"

"Ethics." Silk shrugged. "I always do the things I'm paid to do. You *were* planning to pay me, weren't you?"

Urgit stared at Silk for a moment and then he threw back his head and laughed. "You're absolutely outrageous, Kheldar," he said. "Here you are, about two steps from the headsman's block, and you have the nerve to try to extort money from me."

Silk sighed and looked around tragically. "Why is it that the word 'pay' always brings that same look of consternation into the eyes of kings the world over?" he asked. "Surely your Majesty would not expect me to perform this truly unique service for you without some small recompense, would you?"

"Wouldn't you say that getting to keep your head is more than adequate payment?"

"Oh, I'm fairly safe, I think. Since I'm the only one in the world who can guarantee delivery of your message, I'm far too valuable to kill, wouldn't you say?"

Lady Tamazin suddenly laughed, a whimsical expression on her face as she looked at the two of them.

"Something amusing, mother?" Urgit asked her.

"Nothing, Urgit. Nothing at all."

The king's eyes were still indecisive. He looked hopefully at his seneschal. "What do you think, Oskatat?" he asked. "Can I trust this little knave?"

"It's your Majesty's decision," the big Murgo replied stiffly.

"I'm not asking you as your king," Urgit told him. "I'm asking as a friend."

Oskatat winced. "That's cruel, Urgit," he said. "You're forcing me to decide between duty and friendship."

"All right, then. Let's put it on that basis. What should I do?"

"As king, you should obey the law—even if it means flying in the face of your own best interests. As a man, however, you should seize every opportunity that presents itself to avert disaster."

"Well? What should I do? Should I be a king or a man? Which do you advise?"

It hung there in the air between them. The seneschal refused to meet Urgit's eyes. Instead, he cast one quick, appealing look at Lady Tamazin. "Torak forgive me," he muttered finally. He straightened and looked his king full in the face. "Save yourself, Urgit," he said. "If this Drasnian can arrange an alliance with Belgarion, then pay him whatever he demands and send him on his way. Belgarion may deceive you at some later date, but Kal Zakath seeks your head now. You need that alliance, no matter what the cost."

"Thank you, Oskatat," the king said with genuine gratitude. He turned back to Silk. "How quickly do you think you could reach Belgarion with my message?" he asked.

"Your Majesty," Silk replied, "I can have your message in Belgarion's hands more quickly than you could possibly imagine. Now, shall we talk about money?" His long, pointed nose began to twitch in a manner Garion recognized at once.

"How much do you want?" Urgit asked warily.

"Oh," Silk pretended to think about it, "I suppose a hundred Tolnedran goldmarks ought to cover it."

Urgit gaped at him. "A hundred marks? You're insane!"

Silk casually examined the fingernails of one hand. "The figure's open to negotiation, your Majesty," he admitted. "I just wanted to establish a general price range sort of to get things off to a smooth start."

Urgit's eyes took on a strange light. He leaned forward, tugging absently at his nose. "I might be able to see my way clear to pay you ten—or so," he countered. "I don't really have all that much Tolnedran coin in my vaults."

"Oh, that's all right, your Majesty," Silk said magnanimously. "I'd be willing to accept Angarak coins—at a slight discount, of course."

"Discount?"

"Angarak gold is obviously adulterated, King Urgit. That's why it's red instead of yellow."

Urgit eyed him narrowly. "Why don't you draw up a chair, old boy?" he suggested. "This might take a while." Strangely enough, his nose had also begun to twitch.

What followed was a display of astonishing virtuosity on the part of both negotiators. Garion had seen Silk in this sort of situation many times before and had always believed that his sharp-nosed friend was without peer when it came to getting the best of every bargain he struck. Urgit, however, quickly demonstrated that he too was an expert at the game. When Silk pointed out in suitably exaggerated terms the dangers he would have to face on his way to deliver the message, Urgit countered by offering an escort of Murgo soldiers rather than increased compensation. Silk dropped that line of attack and concentrated for a time on the unusual expenses he would incur—fresh horses, food and lodging, bribes and the like. In each case the Murgo King proposed assistance rather than money—horses, food and lodging at Murgo embassies or trade missions, and the good offices of Murgo officials to step around the necessity for bribes. Silk made some pretense at considering that, his watchful eyes never leaving his adversary's face. Then he fell back to his previously prepared position, re-emphasizing his friendship with the Rivan King and the fact that he, perhaps better than any man in the world, could present the proposed alliance to Belgarion in the most favorable light. "After all," he concluded, "what it finally comes down to is how much the alliance is worth to you, doesn't it?"

"It's worth a very great deal," Urgit admitted with deceptive candor, "but, although I'd be the first to admit that you're probably the perfect messenger, there's no guarantee that Belgarion will agree to an alliance, now is there?" He paused, his expression announcing that a notion had just struck him. "I'll tell you what," he said then with an artfully feigned enthusiasm, "why don't we set a relatively modest figure for the actual delivery of the message—oh, let's say the ten marks I suggested previously."

Silk's face grew flinty, but Urgit lifted one hand. "Hear me out, your Highness," he said. "As I just suggested, we agree on that figure as payment for carrying the message. Then, if Belgarion agrees to an alliance, I'd be more than happy to pay you the rest of the money you asked for."

"That's hardly fair, your Majesty," Silk protested. "You're putting the entire question into the hands of a third party. I can guarantee delivery, but not acceptance. Belgarion is a sovereign king. I can't tell him what to do, and I have no way of knowing how he would react to your proposal."

"Didn't you say that you were his oldest friend? Surely you know him well enough to have at least some idea of how he would view the matter."

"You're shifting the entire basis of the negotiations, your Majesty," Silk accused him.

"Yes, I know." Urgit smirked.

"The payment for actually cementing an alliance between you and Belgarion would have to be much, much higher," Silk countered. "What you propose is extremely hazardous, after all."

"Hazardous? I don't follow you, old boy."

"Belgarion is not entirely a free agent. Even though he's the Overlord of the West, he's still answerable to the other kings—particularly the Alorns; and let's be honest about it, Alorns despise Murgos. If I persuade him to accept an alliance with you, those other Alorn Kings might very well believe that I'm a traitor. I could find myself dodging their assassins for the rest of my life."

"I find that very hard to believe, Kheldar."

"You don't know them. The Alorns are a fearfully unforgiving race. Even my aunt would give orders to have me hunted down if she thought that I'd betrayed a basic Alorn concept of the world. What you propose is absolutely out of the question—unless we start talking about really significant amounts of money, of course."

"Just how significant?" Urgit asked warily.

"Well now, let's see—" Silk pretended to consider the matter. "Naturally I'd have to abandon all my enterprises in the Kingdoms of the West. If the Alorn Kings declare me an outlaw, all my assets would be expropriated anyway. My commercial ventures are far-flung, and it's going to take some time to establish their fair value. Then, of course, I'll have the expense of setting up operations in a part of the world where the Alorns can't track me down."

"That's simplicity in itself, Kheldar. Come to Cthol Murgos. I'll protect you."

"No offense, your Majesty, but Cthol Murgos doesn't suit me. I was thinking perhaps of Mal Zeth or maybe Melcene. I could probably do quite well in Melcene."

"Silk," Belgarath said abruptly, "what's the point of all this?"

"I was just—"

"I know what you were doing. You can amuse yourself some other time. Right now we've got a ship to catch."

"But, Belg—" Silk caught himself abruptly with a quick sidelong glance at Urgit.

"You're not in a position to be giving orders, old man," the Murgo King said. Then he looked around suspiciously.

"There's something going on here that I don't like. I don't think anybody's going anyplace today. I'm not going to turn any of you loose until I get to the bottom of all this."

"Don't be absurd, Urgit," his mother interrupted him. "These people must leave at once."

"Don't interfere, mother."

"Then stop acting like a child. Sadi must get past Rak Cthaka before the fighting starts there, and Kheldar must be on his way to Belgarion within the hour. Don't throw away this opportunity out of sheer pique."

Their eyes locked. Urgit's face was suddenly angry, and his mother's unrelenting. After a long moment, his eyes dropped. "This isn't like you, mother," he mumbled. "Why are you deliberately trying to humiliate me in public?"

"I'm not, Urgit. I'm just trying to bring you to your senses. A king must always bow to reality—even if it injures his pride."

He gave her a long, penetrating look. "The time isn't really all that pressing, mother," he said. "Sadi has time to spare, and Kheldar really doesn't have to leave for a day or so. If I didn't know better, I'd say that you have some personal reason for not wanting me to talk to them any more."

"Nonsense!" But her face had grown quite pale.

"You're upset, mother," he pressed. "Why is that?"

"She can't tell you," Eriond said suddenly. The young man was seated on a bench in front of a nearby window with the autumn sun streaming golden on his pale hair.

"What?"

"Your mother can't tell you," Eriond repeated. "There's a secret she's had locked in her heart since before you were born."

"No!" Lady Tamazin gasped involuntarily. "You musn't!"

"What is this secret?" Urgit demanded, his eyes flickering suspiciously from face to face.

A slow flush crept up Eriond's cheeks. "I'd really rather not say," he replied in a slightly embarrassed tone.

Velvet had been watching the exchange with wholly absorbed fascination; even as a startling suspicion dawned in Garion's mind, she suddenly began to laugh.

"What's so funny, young lady?" Urgit asked irritably.

"A peculiar thought just occurred to me, your Majesty," she replied. She turned to Lady Tamazin. "Didn't you say that you knew Prince Kheldar's father, my Lady?"

Tamazin's chin lifted suddenly. Her face was still deadly pale, and she did not answer.

"How long ago would you say that was?" Velvet asked.

Tamazin's lips remained tightly closed.

Velvet sighed, then looked at Silk. "Kheldar," she said, "quite a long time back your father visited Rak Goska, didn't he? I think it had something to do with some trade negotiations on behalf of King Rhodar. Do you happen to recall just how many years ago that was?"

He looked puzzled. "I don't know," he replied. "It must have been—" He thought about it. "I remember that my mother and I stayed at the palace in Boktor while he was gone. I think I was eight or so at the time. That would make it about forty years, I guess. What's this all about, Liselle?"

"Interesting," she murmured, ignoring his question. "My Lady Tamazin," she said, "you keep telling your son that he isn't going to go mad—but doesn't every male in the Urga line fall prey to that hereditary affliction? What is it that makes you so positive that he's somehow going to escape the family curse?"

Tamazin's face grew even paler, and her lips were resolutely sealed.

"My Lord High Seneschal," Velvet said to Oskatat, "just out of curiosity, how old is his Majesty?"

Oskatat's face had also gone deadly pale. He looked at Lady Tamazin with a stricken expression, and then his lips also clamped shut.

"I'm thirty-nine," Urgit snapped. "What difference does it—" Then he suddenly stopped, his eyes going very wide. He turned with a look of stunned incredulity. "*Mother!*" he gasped.

Sadi began to laugh.

"I just adore happy endings, don't you?" Velvet said brightly to Ce'Nedra. She looked impishly at Silk. "Well, don't just sit there, Kheldar. Go embrace your brother."

The Lady Tamazin rose slowly from her chair, her face proud. "Summon the executioner, Oskatat," she said. "I am ready."

"No, my Lady," he replied. "I won't do that."

"It's the law, Oskatat," she insisted. "A Murgo woman who dishonors her husband is to be put to death immediately."

"Oh, sit down, mother," Urgit said, abstractedly gnawing at one of his knuckles. "This is no time for histrionics."

Silk's eyes were a bit wild. "You're very quick, Liselle," he said in a strained voice.

"Not really," she admitted. "I should have guessed quite some time ago. You and his Majesty could almost use each other for shaving mirrors, and he negotiates almost as shrewdly as you do." She looked at the stunned Murgo King, her cheeks dimpling. "If your Majesty ever grows weary of the throne, I'm certain that my uncle could find work for you."

"This alters things quite a bit, Urgit," Belgarath said. "The prejudices of your subjects are well known. If they find out that you're not a real Murgo, it might agitate them just a bit, wouldn't you say?"

Urgit had been staring at Silk. "Oh, just shut up, old man," he said absently. "Let me think my way through this."

"I'm sure that your Majesty realizes that you can rely totally on our discretion," Sadi said smoothly.

"Of course," Urgit replied drily. "Just as long as I do exactly what you tell me to do."

"Well, there's that, naturally."

Urgit looked at his seneschal. "Well, Oskatat," he said, "will you now dash to the highest window of the Drojim to proclaim this to the entire city?"

"Why should I?" Oskatat shrugged. "I've known since you were a little boy that you were not the son of Taur Urgas."

Lady Tamazin gasped, her hand going suddenly to her lips.

"You've known, Oskatat? And you've kept my shame a secret?"

"My Lady," he said with a stiff bow, "I would not have betrayed you even on the rack."

She gave him a peculiar look. "And why is that, Oskatat?" she asked gently.

"You are of the House of Hagga," he replied, "as am I. Loyalty to blood is very strong in Cthol Murgos."

"And is that all, Oskatat? Is that the only reason you befriended me and protected my son?"

He looked her full in the face. "No, my Lady," he said almost proudly, "it is not."

She lowered her eyelashes.

"There were other reasons for my keeping your secret, however," he continued, "less personal, perhaps, but just as compelling. The Urga Dynasty has brought Cthol Murgos to the brink of disaster. I saw in young Urgit the best hope for the kingdom. I might have wished him to be stronger, but his agility of mind showed much promise. In the long run a clever king is often preferable to a strong one without any brains."

Belgarath rose from his chair. "I hate to break up these festivities," he said, "but it's time for us to leave. Too many secrets are starting to come out into the open." He looked at Urgit. "Did you send that messenger to the Temple? If Agachak's Dagashi wants to go along with us, he's going to have to get down to the harbor at once."

Urgit started to rise from his chair, his face angry. Then he stopped, his eyes narrowing. "Just who are you, old man?" he demanded. "You look like a vagabond, but you've been throwing commands around here like an emperor."

Lady Tamazin, however, had been looking at Belgarath with eyes suddenly gone wide. Then she turned to stare in awe at Aunt Pol. "Urgit!" she said in a half-strangled whisper.

"What is it, mother?"

"Look at him. Look very closely—and then look at his daughter here."

"His daughter? I didn't know they were related."

"Neither did I—until just now." The Queen Mother looked directly at Polgara. "He is your father, isn't he, Lady Polgara?"

Polgara straightened, and the white lock at her brow caught the candlelight. "I think this has gone far enough, father," she said to the old man with a wry expression. "There's not much point in trying to hide things any more, is there?"

"Old friend," Silk said lightly, "you really ought to do something about your appearance, you know. Your description's been noised about the world for all these centuries, so people are bound to recognize you every so often. Have you ever considered shaving off your beard?"

Urgit was staring at the old man with an expression of near-terror.

"Oh, don't do that," Belgarath said in disgust.

Urgit flinched.

"And don't do that either. No matter what you've been told, I don't make a practice of biting off the heads of Murgo babies just for amusement." He tugged thoughtfully at one ear, looking first at Urgit, then at Lady Tamazin, and finally at Oskatat and Prala. "I think there's going to have to be a small change of plans," he said. "I believe that you people are all going to develop an irresistible craving for sea-travel—just as a precaution. You have some secrets you want kept, and so do we. This way we can sort of keep an eye on each other."

"You're not serious!" Urgit burst out.

"Yes, as a matter of fact, I am. I don't like leaving loose ends behind me."

The door opened, and Garion spun quickly, but stopped his hand halfway to his sword hilt. The Murgo officer who had just entered looked curiously at the people in the room, sensing the tension. "Uh—excuse me, your Majesty," he said a bit warily.

Urgit looked at him, a swift flash of hope fleeting across

his face. Then he cast a quick, fearful glance at Belgarath. "Yes, Colonel," he replied in a carefully neutral voice.

"A message has just arrived from the Hierarch, your Majesty. I am directed to advise you that the Dagashi Kabach will be at the harbor within the hour."

Durnik and Toth, moving in unison, had carefully sidled up until one of them stood on each side of Oskatat, and Polgara had crossed to Lady Tamazin's chair.

Urgit's face was faintly sick with fright. "Very good, Colonel," he replied. "Thank you for your trouble."

The officer bowed and then turned toward the door.

"Colonel," Prala's clear voice stopped him.

He turned back, his face respectful. "Yes, Princess?"

Velvet was moving toward the Murgo girl with a deceptive casualness. Garion inwardly flinched at the potential for sudden, awful violence that hung heavily in the air—even as he measured the distance to the unsuspecting colonel.

"Have you had any reports about the weather conditions along the coast to the south?" Prala asked calmly.

"There's some wind, your Highness," the colonel replied, "and there are almost always rain squalls around the tip of the peninsula."

"Thank you, Colonel."

He bowed and quietly left the room.

Garion let out his breath explosively.

"Lord Belgarath." Prala's voice was crisp. "You cannot expose the Lady Tamazin to that kind of weather. I will not permit it."

Belgarath blinked. "Will not permit?" he asked incredulously.

"Absolutely not. If you persist, I'll scream the roof down." She turned coolly to Velvet. "Don't come one step closer, Liselle," she warned. "I can scream at least twice before you can kill me, and that will bring every guard in the Drojim to this room on the run."

"She's right, you know, father," Polgara said very calmly. "Tamazin could not possibly endure the rigors of the voyage."

"Couldn't we—"

"No, father," she said firmly, "it's absolutely out of the question."

He muttered a sour curse and jerked his head at Sadi. The two of them moved down to the far end of the room for a brief, murmured conversation.

"You've got a knife under your doublet, haven't you, Kheldar?" Urgit asked.

"Two, actually," Silk replied in a matter-of-fact tone, "and one in my boot and another on a string at the back of my neck. I like to be prepared for little emergencies when they arise—but why dwell on an unpleasantness that never happened?"

"You're a dreadful man, Kheldar."

"I know."

Belgarath came back from his low-voiced conference with Sadi. "Lady Tamazin," he said.

The Queen Mother's chin lifted. "Yes?" she replied.

"Under the circumstances, I believe we can rely on your discretion," he said. "You've already proved that you know how to keep a secret. You *do* realize that your life—and your son's—depends on your not revealing what you've learned here, don't you?"

"Yes, I suppose I do."

"We're going to need to leave someone ostensibly in charge here anyway, so things will work out, I suppose."

"What you propose is quite impossible, Lord Belgarath."

"I do wish people would stop using that word. What's the problem now?"

"Murgos will not take orders from a woman."

Belgarath grunted sourly. "Oh, yes. I'd forgotten about that peculiar Murgo prejudice."

"My Lord Oskatat," Sadi said.

The seneschal's face was stony as he glanced briefly at Durnik and Toth standing one on each side of him.

"Wouldn't you be the logical one to attend to the affairs of state during his Majesty's absence?"

"It's possible."

"Just how far does your loyalty to your kinswoman, the Lady Tamazin, go?"

Oskatat scowled at him.

"Eriond," Ce'Nedra said then.

"Yes?"

"Can the seneschal be trusted not to send a fleet after us as soon as we leave?"

Garion looked up sharply. He had forgotten his young friend's peculiar ability to see directly into the minds and hearts of others.

"He won't say anything," Eriond replied confidently.

"Are you sure?" Ce'Nedra asked.

"Absolutely. He'd rather die than betray Tamazin."

A dull flush crept up into the big Murgo's scarred cheeks, and he turned his face so that he could avoid the Queen Mother's eyes.

"All right then." Belgarath's tone was decisive. "Urgit will go with us." He looked at the seneschal. "We'll drop him off not far from Rak Cthaka. You have my word on that. You stay here with Tamazin. It's up to you, but I'd recommend that you follow through on the plan to send reinforcements to the city by sea. Otherwise, your king may have to hold off the Malloreans all by himself."

"What about Prala?" Ce'Nedra asked.

Belgarath scratched his ear. "There's no real point in taking her along," he said. "I'm sure that if she stays here, Tamazin and Oskatat can keep her from blurting out any secrets."

"No, my Lord Belgarath," the slender Cthan Princess said firmly. "I will not stay behind. If his Majesty is going to Rak Cthaka, then so am I. I will not give you my word to remain silent. You have no choice but to take me along—or to kill me."

"What's this?" Urgit asked, puzzled.

Silk, however, had already guessed. "If you want to start running right now, Urgit, I'll try to hold her until you get a good head start."

"What are you talking about, Kheldar?"

"If you're very, very lucky, my brother, Kal Zakath won't get you, but I'm afraid that your chances of escaping this young lady are far more slender. Take my advice and start running right now."

CHAPTER SIXTEEN

A heavy bank of gray cloud had moved in off the Great Western Sea, and a stiff offshore breeze tugged at their garments as they mounted their horses in the courtyard of the Drojim.

"You know what to do, Oskatat?" Urgit asked his seneschal.

The big Murgo nodded. "The ships carrying the reinforcements will depart within two days, your Majesty. You have my word on that."

"Good. I'd rather not fight this battle all by myself. Try not to use any more of those warrants than you absolutely have to."

"Trust me." Oskatat's face creased into a bleak smile.

Urgit's quick answering grin was wolfish. "And look after my mother," he added.

"I've done that for many years—without her even being aware of it."

Gravely the Murgo King leaned down from his saddle and shook hands with his friend. Then he straightened resolutely. "All right," he said to the officer in charge of the guard detachment, "let's go."

They clattered out of the courtyard, and Silk drew in beside his brother. "What was that business about warrants?" he asked curiously.

Urgit laughed. "The generals might want to refuse to obey Oskatat's orders," he explained, "so I signed warrants for the execution of every one of them and left them with him to use as he sees fit."

"Clever."

"I should have thought of it years ago." Urgit looked up at the racing clouds overhead, with his robe flapping in the rising wind. "I'm not a very good sailor, Kheldar," he admitted with a shudder. "I tend to throw up a lot in rough weather."

Silk laughed. "Then just remember always to stand at the leeward rail."

The murky sky seemed somehow to Garion to be suited to the bleakness of Rak Urga. A city so devoid of any kind of beauty seemed unnatural when the sky was clear and the sun was shining. Now, however, it squatted under the roiling clouds like some torpid stone toad. The black-robed Murgos in the narrow streets stood aside for their king. Some of them bowed; others stood stony-faced and unbending as the party passed.

They rode through a square and then on down the stone-paved street that led to the Temple. "Captain," Urgit called to the officer in the lead, "have one of your men stop by and tell the Hierarch that we're leaving. He has someone in the Temple that he wants to send along with us."

"As your Majesty commands," the officer replied.

The cobbled street they were following rounded a corner, and they were able to see the harbor. It lay in a sheltered bay behind the headland standing at the narrow mouth of the Gulf of Urga and was dotted with black-painted Murgo ships. The familiar smell of the meeting of sea and land, a mixture of brine, seaweed, and dead fish, rose to meet Garion's nostrils, and his blood began to race at the prospect of once again going to sea.

The black ship moored at the side of the stone quay onto which they rode was larger than most of the other vessels in the harbor. It was a squat, broad-beamed scow with slanting masts and tarred planking. Silk eyed it distrustfully. "Do you really call that thing a ship?" he asked his brother.

"I warned you about Murgo boats."

There was a brief disagreement about the horses when they reached the ship. "Totally out of the question, your Majesty," the ship captain, a huge, evil-looking man, declared adamantly. "I don't carry livestock on board my ship." He stood towering over his king with a self-important expression slightly tinged with contempt on his face.

Urgit's expression became one of distress.

"I'd say that it's time for another exercise of the royal assertiveness," Silk murmured to him.

Urgit gave him a quick look and then squared his shoulders, He turned back to the hulking ship's master. "Load these horses on your ship, Captain," he repeated his command in a firmer tone.

"I just told you that I don't—"

"Did I say it too fast for you? Listen carefully this time. Put-the-horses-on-the-boat. If you don't do exactly what I tell you to do, I'll have you nailed to the prow of your ship in place of a figurehead. Do we understand each other?"

The captain stepped back, his look of arrogance becoming one of doubt and apprehension. "Your Majesty—"

"Do it, Captain!" Urgit barked, "Now!"

The captain drew himself up sharply, saluted, and then

turned to his crew. "You heard the king," he said harshly. "Load the horses." He stalked away, muttering to himself.

"You see," Silk said. "It gets easier every time you do it, doesn't it? All you have to remember is that your commands are not subjects for debate."

"You know," Urgit said with a tight grin, "I could actually get to like that."

The sailors began to push the skittish horses up the narrow gangplank and then down a steeply slanting ramp into the hold of the vessel. They had loaded perhaps half of the animals when Garion heard the sound of a sullen drum coming from the narrow, cobbled steet leading down to the quay. A double file of black-robed Grolims in polished steel masks marched down the hill toward the water, moving with that peculiar, swaying gait Garion had seen in the Temple. Belgarath took Urgit by the sleeve and drew him out of earshot of his guards and the busy sailors. "We don't need any surprises, here, Urgit," he said firmly, "so let's get through the formalities with Agachak as quickly as possible. Tell him that you're going to Rak Cthaka to take personal command of the defense of the city. Let's get your Dagashi on board ship and get out of here."

"I don't really have any choice about this, do I?" Urgit asked unhappily.

"No," Belgarath replied. "Not very much at all."

The cadaverous Agachak rode in a litter carried by a dozen Grolims. At his side, her head erect, came the scarred priestess Chabat. Her eyes were ravaged from weeping, and her face was dreadfully pale. The look she directed at Sadi, however, was filled with implacable hatred.

Behind Agachak's litter there came a hooded figure that did not walk with the stiff-legged, swaying gait of the Grolims in the Hierarch's entourage, and Garion surmised that this man was the mysterious Kabach. He looked at the man curiously, but could not see the face concealed beneath the hood.

As the litter reached the gangway, Agachak signaled his

bearers to a halt. "Your Majesty," he greeted Urgit hollowly as his litter was lowered to the stones.

"Dread Hierarch."

"I received your message. Is the situation in the south as grave as I was led to believe?"

"I'm afraid so, Agachak. I'm going to take advantage of this ship to go to Rak Cthaka and take personal command."

"You, your Majesty?" Agachak looked startled. "Is that altogether wise?"

"Perhaps not, but I'm sure I can't do much worse than my generals have done. I've left orders that reinforcements are to be sent to the city by ship."

"By ship? A daring innovation, your Majesty. I'm surprised that your generals agreed to it."

"I didn't ask them to agree. I finally realized that their duty to advise me doesn't give them the authority to order me around."

Agachak looked at him, his eyes thoughtful. "This is a new side of you, your Majesty," he noted, stepping out of his litter to stand on the stones of the quay.

"I thought it was time for a change."

It was at that point that Garion felt a warning tingle and an oppressive kind of weight that seemed centered just above his ears. He glanced quickly at Polgara, and she nodded. It did not appear to be emanating from the Hierarch, who seemed wholly engrossed in his conversation with Urgit. Chabat stood to one side with her burning eyes fixed balefully on Sadi, but there was no hint of any mounting of her will. The quiet probing was coming from somewhere else.

"We should be able to reach Rak Cthaka in five or six days," Urgit was saying to the red-robed Hierarch. "As soon as we arrive, I'll get Ussa and his people started toward Rak Hagga with our Dagashi. They might have to swing south a bit to avoid the Mallorean advance, but they won't lose too much time."

"You must be very careful at Rak Cthaka, your Majesty,"

Agachak cautioned. "It's not only the fate of Cthol Murgos you carry on your shoulders; it's the fate of the entire world."

"I don't concern myself too much with fate, Agachak. A man whose main concern has always been staying alive for the next hour or so doesn't have much time to worry about next year. Where's Kabach?"

The man in the hooded robe stepped out from behind the litter. "I'm here, your Majesty," he said in a deep, resonant voice. There was something familiar about that voice, and a warning prickle ran up between Garion's shoulder blades.

"Good," Urgit said. "Have you any final instructions for him, Agachak?"

"I have said to him all that needs to be said," the Hierarch responded.

"That covers everything, then." Urgit looked around. "All right," he said, "let's all get on board that ship."

"Perhaps not just yet, your Majesty," the black-robed Dagashi said to him, stepping forward and pushing back his hood. Garion suppressed a start of surprise. Although his black beard had been shaved off, there was no question about the man's identity. It was Harakan.

"There is one last thing your Majesty should know before we board," Harakan declared in a voice clearly intended to be heard by everyone on the quay. "Were you aware of the fact that the man with the sword over there is Belgarion of Riva?"

Urgit's eyes went very wide as a ripple of amazement went through the priests and the soldiers standing on the slippery stones of the quay. The Murgo King, however, was quick to recover. "That's a very interesting thing to suggest, Kabach," he said carefully. "I'd be interested to know what makes you so sure."

"It's absolute nonsense," Sadi spluttered.

Agachak's sunken eyes were boring into Garion's face. "I have seen Belgarion myself," he intoned hollowly. "He was much younger then, but there *is* a resemblance."

"A resemblance certainly, Dread Hierarch," Sadi agreed

quickly, "but that's all. The young man has been in my service since he was a boy. Oh, I'll admit that there are some superficial similarities of features, but I can assure you that this most definitely is *not* Belgarion."

Silk was standing just behind Urgit, and his lips were moving very fast as he whispered to his new-found brother. The Murgo King was a skilled enough politician to control his expression, but his eyes darted nervously this way and that as he began to realize that he stood at the very center of an incipient explosion. Finally, he cleared his throat. "You still haven't told us what makes you believe that this is Belgarion, Kabach," he said.

"I was in Tol Honeth some years ago," Harakan shrugged. "Belgarion was there at the same time—for a funeral, I think. Someone pointed him out to me."

"I think the noble Dagashi is mistaken," Sadi said. "His identification is based entirely on a fleeting glance from a distance. That hardly qualifies as definitive proof. I tell you that this is not Belgarion."

"He lies," Harakan said flatly. "I am of the Dagashi. We are trained observers."

"That raises an interesting point, Agachak," Urgit said, his eyes narrowing as he looked at Harakan. "In spite of everything, the Dagashi are still Murgos, and every Murgo alive slashes his face as a blood offering to Torak." He turned and pointed at two faint, thin white lines on his cheek. The king's scarcely visible scars gave mute evidence that his self-mutilation had been none too fervent. "Look at our Dagashi there," he continued. "I don't see a single mark on his face, do you?"

"I was instructed by my elder not to make the customary blood offering," Harakan said quickly. "He wanted me unmarked so that I could move around freely in the Kingdoms of the West."

"I'm sorry, Kabach," Urgit said with heavy scepticism, "but that story doesn't hold water at all. The blood offering to Torak is a part of the rite of passage into manhood. Were you so precocious as a child that your elder decided to make you a spy before you were ten years old? And even if he had, you would still have been required to go through the rite before you could marry or even enter the Temple. The scars may not be on your face, but if you're a Murgo, you've got scars on you someplace. Show us your scars, noble Dagashi. Let us see the proof of your fidelity to Torak and your uncontaminated Murgo blood."

"Dread Hierarch," Sadi said with a thoughtful expression on his face, "this is not the first accusation leveled at one of my servants." He looked meaningfully at Chabat. "Is it possible that there is a faction among your Grolims that does not want this mission to succeed—some group hiding behind false beards?"

"Beard!" Silk exclaimed, snapping his fingers. "That's why I couldn't place him! He's shaved off his beard!"

Urgit turned to look inquiringly at him. "What are you talking about, fellow?"

"Excuse me, your Majesty," Silk said with exaggerated humility. "I just realized something, and it surprised me. I think I can clarify things here."

"I certainly hope someone can. All right, go ahead."

"Thank you, your Majesty." Silk looked around with a beautifully feigned expression of nervousness. "I'm an Alorn, your Majesty," he said, then held up one hand quickly. "Please hear me out," he begged, half of the king and half of the surrounding Murgos. "I'm an Alorn, but I'm not a fanatic about it. The way I look at it, there's plenty of room in the world for Alorns and Murgos. Live and let live, I always say. Anyway, last year I hired myself out as a soldier in King Belgarion's army—the one that he raised to lay seige to the Bear-cult at Rheon in northeastern Drasnia. Well, to make it short, I was present when Belgarion and his friend from Sendaria—Durnik, I think his name is—captured the cult-leader, Ulfgar. He had a beard then, but I swear to you that this Kabach is the selfsame man. I ought to know. I helped to carry him into a house after Durnik knocked him senseless."

"What would a Dagashi be doing in Drasnia?" Urgit asked with an artfully puzzled expression on his face.

"Oh, he's not a Dagashi, your Majesty," Silk explained. "When King Belgarion and his friends questioned him, it came out that he's a Mallorean Grolim. Harakan, I think his name is."

"Harakan?" Agachak said, turning quickly to fix the counterfeit Dagashi with his suddenly smoldering eyes.

"Ridiculous," Harakan scoffed. "This little weasel is one of Belgarion's servants. He's lying to protect his master."

"Is the name Harakan in any way significant, Agachak?" Urgit asked.

The Hierarch straightened, his eyes intent. "Harakan is Urvon's underling," he replied, "and I've heard that he's been seen here in the west."

"I think we've got a problem on our hands here, Agachak," Urgit said. "These charges—both of them—are too serious to be ignored. We've got to get to the truth here."

The priestess Chabat's eyes were narrowed, and her expression cunning. "Finding that truth is a simple matter, your Majesty," she declared. "My master Agachak is the most powerful sorcerer in all of Cthol Murgos. He will have no difficulty in probing the minds of all who are here to find out who is speaking truth and who is lying."

"Can you really do that, Agachak?" Urgit asked.

Agachak shrugged. "It's a simple matter."

"Then by all means, do it. I'm not going on board that scow over there until I find out exactly who my shipmates are going to be."

Agachak took a deep breath and began to draw in his will.

"Master!" a Grolim with a purple satin lining on the hood of his robe exclaimed, leaping forward with one hand outstretched. "Beware!"

"How dare you?" Chabat shrieked at him, her eyes blazing.

The Grolim ignored her. "Master," he said to Agachak, "there is great danger in what the priestess proposes. Should either of these men be telling the truth, you will be probing the mind of a powerful sorcerer, and your own mind will be totally vulnerable. A single thought could erase your entire consciousness."

Agachak slowly relaxed his will. "Ah, yes," he murmured. "I had not considered that danger." He turned to Chabat, catching the brief flicker of disappointment that crossed her face. "How curious that my Holy Priestess did not think of that before she suggested the probing—or did you, Chabat? Have you given up the notion of raising a demon to destroy me, then? Will you now fall back on so commonplace a thing as simple deceit? I'm terribly disappointed in you, my beloved."

She shrank back, her scar-laced face frightened.

"This matter has to be settled, Agachak," Urgit said. "I'm not going to go near that ship until I find out the truth here. I haven't succeeded in staying alive for all these years by being foolhardy."

"The question is largely academic now anyway," Agachak replied. "None of these people will be leaving."

"Agachak, I have to get to Rak Cthaka immediately."

"Then go. I will find another party of slavers and hire another Dagashi."

"That could take months," Urgit protested. "Personally, I'm inclined to believe these slavers. Ussa has been very honest with me, and the young man over there has none of the bearing of a king. This one who calls himself Kabach, however, is highly suspect. If you were to look along the trail between here and Mount Kahsha, I think you might find the real Kabach in a shallow grave someplace. This man—whoever he is—has come very close to forestalling the mission to Rak Hagga with his accusation. Wouldn't that be exactly what Urvon would want?"

"There's a logic to what you say, your Majesty, but I don't think I want any of them going on board that ship until I find out the truth."

"Why not let *them* settle it for us, then?"

"I don't follow you."

"One of them—or possibly both—is a sorcerer. Let them fight each other, and we'll see which one tries to destroy the other by sorcery."

"Trial by combat?"

"Why not? It's a bit antique, but the circumstances here seem to be appropriate."

"There is merit in your plan, your Majesty."

Urgit suddenly grinned. "Why don't we clear a space?" he suggested. "We wouldn't want to get singed when these two start hurling thunderbolts at each other." He came over and took Garion's arm. "Just stay calm," he whispered, "and don't do anything conspicuous. Try to force him to use sorcery." Then he pushed Garion forward into the circle that had quickly been formed on the stone quay. "Here is the supposed King of Riva," he said to Agachak. "Now, if the ostensible Mallorean Grolim will be so good as to step forth, we'll find out who's been telling the truth."

"I have no sword," Harakan said sullenly.

"Simplicity in itself. Somebody give him a sword."

Several were offered at once.

"I think you're in deep trouble, Harakan," Urgit smirked. "If you so much as twitch one finger, you'll reveal yourself as a Mallorean Grolim, and my soldiers will shoot you full of arrows. On the other hand, if this is really Belgarion and you don't use sorcery to defend yourself, he'll burn you right down into a little pile of cinders. All in all, I think you're in for a very bad afternoon."

Garion ground his teeth together and began talking fervently to the Orb, telling the stone over and over again not to do anything out of the ordinary. Then he steeled himself and reached back over his shoulder. The great blade made a steely hiss as it came out of the scabbard.

Harakan handled his borrowed sword nervously, but the way he held it and his stance clearly indicated that he was a competent swordsman. A sudden anger filled Garion. This was the man who had been responsible for the attempt on Ce'Nedra's life and for the murder of Brand. He dropped into a half crouch with Iron-grip's sword extended in front of him. Harakan desperately tried to slap that great blade away with his own sword, and there was a steely ring as the two swords came together. Implacably, Garion stalked his enemy. His anger was so great that he had even forgotten the reason for this duel. He was no longer interested in unmasking Harakan. All he wanted to do was to kill him.

There was a rapid exchange of thrusts and parries, and the entire harbor rang with the steel song of the swords. Step by step Harakan retreated, and his eyes began to fill with fear. But finally Garion lost all patience with fencing. With his eyes ablaze he seized the hilt of his huge sword in both hands and swung it back over his shoulder. Had he delivered that blow, nothing could have stopped it.

Harakan's cheeks blanched as he looked directly into the face of death. "Curse you!" he shouted at Garion, then flickered and vanished, to reappear briefly at the far end of the quay. He shimmered and swooped away in the form of a swift sea hawk.

"That sort of answers the question, doesn't it, Agachak?" Urgit said quite calmly.

Agachak, however, his eyes ablaze with hate, also flashed into the form of a hawk. With two powerful strokes of his pinions, he drove himself into the air, shrieking for blood as he raced after the fleeing Harakan.

Garion's hands were shaking. He turned and stalked toward Urgit with a scorching fury rising in his throat. With a great effort he restrained his sudden desire to take hold of the front of the smaller man's doublet and hurl him far out into the harbor.

"Now—now don't be hasty," Urgit said, backing fearfully away.

Garion spoke from between clenched teeth in a dreadfully quiet voice. "Don't *ever* do that again."

"Naturally not," Urgit agreed hastily. He stopped, a curious expression suddenly crossing his rat-like face. "Are you *really* Belgarion?" he asked in a hoarse whisper.

"Would you like some proof?"

"No, no—that's quite all right." Urgit's words came tumbling out. He stepped quickly around the still infuriated Garion and crossed the quay to where Chabat stood. "Let us pray that your Hierarch succeeds in capturing that imposter," he said. "Give him my regards upon his return. I'd wait, but I must board ship and depart at once."

"Of course, your Majesty," she replied in a voice that was nearly a purr. "I will take charge of these slavers until the Hierarch's return."

He stared at her.

"Since the entire purpose of this mission was to convey the Dagashi assassin to Rak Hagga, there's no point in their going now, is there? They will have to remain here while we send to Kahsha for another Dagashi." She looked at Sadi with an unconcealed smirk. "I will place them under my personal protection."

Urgit looked at her narrowly. "Holy Priestess," he said to her, "to be quite candid about it, I don't think you can be trusted. Your personal enmity toward this Nyissan is painfully obvious, and he's far too important to risk. I don't think that you would be able to restrain yourself, once both Agachak and I are gone from Rak Urga. I think I'll just take Ussa and his people with me—just to be on the safe side. When the Dagashi arrives from Mount Kahsha, send him along."

Chabat's eyes hardened, and her face grew angry. "The purpose of the mission to Rak Hagga is to fulfill a prophecy," she declared, "and the fulfillment of prophecy is clearly in the domain of the Church."

Urgit drew in a deep breath. Then he straightened from his usual slouching posture. "The mission is also a State matter, Holy Priestess. Agachak and I have been co-operating in this affair, and in his absence I assert the authority of the crown. Ussa and his people will go with me, and you will take your Grolims back to the Temple to await the return of your Hierarch."

Chabat seemed taken aback by his sudden show of

strength. She had obviously expected to brush aside any feeble objections he might raise, but this seemed to be a new Urgit. Her face hardened, and the flamelike scars writhed on her pale cheeks. "So," she said, "it appears that our king is finally maturing. I think, however, that you will come to regret your passage into manhood at this particular time. Watch closely, High King of Cthol Murgos." She bent, holding something in her hand, and began to mark symbols on the stones of the quay—symbols that glowed with an unholy light.

"Garion!" Silk cried in alarm, "Stop her!"

But Garion had also seen the glowing circle Chabat had drawn on the wet stones and the burning five-pointed star she was inscribing in its center and he recognized the meaning of those symbols immediately. He took a halfstep toward Chabat, even as she stepped into the protection of the circle and began muttering words in some unknown language.

As fast as he was, however, Polgara was even faster. "Chabat!" she said sharply, "Stop! This is forbidden!"

"Nothing is forbidden to one who has the power," the priestess replied, her scarred and beautiful face filled with an overwhelming pride, "and who here can prevent me?"

Polgara's face grew grim. "I can," she said calmly. She raised her hand in a curious lifting gesture, and Garion felt the surge of her will. The sullen swells washing against the stones of the quay slowly rose until they broke across the top to swirl about the ankles of those who stood there. The burning symbols Chabat had marked on the stones vanished as the water washed over them.

The Grolim priestess drew in her breath sharply and stared at Aunt Pol, realization slowly dawning in her eyes. "Who are you?"

"One who would save your life, Chabat," Polgara answered. "The punishment for raising demons has always been the same. You might succeed once or twice—or even a few more times—but in the end, the demon will turn on you and tear you to pieces. Not even Torak in all his twisted madness would have dared to step across this line."

"But I *do* dare! Torak is dead, and Agachak is not here to prevent me. No one can stop me."

"I can, Chabat," Polgara said quietly. "I will not permit you to do this."

"And how will you stop me? I have the power."

"But mine is greater." Polgara let her cloak fall to the stones at her feet, bent, and removed her shoes. "You may have been able to control your demon the first time you raised him," she said, "but your control is only temporary. You are no more than the doorway through which he enters this world. As soon as he feels his full strength, he will destroy you and be loosed upon this world to raven as he chooses. I beg of you, my sister, do not do this. Your life—and your very soul—are in deadly peril."

"I have no fear," Chabat rasped. "Not of my demon and not of you."

"Then you're a fool—on both counts."

"You challenge me?"

"If I must. Will you meet me on my own ground, Chabat?" Polgara's blue eyes were suddenly like ice, and the white lock at her brow flamed incandescently as she gathered in her will. Once again she raised her hand and the lead-gray swells again raised obediently to the edge of the quay. With that same dreadful calm, she stepped out onto the surface of the water and stood there, as if what lay under her feet was firm earth. A sudden moan rose from the Grolims as she turned to look at the awe-stricken priestess. "Well, Chabat," she said, "will you join me here? *Can* you join me?"

Chabat's scarred face grew ashen, but her eyes clearly showed that she could not refuse Aunt Pol's challenge. "I will," she rasped through clenched teeth. Then she, too, stepped off the quay, but floundered awkwardly as she sank to the knees in the dirty waters of the harbor.

"Is it so very difficult for you, then?" Polgara asked her. "If this little thing takes all of your will, how do you imagine that you will have enough power to control a demon? Abandon this desperate plan, Chabat. There is still time to save your own life."

"Never!" Chabat shrieked with flecks of froth coming to her lips. With an enormous effort, she lifted herself until she stood on the surface and laboriously strode out several yards. Then, with her face once again twisted into that overwhelming triumph, she drew the symbols on the face of the water, inscribing them with sooty orange flame. Her voice rose again in the evil incantation of the summoning, rising and falling in its hideous cadences. The red scars on her cheeks seemed to grow pale, then suddenly glowed with a burning white light as she continued to recite the spell.

"Kheldar, what's happening?" Urgit's voice was shrill as he stared at the impossibility that was occurring before his eyes.

"Something very unpleasant," Silk told him.

Chabat's voice had risen to a shriek, and the surface of the harbor suddenly erupted before her in a seething cauldron of steam and fire. Out of the midst of those flames there arose something so hideous that it was beyond comprehension. It was vast and clawed and fanged, but the worst of all were its red, glowing eyes.

"Kill her!" Chabat cried, pointing at Polgara with a trembling hand. "I command thee to kill this witch!"

The demon looked at the priestess standing safely within the flaming circle of her protective symbols and then, with the still-boiling water surging around his vast trunk, he turned and started toward Polgara. But, with her face still calm, she raised one hand. "Stop!" she commanded, and Garion felt the enormous jolting force of her will.

The demon suddenly howled, his fanged muzzle lifted toward the gray clouds in a sudden agony of frustration.

"I said kill her!" Chabat shrieked again.

The monster slowly sank into the water, extending his two huge arms just beneath the surface. He began to turn, rotating slowly in the seething water. Faster and faster he spun, with the water sizzling around him. A vortex began to appear around him as he whirled, a sudden maelstrom very nearly as dreadful as the Cherek Bore.

Chabat howled her triumph, dancing on the surface of the water in an obscene caper, unaware that the flames with which she had drawn her symbols had been suddenly whirled away by the surging vortex.

As the spinning waters reached the spot where Polgara stood, she began to be drawn toward the deadly whirlpool and the slavering demon still whirling in its center.

"Pol!" Durnik shouted. "Look out!"

But it was too late. Caught in that inexorable maelstrom, she was carried round and round, slowly at first but then faster and faster as she was pulled in long spirals toward the center. As she neared it, however, she once again raised her hand and very suddenly she disappeared beneath the surging surface.

"Pol!" Durnik shouted again, his face suddenly gone deathly white. Struggling to pull off his tunic, he ran toward the edge of the quay. Belgarath, however, his face grimly set, caught the smith's arm. "Stay out of it, Durnik!" he snapped, his voice cracking like a whip.

Durnik struggled with him, trying to pull himself free. "Let me go!" he yelled.

"I said not to interfere!"

Beyond the edge of the demon-created vortex, a single rose bobbed to the surface. It was a curiously familiar flower, its petals white on the outside and a deep, blushing crimson in the center. Garion stared at it, a sudden wild hope springing up in him.

At the center of the swirling vortex, the monstrous demon suddenly stopped, his burning eyes filled with bafflement. Without any warning he rose, arched foward, and plunged headfirst into the seething water.

"Find her!" the flame-marked Chabat screamed after her enslaved fiend. "Find her and kill her!"

The leaden waters of the harbor boiled and steamed as the huge demon surged this way and that beneath the surface.

Quite suddenly, the movement stopped, and the air and the water grew deadly calm.

Chabat, still standing on the water and with the glowing light still illuminating the cruel scars on her cheeks, lifting both arms above her head in a gesture of exaltation. "Die, witch!" she shouted. "Feel the fangs of my servant rend your flesh!"

Suddenly a monstrous, scaly claw came up out of the water directly in front of her. "No!" she shrieked, "you cannot!" Then she looked in horror at the water upon which she stood, realizing at last that her protective symbols had been swept away. She took a faltering step backward, but the huge hand closed on her, its needle-sharp claws biting deeply into her body. Her blood spurted, and she screamed in agony, writhing in that awful grasp.

Then, with a huge bellow, the demon rose from the depths with his great, fanged muzzle agape. He lifted the struggling priestess aloft with a howl of hellish triumph. The Grolims and the Murgo soldiers on the quay broke and fled in terror as the monster started toward them.

The single rose that had floated to the surface of the harbor, however, had begun to glow with a strange blue light. It seemed to grow larger as the glow intensified. Then, her face calm, Polgara appeared in the very center of that coruscating incandescence. A few feet to her left there also appeared a nimbus of flickering light. Before the stunned eyes of those on the quay, the nimbus suddenly coalesced, and there, standing beside Polgara, Garion saw the glowing form of the God Aldur.

"Must it be so, Master?" Polgara asked in a voice that clearly revealed her reluctance.

"It must, my daughter," Aldur replied sadly.

Polgara sighed. "Then so be it, Master." She extended her left hand, and the God enclosed it in his. The gathering-in of her will roared in Garion's mind like a tornado, and the force of it pushed against him with an awful power. Enclosed in blue light and linked by their touching hands, Polgara and

Aldur stood side by side on the surface of the water, facing the hideous demon who still held the weakly struggling Chabat high in the air.

"I abjure thee, creature of darkness," Polgara said in a great voice. "Return to the hell that spawned thee and never more corrupt this world by thy foul presence. Begone and take with thee the one who summoned thee." She raised her hand, and the force of her will, combined with the will of the God Aldur, blazed forth from her palm. There was a vast thunderclap as the demon suddenly exploded into a huge ball of fire with the waters of the harbor geysering up around it. Then he was gone, and with him disappeared the priestess Chabat.

When Garion looked back, Aldur no longer stood at Polgara's side. She turned and slowly walked back across the waves toward the quay. As she approached, Garion clearly saw that her eyes were filled with anguish.

Part Three

THE ISLE OF VERKAT

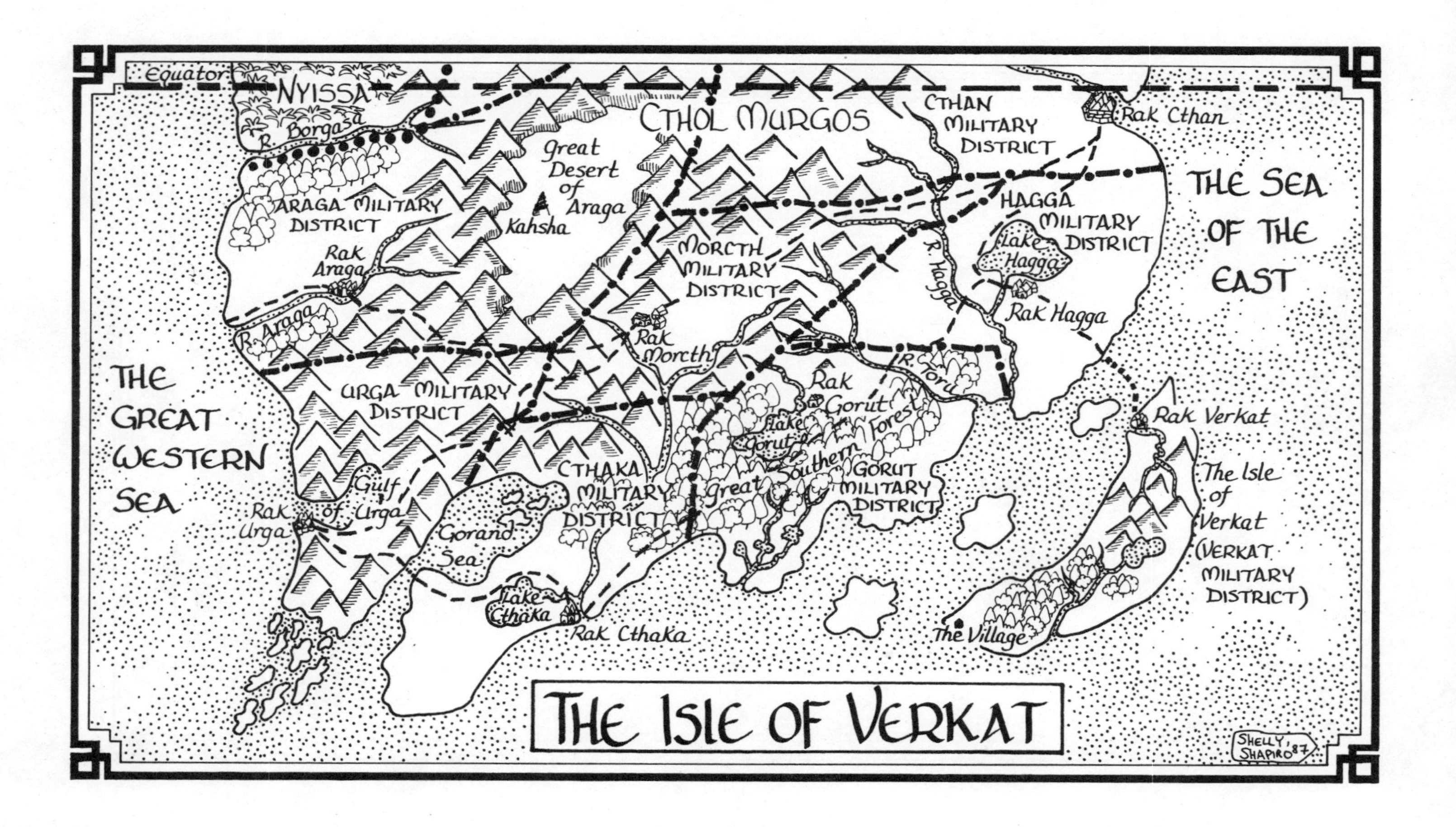
THE ISLE OF VERKAT
Equator
NYISSA
R. Borgasa
CTHOL MURGOS
CTHAN MILITARY DISTRICT
Rak Cthan
THE SEA OF THE EAST
ARAGA MILITARY DISTRICT
Great Desert of Araga
Kahsha
Rak Araga
R. Araga
MORCTH MILITARY DISTRICT
Rak Morcth
HAGGA MILITARY DISTRICT
Lake Hagga
R. Hagga
Rak Hagga
R. Toru
THE GREAT WESTERN SEA
URGA MILITARY DISTRICT
Rak Gorut
Lake Gorut
Great Southern Forest
GORUT MILITARY DISTRICT
Rak Verkat
The Isle of Verkat (VERKAT MILITARY DISTRICT)
Gulf of Urga
Rak Urga
CTHAKA MILITARY DISTRICT
Gorand Sea
Lake Cthaka
Rak Cthaka
The Village
SHELLY SHAPIRO 87

CHAPTER SEVENTEEN

The barren coast of the Urga peninsula slid by on their left the following morning as the Murgo scow beat steadily southward with a good following breeze. Cliffs rose sharply out of the crashing surf, and there was only the scantiest of vegetation to break the monotony of the desolation of rust-colored rock. The autumn sky was a deep, chill blue, but the sun stood far to the north, for winter came early to these extreme southern latitudes.

Garion, as he always did when he was at sea, had risen at first light of day and gone up on deck. He stood at the rail amidships, half-bemused by the sparkle of the morning sun on the waves and by the steady creak and roll of the vessel under his feet.

The slanting door that opened onto the short flight of steps leading down to the aft companionway creaked, and Durnik came out on deck, bracing himself against the awkward roll of the ship and squinting in the bright sunlight. The smith wore his usual plain brown tunic, and his face was somber.

Garion crossed the deck to his friend's side. "Is she all right?" he asked.

"She's very tired," Durnik replied wearily. His own nearly exhausted face clearly showed that he had slept very little himself. "She tossed and fretted for a long time before she finally went to sleep last night. That was a terrible thing she had to do."

"Did she talk to you about it at all?"

"Some. The demon had to be sent back to where he came from. Otherwise he'd have spread horror and death across the whole world. Since Chabat summoned him, he could have used her as a doorway to come into this world any time he wanted to. That's why Chabat had to go with him—to close that doorway."

"Exactly where do they come from—demons, I mean?"

"She didn't say very much about that, but I got the feeliing that I wouldn't really want to know about it."

"Is she sleeping now?"

Durnik nodded. "I'm going to go talk with the ship's cook. I want to have something hot for her to eat when she wakes up."

"You'd better get some sleep yourself."

"Perhaps. Would you excuse me, Garion? I don't want to stay away too long—just in case she wakes up and needs me." He went on forward toward the ship's galley.

Garion straightened and looked around. The Murgo sailors worked with fearful looks on their faces. What had taken place the previous afternoon had washed away all traces of the stiff arrogance that usually marked a Murgo's expression, and they all cast frightened, sidelong glances at every one of their passengers, as if expecting them to turn into ogres or sea monsters without any warning.

Silk and Urgit had emerged from the companionway door while Garion and Durnik had been talking and stood at the rail near the stern, idly watching the bubbly wake tracing its path across the dark green swells and the white-winged gulls screeching and hovering in a greedy cloud behind them. Garion moved a bit closer, but did not actually join them.

"Uninviting sort of place," Silk observed, looking at the stark cliffs rising from the sea. The little man had discarded the shabby clothing he had worn when they had begun this journey and he now wore a plain, unadorned gray doublet.

Urgit grunted morosely. Idly, he tossed chunks of stale bread into their wake, watching without much interest as the squawking gulls trailing the ship swooped down to fight over them. "Kheldar," he said, "does she do that all the time?"

"Who's that?"

"Polgara." Urgit shuddered. "Does she obliterate everybody who displeases her?"

"No," Silk replied. "Polgara doesn't do that—none of them do. It's not allowed."

"I'm sorry, Kheldar. Allowed or not, I know what I saw yesterday."

"I talked to Belgarath about it," Silk told him, "and he explained it. Chabat and the demon weren't actually destroyed. They were just sent back to the place where the demon came from. The demon absolutely had to be sent back; unfortunately, Chabat had to go with him."

"Unfortunately? I didn't feel all that much sympathy for her."

"I don't think you quite understand, Urgit. Killing somebody is one thing, but destroying someone's soul is quite something else. That's what made Polgara miserable. She was forced to condemn Chabat to eternal pain and horror. That's the most terrible thing anybody can be forced to do."

"Who was that who came up out of the water with her?"

"Aldur."

"You're not serious!"

"Oh, yes. I've seen him once or twice. It was Aldur, all right."

"A God? Here? What was he doing?"

"He had to be here." Silk shrugged. "No human, however powerful, can face a demon unaided. When the magicians of the Morindim raise a demon, they always are very careful to set rigid limits on him. Chabat just unleashed hers without any limits at all. Only a God can deal with a demon with that kind of freedom; and since the Gods work through us, Polgara had to be involved as well. It was a very tricky business."

Urgit shuddered. "I don't think I'm going to be able to deal with this."

They stood side by side, leaning on the rail and looking out at the long waves rolling in off the Great Western Sea to crash against the barren cliffs. As Garion looked at the two of them, he wondered how it had been possible for anyone to miss the relationship. Although they were not exactly identical, their features were so much alike that there could be no doubt they were brothers.

"Kheldar," Urgit said finally, "what was our father really like?"

"He was taller than either of us," Silk replied, "and very distinguished-looking. His hair was sort of iron-gray, and this nose we've all got made him look more like an eagle than a rat."

"We do look a bit like rodents, don't we?" Urgit agreed with a brief smile. "That's not what I meant, though. What was he really like?"

"Polished. He had exquisite manners, and he was very civilized and urbane. I never heard him use a harsh word to anyone." Silk's face was melancholy.

"But he was deceitful, wasn't he?"

"What makes you say that?"

"He did cheat, after all. I'm not the product of any sort of lasting fidelity."

"You don't exactly understand," Silk disagreed. He looked thoughtfully out at the green swells topped by an occasional whitecap. "For all his polish, our father was very much an adventurer. He'd accept any challenge—just for the fun involved—and he had an insatiable wanderlust. He was always looking for something new. I think that when you put the two of those traits together, you might begin to understand exactly why he was attracted to your mother. I visited the palace in Rak Goska when Taur Urgas was still alive. His wives were all either closely guarded or kept under lock and key. It was the sort of thing our father would have viewed as a challenge."

Urgit made a sour face. "You aren't bolstering my ego very much, Kheldar. I'm here because a Drasnian gentleman liked to pick locks."

"Not entirely. I didn't have much chance to talk with your mother about it, but I gather that she and our father were genuinely fond of each other. Taur Urgas was never fond of anyone. At least our father and your mother were having fun."

"Maybe that explains my sunny disposition."

Silk sighed. "He didn't have too much fun after my mother's illness, though. That put an end to all the wandering and adventures."

"What kind of illness was it?"

"A pestilence that breaks out in Drasnia from time to time. It disfigures its victims horribly. My mother was blinded by its effects, fortunately."

"Fortunately?"

"She couldn't look into a mirror. Our father stayed by her side for the rest of his life and never once gave any hint about what he saw whenever he looked at her." Silk's face was bleak, and his jaws were tightly clenched together. "It was the bravest thing I've ever seen any man do—and it was all the worse because it went on and on and on until the day he died." He looked away quickly. "Do you suppose we could talk about something else?"

"I'm sorry, Kheldar," Urgit said sympathetically. "I didn't mean to open old wounds."

"What was it like growing up in Rak Goska?" Silk asked after a moment.

"Grim," Urgit replied. "Taur Urgas had begun to show signs of his madness much earlier than was usual in the Urga family, and there were all kinds of rituals we had to observe."

"I've seen some of them."

"Not just the ones in the Temple, Kheldar—although there were plenty of those as well. I'm talking about his personal peculiarities. No one was ever supposed to stand to his right, and it was worth a man's life to let his shadow fall on the royal person. My brothers and I were taken from our mothers at the age of seven and set to training—military exercises for the most part—involving a great deal of grunting and sweating. Lapses of any kind were punished with flogging—usually at the supper table."

"That might tend to cool one's appetite."

"It does indeed. I don't even eat supper any more—too many unpleasant memories. My brothers and I all started plotting against each other very early. Taur Urgas had many wives and whole platoons of children. Since the crown falls to the eldest surviving son, we all schemed against our older brothers and tried to protect ourselves against the plots of the younger ones. One charming little fellow ran a knife into one of the others when he was nine."

"Precocious," Silk murmured.

"Oh, he was indeed. Taur Urgas was delighted, of course. For a time, the little back-stabber was his favorite. That made me and my older brothers quite nervous, since it was entirely possible that our insane sire might have seen fit to have us all strangled to make room for the little monster, so we took steps."

"Oh?"

"We caught him alone in the upper floors of the palace one day and threw him out a window." Urgit looked somberly out over the long swells sweeping in off the Great Western Sea. "From the day we were taken from our mothers, we lived a life of constant fear and senseless brutality. We were supposed to be perfect Murgos—strong, brave, insanely loyal, and absolutely dedicated to Torak. Each of us had a Grolim for a tutor, and we had to listen to hours of gibberish about the God of Angarak every day. It wasn't what you might call a pleasant childhood."

"Taur Urgas never showed any kind of affection?"

"Not to me, he didn't. I was always the smallest, and he had a great deal of contempt for me. Murgos are supposed to be big and muscular. Even after I'd managed to work my way up to the point where I was heir apparent, he never had a civil word for me and he encouraged my younger brothers to try to murder me."

"How did you manage to survive?"

"By my wits—and by using a key I managed to steal."

"A key?"

"To the palace strong room. You'd be amazed at how much help a man with unlimited funds at his command can get—even in Cthol Murgos."

Silk shivered. "It's getting definitely chilly out here on deck," he said. "Why don't we go inside and share a flagon of spiced wine?"

"I don't drink, Kheldar."

"You don't?" Silk sounded amazed.

"I need to keep my wits about me. A man with his head stuck in a wine barrel can't see someone creeping up behind him with a knife, can he?"

"You're quite safe with me, brother."

"I'm not safe with anyone, Kheldar—particularly not with a brother. Nothing personal, you understand—just the result of a very nervous childhood."

"All right," Silk said amiably. "Let's go inside, and you can watch *me* drink. I'm very good at it."

"I can imagine. You're an Alorn, after all."

"So are you, dear brother." Silk laughed. "So are you. Come along, and I'll introduce you to all the fun that goes with your heritage."

Garion was on the verge of turning to follow them, but at that moment Belgarath came out on deck, stretching and yawning. "Is Pol up yet?" he asked Garion.

Garion shook his head. "I talked with Durnik a little while ago. He said that she's very tired after what she did yesterday."

Belgarath frowned slightly. "It really shouldn't have tired her all that much," he said. "It was spectacular, I'll admit, but hardly exhausting."

"I don't think it's that kind of exhaustion, Grandfather. Durnik said she was troubled for about half the night."

The old man scratched at his beard. "Oh," he said, "sometimes I lose sight of the fact that Pol's a woman. She can't seem to put things behind her, and sometimes her compassion gets the better of her."

"That's not necessarily a bad trait, Grandfather."

"Not for a woman, perhaps."

"I seem to remember something that happened in the fens once," Garion told him. "Didn't you sort of go out of your way to do something for Vordai—more or less out of compassion?"

Belgarath looked around guiltily. "I thought we agreed that you weren't going to mention that."

"You know something, Grandfather?" Garion said with a faint smile. "You're a fraud. You pretend to be as cold as ice and as hard as a rock, but underneath you've got the same emotions as all the rest of us."

"Please, Garion, don't bandy that about too much."

"Does it bother you being human?"

"Well, not really, but after all, I do sort of have a reputation to maintain."

By late afternoon the coast line they had been following had grown even more jagged, and the surf boiled and thundered against the rocks. Silk and Urgit came up out of the aft companionway, and Garion noted that both were a trifle unsteady as they walked.

"Hello there, Belgarion," Urgit said expansively. "How would you like to join us? Kheldar and I have decided that we'd like to sing for a bit."

"Uh—thanks all the same," Garion replied carefully, "but I don't sing very well."

"That doesn't matter, old boy. It doesn't matter in the slightest. I might not be very good at it myself. I can't say for sure, because I've never sung a note in my whole life." He giggled suddenly. "There are a lot of things I've never done before, and I think it might be time I tried a few."

Ce'Nedra and the Murgo girl, Prala, came up on deck. Instead of her customary black, Prala was dressed in a stunning gown of pale rose, and her jet-black hair was caught in an intricate coil at the nape of her neck.

"My ladies," Urgit greeted them with a formal bow, marred only slightly by an unsteady lurch.

"Careful, old boy," Silk said, catching him by the elbow. "I don't want to have to fish you out of the sea."

"You know something, Kheldar?" Urgit said, blinking owlishly. "I don't think I've ever felt quite this good." He looked at Ce'Nedra and the dark-haired Prala. "You know something else? Those are a couple of awfully pretty girls there. Do you think they might like to sing with us?"

"We could ask them."

"Why don't we?"

The pair of them descended on Ce'Nedra and her Murgo companion, imploring them outrageously to join them in song. Prala laughed as the Murgo King lurched forward and back with the roll of the ship. "I think you two are drunk," she declared.

"Are we drunk?" Urgit asked Silk, still swaying on his feet.

"I certainly hope so," Silk replied. "If we aren't, we've wasted a great deal of very good wine."

"I guess we're drunk then. Now that's been settled, what shall we sing?"

"Alorns!" Ce'Nedra sighed, rolling her eyes skyward.

It was raining the following morning when they awoke, a chill drizzle that hissed into the sea and collected to run in heavy droplets down the tarred ropes of the rigging. Polgara joined them for breakfast in the larger cabin at the extreme aft end of the companionway, though she seemed silent and withdrawn.

Velvet looked brightly around the cabin, where stoutly constructed windows instead of portholes stretched across the stern and heavy beams held up a ceiling which was actually the deck above. She looked pointedly at the two conspicuously empty chairs at the breakfast table. "What's become of Prince Kheldar and his wayward royal brother?" she asked.

"I think they lingered a bit too long over their wine cups yesterday," Ce'Nedra replied with a slightly malicious smirk. "I'd imagine that they're feeling just a bit delicate this morning."

"Would you believe that they were singing?" Prala said.

"Oh?" Velvet said. "Were they doing it well?"

Prala laughed. "They frightened away the seagulls. I've never heard such dreadful noise."

Polgara and Durnik had been talking quietly at the far end of the table. "I'm perfectly fine, Durnik," she assured him. "You go right ahead."

"I don't want to leave you alone, Pol," he told her.

"I won't be alone, dear. Ce'Nedra, Prala, and Liselle will all be with me. If you don't find out for yourself, you'll wonder about it for the rest of your life and always regret the fact that you passed the opportunity by."

"Well—if you're sure, Pol."

"I'm certain, dear," she said, laying her hand fondly on his and kissing his cheek.

After breakfast, Garion pulled on a cloak and went out on deck. He stood squinting up into the drizzle for a few minutes, then turned as he heard the companionway door open behind him. Durnik and Toth emerged with fishing poles in their hands. "It only stands to reason, Toth," Durnik was saying. "With that much water, there almost have to be fish."

Toth nodded, then made a peculiar gesture, extending both his arms out as if measuring something.

"I don't quite follow you."

Toth made the gesture again.

"Oh, I'm sure they wouldn't be all that big," the smith disagreed. "Fish don't get that big, do they?"

Toth nodded vigorously.

"I don't mean to doubt you," Durnik said seriously, "but I'd have to see that."

Toth shrugged.

"Quite a beautiful morning, isn't it, Garion?" Durnik said, smiling up at the dripping sky. Then he went up the three steps to the aft deck, nodded pleasantly to the steersman at the tiller, and then made a long, smooth cast out into the frothy wake. He looked critically at his trailing lure. "I think we're going to need some weight on the lines to hold them down, don't you?" he said to Toth.

The giant smiled slightly, then nodded his agreement.

"Have Silk and Urgit managed to get up yet?" Garion called to them.

"Hmm?" Durnik replied, his eyes fixed intently on his brightly colored lure bobbing far back in their wake.

"I said, are Silk and his brother up yet?"

"Oh—yes, I think I heard them stirring around in their cabin. Toth, we're definitely going to need something to weight down the lines."

Belgarath came up on deck just then, with his shabby old cloak pulled tightly around his shoulders. He looked sourly out through the drizzle at the half-concealed coast sliding by to port and went forward to stand amidships.

Garion joined him there. "How long do you think it's going to take us to get to Verkat, Grandfather?" he asked.

"A couple of weeks," the old man replied, "if this weather doesn't get any worse. We're a long way south and we're coming up on the stormy season."

"There's a faster way, though, isn't there?" Garion suggested.

"I don't quite follow you."

"You remember how we got from Jarviksholm to Riva? Couldn't you and I do it that way? The others could catch up later."

"I don't think we're supposed to. I think the others are supposed to be with us when we catch up with Zandramas."

Garion suddenly banged his fist on the rail in frustration. "Supposed to!" he burst out. "I don't care about what we're *supposed* to do. I want my son back. I'm tired of creeping around trying to satisfy all the clever little twists and turns of the Prophecy. What's wrong with just ignoring it and going right straight to the point?"

Belgarath's face was calm as he looked out at the rust-colored cliffs half-hidden in the gray drizzle. "I've tried that a few times myself," he admitted, "but it never worked—and usually it put me even further behind. I know you're impatient, Garion, and sometimes it's hard to accept the idea that following the Prophecy is really the fastest way to get where you want to go, but that's the way it always seems to work out." He put his hand on Garion's shoulder. "It's sort of like digging a well. The water's at the bottom, but you have to start at the top. I don't think anybody's ever had much luck digging a well from the bottom up."

"What's that got to do with it, Grandfather? I don't see any connection at all."

"Maybe you will if you think about it for a while."

Durnik came running forward. His eyes were wide in stunned amazement, and his hands were shaking.

"What's wrong?" Belgarath asked him.

"That was the biggest fish I've ever seen in my life!" the smith exclaimed. "He was as big as a horse!"

"He got away, I take it."

"Snapped my line on the second jump." Durnik's voice had a peculiar pride in it, and his eyes grew very bright. "He was beautiful, Belgarath. He came up out of the water as if he'd just been shot out of a catapult and he actually walked across the waves on his tail. What a tremendous fish!"

"What are you going to do?"

"I'm going to catch him, of course—but I'm going to need a stouter line—maybe even a rope. What a fish! Excuse me."

He hurried toward the bow to talk to the Murgo ship captain about some rope.

Belgarath smiled. "I love that man, Garion," he said. "I really love him."

The door to the aft companionway opened again, and Silk and his brother emerged. Although Garion was usually the first one on deck, he had noticed that, sooner or later during the course of any day, everyone came out to take a turn or two in the bracing salt air.

The two weasel-faced men came forward along the rain-slick deck. Neither of them looked particularly well. "Are we making any headway?" Silk asked. His face was pale, and his hands were trembling noticeably.

"Some," Belgarath grunted. "You two slept late this morning."

"I think we should have slept longer," Urgit replied with a mournful look. "I seem to have this small headache—in my left eye." He was sweating profusely, and there was a faint greenish cast to his skin. "I feel absolutely dreadful," he declared. "Why didn't you warn me about this, Kheldar?"

"I wanted to surprise you."

"Is it always like this the next morning?"

"Usually," Silk admitted. "Sometimes it's worse."

"Worse? How could it possibly get any worse? Excuse me." Urgit hurried to the rail and leaned over it, retching noisily.

"He's not handling this too well, is he?" Belgarath noted clinically.

"Inexperience," Silk explained.

"I honestly believe I'm going to die," Urgit said weakly, wiping at his mouth with a shaking hand. "Why did you let me drink so much?"

"That's a decision a man has to make for himself," Silk told him.

"You seemed to be having a good time," Garion added.

"I really wouldn't know. I've lost track of several hours. What did I do?"

"You were singing."

"Singing? Me?" Urgit sank onto a bench and dropped his face into his trembling hands. "Oh dear," he moaned. "Oh dear, oh dear, oh dear."

Prala came out of the aft door wearing a black coat and a smug little smile. She carried a pair of tankards forward through the drizzle to the two suffering men. "Good morning, my Lords," she said brightly with a little curtsey. "Lady Polgara says that you're to drink this."

"What's in it?" Urgit asked suspiciously.

"I'm not sure, your Majesty. She and the Nyissan mixed it up."

"Maybe it's poison," he said hopefully. "I would sort of like to die quickly and get it over with." He seized a tankard and gulped it down noisily. Then he shuddered, and his face went deathly pale. His expression was one of sheer horror, and he began to shake violently. "That's terrible!" he gasped.

Silk watched him closely for a moment, then took the other tankard and carefully dumped it out over the side.

"Aren't you going to drink yours?" Urgit asked accusingly.

"I don't think so. Polgara has a peculiar sense of humor sometimes. I'd rather not take any chances—until I see how many fish come floating to the top."

"How are you feeling this morning, your Majesty?" Prala asked the suffering Urgit with a feigned look of sympathy on her face.

"I'm sick."

"It's your own fault, you know."

"Please don't."

She smiled sweetly at him.

"You're enjoying this, aren't you?" he accused.

"Why, yes, your Majesty," she replied with a little toss of her head, "As a matter of fact, I am." Then she took the two tankards and went back along the rail toward the stern.

"Are they all like that?" Urgit asked miserably. "So cruel?"

"Women?" Belgarath shrugged. "Of course. It's in their blood."

Somewhat later that gloomy morning, after Silk and Belgarath had returned aft to seek refuge from the weather in one of the cabins and also, Garion suspected, for a touch of something to ward off the chill, Urgit sat miserably on a rain-wet bench with his head in his hands while Garion moodily paced the deck not far away. "Belgarion," the Murgo King said plaintively, "do you have to stamp your feet so hard?"

Garion gave him a quick, amused smile. "Silk really should have warned you about this," he said.

"Why do people call him Silk?"

"It's a nickname he picked up from his colleagues in Drasnian Intelligence."

"Why would a member of the Drasnian royal family want to be a spy?"

"It's their national industry."

"Is he really any good at it?"

"He's just about the best there is."

Urgit's face had definitely grown green. "This is dreadful," he groaned. "I can't be sure if it's the drink or seasickness. I wonder if I'd feel better if I stuck my head in a bucket of water."

"Only if you held it down long enough."

"That's a thought." Urgit laid his head back on the rail to let the rain drizzle into his face. "Belgarion," he said finally, "what am I doing wrong?"

"You drank a little too much."

"That's not what I'm talking about. Where am I making my mistakes—as a king, I mean?"

Garion looked at him. The little man was obviously sincere, and the sympathy for him which had welled up back in Rak Urga rose again. Garion finally admitted to himself that he liked this man. He drew in a deep breath and sat down beside the suffering Urgit. "You know part of it already," he said. "You let people bully you."

"It's because I'm afraid, Belgarion. When I was a boy, I let them bully me because it kept them from killing me. I guess it just got to be a habit."

"Everybody's afraid."

"You aren't. You faced Torak at Cthol Mishrak, didn't you?"

"It wasn't altogether my idea—and believe me, you can't even begin to guess how frightened I was when I was on my way there for that meeting."

"You?"

"Oh, yes. You're beginning to get some control over that problem, though. You handled that general—Kradak, wasn't it?—fairly well back at the Drojim. Just keep remembering that you're the king, and that you're the one who gives the orders."

"I can try, I guess. What else am I doing wrong?"

Garion thought about it. "You're trying to do it all yourself," he replied finally. "Nobody can do that. There are just too many details for one man to keep up with. You need help—good, honest help."

"Where am I going to find good help in Cthol Murgos? Whom can I trust?"

"You trust Oskatat, don't you?"

"Well, yes, I suppose so."

"That's a start, then. You see, Urgit, what's happening is that you've got people in Rak Urga who are making decisions that you should be making. They're taking it upon themselves to do that because you've been too afraid or too busy with other things to assert your authority."

"You're being inconsistent, Belgarion. First you say that I should get some people to help me, then you turn around and tell me that I shouldn't let other people make my decisions."

"You weren't listening. The people who are making your decisions for you aren't the people you might have chosen. They've just stepped in on their own. In a lot of cases, you probably don't even know who they are. That simply won't work. You have to choose your people rather carefully. Their first qualification has to be ability. Right behind that comes personal loyalty to you—and to your mother."

"Nobody's loyal to me, Belgarion. My subjects despise me."

"You might be surprised. I don't think there's any question about Oskatat's loyalty—or his ability. That's probably a good place to start. Let him pick your administrators. They'll start out by being loyal to him, but in time they'll come to respect you as well."

"I hadn't even considered that. Do you think it might work?"

"It won't hurt to try. To be perfectly honest with you, my friend, you've made a mess of things. It's going to take you a while to straighten them out, but you've got to start somewhere."

"You've given me quite a bit to think about, Belgarion." Urgit shivered and looked around. "It's really miserable out here," he said. "Where did Kheldar go?"

"Back inside. I think he's trying to get well."

"You mean that there's actually something that will cure this?"

"Some Alorns recommend some more of what made you sick in the first place."

Urgit's face went pale. "More?" he said in a horrified voice. "How can they?"

"Alorns are notoriously brave people."

Urgit's eyes grew suspicious. "Wait a minute," he said. "Wouldn't that just make me feel exactly the same way tomorrow morning?"

"Probably, yes. That could explain why Alorns are usually so foul-tempered when they first get up."

"That's stupid, Belgarion."

"I know. Murgos don't have an absolute monopoly on stupidity." Garion looked at the shivering man. "I think you'd better go inside, Urgit," he advised. "You don't want a chill on top of all your other problems."

The rain let up by late afternoon. The Murgo captain looked up at the still-threatening sky and then at the cliffs and the jagged reefs jutting out of the turbulent water and prudently ordered his crew to lower the sails and drop the anchor.

Durnik and Toth rather regretfully rolled up their stout fishing lines and stood looking proudly at the dozen or so gleaming silver fish lying on the deck at their feet.

Garion drifted back to where they stood and looked admiringly at their catch. "Not bad," he said.

Durnik carefully measured the biggest fish with his hands. "About three feet," he said, "but they're minnows compared to the big one that got away."

"It always seems to work out that way," Garion said. "Oh," he added, "one thing, Durnik. I'd clean them before I showed them to Aunt Pol. You know how she feels about that."

Durnik sighed. "You're probably right," he agreed.

That evening, after they had all dined on some of the catch, they sat around the table in the aft cabin conversing idly.

"Do you think Agachak's caught up with Harakan yet?" Durnik asked Belgarath.

"I sort of doubt it," the old man replied. "Harakan's tricky. If Beldin couldn't catch him, I don't think Agachak's going to have much luck either."

"Lady Polgara," Sadi suddenly protested in a tone of outrage, "make her stop that."

"What's that, Sadi?"

"The Margravine Liselle. She's subverting my snake."

Velvet, with a mysterious little smile on her face, was delicately feeding Zith fish eggs taken from one of the large fish Durnik and Toth had caught. The little green snake was purring contentedly and was half-raised in anticipation of the next morsel.

CHAPTER EIGHTEEN

The wind came up during the night, a raw, gusty wind, smelling strongly of dusty old ice, and the drizzle which had fallen for most of the previous day turned to sleet that rattled in the rigging and clattered on the deck like handfuls of pebbles. As usual, Garion rose early and tiptoed on unshod feet from the tiny cabin he shared with his sleeping wife. He made his way down the dark companionway past the doors to the cabins where the others slept and entered the aft cabin. He stood for a time at the windows running across the stern of the ship, looking out at the wind-tossed waves and listening to the slow creak of the tiller post running down through the center of the cabin to the rudder that probed the dark water beneath the stern.

As he sat down to put on his boots, the door opened and Durnik came in, brushing the ice pellets of the sleet squall chattering on the decks from the folds of his cloak. "It's going to be slow going for a while, I'm afraid," he said to Garion. "The wind's swung around and it's coming directly up out of the south. We're running right straight into it. The sailors are breaking out the oars."

"Could you get any idea of how far it is to the tip of the peninsula?" Garion asked, standing up and stamping his feet to settle his boots into place.

"I talked with the captain a bit. From what he said, it's only a few leagues. There's a cluster of islands that runs off the south end of it, though, and he wants to let this blow over before he tries to thread his way through the passage. He's not much of a sailor, and this isn't much of a boat, so I guess he's a little timid."

Garion leaned forward, put his hands on the sill of one of the stern windows and looked out again at the stormy sea. "This could blow for a week," he observed. He turned to look at his friend. "Has our captain recovered his composure at all?" he asked. "He was a little wild-eyed when we sailed out of Rak Urga."

Durnik smiled. "I think he's been talking to himself very hard. He's trying to convince himself that he didn't really see what happened back there. He still tends to cringe a lot when Pol goes out on deck, though."

"Good. Is she awake?"

Durnik nodded. "I fixed her morning tea for her before I went out on deck."

"How do you think she'd react if I asked her to bully the captain for me—just a little bit?"

"I don't know that I'd use the word 'bully,' Garion," Durnik advised seriously. "Try 'talk to' or 'persuade' instead. Pol doesn't really think of what she does as bullying."

"It is, though."

"Of course, but she doesn't think of it that way."

"Let's go see her."

The cabin Polgara shared with Durnik was as tiny and cramped as all the rest aboard this ungainly vessel. Two-thirds of the space inside was given over to the high-railed bed, built of planks and seeming to grow out of the bulkheads themselves. Polgara sat in the center of the bed in her favorite blue dressing gown, holding a cup of tea and gazing out the porthole at the sleet-spattered waves.

"Good morning, Aunt Pol," Garion greeted her.

"Good morning, dear. How nice of you to visit."

"Are you all right, now?" he asked. "What I mean is, I understand that you were quite upset about what happened back at the harbor."

She sighed. "I think the worst part was that I had no choice in the matter. Once Chabat raised the demon, she was doomed—but I was the one who had to destroy her soul." Her expression was somber with a peculiar overtone of a deep and abiding regret. "Could we talk about something else?" she asked.

"All right. Would you like to speak to someone for me?"

"Who's that?"

"The ship's captain. He wants to drop his anchor until this weather clears, and I'd rather not wait."

"Why don't you talk with him yourself, Garion?"

"Because people tend to listen to you more attentively than they do me. Could you do it, Aunt Pol—talk to him, I mean?"

"You want me to bully him."

"I wouldn't exactly say 'bully,' Aunt Pol," he protested.

"But that's what you mean, Garion. Always say what you mean."

"Will you?"

"All right, if you want me to. Now, will you do something for me?"

"Anything, Aunt Pol."

She held out her cup. "Do you suppose you could fix me another cup of tea?"

After breakfast, Polgara put on her blue cloak and went out on deck. The Murgo captain changed his plans almost as soon as she began to speak to him. Then he climbed the mainmast and spent the rest of the morning with the lookout in the wildly swaying crow's nest high aloft.

At the southern tip of the Urga peninsula, the steersman swung his tiller over, and the ship heeled sharply to port. It was not hard to understand why the captain had originally wanted to avoid the passage through the islands in anything remotely resembling rough weather. The currents and tides swirled through the narrow channels, the wind tore the tops of the dark-rolling waves to tatters, and the surf boomed and crashed on the knife-edged rocks rearing up out of the sea. The Murgo sailors rowed fearfully, casting wild-eyed looks at the looming cliffs on all sides of them. After the first league or so, the captain clambered down the mast to stand tensely beside the steersman as the ship cautiously crawled through the gale-lashed islands.

It was midafternoon when they finally passed the last of the rocky islets, and the sailors began to row away from the land toward open water where the wind-driven sleet sizzled into the whitecaps.

Belgarath and Garion, with their cloaks pulled tightly about them, stood on the deck watching the oarsmen for a few minutes; then the old man went to the companionway door. "Urgit!" he shouted down the narrow hall, "come out here!"

The Murgo King stumbled up the stairs out onto the deck, his eyes fearful.

"Don't your people know how to set their rigging so that they can quarter into the wind?" Belgarath demanded.

Urgit looked at him blankly. "I have absolutely no idea what you're talking about," he said.

"Durnik!" Belgarath shouted.

The smith, standing with Toth at the stern of the ship, was intently watching his trailing lure and did not answer.

"Durnik!"

"Hmmm?"

"We have to reset the rigging. Come and show the captain how it's done."

"In a minute."

"Now, Durnik!"

The smith sighed and began to coil up his line. The fish struck without warning, and Durnik's excited whoop was whipped away by the rising wind. He seized the line and jerked hard to set his hook. The great, silver-sided fish came boiling up out of the water, shaking his head angrily and threshing his way across the wind-driven chop. Durnik's shoulders bowed as he pulled hard on his line, struggling manfully to haul the huge fish in hand over hand.

Belgarath started to swear.

"I'll show the captain how to set his rigging, Grandfather," Garion said.

"How much do you know about it?"

"I've been on at least as many ships as Durnik has. I know how it's done." He went toward the bow to talk to the Murgo captain who now stood staring ahead at the tossing sea. "You want to slack off your lines on this side over here," Garion explained to him, "and draw them in on the other. The idea is to angle your sails so that they catch the wind. Then you put your rudder over to compensate."

"Nobody's ever done it that way before," the captain declared stubbornly.

"The Alorns do, and they're the best sailors in the world."

"The Alorns control the wind by sorcery. You can't use your sails unless the wind is behind you."

"Just try it, Captain," Garion said patiently. He looked at the heavy-shouldered sailor and saw that he was wasting his time. "If you'd rather not do it because I ask you to," he added, "I could probably persuade Lady Polgara to ask you—as a personal favor."

The captain stared at him. Then he swallowed hard. "How was it you said you wanted the rigging reset, my Lord?" he asked in a much milder tone.

It took perhaps a quarter of an hour to set the lines to Garion's satisfaction. Then, with the dubious captain in tow, he went aft and took the tiller from the steersman. "All right," he said, "raise the sails."

"It's not going to work," the captain predicted under his breath. Then he lifted his voice to a bellow. "Hoist the sails!"

The pulleys began to creak, and the sails, flapping in the wind, crawled up the masts. Then they boomed and bellied out, angled sharply to catch the wind. Garion pulled the tiller over as the ship heeled sharply to leeward. The prow knifed sharply through the heaving waves.

The Murgo captain gaped up at his sails. "I don't believe it!" he exclaimed. "Nobody's ever done that before."

"You see how it works now, don't you?" Garion asked him.

"Of course. It's so simple that I can't understand why I didn't think of it myself."

Garion had an answer, but he decided to keep it to himself. The captain had already had a bad enough day. He turned to the steersman. "You have to keep your tiller over like this to compensate for the force of the wind coming in on your starboard beam," he explained.

"I understand, my Lord."

Garion relinquished the tiller and stepped back to watch Durnik and Toth. They were still hauling at their line, and the great fish, no longer dancing on the sleet-swept surface, swept back and forth in long arcs across the boiling wake; the stout rope connecting his jaw to the two fishermen sizzled through the water as if it were hot.

"Nice fish," Garion called to the struggling pair.

Durnik's quick answering grin was like the sun coming up.

They quartered into an increasingly stiff wind for the remainder of the day. As the light began to fade, they were far from land. Garion was by now certain that the captain and the steersman could manage and he went forward to join the little group standing amidships around Durnik's huge fish.

"Now that you've got him, where are you going to find a pan big enough to cook him in?" Silk was asking the smith.

A brief frown crossed Durnik's face, but then he smiled again. "Pol will know how to take care of it," he said and went back to admiring the monster lying on the deck. "Pol knows how to take care of everything."

The sleet had abated, and the dark-rolling waves stretched sullenly to the faintly luminous line of the horizon that divided the black waves from an even blacker sky. The Murgo captain came forward in the windy twilight with a worried look on his face. Respectfully, he touched Urgit's sleeve.

"Yes, Captain?"

"I'm afraid there's trouble, your Majesty."

"What kind of trouble?"

The captain pointed toward the line of the southern horizon. A half-dozen ships were running before the wind, coming directly toward them.

Urgit's face grew slightly sick. "Malloreans?"

The captain nodded.

"Do you think they've seen us?"

"Almost certainly, your Majesty."

"We'd better go talk to Belgarath," Silk said. "I don't think any of us counted on this."

The conference in the aft cabin was tense. "They're making much better time than we are, Grandfather," Garion said. "We're quartering the wind, and they're running with it dead astern. I think we're going to have to turn north—at least until we can get out of their sight."

The old man was staring at a tattered map the captain had brought with him. He shook his head. "I don't like it," he said. "This gulf we're in right now funnels into the mouth of the Gorand Sea, and I don't want to get trapped in there." He turned to Silk. "You've been to Mallorea a few times. How good are their ships?"

Silk shrugged. "About the same as this one. I'm not trying to be offensive, Captain, but Angaraks aren't the same kind of sailors—or shipbuilders—that Chereks are." He considered it. "There might be a way to escape them," he said. "Malloreans are timid sailors, so they won't spread all sail at night. If we turned north and put up every ounce of canvas we can, we could be a long way ahead of them—no more than a blinking light on the horizon once it gets dark. Then we drop the sails, reset the rigging and put out every light on board ship."

"But we can't do that," the captain objected. "It's against the law."

"I'll write you an excuse, Captain," Urgit said drily.

"It's too dangerous, your Majesty. If we run without lights, we could collide with another ship out there in the dark. We could be sunk."

"Captain," Urgit said in a patient tone, "there are six Mallorean ships chasing us. What do you imagine they're going to do if they catch up with us?"

"They'll sink us, of course."

"What difference does it make, then? At least if we put out the lights, we'll have a chance. Go ahead, Kheldar."

Silk shrugged. "There isn't much more. After we blow out the running lights, we hoist sail and run east again. The Malloreans won't be able to see us, and they'll charge right on across our wake. By tomorrow morning, they won't have any idea about where we are."

"It might just work," Belgarath conceded.

"It's dangerous," the captain said disapprovingly.

"Sometimes even breathing is dangerous, Captain," Urgit told him. "Let's try it and see what happens. What I can't understand, though, is what Mallorean ships are doing this far west."

"It's possible that they're marauders sent to harry the coast lines," Sadi suggested.

"Perhaps," Urgit said dubiously.

They ran due north before the rising wind that swept up from the south polar icecap. The deck lanterns swung and bobbed in the wind, peopling the storm-whipped rigging with wildly dancing shadows. The six Mallorean vessels, running cautiously under half sail, dropped behind until their running lights looked no larger than tiny twinkling stars on the horizon far astern. Then, about midnight, the captain gave the order to drop the sails. The sailors quickly reset the rigging and the ship's master came aft to where Garion stood beside the steersman. "Everything's ready, my Lord," he reported.

"All right then. Let's blow out all the lights and see if we can sneak out of here."

The Murgo's stiff face creased uncertainly into a rueful grin. "When we get out of this—*if* we get out of it—I think I'll take to my bed for a month," he said. He raised his voice to a shout. "Extinguish all the deck lights!" he commanded.

The resulting blackness was so intense as to be very nearly palpable.

"Hoist the sails!" the captain shouted.

Garion could hear the creaking pulleys and the flapping of canvas. Then there was the heavy boom of the sails catching the wind and the ship heeled over as she swung to starboard.

"There's no way to be sure of our direction, my Lord," the captain warned. "We haven't got a fixed point of any kind to refer to."

"Use those," Garion suggested, pointing at the winking deck lights on the Mallorean vessels trailing far behind. "We might as well get some use out of them."

Their darkened scow moved eastward with her sharply angled sails cracking in the wind. The deck lights of the Mallorean ships that had been pursuing them continued their cautious northward course, crossed far behind, and winked out of sight.

"May Torak guide them to a reef," the captain muttered fervently.

"It worked!" Urgit said delightedly, clapping the seaman on the shoulder. "By the Gods, it actually worked!"

"I just hope that nobody catches me running at night without any lights," the captain brooded.

Dawn came smudged and bleary to the murky eastern horizon, rising slowly up out of a low-lying shadow some ten leagues or so ahead. "That's the coast of Cthaka," the captain said, pointing.

"Is there any sign of those Mallorean ships?" Urgit asked, peering around at the heaving sea.

The captain shook his head. "They passed astern of us during the dogwatch, your Majesty. They're halfway up the Gorand Sea by now." The seaman looked at Garion. "You wanted to get closer in to shore and then swing around to starboard again, my Lord?"

"To starboard, of course."

The captain squinted up at the sails. "We'll have to reset the rigging again, I suppose."

"I'm afraid not," Garion told him regretfully. "When we turn south, we'll be sailing directly into the wind. You'll have to furl your sails and break out the oars." He noted the disappointed expression on the seaman's face. "I'm sorry, Captain, but there are limits. Your sails are the wrong shape, and when you get right down to it, rowing in this case will actually be faster. How far north were we swept last night?"

"A goodly way, my Lord," the captain replied, peering at the indistinct coastline lying ahead. "You can put a lot of water behind you moving under full sail before a wind like that. I wouldn't be surprised to see the mouth of the Gorand Sea somewhere ahead."

"We don't want to go in there. Let's not start playing tag with those Mallorean ships again—particularly in tight quarters. I'm going below for a bite of breakfast and some dry clothes. Send someone down if anything happens."

"I will, my Lord."

They had fish for breakfast that morning. At Polgara's suggestion, Durnik's huge catch had been cut into steaks and then delicately broiled over a low flame.

"Delicious, isn't he?" Durnik asked proudly.

"Yes, dear," Polgara agreed. "He's a very nice fish."

"Did I tell you how I caught him, Pol?"

"Yes, dear—but that's all right. You can tell me again, if you'd like."

As they were just finishing their meal, the Murgo captain entered, wearing a tarred cape and an anxious expression. "There's more of them, my Lord," he blurted to Garion.

"More of what?"

"Malloreans. There's another squadron coming up the Cthaka coast."

Urgit's face blanched, and his hands started to tremble.

"Are you sure they aren't the same ones who were chasing us last night?" Garion asked, getting quickly to his feet.

"There's no way they could be, my Lord. It's a different group of ships."

Silk was looking narrowly at the ship's master. "Captain," he said, "have you ever been in business for yourself?"

The captain threw a brief, guilty glance at Urgit. "I don't know what you're talking about," he mumbled.

"This is no time for false modesty, Captain," Silk said. "We're charging headlong into the midst of a Mallorean squadron. Are there any coves or inlets around here where we could get out of sight?"

"Not along this coast, your Highness; but right after you go through the channel into the Gorand Sea, there's a small bay to starboard. It's well hidden by some reefs. If we were to unstep the masts and tie bushes along the sides, I think we could escape notice."

"Let's do it then, Captain," Belgarath said shortly. "What's the weather look like?"

"Not very pleasant. There's a heavy cloud bank coming up from the south. I think we can expect a gale before noon."

"Good."

"Good?"

"We're not alone in these waters," Belgarath reminded him. "A nice gale ought to give the Malloreans something to do beside line the rails of their ships looking for us. Go give the orders, Captain. Let's turn around and make a run for it."

"How were you so sure that the captain knew about a secluded cove or bay somewhere?" Urgit asked Silk after the seaman had left.

Silk shrugged. "You levy taxes on merchandise that gets moved from one place to another, don't you?"

"Of course. I need the revenue."

"A resourceful man with his own boat can sort of forget to

stop by the customs dock at the end of a voyage—or he can locate some quiet place to store things until he finds customers for them."

"That's smuggling!"

"Why, yes, I believe some people do call it that. Anyway, I'd guess that every sea captain in the world has dabbled in the business at one time or another."

"Not Murgos," Urgit insisted.

"Then how is it that your captain knew of a perfect hiding place not five leagues from our present location—and probably knows of hundreds more?"

"You're a corrupt and disgusting man, Kheldar."

"I know. Smuggling is a very profitable business, though. You ought to give some thought to going into it."

"Kheldar, I'm the king. I'd be stealing from myself."

"Trust me," Silk said. "It's a bit complicated, but I can show you how to set things up so that you can make a very handsome profit."

The ship rolled then, and they all looked out through the windows along the stern to watch the waves sweep by as the steersman pulled his tiller over hard and the ship came about. Far astern they could see a half-dozen red sails looking tiny in the distance.

"Are there any Grolims on board those ships, Pol?" Belgarath asked his daughter.

Her lavender eyes became distant for a moment, then she passed one hand over her brow. "No, father," she replied, "just ordinary Malloreans."

"Good. We shouldn't have too much trouble hiding from them, then."

"That storm the captain mentioned is coming up behind them," Durnik said.

"Won't it just hurry them along?" Urgit asked nervously.

"Probably not," the smith answered. "Most likely they'll come about to head into the wind. That's the only safe way to ride out a storm."

"Won't we have to do the same thing?"

"We're outnumbered six to one, my brother," Silk pointed out. "We're going to have to take a few chances, I think."

The advancing wave of darkness that marked the leading edge of the oncoming storm engulfed the red sails far astern and came racing up the coast. The waves grew higher, and the Murgo ship bucked and plunged as the wind picked up. The timbers shrieked and groaned in protest as the heavy seas wrenched at their vessel, and high overhead there was the heavy booming of the sails. Garion actually listened to that booming sound for several minutes before the significance of it began to dawn on him. It was an ominous grinding noise from amidships that finally alerted him. "That idiot!" he exclaimed, leaping to his feet and snatching up his cloak.

"What's the matter?" Sadi asked in alarm.

"He's carrying full sail! If his mainmast doesn't break, we'll be driven under!" Garion whirled, dashed out of the cabin, and staggered along the lurching companionway to the three steps leading up to the deck. "Captain!" he shouted as he dashed out onto the rain-swept deck. He caught one of the hastily strung lifelines as a wave broke over the stern and came rushing knee-deep down the deck, sweeping his feet out from under him. "Captain!" he shouted again, hauling himself hand over hand up the rope toward the aft deck.

"My Lord?" the captain shouted back with a startled look.

"Shorten your sail! Your mainmast is starting to tear free!"

The captain stared aloft, his face filled with sudden chagrin. "Impossible, my Lord," he protested as Garion reached him. "The men can't furl sail in this storm."

Garion rubbed the rain out of his eyes and looked back up over his shoulder at the tautly bellied mainsail. "They'll have to cut it away, then."

"Cut it? But, my Lord, that's a new sail."

"Right now it's the sail or the ship. If the wind uproots your mainmast, it's going to tear your ship apart—and if it doesn't, we'll be driven under. Now get that sail off the mast—or I will."

The captain stared at him.

"Believe me," Garion told him, "if I have to do it, I'll sweep your deck clean—masts, rigging, sails, and all."

The captain immediately began giving orders.

Once the mainsail had been cut free and allowed to kite off into the storm, the dreadful shuddering and grinding eased, and the vessel ran before the wind more smoothly, propelled only by a small foresail.

"How far is it to the mouth of the Gorand Sea?" Garion asked.

"Not far, my Lord," the captain replied, mopping his face. He looked around at the storm-lashed morning and the low, nearly invisible coast sliding by on their right. "There it is," he said, pointing at a scarcely visible hillock jutting up a mile or so ahead. "You see that headland—the one with the white bluff facing us? The channel's just on the other side of it." He turned to the sailors clinging to the aft rail. "Drop the sea anchor," he commanded.

"What's that for?" Garion asked him.

"We've got too much headway, my Lord," the seaman explained. "The channel's a little difficult, and we have to turn sharply to get through it. We have to slow down. The sea anchor drags behind and keeps us from going quite so fast."

Garion thought about it, frowning. Something seemed wrong, but he couldn't quite put his finger on it. He watched as the sailors rolled what appeared to be a long canvas sack on a heavy rope over the stern rail. The sack streamed out behind them; the rope went taut, and the ship shuddered and slowed perceptibly.

"That's better," the captain said with some satisfaction.

Garion shielded his eyes from the icy rain being driven into his face and peered back behind them. The Malloreans were nowhere in sight. "Just how tricky is this channel you mentioned?" he asked.

"There are some reefs in the center, my Lord. You have to hug the coast on one side or the other to avoid them. We'll stay close to the south shore, since that bay I mentioned is on that side."

Garion nodded. "I'll go warn the others that we're about to make a turn to the right. A sudden change of direction might toss them around a bit down there."

"Starboard," the captain said disapprovingly.

"What? Oh, no. To most of them, it's to the right." Garion started forward, peering out through the rain at the low coast sliding past. The bluff and the rounded headland looming above it was almost dead amidships now. He could see the channel just ahead cluttered with jagged, up-thrusting rocks. He swung down into the narrow, dark companionway and shook as much water out of his cloak as possible as he stumbled aft. He opened the main cabin door and poked his head inside. "We're at the mouth of the Gorand Sea," he announced. "We'll be turning to starboard here." Then he cursed at forgetting.

"Which way is starboard?" Ce'Nedra asked.

"Right."

"Why didn't you say right, then?"

He let that pass. "When we come about, we could bounce around a bit, so you'd all better hang on to something. There's a reef in the center of the channel, so we're going to have to swing in tight to the south shore to avoid—" Then it came to him, even as the ship heeled over and plunged into the channel. "Belar!" he swore. He spun, reaching over his shoulder for Iron-grip's sword, and then plunged back down the companionway. He banged out through the slanting companionway doors and jumped up to the rain-swept aft deck with the great blade aloft. "Cut it!" he screamed. "Cut the rope to the sea anchor!"

The captain gaped at him, uncomprehending.

"Cut the cursed rope!" Garion bellowed. Then he was on them, and they stumbled clumsily over each other, trying to get out of his way. The ship had already swept in a tight curve close in to the headland, avoiding the reefs and up-thrusting boulders in mid-channel. The submerged sea anchor, however, pulled by the force of the waves running before the wind, continued on across the mouth of the channel. The rope that had slackened until it was lost in the whitecaps suddenly snapped taut, jerking the Murgo scow askew. The force of that sudden sideways jerk threw Garion off his feet, and he crashed into the tangle of arms and legs at the rail. "Cut it!" he shouted, struggling to free himself. "Cut the rope!"

But it was too late. The heavy sea anchor, pulled by the irresistable force of the storm-driven waves, had not only jerked the Murgo vessel to a halt but was now pulling her inexorably backward—not toward the safe channel through which she had just passed, but instead directly toward the jagged reefs.

Garion staggered to his feet, kicking the floundering sailors out from around his ankles. Desperately he swung a massive blow at the tautly thrumming rope, shearing away not merely the rope itself but the stout windlass to which it was attached.

"My Lord!" the captain protested.

"Get that tiller!" Garion shouted. "Turn starboard! Turn! Turn! Turn!" He pointed at the deadly reefs foaming directly in their path.

The captain gaped at the huge knife-edged rocks standing in his vessel's course. Then he whirled and tore the tiller from the hands of his frozen steersman. Instinctively, he swung the tiller hard over for a turn to port.

"Starboard!" Garion shouted. "Turn to starboard!"

"No, my Lord," the captain disagreed. "We have to turn to port—to the left."

"We're going backward, you jackass! Turn right!"

"Starboard," the captain corrected absently, still wrestling with an idea he was not yet fully prepared to grasp—all the while still firmly holding the tiller locked into the fatal course he had originally set.

Garion began to clamber over the still-floundering sailors, desperately trying to reach the bemused captain, but there came a sudden tearing sound from below the waterline and a lurching jolt as their ship crashed stern-first into the reef. Timbers shrieked and snapped as the sharp rocks knifed into the vessel's bottom. Then they hung there, impaled on the rocks, while the waves began the deadly pounding that would soon break the ship to pieces.

CHAPTER NINETEEN

Garion struggled to his feet, shaking his head to clear it of the ringing sound and to chase the dancing sparks from before his eyes. The sudden jolt of the ship's striking the reef had tumbled him headlong into the aft rail, and there was a great, stinging welt across the top of his scalp. The air around him was filled with sounds. There were shouts from the deck and cries for help coming from the water. The ship groaned and shook as she hung on the reef, and the surging waves pounded her splintered bottom on the unseen rocks beneath her keel. Wincing, Garion shook his head again and began to slip and slide his way across the heaving aft deck toward the companionway door. As he reached it, however,

Belgarath and Durnik came crashing out. "What's happened?" the old man demanded.

"We hit a reef," Garion said. "Is anybody down there hurt?"

"They're all right—a little tumbled about is all."

Garion touched the welt on top of his head, wincing at the sharp sting. Then he looked at his fingers, noting that there didn't seem to be any blood.

"What's the matter?" Belgarath asked.

"I hit my head."

"I thought we all decided that you weren't going to do that any more."

A deadly, jarring boom came from under their feet and with it the sound of splintering timbers.

"Belgarath," Durnik said with alarm, "we're caught on the reef. This surf is going to pound the ship to pieces."

Belgarath looked around quickly. "Where's the captain?" he demanded.

Garion turned to look aft. "He was right there at the tiller, Grandfather," he said. He clambered up the short incline to the aft deck and caught hold of the steersman, who was stumbling forward. "Where's the captain?" he shouted.

"Lost. He was thrown over the aft rail when we hit the reef." The steersman's eyes were filled with shock and fright. "We're all doomed!" he cried, clinging to Garion.

"Oh, stop that!" Garion snapped. "The captain's gone, Grandfather," he shouted over the noise of the storm and the confusion on deck. "He fell over the side."

Belgarath and Durnik came quickly up the three steps to the aft deck. "We'll have to take care of it ourselves, then," the old man said. "How much time do you think we've got, Durnik?"

"Not much. There are a lot of timbers breaking down in the hold, and you can hear water pouring in."

"We have to get her off this reef, then—before the rocks break any more holes in her bottom."

"The reef's the only thing that's keeping us up right now,

Belgarath," the smith objected. "If we lift her off, she'll sink in minutes."

"Then we'll have to beach her. Come along, both of you." He led them aft and took hold of the tiller bar. He jiggled it back and forth a couple times and then swore. "The rudder's gone." He drew in a deep breath to calm himself and then turned to Garion and Durnik. "We'll do this all at one time and all together," he told them. "If we start heaving and hauling and bouncing her around, we'll just tear her up all the more." He wiped the rain and spray out of his face and peered toward the shore, perhaps a mile distant. He pointed at the up-thrusting headland with the white bluff on one side dropping straight down into the thundering surf. "There's a beach just to the left of that bluff," he said. "We'll try for that. It's not too well sheltered, and there are a lot of rocks sticking up out of the sand, but it's the closest."

Durnik leaned far out over the aft rail and peered down. "She's been badly broached, Belgarath," he reported gravely. He squinted across the intervening water toward the beach. "Our only hope is speed. Once she's clear of the reef, she'll start to go down. We're going to have to push her toward the beach as fast as we can—and without a rudder, it's going to be very hard to control our direction."

"Do we have any other options?" Belgarath asked him.

"Not that I can think of, no."

"Let's do it then." The old man looked at them. "Are we ready?"

Garion and Durnik both nodded, then straightened, concentrating hard as each of them drew in and focused his will. Garion began to tingle all over and clenched himself tightly, holding in the pent-up force.

"Now!" Belgarath barked.

"Lift!" the three of them said in unison.

The battered stern of the ship came sluggishly up out of the churning waves with her shattered timbers shrieking as the hull pulled free of the jagged reef.

"There!" Belgarath snapped, pointing at the half-obscured beach.

Garion thrust, bracing his will astern at the boiling reef. The ship settled sickeningly as she came free, going down rapidly by the stern; then, slowly at first, but quickly gaining speed, she surged forward. Even over the sound of the howling wind, he could hear the rushing wash of water along her sides as she raced toward the safety of the beach.

When they hit the currents in the main channel, however, the rudderless ship began to veer and yaw, threatening to swing broadside. "Keep her straight!" Belgarath shouted. The veins were standing out in his forehead, and his jaws were tightly clenched.

Garion labored at it. As long as their broken ship moved fast enough, they could keep the water from pouring in through the shattered stern, but if she went broadside to the waves, the loss of momentum would be fatal. The sea would inexorably drag her under. Garion gripped the bow with the force of his will, holding the ship rigidly on course, even as he continued to drive toward the beach with all his strength.

Three hundred more yards. Sweating and straining, Garion could see the foaming surf seething on the sandy, boulder-strewn beach.

Two hundred yards. He could hear the thunder of the waves.

One hundred yards. He could feel the ponderous, upward-heaving swell of the great wave that rose beneath them and rushed them toward the safety only scant yards away.

And then, even as the prow touched the froth-covered sand, the great swell that had driven them up onto the beach subsided, and there was a dreadful, shocking crash from amidships as they came down onto a submerged boulder lurking beneath the surf. Again Garion was thrown face down on the deck and half stunned by the impact.

The surf still boomed about them, and the snapping and splintering of timbers amidships was deafening, but they were safe. The prow of the stricken vessel was firmly embedded in the wet sand of the beach. As Garion painfully hauled himself to his feet, he felt drained and weak from his efforts. Then the deck beneath his feet gave a peculiar, sickening lurch, and there were more cracking and splintering noises coming from amidships.

"I think we broke the keel when we hit that rock," Durnik said shakily. His face was gray with exhaustion, and he was shaking visibly. "We'd better get everybody off the ship and onto the beach."

Belgarath rose from the scuppers. There was a ruddy contusion on his cheek, rain and spray streaming down his face, and a vast anger in his eyes. He was swearing sulfurously. Then his rage suddenly vanished. "The horses!" he exclaimed. "They're down in the hold! Durnik!"

But the smith was already running forward toward the sprung hatchway amidships. "Get Toth to come and help me!" he shouted back over his shoulder. "We have to get those horses out!"

"Garion!" Belgarath barked. "Let's get everybody out of the cabins and onto dry land. I don't think we've got a lot of time before this wreck starts to break apart."

They started forward, moving carefully on the slanting deck of the broken ship, with the wind-whipped spray and driving rain stinging their faces. They ducked into the slanting aft door and down the companionway. The narrow hall echoed and rang with the noise of cracking timbers coming from amidships.

The aft cabin was a total shambles. The shock of striking the reef and the even worse one that had broken the ship's back had torn most of the bolted-down furniture loose. Sprung timbers flopped and clattered, and the windows across the stern had all been broken and wrenched from their casings. Spray and rain were splashing in through those gaping holes.

Ce'Nedra and Prala looked frightened as they clung to each other, Urgit held tightly to the keel-post as if expecting yet another crashing impact, and Sadi half-lay in a corner with his arms protectively wrapped around his red leather case. Polgara, however, looked dreadfully angry. She was also wet. The water pouring in through the shattered stern had drenched her clothes and her hair, and her expression was that of one who has been enormously offended. "Exactly what did you do, old man?" she demanded of Belgarath as he and Garion entered through the broken door.

"We hit a reef, Pol," he replied. "We were taking water, so we had to beach the ship."

She considered that for a moment, obviously trying to find something wrong with it.

"We can talk about it later," he said. He looked around. "Is everyone all right? We've got to get off this wreck immediately."

"We're as well as can be expected, father," she said. "What's the problem? I thought you said we were on the beach."

"We hit a submerged rock and broke the keel. This part of the ship's still in the water, and about the only thing that's holding this tub in one piece right now is the pitch in her seams. We've got to get forward and off the ship at once."

She nodded. "I understand, father." She turned to the others. "Gather up whatever you can carry," she instructed. "We have to get ashore."

"I'll go help Durnik with the horses," Garion said to Belgarath. "Toth, Eriond, come with me." He turned toward the door, but paused a moment to look at Ce'Nedra. "Are you all right?" he asked her.

"I think so," she replied, sounding frightened and rubbing at an ugly bruise on her knee.

"Stay with Aunt Pol," he instructed curtly and then went out.

The scene in the ship's hold was even worse than he had expected. Knee-deep water swirled and sloshed in the half-light coming in through the splintered hull. Boxes, bags, and bales floated everywhere, and the top of the sloshing, bilge-smelling water was littered with splinters from the broken timbers. Durnik had herded the wild-eyed horses forward, and they were bunched together in the ship's bow where the water was the shallowest. "We lost three of them," he reported, "two with broken necks and one that drowned."

"Horse?" Eriond asked quickly.

"He's all right, Eriond," Durnik assured him. He turned back to Garion. "I've been trying to gather up our packs. Everything's pretty wet, I'm afraid. The food packs were all back in the stern, though. There's no way to get to them."

"We can deal with that later," Garion said. "The main thing now is to get the horses out."

Durnik squinted at the jagged edges of the two-foot square keel grinding together as the aft end of the ship swung sluggishly in the surging waves. "Too dangerous," he said shortly. "We'll have to go out through the bow. I'll get my axe."

Garion shook his head. "If the aft end breaks loose, the bow-section's likely to roll. We could lose another four or five horses if that happens and we might not have too much time left."

Durnik drew in a deep breath and squared his broad shoulders. His face was not happy.

"I know," Garion said, putting his hand on his friend's arm. "I'm tired, too. Let's do it up forward. There's no point in breaking out of the hull someplace where we'll have to jump into deep water."

It was not quite as difficult as they had expected. The assistance of Toth made a noticeable difference. They selected a space in the ship's side between a pair of stout ribs and went to work. As Durnik and Garion began carefully to break out the ship's timbers between those ribs with the force of concentrated will, Toth attacked the same area with a large iron pry bar. The combination of sorcery and the mute's enormous physical strength quickly opened a low, narrow opening in the ship's bow.

Silk stood on the beach out of range of the splinters their efforts had sent flying. His cloak was whipping wildly in the wind, and the surf was swirling about his ankles. "Are you all right?" he shouted over the noise of the storm.

"Good enough," Garion shouted back. "Give us a hand with the horses."

It eventually took blindfolds. Despite the best efforts of Durnik and Eriond to calm them, the terrified horses could be moved only if they could not see the dangers in the sloshing water surging around their knees. One by one they had to be led and coaxed through the litter lying half-awash in the shattered hold and out into the foaming surf. When the last of their animals was clear and stood flinching on the sand with the driving rain lashing at his flanks, Garion turned back to the sluggishly heaving wreck. "Let's get the packs out," he shouted at the others. "Save what you can, but don't take any chances."

The Murgo sailors, after leaping from the bow of the ship to the sand, had retreated up the beach and taken dubious shelter on the leeward side of a large, up-thrusting rock. They stood clustered together, sullenly watching the unloading. Garion and the others heaped up the packs above the frothy line that marked the highest point reached by the waves.

"We lost three horses and all the food packs," Garion reported to Belgarath and Polgara. "I think we got everything else—except what we had to leave behind in the cabins."

Belgarath squinted upward into the rain. "We can redistribute the packs," he said, "but we're going to need food."

"Is the tide going in or out?" Silk asked as he deposited the last pack on their heap of belongings.

Durnik squinted at the storm-tossed channel leading into the Gorand Sea. "I think it's just turning."

"We don't really have too much of a problem, then," the little man said. "Let's find someplace out of the wind and wait for the tide to go out. Then we can come back and ransack the wreck at our leisure. She ought to be completely out of the water at low tide."

"There's just one thing wrong with your plan, Prince Kheldar," Sadi told him, squinting toward the upper end of the beach. "You're forgetting those Murgo sailors. They're stranded on a deserted coast with at least a dozen Mallorean ships cruising up and down the shore line looking for them. Malloreans enjoy killing Murgos almost as much as Alorns do, so those sailors are going to want to get far away from here. It might be wise to get these horses quite some distance away—if we want to keep them."

"Let's load the pack horses and get mounted," Belgarath decided. "I think Sadi's right. We can come back and pick over what's left of the ship later."

They broke down the packs and redistributed the weight to make up for the three lost animals, then began to saddle their mounts.

The sailors, led by a tall, heavy-shouldered Murgo with an evil-looking scar under his left eye, came back down the beach. "Where do you think you're taking those horses?" he demanded.

"I can't really see where that's any of your business," Sadi replied coolly.

"We're going to make it our business, aren't we, mates?"

There was a rumble of agreement from the rain-soaked sailors.

"The horses belong to us," Sadi told him.

"We don't care about that. There are enough of us so that we can take anything we want."

"Why waste time with talk?" one of the sailors behind the scar-faced man shouted.

"Right," the big Murgo agreed. He drew a short, rusty sword from the sheath at his hip, looked back over his shoulder as he raised it aloft, and shouted, "Follow me!" Then he fell writhing and bellowing in pain to the wet sand, clutching at his broken right arm. Toth, without any change of expression and with an almost negligent side-arm flip, had sent the iron pry bar he still held in one hand spinning through the air with a whirring flutter that ended with a sharp crack as the sword-wielding Murgo's arm snapped.

The sailors drew back, alarmed by their leader's sudden collapse. Then a stubble-cheeked fellow in the front rank lifted a heavy boat hook. "Rush them!" he bellowed. "We want those horses and we outnumber them."

"I think you might want to count again," Polgara said in a cool voice. Even as Garion stepped forward, drawing his sword out of its sheath, he felt a peculiar shadowy presence to his left. He blinked unbelievingly. As real as if he were actually there, the huge, red-bearded shape of Barak stood at his side.

A clinking sound came from the right, and there, his armor gleaming wet in the rain, stood Mandorallen, and somewhat beyond him, the hawk-faced Hettar. "What thinkest thou, my Lords?" the figure that appeared to be the invincible Baron of Vo Mandor said gaily. "Should we afford these knaves the opportunity to flee, ere we fall upon them and spill out their lifeblood?"

"It seems like the decent thing to do," the apparition of Barak rumbled its agreement. "What do you think, Hettar?"

"They're Murgos," the shade of Hettar said in his quiet, chilling voice as he drew his saber. "Kill them all right here and now. That way we won't have to waste time chasing them down one by one later."

"Somehow I knew you were going to look at it that way." Barak laughed. "All right, my Lords, let's go to work." He drew his heavy sword.

The three images, larger actually than they were in life, advanced grimly on the shrinking sailors. In their midst, painfully aware that he was in fact quite alone, Garion moved forward, his huge sword held low. Then, on the far side of the apparition of Barak, he saw Toth advancing with his huge staff. Beyond him, Sadi held a small poisoned dagger. At the opposite end of the line, Durnik and Silk moved into place.

The image of Barak glanced over at Garion. "Now, Garion!" Polgara's whispered voice came from those bearded lips.

Instantly he understood. He relaxed the restraints he usually kept on the Orb. The great sword he held leaped into flame, spurting blue fire from its tip almost into the faces of the now-terrified Murgos.

"Will all of you who would like to die immediately and save

yourselves the inconvenience and discomfort of being chased down and slowly hacked to pieces please step forward?" the red-bearded shadow at Garion's side roared in tones more grandiose than Barak himself could ever have managed. "We can have you in the arms of your one-eyed God in the blinking of an eye."

It hung there for a moment; then the sailors fled.

"Oh, Gods!" Garion heard Polgara's ringing voice coming from behind him. "I've wanted to do that for a thousand years!" He turned and saw her, standing with the raging sea and racing black clouds behind her and the wind tearing at her blue cloak. The rain had plastered her hair to her face and neck, but her glorious eyes were triumphant.

"My Pol!" Belgarath exulted, catching her in a rough embrace. "Gods, what a son you'd have made!"

"I'm your daughter, Belgarath," she replied simply, "but could any son have done better?"

"No, Pol," he laughed suddenly, crushing her to him and soundly planting a kiss on her rain-wet cheek. "Not one bit."

They stopped, startled and even a little embarrassed that the enormous love they had each tried to conceal for millennia had finally come out into the open on this storm-swept beach here at the bottom of the world. Almost shyly they looked at each other and then, unable to hold it in, they began to laugh.

Garion turned away, his eyes suddenly brimming.

Urgit was bending over the sailor with the broken arm. "If you wouldn't mind taking some advice from your king, my man," he said urbanely, "might I remind you that the sea out there is crawling with Malloreans, and Malloreans take a childlike delight in crucifying every Murgo they come across. Don't you think it might be prudent for you and your shipmates to remove yourselves from the vicinity of all that scrap lumber?" He looked meaningfully at the wreck.

The sailor cast a sudden, frightened glance at the storm-tossed channel and scrambled to his feet. Cradling his broken arm, he scurried back up the beach to rejoin his frightened mates.

"He shows a remarkable grasp of the situation, doesn't he?" Urgit said to Silk.

"He does seem uncharacteristically alert," Silk agreed. He looked at the rest of them. "Why don't we mount up and get off this beach?" he suggested. "That wreck stands out like a beacon, and our injured friend and his companions might decide to give horse rustling another try." He looked appraisingly at the hulking images Polgara had conjured up. "Just out of curiosity, Polgara, could those apparitions of yours actually have done any good if it had gotten down to a fight?"

Polgara was still laughing, her lavender eyes alight. "To be perfectly honest with you, my dear Silk," she replied gaily, "I haven't got the faintest idea."

For some reason her answer sent them all off into helpless gales of laughter.

CHAPTER TWENTY

The slope leading to the top of the headland was covered with rank grass, drooping under the rain that swept in from the south. As they started up from the beach, Garion looked back. The Murgo sailors had swarmed over the wreck to salvage whatever they could, stopping often to look fearfully out at the storm-racked channel.

At the top of the headland, the full force of the gale struck them, tearing at their clothes and raking them with sheets of rain. Belgarath pulled to a halt, held one hand above his eyes to shield them, and surveyed the treeless expanse of grassland lying sodden and wind-whipped ahead.

"This is totally impossible, father," Polgara declared, drawing her wet cloak more tightly about her. "We're going to have to find shelter and wait this out."

"That might be difficult, Pol." He gazed out over a grassland that showed no signs of any sort of human habitation. The broad valley lying below them was laced with deep gullies where turbulent creeks had cut down through the turf and exposed the rounded boulders and beds of gravel lying beneath the thin topsoil and its tenacious cover of grass. The wind sheeted across that grass, tossing it like waves, and the rain, mingled with icy sleet, raked at it. "Urgit," the old man said, "are there any villages or settlements hereabouts?"

Urgit wiped his face and looked around. "I don't think so," he replied. "The maps don't show anything in this part of Cthaka except the high road leading inland. We might stumble across some isolated farmstead, but I doubt it. The soil here is too thin for crops, and the winters are too severe for cattle."

The old man nodded gloomily. "That's more or less what I thought."

"We might be able to pitch the tents," Durnik said, "but we'll be right out in the open, and there's no firewood anywhere out there."

Eriond had been patiently sitting astride his stallion, staring out at the featureless landscape with a peculiar look of recognition. "Couldn't we take shelter in the watchtower?" he asked.

"What watchtower?" Belgarath asked him, looking around again, "I don't see anything."

"You can't see it from here. It's mostly all tumbled down. The cellar's still all right, though."

"I don't know of any watchtowers on this coast," Urgit said.

"It hasn't been used for a long time."

"Where, Eriond?" Polgara asked. "Can you show us where it is?"

"Of course. It's not too far." The young man turned his stallion and angled up toward the very top of the headland. As they climbed the hill, Garion looked down and saw a fair number of stone blocks protruding up out of the grass. It was difficult to say for sure, but at least some of those blocks bore what looked vaguely like chisel marks.

When they reached the top, the gale shrieked around them, and the tossing grass whipped at their horses' legs.

"Are you sure, Eriond?" Polgara shouted over the wind.

"We can get in from the other side," he replied confidently. "It might be better to lead the horses, though. The entrance is fairly close to the edge of the bluff." He slid out of his saddle and led the way across the grassy, rounded top of the hill. The rest of them followed him. "Be careful here," he warned, moving around a slight depression. "Part of the roof is sagging a bit."

Just past that grass-covered depression was a bank that angled steeply downward to a narrow ledge. Beyond that, the bluff broke away sharply. Eriond picked his way down the bank and led his horse along the ledge. Garion followed him; when he reached the ledge, he glanced over the edge of the bluff. Far below, he saw the wreck lying on the beach. A broad line of footprints stretched away from it at the water's edge to disappear in the rain.

"Here it is," Eriond said. Then he disappeared, leading his horse, it seemed, directly into the grass-covered bank.

The rest of them followed curiously and found a narrow, arched opening that had quite obviously been built by human hands. The long grass above and on each side of the arch had grown over it until it was barely visible. Gratefully, Garion pushed his way through that grass-obscured opening into a calm, musty-smelling darkness.

"Did anyone think to bring any torches?" Sadi asked.

"They were with the food-packs, I'm afraid," Durnik apologized. "Here, let's see what I can do." Garion felt a light surge and heard a faint rushing sound. A dimly glowing spot of light appeared, balanced on the palm of Durnik's hand. Gradually that dim light grew until they could see the interior of the ancient ruin. Like so many structures that had been built in antiquity, this low-ceilinged cellar was vaulted. Stone arches supported the ceiling, and the walls were solidly buttressed. Garion had seen precisely the same construction in King Anheg's eons-old palace in Val Alorn, in the ruins of Vo Wacune, in the lower floors of his own Citadel at Riva, and even in the echoing tomb of the one-eyed God in Cthol Mishrak.

Silk was looking speculatively at Eriond. "I'm sure you have an explanation," he said. "How did you know that this place was here?"

"I lived here for a while with Zedar. It was while he was waiting until I'd grow old enough to steal the Orb."

Silk looked slightly disappointed. "How prosaic," he said.

"I'm sorry," Eriond said as he led the horses over to one side of the vaulted room. "Would you like to have me make up some kind of story for you instead?"

"Never mind, Eriond," the little man told him.

Urgit had been examining one of the buttresses. "No Murgo ever built this," he declared. "The stones fit too closely."

"It was built before the Murgos came to this part of the world," Eriond said.

"By the slave race?" Urgit asked incredulously. "All they know how to make are mud huts."

"That's what they wanted you to think. They were building towers—and cities—when Murgos were still living in goatskin tents."

"Could somebody please make a fire?" Ce'Nedra asked through chattering teeth. "I'm freezing." Garion looked at her closely and saw that her lips had a bluish tinge to them.

"The firewood's over here," Eriond said. He went behind one of the buttresses and emerged with an armload of white-bleached sticks. "Zedar and I used to carry driftwood up from the beach. There's still quite a bit left." He went to the fireplace in the back wall, dropped the wood, and bent over to peer up the chimney. "It seems to be clear," he said.

Durnik went to work immediately with his flint, steel, and tinder. In a few moments, a small curl of orange flame was licking up through the little peaked roof of splinters he had built on the bed of ash in the fireplace. They all crowded around that tiny flame, thrusting twigs and sticks at it in their eagerness to force it to grow more quickly.

"That won't do," Durnik said with uncharacteristic sternness. "You'll only knock it apart and put it out."

They reluctantly backed away from the fireplace.

Durnik carefully laid twigs and splinters on the growing flame, then small sticks, and finally larger ones. The flames grew higher and began to spread quickly through the bone-dry wood. The light from the fireplace began to fill the musty cellar, and Garion could feel a faint warmth on his face.

"All right, then," Polgara said in a crisp, businesslike way, "what are we going to do about food?"

"The sailors have left the wreck," Garion said, "and the tide's gone out enough so that all but the very aft end of the ship is out of the water. I'll take some packhorses and go back down there to see what I can find."

Durnik's fire had begun to crackle. He stood up and looked at Eriond. "Can you manage here?" he asked.

Eriond nodded and went behind the buttress for more wood.

The smith bent and picked up his cloak. "Toth and I can go with you, Garion," he said, "just in case those sailors decide to come back. But we're going to have to hurry. It's going to start getting dark before too long."

The gale still howled across the weather-rounded top of the headland, driving rain and sleet before it. Garion and his two friends picked their way carefully down the slope again toward the forlorn-looking ship, lying twisted and broken-backed on the boulder that had claimed her life.

"How long do you think this storm is going to last?" Garion shouted to Durnik.

"It's hard to say," Durnik shouted back. "It could blow over tonight or it could keep it up for several days."

"I was afraid you might say that."

They reached the wreck, dismounted, and entered the hold

through the opening they had previously made in the bow. "I don't think we'll find too much down here," Durnik said. "Our own food is all spoiled, and I don't think the sailors stored anything perishable in the hold."

Garion nodded. "Can we get Aunt Pol's cooking things?" he asked. "She'll want those, I think."

Durnik peered aft at the bilge-soaked bags and bales lying in a tumbled heap in the shattered stern, with surf sloshing over them through the holes rent in the hull in that end of the ship. "I think so," he said. "I'll take a look."

"As long as we're here, we might as well pick up the rest of the things we had in those aft cabins," Garion said. "I'll go gather them up while you and Toth see what the sailors left behind in the galley." He climbed carefully over the splintered timbers at the point where the keel had broken and went up a ladder to the hatch above. Then he slipped and slid down the deck to the aft companionway.

It took him perhaps a quarter of an hour to gather up the belongings they had left behind when they had fled the wreck. He wrapped them all in a sheet of sailcloth and went back up on deck. He carried his bundle forward and dropped it over the side onto the wet sand of the beach.

Durnik poked his head out of the forward companionway. "There isn't much, Garion," he said. "The sailors picked it over pretty thoroughly."

"We'll have to make do with whatever we can find, I guess." Garion squinted up through the rain. The sky was growing noticeably darker. "We'd better hurry," he added.

They reached the top of the headland in a gale-torn twilight and carefully led their horses along the edge of the bluff to the entrance of the cellar as the last tatters of daylight faded from the sky. The inside of the vaulted chamber was warm now and filled with the light of the fire dancing on the hearth. The others had strung lines from the arches during their absence, and their blankets and clothing hung dripping and steaming along the walls.

"Any luck?" Silk asked as Garion led his horse inside.

"Not much," Garion admitted. "The sailors cleaned out the galley pretty thoroughly."

Durnik and Toth led in the other horses and lifted down a number of makeshift packs. "We found a bag of beans," the smith reported, "and a crock full of honey. There was a sack of meal back in a corner and a couple of sides of bacon. The sailors left the bacon behind because it was moldy, but we ought to be able to cut most of the mold away."

"That's all?" Polgara asked.

"I'm afraid so, Pol," Durnik replied. "We picked up a brazier and a couple of bags of charcoal—since there doesn't seem to be any firewood in this part of the world."

She frowned slightly, running over the inventory he had just given her.

"It's not very much, Pol," he apologized, "but it was the best we could do."

"I can manage with it, dear," she said, smiling at him.

"I picked up the clothes we left in those aft cabins, too," Garion said as he unsaddled his horse. "A few of them are even dry."

"Good," Polgara said. "Let's all change into whatever dry clothing will fit, and I'll see what I can do about something to eat."

Silk had been looking suspiciously at the sack of meal. "Gruel?" he asked, looking unhappy.

"Beans would take much too long to cook," she replied. "Porridge and honey—and a bit of bacon—will get us through the night."

He sighed.

The following morning, the rain and sleet had let up, although the wind still tore at the long grass atop the headland. Garion, wrapped in his cloak, stood on the ledge outside the entrance to the cellar, looking out over the froth-tipped waves in the gulf and the surf pounding on the beach far below. Off to the southeast, the clouds seemed to be growing thinner, and patches of blue raced along through the dirty-looking murk covering the rest of the sky. Sometime during the night, the tide had once again washed over the wreck of their ship, and the aft end had broken away and been carried off. A number of huddled lumps bobbed limply at the edge of the surf, and Garion resolutely kept his eyes away from those mute remains of the Murgo sailors who had been washed overboard and drowned when the ship had crashed into the reef.

Then, far up the coast, he saw a number of red-sailed ships beating their way along the south shore of the Gorand Sea toward the broken remains of the ship lying on the beach below.

Belgarath and Eriond pushed their way past the sailcloth door Durnik had hung across the arched entrance to the cellar the night before to join Garion on the ledge. "It's quit raining at least," Garion reported, "and the wind seems to be dropping. There's that problem though." He pointed at the Mallorean ships coming up the coast.

Belgarath grunted. "They're certain to come ashore when they see the wreck," he agreed. "I think it's time for us to leave here."

Eriond was looking around with a strange expression on his face. "It hasn't changed much," he noted. He pointed toward a small, grassy bench at the far end of the ledge. "I used to play there," he said, "when Zedar let me come outside, anyway."

"Did he talk to you very much while you were staying here?" Belgarath asked him.

"Not very often." Eriond shrugged. "He kept pretty much to himself. He had some books with him and he used to spend most of his time with them."

"It must have been a lonely way to grow up," Garion said.

"It wasn't so bad. I used to spend a lot of my time watching the clouds—or the birds. In the springtime the birds nest in holes in the face of this bluff. If you lean out over the edge, you can see them coming and going, and I always used to like watching the fledglings when they first tried out their wings."

"Do you have any idea of how far it is to the high road that leads inland?" Belgarath asked him.

"It used to take us about a day to get there. Of course I was small then, and I couldn't walk very fast."

Belgarath nodded. He shaded his eyes with one hand and looked at the Mallorean ships laboring up the coast. "I think we'd better tell the others," he said. "We won't accomplish too much by trying to hold this place against several shiploads of the Mallorean sailors."

It took perhaps an hour to gather up their still-wet clothing and their meager food supply and load the pack horses. Then they pushed their way out past the sailcloth door and led their horses to the far side of the headland. Garion noticed that Eriond looked back once with a faintly regretful expression, then resolutely turned his back on his childhood home to face the grassland lying ahead. "I sort of know the way," he said. "Those creeks out there are running bank-full, though, so we'll have to be careful." He swung lightly up into his saddle. "I'll go on ahead and pick the best route." He leaned forward and stroked his stallion's neck. Then he smiled. "Horse wants to run a bit anyway." He moved off down the hill at a rolling gallop.

"That's a very strange boy," Urgit said as he mounted. "Did he really know Zedar?"

"Oh, yes," Silk replied, "and also Ctuchik." He gave Polgara a sly look. "He's been consorting with strange people all his life, so his peculiarities aren't really all that hard to understand."

The small patches of blue that had touched the southeastern sky when Garion had first awakened had spread now, and columns of bright morning sunlight streamed down through the misty air to stalk ponderously across the stream-laced grassland below. The wind had abated to little more than a gusty breeze, and they rode on down through the still-wet grass at a brisk canter, following the trail of Eriond and his exuberant horse.

Ce'Nedra, dressed now in one of Eriond's tunics and a pair of woolen leggings, pulled in beside Garion.

"I like your outfit, my Queen." He grinned.

"All my dresses were still wet," she said. She paused, her face growing somber. "It's not working out very well, is it, Garion? We were counting so much on that ship."

"Oh, I don't know," he replied. "We saved a bit of time and we managed to get around most of the war zone. Once we get past Rak Cthaka, maybe we'll be able to find another ship. I don't think we actually lost any time."

"But we didn't gain any either, did we?"

"It's hard to say exactly."

She sighed and rode on beside him in silence.

They reached the high road about noon and turned eastward, making good time for the rest of the day. There was no sign that any other travelers had recently used the road, but Silk ranged out in front of them as a precautionary scout. A clump of willows at the side of the road afforded some shelter that night and also provided the poles necessary for erecting their tents. Supper that evening consisted of beans and bacon, a meal which Urgit in particular found less than satisfying. "I'd give anything for a chunk of beef right now," he complained, "even one as badly prepared as the cooks at the Drojim used to offer me."

"Would you prefer a bowl of boiled grass, your Majesty?" Prala asked him pertly, "or perhaps a nice plate of fried willow bark?"

He gave her a sour look, then turned to Garion. "Tell me," he said, "do you and your friends plan to remain long in Cthol Murgos?"

"Not too long, why?"

"Western ladies seem to have a broad streak of independence in their nature—and a regrettable tendency to speak their minds. I find their influence on certain impressionable Murgo ladies to be unwholesome." Then, as if suddenly realizing that he might have gone too far, he threw an apprehensive glance in Polgara's direction. "No offense intended, my Lady," he apologized quickly. "Just an old Murgo prejudice."

"I see," she replied.

Belgarath set aside his plate and looked over at Silk. "You were out in front all day," he noted. "Did you happen to see any game moving around?"

"There were herds of what looked like some sort of large deer moving north," the little man answered, "but they stayed a long way out of bow shot."

"What have you got in mind, old man?" Polgara asked.

"We need fresh meat, Pol," he replied, rising to his feet. "Moldy bacon and boiled beans aren't going to get us very far." He stepped out of the small circle of light and squinted up at the moon-speckled clouds drifting across the stars. "It might be a good night for hunting," he observed. "What do you think?"

A curious smile touched her lips, and she also rose. "Do you think you can still keep up, old wolf?" she asked him.

"Well enough, I suppose," he said blandly. "Come along, Garion. Let's get a little way away from the horses."

"Where are they going?" Urgit asked Silk.

"You don't want to know, my brother. You really don't want to know."

The moon touched the grass waving in the night breeze with silvery light. The scents of the grassland around them came sharply to Garion's nostrils as his ten-fold heightened sense of smell tasted the odors of the night. He loped easily at the side of the great silvery wolf while the snowy owl ghosted through the moonlight above them. It was good again to run tirelessly with the wind ruffling his fur and his toenails digging into the damp turf as he and his grandfather wolf ranged out across the moon-silvered grass in the ancient rite of the hunt.

They started a herd of deerlike creatures from their matted grass beds some leagues east of their camp and pursued them hard for miles across the rolling hills. Then, as the terrified animals plunged across a rain-swollen creek, an old buck, pushed to exhaustion, missed his footing, tumbled end over end, throwing up a great spray of water, and came to rest against the far bank, his antlers dug into the shore and his grotesquely twisted head proclaiming that his fall had snapped his neck.

Without thinking, Garion leaped from the bank into the swollen creek, drove himself rapidly across, and caught the dead buck by the foreleg with his powerful jaws. Straining, he dragged the still-warm carcass up onto the bank before the rushing creek could sweep it away.

Belgarath and Polgara, who had once again resumed their natural forms, came sauntering up the gravel bank as calmly as if they were on an evening stroll. "He's very good, isn't he?" Polgara observed.

"Not bad," Belgarath admitted. Then he drew his knife from his belt and tested its edge with his thumb. "We'll dress the deer out," he said to her. "Why don't you go back and get Durnik and a pack horse?"

"All right, father," she agreed, shimmered in the moonlight, and swooped away on silent wings.

"You're going to need your hands, Garion," the old man said pointedly.

"Oh," Garion said in the manner of wolves and rose from his haunches. "Sorry, Grandfather. I forgot." He changed back into his own form a little regretfully.

There were some queer looks the following morning when Polgara served up steaks instead of porridge, but no one chose to say anything about the sudden change of diet.

They rode on for the next two days, with the last wrack and tatter of the dying storm flowing overhead. About noon, they crested a long hill and saw before them the broad blue expanse of a great body of water.

"Lake Cthaka," Urgit said. "Once we circle that, we're only two days from Rak Cthaka itself."

"Sadi," Belgarath said, "have you got your map?"

"Right here, Ancient One," the eunuch replied, reaching inside his robe.

"Let's have a look." The old sorcerer swung down from his horse, took the parchment map from Sadi, and opened it. The wind coming off the lake rattled and fluttered it, threatening to tear it from his grasp. "Oh, stop that," he snapped irritably. Then he stared at the map for several long moments. "I think we're going to have to get off the road," he said finally. "The storm and the wreck delayed us, and we can't be absolutely certain how far the Malloreans have marched since we left Rak Urga. I don't want an army catching us with the lake at our backs. The Malloreans don't have any reason to be on the south side of the lake, so we'll go that way instead." He pointed at a large area on the map covered with a representation of trees. "We'll find out what the situation is in Rak Cthaka," he said, "and if we need to, we'll be able to get into the Great Southern Forest."

"Belgarath," Durnik said urgently, pointing toward the north, "what's that?"

A low smudge of black smoke was streaming low to the horizon in the stiff breeze.

"Grass fire perhaps?" Sadi suggested.

Belgarath began to swear. "No," he said shortly, "it's not the right color." He pulled the map open again. "There are some villages up there," he said. "I think it's one of them."

"Malloreans!" Urgit gasped.

"How could they have gotten this far west?" Silk asked.

"Wait a minute," Garion said as a sudden thought came to him. He looked at Urgit. "Who wins when you fight the Malloreans in the mountains?" he asked.

"We do, of course. We know how to use the mountains to our advantage."

"But when you fight them on the plains, who wins?"

"They do. They've got more people."

"Then your armies are safe only as long as they stay in the mountains?"

"I already said that, Belgarion."

"If I were the one who was fighting you then, I'd try to figure out a way to lure you down onto the plains. If I moved around, making threatening noises at Rak Cthaka, you'd almost have to respond, wouldn't you? You'd send all your troops out of Urga and Morcth to defend the city. But if, instead of attacking the city, I moved my forces north and west, I could intercept and ambush you out in the open on flat ground. I could pick my battlefields and destroy both your armies in a single day."

Urgit's face had grown very pale. "*That's* what those Mallorean ships were doing in the Gorand Sea!" he exclaimed. "They were there to spy out the movements of my troops coming from Rak Urga. Zakath's setting traps for me." He spun, his eyes wild. "Belgarath, you've got to let me go warn my troops. They're completely unprepared for an attack. The Malloreans will wipe my army out, and they're the only force between here and Rak Urga."

Belgarath tugged at one earlobe, squinting at him.

"Please, Belgarath!"

"Do you think you can move fast enough to get ahead of the Malloreans?"

"I have to. If I don't, Cthol Murgos will fall. Blast it, old man, I've got a responsibility."

"I think you're finally beginning to learn, Urgit," Belgarath told him. "We might make a king out of you, after all. Durnik, give him whatever food we can spare." He turned back to Silk's anxious brother. "Don't take chances," he cautioned. "Stay off the hilltops where you'll be outlined against the sky. Make the best time you can, but don't kill your horse in the process." He stopped, then gruffly grasped the weasel-faced man by the shoulders. "Good luck," he said shortly.

Urgit nodded, then turned toward his horse.

Prala was right behind him.

"What do you think you're doing?" he demanded.

"I'm going with you."

"You most certainly are not!"

"We're wasting time."

"There's probably going to be a battle, girl. Use your head."

"I'm a Murgo, too," she declared defiantly, "I'm descended from the Cthan Dynasty. I'm not afraid of battles!" She caught the reins of her horse and lifted the long black leather case down from her saddle. She untied the fastenings and snapped the case open. Inside lay a sword, its hilt encrusted with rubies. She lifted it from the case and held it aloft. "This is the sword of the last king of the Cthan Dynasty," she announced dramatically. "He took the field with it at Vo Mimbre. Do not dishonor it." She reversed the blade and offered him the hilt across her forearm.

He stared first at her and then at the sword.

"It was to have been my gift to you on our wedding day," she said to him, "but you need it now. Take the sword, King of the Murgos, and get on your horse. We have a battle to win."

He took the sword and held it up. The rubies caught the sun like drops of blood on the hilt. Then he suddenly turned, as if on an impulse. "Cross swords with me, Belgarion," he said, "for luck."

Garion nodded and drew his great sword. The fire that ran up its blade was a bright blue; when he touched Urgit's extended weapon with it, the smaller man winced as if the hilt of his sword had suddenly burned his hand. Then he stared at it incredulously. The stones on the hilt of his sword were no longer rubies, but bright blue sapphires. "Did you do that?" he gasped.

"No," Garion replied. "The Orb did. It seems to like you for some reason. Good luck, your Majesty."

"Thanks, your Majesty," Urgit answered. "And good luck to you, too—all of you." He started toward his horse again, then turned back and wordlessly caught Silk in a rough embrace. "All right, girl," he said to Prala, "let's go."

"Good-bye, Ce'Nedra," Prala called as she mounted her horse. "Thank you—for everything." The two of them wheeled their horses and raced off toward the north.

Silk sighed. "I'm afraid I'm going to lose him," he said mournfully.

"To the Malloreans, you mean?" Durnik asked.

"No—to that girl. She had a marrying sort of expression on her face when they left."

"I think it's sweet," Ce'Nedra sniffed.

"Sweet? I think it's revolting." He looked around. "If we're going around the south end of the lake, we'd better get started."

They galloped south along the lake shore through the long, golden-slanting beams of afternoon sunlight until they were a couple of leagues from the place where Urgit and Prala had so abruptly left them. Then Silk, ranging once again ahead of them, crested a hill and motioned them to come ahead, but cautiously.

"What is it?" Belgarath asked when they joined him.

"There's something else burning up ahead," the little man reported. "I didn't get too close, but it looks like an isolated farmstead."

"Let's go look," Durnik said to Toth, and the two of them rode off in the direction of the smudge of smoke lying low on the horizon to the east.

"I'd certainly like to know if Urgit's doing all right," Silk said with a worried frown.

"You really like him, don't you?" Velvet asked him.

"Urgit? Yes, I think I do. We're very much alike in many ways." He looked at her. "I suppose that you're going to mention all of this in your report to Javelin?"

"Naturally."

"I really wish you wouldn't, you know."

"Why on earth not?"

"I'm not entirely sure. It's just that for some reason I don't think I want Drasnian Intelligence using my relationship to the King of Cthol Murgos for its own advantage. I think I want to keep it private."

A silver twilight was settling over the lake when Durnik and Toth returned with grim faces. "It was a Murgo farmstead," Durnik reported. "Some Malloreans had been there. I don't think they were regular troops—probably deserters of some kind. They looted and burned, and regular troops don't usually do that, if they've got officers around to control them. The house is gone, but the barn is still partially intact."

"Is there enough of it left to shelter us for the night?" Garion wanted to know.

Durnik looked dubious, then shrugged. "The roof's still mostly there."

"Is something wrong?" Belgarath asked him.

Durnik made a small gesture and then walked away until he was out of earshot of the rest. Garion and Belgarath followed him.

"What's the matter, Durnik?" Belgarath asked.

"The barn's good enough to give us shelter," the smith said quietly, "but I think you ought to know that those Mallorean deserters impaled everybody on the farmstead. I don't think you want the ladies to see that. It isn't very pleasant."

"Is there someplace where you can get the bodies under cover?" the old man asked.

"I'll see what we can do," Durnik sighed. "Why do people do that sort of thing?"

"Ignorance, usually. An ignorant man falls back on brutality out of a lack of imagination. Go with them, Garion. They might need some help. Wave a torch to let us know when you get finished."

The fact that it was nearly dark helped a little. Garion was unable to see the faces of the people on the stakes. There was a sod-roofed cellar at the back of the still-smoldering house, and they put the bodies there. Then Garion took up a torch and walked some distance from the house to signal to Belgarath. The barn was dry, and the fire Durnik built in a carefully cleared area on the stone floor soon warmed it.

"This is actually pleasant," Ce'Nedra declared with a smile as she looked around at the dancing shadows on the walls and rafters. She sat on a pile of fragrant hay and bounced tentatively a few times. "And this will make wonderful beds. I hope we can find a place like this every night."

Garion walked over to the door and looked out, not trusting himself to answer. He had grown up on a farm not really all that much different from this one, and the thought of a band of marauding soldiers swooping down on Faldor's farm, burning and killing, filled him with a vast outrage. A sudden image rose in his mind. The shadowy faces of the dead Murgos hanging on those stakes might very well have been the faces of his childhood friends, and that thought shook him to the very core of his being. The dead here had been Murgos, but they had also been farmers, and he felt a sudden kinship with them. The savagery that had befallen them began to take on the aspect of a personal affront, and dark thoughts began to fill his mind.

CHAPTER TWENTY-ONE

By morning it was raining again, a drizzly sort of rain that made the surrounding countryside hazy and indistinct. They rode out from the ruins of the farmstead, dressed again in their slaver's robes, and turned northward along the eastern shore of the lake.

Garion rode in silence, his thoughts as somber as the leaden waters of the lake lying to his left. The rage he had felt the previous evening had settled into an icy resolve. Justice, he had been told, was an abstraction, but he was determined that, should the Mallorean deserters responsible for the atrocity at the farm ever cross his path, he would turn the abstract into an immediate reality. He knew that Belgarath and Polgara did not approve of the sort of thing he had in mind, so he kept his peace and contemplated the idea of vengeance, if not justice.

When they reached the muddy road coming in off the northern end of the lake and stretching out toward the southeast and the city of Rak Cthaka, they found it clogged with a horde of terrified civilians, dressed for the most part in ragged clothing and carrying bundles of what few possessions they had been able to salvage.

"I think we'll stay off the road," Belgarath decided. "We could never make any time through that mob."

"Are we going on to Rak Cthaka?" Sadi asked him.

Belgarath looked at the crowd streaming along the road. "I don't think you could find a raft in Rak Cthaka right now, much less a ship. Let's go on into the forest and work our way south through the trees. I don't much like staying out in the open in hostile territory, and fishing villages are better places to hire boats than the piers of a major city."

"Why don't you and the others ride on," Silk suggested. "I'd like to ask a few questions."

Belgarath grunted. "That might not be a bad idea. Just don't be too long at it. I'd like to reach the Great Southern Forest sometime before the end of winter, if I can possibly manage it."

"I'll go with him, Grandfather," Garion offered. "I need to get my mind off some things I've seen lately, anyway."

The two of them rode through the knee-high grass toward the broad stream of frightened refugees fleeing southward. "Garion," Silk said, reining in his horse, "isn't that a Sendar—the one pushing the wheelbarrow?"

Garion shielded his eyes from the rain and peered at the sturdy fellow Silk had pointed out. "He sort of looks like a Sendar," he agreed. "What would a Sendar be doing down here in Cthol Murgos?"

"Why don't we go ask him? Sendars love to gossip, so he can probably give us some idea of what's happening." The little man walked his horse over until he was riding beside the stout man with the wheelbarrow. "Morning, friend," he said pleasantly. "You're a long way from home, aren't you?"

The stout man set down his barrow and eyed Silk's green Nyissan robe apprehensively. "I'm not a slave," he declared, "so don't get any ideas."

"This?" Silk laughed, plucking at the front of the robe. "Don't worry, friend, we're not Nyissans. We just found these on some bodies back there a ways. We thought they might be a help if we happened to run into somebody official. What in the world are you doing in Cthol Murgos?"

"Running," the Sendar said ruefully, "just like all the rest of this rabble. Didn't you hear about what's been happening?"

"No. We've been out of touch."

The stout man lifted the handles of his barrow again and trudged along the grassy shoulder of the road. "There's a whole Mallorean army marching west out of Gorut," he said. "They burned the town I lived in and killed half the people. They didn't even bother with Rak Cthaka, so that's where we're all going. I'm going to see if I can find a sea captain who's going in the general direction of Sendaria. For some reason, I'm suddenly homesick."

"You've been living in a Murgo town?" Silk asked with some surprise.

The fellow made a face. "It wasn't altogether by choice," he replied. "I had some trouble with the law in Tolnedra when I was there on business ten years ago and I took passage on board a merchantman to get out of the country. The captain was a scoundrel; when my money ran out, he sailed off and left me on the wharf at Rak Cthaka. I drifted on up to a town on the north side of the lake. They let me stay because I was willing to do things that are beneath Murgo dignity, but were too important to trust a slave to do. It was sort of degrading, but it was a living. Anyway, a couple days ago the Malloreans marched through. When they left, there wasn't a single building standing."

"How did you escape?" Silk asked him.

"I hid under a haystack until dark. That's when I joined

this mob." He glanced over at the crowd of refugees slogging through the ankle-deep mud of the road. "Isn't that pathetic? They don't even have sense enough to spread out and walk on the grass. You certainly wouldn't see soldiers doing that, let me tell you."

"You've had some military experience, then?"

"I most certainly have," the stout man replied proudly. "I was a sergeant in Princess Ce'Nedra's army. I was at Thull Mardu with her."

"I missed that one," Silk told him with aplomb. "I was busy someplace else. Are there any Malloreans between here and the Great Southern Forest?"

"Who knows? I don't go looking for Malloreans. You don't really want to go into the forest, though. All this killing has stirred up the Raveners."

"Raveners? What's that?"

"Ghouls. They feed on dead bodies most of the time, but I've heard some very ugly stories lately. I'd make a special point of staying out of the forest, my friend."

"We might have to keep that in mind. Thanks for the information. Good luck when you get to Rak Cthaka, and I hope you make it back to Camaar."

"Right now, I'd settle for Tol Honeth. Tolnedran jails aren't really all that bad."

Silk grinned at him quickly, turned his horse, and led Garion away from the road at a gallop to rejoin the others.

That afternoon they forded the River Cthaka some leagues upstream from the coast. The drizzle slackened as evening approached, though the sky remained cloudy. Once they had reached the far side of the river, they could see the irregular, dark shape of the edge of the Great Southern Forest, looming up beyond perhaps a league of open grassland.

"Shall we try for it?" Silk asked.

"Let's wait," Belgarath decided. "I'm just a little concerned about what that fellow you talked with said. I'm not sure I want any surprises—particularly in the dark."

"There's a willow thicket downstream a ways," Durnik

said, pointing at a fair-sized grove of spindly trees bordering the river a half mile or so to the south. "Toth and I can pitch the tents there."

"All right," Belgarath agreed.

"How far is it to Verkat now, Grandfather?" Garion asked as they rode down along the rain-swollen river toward the willows.

"According to the map, it's about fifty leagues to the southeast before we reach the coast opposite the island. Then we'll have to find a boat to get us across."

Garion sighed.

"Don't get discouraged," Belgarath told him. "We're making better time than I'd originally expected, and Zandramas can't run forever. There's only so much land in the world. Sooner or later we'll chase her down."

As Durnik and Toth pitched the tents, Garion and Eriond ranged out through the sodden willow thicket in search of firewood. It was difficult to find anything sufficiently dry to burn, and the effort of an hour yielded only enough twigs and small branches from under fallen trees to make a meager cook fire for Polgara. As she began to prepare their evening meal of beans and venison, Garion noted that Sadi was walking about their campsite, combing the ground with his eyes. "This isn't funny, dear," he said quite firmly. "Now you come out this very minute."

"What's the matter?" Durnik asked him.

"Zith isn't in her bottle," Sadi replied, still searching.

Durnik rose from where he was sitting quite rapidly. "Are you sure?"

"She thinks it's amusing to hide from me sometimes. Now, you come out immediately, you naughty snake."

"You probably shouldn't tell Silk," Belgarath advised. "He'll go directly into hysterics if he finds out that she's loose." The old man looked around. "Where is he, by the way?"

"He and Liselle went for a walk," Eriond told him.

"In all this wet? Sometimes I wonder about him."

Ce'Nedra came over and sat on the log beside Garion. He put his arm about her shoulders and drew her close to him. She snuggled down and sighed. "I wonder what Geran is doing tonight," she said wistfully.

"Sleeping, probably."

"He always looked so adorable when he was asleep." She sighed again and then closed her eyes.

There was a crashing back in the willows, and Silk suddenly ran into the circle of firelight, his eyes very wide and his face deathly pale.

"What's the matter?" Durnik exclaimed.

"She had that snake in her bodice!" Silk blurted.

"Who did?"

"Liselle!"

Polgara, holding a ladle in one hand, turned to regard the violently trembling little man with one raised eyebrow. "Tell me, Prince Kheldar," she said in a cool voice, "exactly what were you doing in the Margravine Liselle's bodice?"

Silk endured that steady gaze for a moment; then he actually began to blush furiously.

"Oh," she said, "I see." She turned back to her cooking.

It was past midnight, and Garion was not sure what it was that had awakened him. He moved slowly to avoid waking Ce'Nedra and carefully parted the tentflap to look out. A dense, clinging fog had arisen from the river, and all that he could see was a curtain of solid, dirty white. He lay quietly, straining his ears to catch any sound.

From somewhere off in the fog, he heard a faint clinking sound; it took him a moment to identify it. Finally he realized that what he was hearing was the sound of a mounted man wearing a mail shirt. He reached over in the darkness and took up his sword.

"I still think you ought to tell us what you found in that house before you set it on fire," he heard someone say in a gruff, Mallorean-accented voice. The speaker was not close, but sounds at night traveled far, so Garion could clearly understand what was being said.

"Oh, it wasn't much, Corporal," another Mallorean voice replied evasively. "A bit of this; a bit of that."

"I think you ought to share those things with the rest of us. We're all in this together, after all."

"Isn't it odd that you didn't think of that until after I managed to pick up a few things? If you want to share in the loot, then you should pay attention to the houses and not spend all your time impaling the prisoners."

"We're at war," the corporal declared piously. "It's our duty to kill the enemy."

"Duty," the second Mallorean snorted derisively. "We're deserters, Corporal. Our only duty is to ourselves. If you want to spend your time butchering Murgo farmers, that's up to you, but I'm saving up for my retirement."

Garion carefully rolled out from under the tent flap. He felt a peculiar calm, almost as if his emotions had somehow been set aside. He rose and moved silently to where the packs were piled and burrowed his hand into them one by one until his fingers touched steel. Then, carefully, so that it made no sound, he drew out his heavy mail shirt. He pulled it on and shrugged his shoulders a couple of times to settle it into place.

Toth was standing guard near the horses, his huge bulk looming in the fog.

"There's something I have to take care of," Garion whispered softly to the mute giant.

Toth looked at him gravely, then nodded. He turned, untied a horse from the picket line, and handed him the reins. Then he put one huge hand on Garion's shoulder, squeezed once in silent approval, and stepped back.

Garion did not want to give the Mallorean deserters time to lose themselves in the fog, so he pulled himself up onto the unsaddled horse and moved out of the willow thicket at a silent walk.

The fading voices that had come out of the fog had seemed to be moving in the direction of the forest, and Garion rode quietly after them, probing the foggy darkness ahead with his ears and with his mind.

After he had ridden for perhaps a mile, he heard a raucous laugh coming from somewhere ahead and slightly to the left. "Did you hear the way they squealed when we impaled them?" a coarse voice came out of the clinging mist.

"That does it," Garion grated from between clenched teeth as he drew his sword. He directed his horse toward the sound, then nudged his heels at the animal's flanks. The horse moved faster, his hooves making no sound on the damp earth.

"Let's have some light," one of the deserters said.

"Do you think it's safe? There are patrols out looking for deserters."

"It's after midnight. The patrols are all in bed. Go ahead and light the torch."

After a moment, there was a fatally ruddy beacon glowing in the dark and reaching out to Garion.

His charge caught the deserters totally by surprise. Several of them were dead before they even knew that he was upon them. There were screams and shouts from both sides as he crashed through them, chopping them out of their saddles with huge strokes to the right and the left. His great blade sheared effortlessly through mail, bone, and flesh. He sent five of them tumbling to the ground as he thundered through their ranks. Then he whirled on the three who still remained. After one startled look, one of them fled; another dragged his sword from its sheath, and the third, who held the torch, sat frozen in astonished terror.

The Mallorean with the sword feebly raised his weapon to protect his head from the dreadful blow Garion had already launched. The great overhand sweep, however, shattered the doomed man's sword blade and sheared down through his helmet halfway to his waist. Roughly, Garion kicked the twitching body off his sword and turned on the torch bearer.

"Please!" the terrified man cried, trying to back his horse away. "Have mercy!"

For some reason, that plaintive cry infuriated Garion all the more. He clenched his teeth together. With a single broad swipe, he sent the murderer's head spinning off into the foggy darkness.

He pulled his horse up sharply, cocked his head for a moment to pick up the sound of the last Mallorean's galloping flight, and set out in pursuit.

It took him only a few minutes to catch up with the fleeing deserter. At first he had only the sound to follow, but then he was able to make out the dim, shadowy form racing ahead of him in the fog. He veered slightly to the right, plunged on past the desperate man, then pulled his horse directly into the shadowy deserter's path.

"Who are you?" the unshaven Mallorean squealed as he hauled his mount to a sudden, rearing stop. "Why are you doing this?"

"I am justice," Garion grated at him and quite deliberately ran the man through.

The deserter stared in horrified amazement at the huge sword protruding from his chest. With a gurgling sigh, he toppled to one side, sliding limply off the blade.

Still without any real sense of emotion, Garion dismounted and wiped the blade of his sword on the dead man's tunic. Almost as an afterthought, he caught the reins of the fellow's horse, remounted, and turned back toward the place where he had killed the others. Carefully, one by one, he checked each fallen body for signs of life, then rounded up three more horses and rode back to the camp concealed in the willows.

Silk stood beside the huge Toth near the picket line. "Where have you been?" he demanded in a hoarse whisper as Garion dismounted.

"We needed some more horses," Garion replied tersely, handing the reins of the captured mounts to Toth.

"Mallorean ones, judging from the saddles," Silk noted. "How did you find them?"

"Their riders were talking as they went by. They seemed to be quite amused by a visit they paid to a Murgo farmstead a few days ago."

"And you didn't even invite me to go along?" Silk accused.

"Sorry," Garion said, "but I had to hurry. I didn't want to lose them in the fog."

"Four of them?" Silk asked, counting horses.

"I couldn't find the other four mounts." Garion shrugged. "These ought to be enough to make up for the ones we lost during the shipwreck, though."

"Eight?" Silk looked a bit startled at that.

"I came on them by surprise. It wasn't much of a fight. Why don't we get some sleep?"

"Uh—Garion," Silk suggested, "it might not be a bad idea for you to wash up before you go back to bed. Ce'Nedra's nerves are a little delicate, and she might be upset, if she wakes up and sees you covered with blood the way you are."

The fog was even thicker the following morning. It was a heavy fog, chill and clinging, lying densely along the river bank and bedewing the tangled limbs of the willow thicket at their backs with strings of pearllike droplets.

"It hides us, at least," Garion observed, still feeling that peculiar remoteness.

"It also hides anybody else who might be out there," Sadi told him, "or any *thing*. That forest up ahead has a bad reputation."

"Just how big is it?"

"It's probably the largest forest in the world," Sadi replied, lifting a pack up onto a horse's back. "It goes on for hundreds of leagues." He looked curiously down the picket line. "Is it my imagination, or do we have more horses this morning?"

"I happened across a few last night," Garion replied.

After breakfast, they packed up Polgara's cooking utensils, mounted, and started out across the intervening grassland toward the forest lying hidden in the fog.

As Garion rode, he heard Silk and Durnik talking right behind him. "Just what were you doing last night?" Durnik asked directly. "When you found Zith in Liselle's bodice, I mean?"

"She's going to make a report to Javelin when this is all over," Silk replied. "There are some things I'd rather he didn't know. If I can get on friendly terms with her, maybe I can persuade her to overlook those things in her report."

"That's really rather contemptible, you know. She's just a girl."

"Believe me, Durnik, Liselle can take care of herself. The two of us are playing a game. I'll admit that I hadn't counted on Zith, though."

"Do Drasnians always have to play games?"

"Of course. It helps to pass the time. Winters are very long and tedious in Drasnia. The games we play sharpen our wits and make us better at what we do when we aren't playing." The little man raised his voice slightly. "Garion?" he said.

"Yes?"

"Are we avoiding the place where you found those horses last night? We wouldn't want to upset the ladies so soon after breakfast."

"It was over that way." Garion gestured off to the left.

"What's this?" Durnik asked.

"The extra animals came from a group of Mallorean deserters who used to creep up on isolated Murgo farmlands," Silk replied lightly. "Garion saw to it that they won't be needing horses any more."

"Oh," Durnik said. He thought about it for a moment. "Good," he said finally.

The dark trees loomed out of the fog as the company approached the edge of the forest. The leaves had turned brown and clung sparsely to the branches, for winter was not far off. As they rode in under the twisted branches, Garion looked about, trying to identify the trees, but they were of kinds that he did not recognize. They were gnarled into fantastic shapes, and their limbs seemed almost to writhe up and out from their massy trunks, reaching toward the sunless sky. Their gnarled stems were dotted with dark knots, deeply indented in the coarse bark, and those knots seemed somehow to give each tree a grotesque semblance of a distorted human face with wide, staring eyes and a gaping mouth twisted into an expression of unspeakable horror. The forest floor was deep with fallen leaves, blackened and sodden, and the fog hung gray beneath the branches spreading above.

Ce'Nedra drew her cloak more tightly about her and shuddered. "Do we have to go through this forest?" she asked plaintively.

"I thought you liked trees," Garion said.

"Not these." She looked about fearfully. "There's something very cruel about them. They hate each other."

"Hate? Trees?"

"They struggle and push each other, trying to reach the sunlight. I don't like this place, Garion."

"Try not to think about it," he advised.

They pushed deeper and deeper into the gloomy wood, riding in silence for the most part, their spirits sunk low by the pervasive gloom and by the cold antagonism seeping from the strange, twisted trees.

They took a brief, cold lunch, then rode on toward a somber twilight which seemed hardly more than a deepening of the foggy half-dark spread beneath the hateful trees.

"I guess we've gone far enough," Belgarath said finally. "Let's get a fire going and put up the tents."

It might have been only Garion's imagination or perhaps the cry of some hunting bird of prey, but as the first few flickering tongues of flame curled up around the sticks in the fire pit, it seemed that he heard a shriek coming from the trees themselves—a shriek of fear mingled with a dreadful rage. And as he looked around, the distorted semblances of human faces deeply indented in the surrounding tree trunks seemed to move in the flickering light, silently howling at the hated fire.

After they had eaten, Garion walked away from the fire. He still felt strangely numb inside, as if his emotions had been enclosed in some kind of protective blanket. He found that he could no longer even remember the details of last night's encounter, but only brief, vivid flashes of blood spurting in ruddy torchlight, of riders tumbling limply out of their saddles, and of the torch bearer's head flying off into the fog.

"Do you want to talk about it?" Belgarath asked quietly from just behind him.

"Not really, Grandfather. I don't think you'll approve of what I did, so why don't we just let it go at that? There's no way that I could make you understand."

"Oh, I understand, Garion. I just don't think that you accomplished anything, that's all. You killed—how many was it?"

"Eight."

"That many? All right—eight Malloreans. What did you prove by it?"

"I wasn't really out to prove anything, Grandfather. I just wanted to make sure that they never did it again. I can't even be absolutely certain that they were the men who killed those Murgo farmers. They did kill some people someplace, though, and people who do that sort of thing need to be stopped."

"You did that, all right. Does it make you feel any better?"

"No. I suppose not. I wasn't even angry when I killed them. It was just something that had to be done, so I did it. Now it's over, and I'd just as soon forget about it."

Belgarath gave him a long, steady look. "All right," he said finally. "As long as you keep that firmly in mind, I guess you haven't done yourself any permanent injury. Let's go back to the fire. It's chilly out here in the woods."

Garion slept badly that night, and Ce'Nedra, huddled almost fearfully in his arms, stirred restlessly and often whimpered in her sleep.

The next morning, Belgarath rose and looked about with a dark scowl. "This is absurd," he burst out quite suddenly. "Where *is* the sun?"

"Behind the clouds and fog, father," Polgara replied as she calmly brushed her long, dark hair.

"I know that, Pol," he retorted testily, "but I need to see it—even if only briefly—to get our direction. We could wind up wandering around in circles."

Toth, who had been building up the fire, looked over at

the old man, his face impassive as always. He raised one hand and pointed in a direction somewhat at an oblique from that which they had been following the previous evening.

Belgarath frowned. "Are you absolutely sure?" he asked the giant.

Toth nodded.

"Have you been through these woods before?"

Again the mute nodded, then firmly pointed once more in the same direction.

"And if we go that way, we're going to come out on the south coast in the vicinity of the Isle of Verkat?"

Toth nodded again and went back to tending the fire.

"Cyradis said that he was coming along to aid us in the search, Grandfather," Garion reminded him.

"All right. Since he knows the way, we'll let him lead us through this forest. I'm tired of guessing."

They had gone perhaps two leagues that cloudy morning, with Toth confidently leading them along a scarcely perceptible track, when Polgara quite suddenly reined in her horse with a warning cry. "Look out!"

An arrow sizzled through the foggy air directly at Toth, but the huge man swept it aside with his staff. Then a gang of rough-looking men, some Murgos and some of indeterminate race, came rushing out of the woods, brandishing a variety of weapons.

Without a moment's hesitation, Silk rolled out of his saddle, his hands diving under his slaver's robe for his daggers. As the bawling ruffians charged forward, he leaped to meet them, his heavy daggers extended in front of him like a pair of spears.

Even as Garion jumped to the ground, he saw Toth already advancing, his huge staff whirling as he bore down on the attackers, and Durnik, holding his axe in both hands, circling to the other side.

Garion swept Iron-grip's sword from its scabbard and ran forward, swinging the flaming blade in great arcs. One of the ruffians launched himself into the air, twisting as he did so in a clumsy imitation of a maneuver Garion had seen Silk perform so many times in the past. This time, however, the technique failed. Instead of driving his heels into Garion's face or chest, the agile fellow encountered the point of the burning sword, and his momentum quite smoothly skewered him on the blade.

Silk ripped open an attacker with one of his daggers, spun, and drove his other knife directly into the forehead of another.

Toth and Durnik, moving in from opposite sides, drove several of the assailants into a tight knot, and methodically began to brain them one after another as they struggled to disentangle themselves from each other.

"Garion!" Ce'Nedra cried, and he whirled to see a burly, unshaven man pull the struggling little queen from her saddle with one hand, even as he raised the knife he held in the other. Then he dropped the knife, and both his hands flew up to grasp the slim, silken cord that had suddenly been looped about his neck from the rear. Calmly, the golden-haired Velvet, her knee pushed firmly against the wildly threshing man's back, pulled her cord tighter and tighter. Ce'Nedra watched in horror as her would-be killer was efficiently strangled before her eyes.

Garion grimly turned and began to chop his way through the now-disconcerted attackers. The air around him was suddenly filled with shrieks, groans, and chunks of clothing and flesh. The ragged-looking men he faced flinched back as his huge sword laid a broad windrow of quivering dead in his wake. Then they broke and ran.

"Cowards!" a black-robed man screamed after the fleeing villains. He held a bow in his hand and he raised it, pointing his arrow directly at Garion. Then he suddenly doubled over sharply, driving his arrow into the ground before him as one of Silk's daggers flickered end over end to sink solidly into his stomach.

"Is anybody hurt?" Garion demanded, spinning around quickly, his dripping sword still in his hand.

"They are." Silk laughed gaily, looking around with some satisfaction at the carnage in the forest clearing.

"Please stop!" Ce'Nedra cried to Velvet in an anguished voice.

"What?" the blond girl asked absently, still leaning back against the silken cord drawn tightly about the neck of the now-limp man she had just strangled. "Oh, I'm sorry, Ce'Nedra," she apologized. "My attention wandered a bit, I guess." She released the cord, and the black-faced dead man toppled to the ground at her feet.

"Nice job," Silk congratulated her.

"Fairly routine." She shrugged, carefully coiling up her garrote.

"You seem to be taking it quite calmly."

"There's no particular reason to get excited, Kheldar. It's part of what we were trained to do, after all."

He looked as if he were about to reply, but her matter-of-fact tone obviously baffled him.

"Yes?" she asked.

"Nothing."

CHAPTER TWENTY-TWO

"Stop that!" Durnik said in disgust to Sadi, who was moving about the clearing casually sticking his small, poisoned danger into each of the bodies littering the ground.

"Just making sure, Goodman," Sadi replied coolly. "It's not prudent to leave an enemy behind you who might be feigning death." He moved over to the black-robed man whom Silk had felled. "What's this?" he said with some surprise. "This one's still alive." He reached down to push the dying man's hood aside to look at his face, then pulled back his hand with a sharp intake of his breath. "You'd better have a look at this one, Belgarath," he said.

Belgarath crossed the clearing to the eunuch's side.

"Doesn't that purple lining on the inside of his hood mean that he's a Grolim?" Sadi asked.

Belgarath nodded bleakly. He bent and lightly touched the hilt of Silk's dagger that still protruded from the robed man's stomach. "He doesn't have much time left," he said. "Can you get him conscious enough to answer a few questions?"

"I can try," Sadi told him. He went to his horse and took a vial of yellow liquid from his red case. "Could you get me a cup of water, Goodman?" he asked Durnik.

The smith's face was disapproving, but he fetched a tin cup from one of the packs and filled it from one of their water bags.

Sadi carefully measured a few drops of the yellow liquid into the cup, then swirled it around a few times. He knelt beside the dying man and almost tenderly lifted his head. "Here," he said gently, "drink this. It might make you feel better." He supported the Grolim's head on his arm and held the cup to his lips. Weakly, the stricken man drank, then lay back. After a moment, a serene smile came to his ashen face.

"There, isn't that better?"

"Much better," the dying man croaked.

"That was quite a skirmish, wasn't it?"

"We thought to surprise you," the Grolim admitted, "but we were the ones who got the surprise."

"Your Master—what was his name again? I'm terrible at names."

"Morgat," the Grolim supplied with a bemused look on his face, "Hierarch of Rak Cthan."

"Oh, yes, now I remember. Anyway, Morgat should have given you more men to help you."

"I hired the men myself—at Rak Cthaka. They told me that they were professionals, but—" He began to cough weakly.

"Don't tire yourself," Sadi said. He paused. "What's Morgat's interest in us?" he asked.

"He's acting on the instructions of Agachak," the Grolim replied, his voice little more than a whisper. "Agachak is not one to take chances, and some very serious accusations were made back at Rak Urga, I understand. Agachak has ordered that every Grolim priest of the purple seek you out."

Sadi sighed. "It's more or less what I'd expected," he said mournfully. "People always seem to distrust me. Tell me, how did you ever manage to find us?"

"It was Cthrag Yaska," the Grolim replied, his breathing growing even more labored. "Its accursed song rings across Cthol Murgos like a beacon, drawing every Grolim of the purple directly to you." The dying man drew in a deep breath, and his unfocused eyes suddenly became alert. "What was in that cup?" he demanded sharply. He pushed Sadi's arm away and tried to rise to a sitting position. A great gush of blood spurted from his mouth, and his eyes went blank. He shuddered once with a long, gurgling groan. Then he fell limply back.

"Dead," Sadi noted clinically. "That's the problem with oret. It's a little hard on the heart, and this fellow wasn't in very good shape to begin with. I'm sorry, Belgarath, but it was the best I could do."

"It was enough, Sadi," the old man replied bleakly. "Come with me, Garion," he said. "Let's go someplace quiet. You and I are going to have to have a long talk with the Orb."

"Do you suppose that you could hold off on that, Belgarath?" Sadi asked, looking around nervously. "I think we want to get as far away from here as we can—almost immediately."

"I hardly expect those fellows to come back, Sadi," Silk drawled.

"That's not what concerns me, Kheldar. It's not prudent to remain in the vicinity of so many dead bodies in this forest, and we've lingered much too long already."

"Would you like to explain that?" Garion asked.

"Do you remember the warning the Sendar on the road gave to you and Kheldar?"

"About something he called the Raveners, you mean?"

"Yes. How much did he tell you?"

"He said that they're ghouls—creatures that feed on the dead. But that's just a ghost story, isn't it?"

"I'm afraid not. I've heard the story from people who've actually seen them. We definitely want to get away from here. Most of the people who live in this forest—or near it—don't bury their dead. They burn them instead."

"I've never cared much for that idea," Durnik said.

"It has nothing to do with respect, Goodman—or the lack of it. It's done to protect the living."

"All right," Silk said. "What are these ghouls supposed to look like? There are a lot of animals around that try to dig up dead bodies."

"The Raveners aren't animals, Kheldar. They're men—or at least that's what they look like. Normally, they're quite torpid and only come out at night, but during a war or a pestilence, when there are a large number of bodies unburied, they go into a kind of frenzy. The smell of death attracts them and makes them wild. They'll attack anything when they're like that."

"Father," Polgara said, "is this true?"

"It's possible," he admitted. "I've heard some unpleasant things about these woods myself. I don't usually pursue ghost stories, so I didn't bother to investigate."

"Every country has its stories of ogres and monsters," Silk said sceptically. "Only children are frightened by them."

"I'll strike a bargain with you, Kheldar," Sadi said. "If we make it through these woods without seeing any Raveners, you can laugh at my timidity if you like, but for the sake of the ladies, let's get away from here."

Belgarath was frowning. "I don't altogether accept the notion of ghouls," he said, "but then, I didn't believe there was such a thing as an Eldrak either—until I saw one. We want to move along anyway, and Garion and I can talk with the Orb later."

With Toth once more in the lead, they rode away at a gallop, still following the scarcely visible track that angled off toward the southeast. Their horses' hooves tossed up clots of the leaves lying thick-spread on the forest floor as they plunged through the misty wood. The misshapen trees seemed to gape at them as they pounded past, and, though Garion knew it was only his imagination, those grotesque, almost human features seemed somehow to have taken on expressions of malicious glee.

"Wait!" Silk barked suddenly. "Stop!"

They all reined in.

"I thought I heard something—off that way," Silk said.

They all sat straining their ears, trying to listen over the heavy panting of their horses.

Faintly, from somewhere to the east, a scream came out of the fog.

"There it is again," Silk said. He pulled his horse around.

"What are you doing?" Belgarath asked him.

"I'm going to have a look."

But Toth had moved his horse around until it was blocking the Drasnian's path. Gravely the giant shook his head.

"Toth, we have to know what's happening," Silk said.

Toth shook his head again.

"Toth," Garion said, "is what Sadi told us really true? Is there really such a thing as a Ravener?"

Toth's face grew bleak, and he nodded.

Another scream came out of the dim woods, seeming much closer this time. The scream was filled with horror and agony.

"Who is it?" Ce'Nedra demanded, her voice shrill with fright. "Who's screaming?"

"The men who attacked us," Eriond replied in a sick voice. "The ones who survived the fight. Something's running them down one by one."

"Raveners?" Garion asked him.

"I think so. Whatever it is, it's horrible."

"They're coming this way," Sadi said. "Let's get away from here." He drove his heels into his horse's flanks.

They plunged off into the gloomy wood, no longer even trying to follow the track. Their blind flight took them perhaps a half mile farther into the forest when Polgara suddenly pulled her horse to a halt. "Stop!" she commanded.

"What is it, Pol?" Durnik asked her.

But she pushed forward carefully to peer at a thicket half-obscured in the mist. "There's someone ahead," she whispered.

"A Ravener?" Garion asked in a low voice.

She concentrated for a moment. "No. It's one of the attackers. He's trying to hide."

"How far away is he?"

"Not far." She continued to peer into the shrouding mist. "There," she said. "He's behind that tree at the edge of the thicket—the one with the broken limb hanging down."

Garion vaguely saw a dark patch half-concealed behind a gnarled tree root rising out of the sodden leaves. Then a movement caught his eye, and he glimpsed a shambling figure coming out of the trees. It seemed gray, almost invisible in the hazy fog, and it was so gaunt that it resembled a skeleton. It was dressed in rags, stained with earth and blood. Its pale skull was covered with scanty hair, and it was half-crouched, snuffling audibly as it walked with its arms hanging loosely. Its eyes were vacant and its mouth agape.

Then another emerged from the woods, and yet another. As the creatures advanced, they made a low moaning sound that expressed nothing remotely intelligible, but rather seemed to convey only a dreadful hunger.

"He's going to run!" Polgara said.

With a despairing cry, the hidden assassin leaped to his feet and desperately began to run. The Raveners took up the chase, their moaning coming faster. Their shambling gait quickened, and their emaciated legs carried them through the wood at a surprising rate of speed.

Twisting and dodging, the panic-stricken ruffian fled among the trees, with his hideous pursuers gaining on him at every step. When he finally disappeared far back into the fog and gloom, they were no more than a few yards behind him.

His shriek was a shocking, horrible sound. Again he screamed—and again.

"Are they killing him?" Ce'Nedra's voice was shrill.

Polgara's face had gone absolutely white, and her eyes were filled with horror. "No," she replied in a shaking voice.

"What are they doing?" Silk demanded.

"They're eating him."

"But—" Silk broke off as more shrieks came out of the fog. "He's still—" He stared at her, his eyes gone very wide and the blood draining from his cheeks.

Ce'Nedra gasped. "Alive?" she said in a choked whisper. "They're eating him while he's still alive?"

"That's what I was trying to warn you about, your Majesty," Sadi said grimly. "When they go into their frenzy, they don't make any distinction between the living and the dead. They feed on anything."

"Toth," Belgarath said sharply. "Can they be frightened off?"

The mute shook his head, then turned to Durnik, gesturing rapidly, touching his head and then his stomach.

"He says that they aren't able to think enough to be afraid," the smith told him. "All they know is hunger."

"What are we going to do, father?" Polgara demanded.

"We're going to try to outrun them," he replied, "and if any of them get in our way, we'll have to kill them." He looked back at Toth. "How far can they run?" he asked.

Toth raised one hand and traced an arc over his head, then another, and then another.

"For days," Durnik interpreted.

Belgarath's face became very grim. "Let's go," he said, "and stay together."

Their pace through the dreadful wood was more measured now, and the men all rode with their weapons in their hands.

The first attack came after they had gone no more than a mile. A dozen gray-faced Raveners shambled out from among the trees, moaning their hideous hunger and spreading out to block the path.

Garion spurred forward, swinging his sword in great arcs. Savagely, he chopped a path through the ranks of the slavering Raveners, who reached out mindlessly to pull him from his saddle. A terrible, rotting stink rose from them as he rode them down. He killed fully half of them as he crashed through, then whirled his horse to smash into them again, but pulled up sharply, his gorge rising. The Raveners who had escaped his sword were tearing at the bodies of those who had gone down, ripping out dripping gobbets of flesh and feeding them into their gaping mouths with their clawlike hands, even as they continued their awful moan.

Cautiously Belgarath and the others circled around that dreadful feeding, averting their eyes as they passed.

"It won't work, father," Polgara declared. "Sooner or later one of us is going to make a mistake. We're going to have to shield."

He thought about it for a moment. "You might be right, Pol," he admitted finally. He looked at Garion. "You and Durnik pay attention to how this is done," he instructed. "I want you to be able to take over when we get tired."

They started out at a walk as Belgarath and Polgara adjusted the barrier they were creating with the force of their combined will. They had gone no more than a little way when a gray-faced Ravener came loping out from among the twisted trees, slobbering and moaning. When it was perhaps ten yards from Durnik's horse, it suddenly stumbled back as if it had just run headlong into something solid. Moaning dreadfully, it came forward again and began to claw at the empty air with its filthy, long-nailed hands.

"Durnik," Polgara said quite calmly, "would you deal with it, please?"

"All right, Pol." The smith's face creased into an expression of extreme concentration, and he muttered a single word. The Ravener flickered and popped momentarily out of sight. When it reappeared, it was twenty yards away, beside a large tree. It struggled to lurch forward at them again, but seemed for some reason unable to move.

"That should hold it," Durnik said.

"What did you do?" Silk asked, peering at the struggling creature.

"I stuck its arm into that tree," Durnik replied. "If it wants to attack again, it's either going to have to bring the tree along or leave the arm behind. I didn't really hurt it, but it's going to take it a day or so to get its arm loose."

"Have you got a good hold on our shield, Pol?" Belgarath asked over his shoulder.

"Yes, father."

"Let's pick up the pace a trifle then. A bit of momentum won't hurt."

They moved, first at a trot and then at a loping canter. The shield Belgarath was projecting to the front ran ahead of them like a battering-ram, hurling the rag-clothed Raveners from their path.

"Where do they get those clothes?" Silk asked as he rode.

Toth made a kind of digging motion with one hand.

"He says that they take them off the bodies of the dead that they dig up," Durnik translated.

Silk shuddered. "That would explain the smell, then."

The next few days began to blur in Garion's mind. It was necessary to relieve Polgara and Belgarath every four hours or so, and the weight of the shield he and Durnik erected seemed to grow with each passing mile. The fog continued, making it impossible to see more than a hundred yards in any direction, and the twisted trees, with their semblance of human faces, emerged with a shocking suddenness out of that obscuring mist. Shapes, gray and emaciated, moved through that fog, and the mindless moaning came from all around them as they plunged through the ghoul-haunted wood.

Night was a time of dreadful terror as the Raveners gathered around the shield, clawing at it and moaning their hideous longing. Exhausted by his efforts of the day, Garion was forced to use every ounce of his will—not merely to hold the shield in place when his turn came to maintain it, but also to ward off sleep. Even more than the Raveners, sleep was the enemy. He forced himself to walk up and down. He pinched himself. He even went so far as to put a large pebble in his left boot in hopes that the discomfort would help to keep him awake. Once, all his devices failed, and his head began to sag slowly forward as sleep finally overcame him.

It was the putrid smell that jerked him awake. There, directly before him as his head came up, stood a Ravener. Its eyes were empty of all thought, its gaping mouth revealed broken, rotting teeth, and its black-nailed hands groped out—reaching for him. With a startled cry, he unleashed a heavy blow with his will, hurling the creature backward. Trembling violently, he re-established the barrier that had begun to falter.

Then, at last, they reached the southernmost fringe of the dreadful forest and rode out from under the twisted trees onto a fog-shrouded heath.

"Will they keep up the chase?" Durnik asked his giant friend. The smith's voice dropped from his lips with a great weariness.

Toth made a number of obscure gestures.

"What did he say?" Garion asked.

Durnik's face was bleak. "He says that for as long as the fog lasts, they probably won't give up. They don't like the sun, but the fog's hiding it, so—" He shrugged.

"We have to keep the shield up then, don't we?"

"I'm afraid so."

The heath across which they rode was a blasted, ugly place, covered with low thorn bushes and dotted with shallow tarns filled with rusty-looking water. The fog eddied and billowed, and always at the farthest edge of vision lurked the shadowy forms of the Raveners.

They rode on. Polgara and Belgarath took the burden of the shield, and Garion slumped in his saddle, trembling with exhaustion.

Then, very faintly, he caught the smell of salt brine.

"The sea!" Durnik exulted. "We've reached the sea."

"Now all we need is a boat," Silk reminded him.

Toth, however, pointed ahead confidently and made a curious gesture.

"He says that there's a ship waiting for us," Durnik told them.

"There is?" Silk seemed astonished. "How did he manage that?"

"I really don't know," Durnik replied. "He didn't say."

"Durnik," Silk said, "exactly how do you know what he's saying? Those gestures of his don't make much sense to me at all."

Durnik frowned. "I really don't know," he admitted. "I hadn't even thought about it. I just seem to know what he wants to say."

"Are you using sorcery?"

"No. Maybe it's because we've worked with each other a few times. That always seems to bring men closer together."

"I'll take your word for it."

They crested a moundlike hill to look down at a gravel beach where long rollers came in off the foggy sea to crash against the rounded pebbles and then slide back with a mournful hissing sound as the foam-flecked water slithered down the strand, only to pause and then crash back up again.

"I don't see your ship, Toth," Silk said almost accusingly. "Where is it?"

Toth pointed out into the fog.

"Really?" Silk's voice was sceptical.

The mute nodded.

The Raveners trailing behind grew more agitated as the company started down toward the beach. Their moans became more urgent, and they began to run back and forth along the crest of the hill, reaching out their clawed hands with a kind of desperate longing. They did not, however, pursue any farther.

"Is it my imagination, or does it seem that they're afraid of something?" Velvet suggested.

"They aren't coming down the hill," Durnik agreed. He turned to Toth. "Are they afraid?" he asked.

Toth nodded.

"I wonder what it is," Velvet said.

The giant made a motion with both hands.

"He says that it has to do with something being even more hungry than they are," Durnik said. "They're afraid of it."

"Sharks, maybe?" Silk suggested.

"No. It's the sea itself."

When they reached the gravel strand, they dismounted and stood in a weary little group at the water's edge. "Are you all right, father?" Polgara asked the old man, who was leaning against his saddle, staring out into the fog that lay thick and pale on the dark water.

"What? Oh, yes. I'm fine, Pol—just a little puzzled, that's all. If there *is* a ship out there, I'd sort of like to know who arranged for it and how they knew that we were going to arrive at this particular spot."

"More important than that," Silk added, "I'd like to know how we're going to tell them that we've arrived. That fog's like a blanket out there."

"Toth says they already know we're here," Durnik told him. "They'll probably show up in the next half hour or so."

"Oh?" Belgarath said curiously. "And who sent this ship in the first place?"

"He said it was Cyradis."

"I'm going to have to have a long talk with that young lady one of these days," Belgarath said. "She's starting to make me just a little uneasy about certain things."

"They went back," Eriond told them as he stood stroking the bowed neck of his stallion.

"Who did?" Garion asked.

"The Raveners," the boy replied, pointing back up the hill. "They gave up and started back toward the woods."

"And without even saying good-bye," Silk added with a tight grin. "I don't know what's happened to people's manners these days."

The ship that came ghosting out of the fog was curiously built with a high prow and stern and broad sails on her twin masts.

"What's making it go?" Ce'Nedra asked, staring curiously at the shadowy shape.

"I don't quite follow you," Garion said.

"They aren't rowing," she pointed out, "and there isn't even a hint of a breeze."

He looked sharply back at the ship and saw immediately that she was right. There were no oars protruding from the ghostly ship's sides; but in spite of the dead-calm, foggy air, the sails were bellied outward, and the vessel moved smoothly through the oily-looking water.

"Is it sorcery?" she asked him.

He pushed his mind out, searching for some hint. "It doesn't seem to be," he replied. "At least not any kind that I know about."

Belgarath stood not far away, his expression profoundly disapproving.

"How are they moving the ship, Grandfather?" Garion asked him.

"It's a form of witchcraft," the old man told him, still scowling, "unpredictable and usually not very reliable." He turned to Toth. "You want us to go on board that?" he asked.

Toth nodded.

"Will it take us to Verkat?"

Toth nodded again.

"You mean that it will, if the sprite that's pushing it doesn't get bored with the idea—or decide that it might be funny to take us in the opposite direction."

Toth held out both hands.

"He says to trust him," Durnik supplied.

"I wish people would quit saying that to me."

The ship slowed, and her keel ground gently on the gravel bottom. A broad ramp came sliding out over the side, and its weighted end sank in about three feet of water. Toth, leading his reluctant horse, waded out to the ramp. Then he turned and looked inquiringly back at the rest of them. He motioned with his arm.

"He says we're supposed to board now," Durnik said.

"I heard him," Belgarath growled. "All right, I suppose we might as well." Sourly, he took his horse's reins and waded out into the water.

CHAPTER TWENTY-THREE

The crew of the strange ship all wore rough, cowled tunics made of heavy cloth. The bones of their faces were prominent, giving their features a peculiarly hewn-out look and, like Toth, they were all mutes. They went about their work in absolute silence. Garion, accustomed to the bawling and cursing which accompanied the labors of Cherek sailors, found this stillness peculiar, even slightly unnerving. The ship itself made none of the usual sounds. There was no rasp of oars in their locks, no creak of rigging, no groaning of timbers—only the faint wash and run of water along the sides as they were propelled out across the fog-muffled sea by some force or spirit Garion could not even comprehend.

Once the shore behind had sunk into the fog, there was no reference point, no hint of direction. The silent ship moved on.

Garion stood with his arm about Ce'Nedra's shoulders. The peculiar combination of his near-exhaustion from the ordeal in the wood of the Raveners and the pervading gloom of dark, unbroken water and thick-hanging fog made his mood melancholy and his thoughts abstracted. It was enough merely to stand at the side of his weary wife, holding her in the protecting curve of his arm and to look blankly, uncomprehendingly into the fog.

"What in the world is that?" Velvet exclaimed from somewhere behind him. He turned and looked toward the stern. From out of the pearly fog, there came a ghostly white bird with impossible wings—pinions that appeared longer than a tall man might stretch his arms. The wings did not move, and yet the silent bird came on, gliding through the misty air like a disembodied spirit.

"Albatross," Polgara identified the magnificent creature.

"Aren't they supposed to be bad luck?" Silk asked.

"Are you superstitious, Prince Kheldar?"

"Not exactly, but—" He left it hanging.

"It's a sea bird, nothing more," she told him.

"Why does it have such enormous wings?" Velvet asked curiously.

"It flies great distances over open water," Polgara said. "The wings hold it aloft without any effort. It's very practical."

The great-winged bird tilted in the air, giving forth a strange, lonely cry, a sound that carried in it all the emptiness of a vast, rolling sea.

Polgara inclined her head in response to that strange greeting.

"What did he say, Pol?" Durnik asked her in an oddly subdued voice.

"It was quite formal," she replied. "Sea birds have a great deal of dignity—perhaps because they spend so much time alone. It gives them leisure to formulate their thoughts, I suppose. Land birds babble a great deal, but sea birds try to be profound."

"They're strange creatures, aren't they—birds I mean?"

"Not once you get used to them." She looked out at the alabaster bird coasting in the silent air beside the ship with an indecipherable expression on her face.

The albatross moved his great wings and pulled ahead of the ship to station himself just in front of the prow, hanging apparently motionless in the mist.

Belgarath had been staring up at the sails, which bellied out improbably in the dead-calm air. Finally he grunted and turned to Toth. "How long does the trip to Verkat take?" he asked.

Toth measured out a short space with his hands.

"That's not very specific, my friend."

Toth pointed upward and spread his fingers wide.

"He says about five hours, Belgarath," Durnik translated.

"We're moving faster than it appears then," the old man observed. "I wonder how they managed to persuade the sprite to concentrate on one thing for that long, though. I've never run into one before that could keep hold of an idea for more than a minute."

"Do you want me to ask him?" Durnik offered.

Belgarath squinted back up at the sails. "No," he said. "I guess not. I might not like the answer."

The northwest coast of the Isle of Verkat rose dark and indistinct out of the fog as evening approached. They sailed closer, with the gleaming albatross hovering just ahead, and Garion saw that the low hills behind the gravel strand were thickly covered with dark evergreens wreathed in fog. Some distance back up from the beach, a few scattered lights gleamed golden in the windows of a village, and a line of torches wound down from that village toward the shore. Faintly, Garion could hear the sound of singing. The words were indistinct, but the overall tone of the song conveyed a great sadness and an endless longing.

Their ship moved silently across a shallow bay, then coasted gently up beside a rude stone quay that looked more like a natural rock formation than any man-made structure.

A tall man in a white linen robe stood on the quay. Although his face was unlined and his eyebrows were black as ravens' wings, his flowing hair was as silver as Belgarath's. "Welcome," he greeted them. His voice was deep and peculiarly gentle. "I am Vard. We have long awaited your coming, which the Book of the Heavens revealed to us ages past."

"Now you see why I don't like these people," Belgarath muttered. "I hate it when someone pretends to know everything."

"Forgive us, Holy Belgarath," the man on the quay said with a slight smile. "If it will make you more comfortable, we will conceal what we have read in the stars."

"You've got sharp ears, Vard," the old man noted.

"If you wish to believe so." Vard shrugged. "A place has been made ready for you—and food prepared. Your journey has been long and difficult, and I'm sure you are all very tired. If you will come with me, I will show you the way. My people will bring your mounts and your belongings."

"You are very kind, Vard," Polgara said across the rail of the ship as the mute sailors ran their ramp out to the stones of the quay.

Vard bowed. "We are honored by your presence, Lady Polgara," he replied. "We have stood in awe of you since the beginning of the Third Age."

The path leading up from the bay was narrow and it wound about with no seeming purpose. "I fear that you will find our village rude by comparison with the mighty cities of the west," the white-robed man apologized. "We have ever been indifferent to our surroundings."

"One place is much the same as another," Belgarath agreed, peering ahead toward the cluster of lighted windows glowing in the mist.

The village consisted of a score or so buildings constructed of rough field stone and thatched with straw. They seemed scattered at random with nothing resembling an organized street anywhere in sight. The place was tidy, however, with none of the clutter that inevitably seemed to spring up in such places, and the doorstep of each house showed signs of frequent scrubbing.

Vard led them to a fair-sized house in the center of the village and opened the door for them. "This will be yours for as long as you remain," he said. "The table is prepared, and some of my people will attend you. Should you require anything else, please send for me." Then he bowed, turned, and walked away into the foggy twilight.

The inside of the house was by no means palatial, but it belied the crude-appearing exterior. Each room contained a low, cheery fireplace, exuding warmth and light. The doorways were arched and the walls all whitewashed. The furniture was plain, but stoutly made, and the beds were covered with thick, down-filled comforters.

A table and benches stood in the central room, and a number of covered earthenware pots stood on that table. The smells coming from those pots reminded Garion that he had not eaten a hot meal in several days.

"They're a strange sort of people," Velvet observed, removing her cloak, "but you certainly can't fault their hospitality."

Silk had been eyeing the table. "We wouldn't want to offend them by letting supper get cold, would we? I don't know about the rest of you, but I'm famished."

The supper that had been laid for them was delicious. None of the dishes were anything out of the ordinary, but each was delicately seasoned. The main course was a well-browned haunch of some animal Garion did not recognize, but he found it rich and full-flavored.

"What *is* this delicious roast?" Ce'Nedra asked, helping herself to another piece.

"Goat, I think," Polgara replied.

"Goat?"

"It seems to be."

"But I *hate* goat."

"That's your third slice, dear," Polgara pointed out.

After they had eaten, they sat around the fireplace. Garion felt a vast weariness and knew that he should go to bed, but he was simply too comfortable to move.

"Did you get any hints that Zandramas came through here?" Silk asked him.

"What? Oh—no. Nothing."

"She seems to want to avoid inhabited places," Belgarath noted. "I don't think she'd have come to the village here. Probably tomorrow you're going to have to ride out and see if you can cross her trail."

"Wouldn't she have gone straight to Rak Verkat?" Silk suggested. "That's where all the ships are, and she wants to go to Mallorea, doesn't she?"

"She might have made other arrangements," the old man told him. "She *does* have a price on her head, and the Malloreans at Rak Verkat are probably as interested in collecting it as the ones at Rak Hagga. She's made careful preparations in advance for every step of this journey. I don't think she'd have left anything to chance, once she got this far."

Sadi came back into the room, holding the small earthenware bottle. "Margravine Liselle," he said acidly, "do you suppose I could have my snake back?"

"Oh, I'm ever so sorry, Sadi," she apologized. "I completely forgot I had her." She dipped into the front of her dress and gently removed the little green reptile.

Silk drew back with a sharp intake of his breath.

"I wasn't really trying to steal her," Velvet assured Sadi. "It was just that the poor dear was cold."

"Of course." He took his snake from her.

"I was only trying to keep her warm, Sadi. You certainly wouldn't want her to get sick, would you?"

"Your concern touches my heart." He turned and went back toward the sleeping rooms with Zith lazily coiled about his wrist.

The following morning, Garion went into the shed attached

to the back of the house, saddled his horse, and rode back down to the gravel strand, where the waves rolled endlessly in off the foggy sea to crash against the shore. He stopped, looking first up the beach, then down. He shrugged and turned his horse toward the northeast.

The upper edge of the rock-strewn beach was thick with windrows of white-bleached driftwood. As he rode, he idly ran his eyes along those tangled heaps of branches and broken logs. Occasionally, he noted a squared-off timber lying among the other bits and pieces, mute evidence that some ship had come to grief. The possibility occurred to him that the shipwreck that had set those timbers adrift might have taken place as long as a century ago and that the debris might well have floated half around the world to wash up on this strand of salt-crusted pebbles.

"*That's all very interesting,*" the dry voice in his mind told him, "*but you're going the wrong way.*"

"*Where have you been?*" Garion asked, reining in.

"*Why do we always have to start these conversations with that same question? The answer wouldn't mean anything to you, so why pursue it? Turn around and go back. The trail is on the other side of the village, and you don't have time to ride all the way around the island.*"

"*Is Zandramas still here with my son?*" Garion asked quickly, wanting to get that question out in the open before the elusive voice went off again.

"*No,*" the voice replied. "*She left about a week ago.*"

"We're gaining on her then," Garion said aloud, a sudden hope springing up in him.

"*That would be a logical assumption.*"

"Where did she go?"

"*Mallorea—but you knew that already, didn't you?*"

"Could you get a little more specific? Mallorea's a big place."

"*Don't do that, Garion,*" the voice told him. "*UL told you that finding your son was your task. I'm not permitted to do it for you any more than he was. Oh, incidentally, keep an eye on Ce'Nedra.*"

"Ce'Nedra? What for?"

But the voice had already gone. Garion swore and rode back the way he had come.

A league or so to the south of the village, where a cove sheltered by two jutting headlands ran back into the shore line, the sword strapped across his back tugged at him. He reined in sharply and drew the blade. It turned in his hand to point unerringly due inland.

He trotted his horse up the hill, with the blade of Iron-grip's sword resting on the pommel of his saddle. The trail did not veer. Ahead of him lay a long, grassy slope and then the misty edge of the evergreen forest. He considered the situation for a moment and decided that it might be better to go back and tell the others, rather than pursue Zandramas alone. As he turned his horse toward the village, he glanced down at the shallow waters of the cove. There, lying on its side beneath the water, lay the sunken wreck of a small ship. His face grew bleak. Once again, Zandramas had rewarded those who had aided her by killing them. He kicked his mount into a loping canter and rode back across the foggy meadows lying between the sea and the dark forest toward the village.

It was nearly noon when he reached the house Vard had provided for them, and he swung down out of his saddle, controlling his excitement as best he could.

"Well?" Belgarath, who sat before the fire with a mug in his hand, asked as Garion entered the room.

"The trail's about a league to the south."

Polgara, seated at the table, looked up quickly from the piece of parchment she had been examining. "Are you sure?" she asked.

"The Orb is." Garion unfastened his cloak. "Oh—I had another visit from our friend." He tapped his forehead. "He told me that Zandramas left the island about a week ago and that she's going to Mallorea. That's about all I could get out of him. Where's Ce'Nedra? I want to tell her that we're getting closer."

"She's asleep," Polgara said, carefully folding the parchment.

"Is that part of one of those books Grandfather's been looking for?" he asked.

"No, dear. It's the recipe for that soup we had at supper last night." She turned to Belgarath. "Well, father? Do we take up the trail again?"

He thought about it, staring absently into the fire dancing on the hearth. "I'm not sure, Pol," he answered finally. "We were deliberately brought here to this island for something, and I don't think that locating the trail was the only reason. I think we ought to stay here for another day or so."

"We've gained a great deal of time on Zandramas, father," she reminded him. "Why waste it by just sitting in one place?"

"Call it a hunch, Pol. I've got a very strong feeling that we're supposed to wait here for something—something fairly important."

"I think it's a mistake, father."

"That's your privilege, Pol. I've never told you what to think."

"Only what to do," she added tartly.

"That's *my* privilege. It's a father's duty to guide his children. I'm sure you understand."

The door opened, and Silk and Velvet came in out of the sunless noon. "Did you find the trail?" Silk asked, removing his cloak.

Garion nodded. "She came ashore a league or so down the beach. Then she sank the boat that brought her. It's lying on the bottom with the full crew aboard, about fifty yards from shore."

"She's running true to form, then," Silk noted.

"What have you been up to this morning?" Garion asked him.

"Snooping."

"The term is 'intelligence gathering,' Kheldar," Velvet said primly, also removing her cloak and smoothing the front of her dress.

"It amounts to the same thing, doesn't it?"

"Of course, but 'snooping' has such a nasty ring to it."

"Did you find out anything?" Garion asked.

"Not much," Silk admitted, coming to the fire to warm himself. "All these people are terribly polite, but they're very good at evading direct questions. I can tell you one thing, though. This place isn't a real village—at least not in the sense that we understand it. It's all very carefully set up to look crude and rustic, and the people here go through the motions of tending crops and herds, but it's all for show. Their tools show almost no signs of use, and their animals are just a bit too well groomed."

"What are they doing, then?" Garion asked.

"I think they spend their time in study," Velvet replied. "I was visiting with one of the women, and there was a sort of a chart on the table in her house. I got a look at it before she put it away. It looked like a map of some constellations—a sort of a picture of the night sky."

Belgarath grunted. "Astrologers. I've never had much faith in astrology. The stars seem to say something different every quarter-hour or so." He thought about it for a moment. "Back at Prolgu, the Gorim said that these people are Dals—the same as the ones who live in southern Mallorea—and no one has ever been able to figure out what the Dals are up to. They seem to be docile and placid, but I suspect that's only a mask. There are several centers of learning in Dalasia, and I wouldn't be surprised to find out that this place is very similar. Did either of you see anyone wearing a blindfold—the way Cyradis does?"

"A seer?" Silk said. "I didn't." He looked at Velvet.

She shook her head.

"Toth might be able to give us some answers, father," Polgara said. "He seems to be able to communicate with these people in ways that we can't."

"How do you propose to get answers out of a mute, Polgara?" Silk asked her.

"Durnik seems to be able to talk with him," she replied. "Where are they, by the way?"

"They found a pond on the upper edge of the village," Velvet answered. "They're checking to see if it's occupied. Eriond is with them."

"Inevitably." Polgara smiled.

"Doesn't it get a little tedious?" Velvet asked. "Having him spend all his time fishing, I mean?"

"It's a healthy activity," Polgara said. She looked meaningfully at the mug in Belgarath's hand. "And probably much better for him than the amusements of some others I could name."

"What next, old friend?" Silk asked Belgarath.

"Let's sit tight for a while and keep our eyes and ears open. I've got a nagging sort of feeling that something important's going to happen here."

That afternoon a faint breeze began to stir the fog that had plagued them for the past week or so. When evening approached, the sky had blown clear except for a heavy cloud bank off toward the west, dyed a deep scarlet by the setting sun.

Sadi had spent the day with Vard; when he returned, his expression was frustrated.

"Were you able to get anything out of him?" Silk asked.

"Nothing that I could make any sense out of," the eunuch replied. "I think the grip these people have on reality is rather tenuous. The only thing that seems to interest them is some obscure thing they call the task. Vard wouldn't tell me exactly what this task is, but they seem to have been gathering information about it since the beginning of time."

As twilight began to settle over the Isle, Durnik, with Eriond at his side, returned with his fishing pole across his shoulder and a frustrated look on his face.

"Where's Toth?" Garion asked him.

"He said that he had something to attend to," Durnik replied, carefully examining his tackle. "I think that maybe I need a smaller hook," he mused.

As Polgara and Velvet began preparing supper, Silk looked over at Garion. "Why don't we go stretch our legs?" he suggested.

"You mean right now?"

"I'm a little restless." The weasel-faced man rose from his chair. "Come along," he said. "If you sit in that chair much longer, you're going to put down roots."

Puzzled, Garion followed his friend outside. "What was that all about?" he asked.

"I want to find out what Toth's up to and I don't want Liselle tagging along."

"I thought you liked her."

"I do, but I'm getting a little tired of having her looking over my shoulder every place I go." He stopped. "Where are *they* going?" he said, pointing at a line of torches strung out across the meadow lying between the village and the edge of the forest.

"We could follow them and find out," Garion suggested.

"Right. Let's go."

Vard led the line of torch-bearing villagers toward the dark forest at the upper end of the meadow, and Toth, towering above all the rest, strode beside him. Garion and Silk, bent low to the tall grass, paralleled their course, but remained some distance away.

As the torchlit file of villagers approached the edge of the woods, several dim figures emerged from the shadows under the trees and stood waiting. "Can you make them out at all?" Garion whispered.

Silk shook his head. "Too far," he murmured, "and there's not enough light. We're going to have to get closer." He dropped down onto his stomach and began to worm his way through the grass.

The meadow was still wet from the days of dense fog; by the time Garion and Silk reached the protecting shadows at the edge of the trees, they were both soaking wet.

"I'm not enjoying this much, Silk," Garion whispered somewhat crossly.

"I don't think you'll melt," Silk whispered back. Then he raised his head and peered out through the trees. "Are those people blindfolded?" he asked.

"It sort of looks that way," Garion replied.

"That would mean that they're seers then, wouldn't it? We didn't see any of them in the village, so maybe they live somewhere in these woods. Let's see if we can get a little closer. All of this is definitely stirring up my curiosity."

The villagers, still carrying their torches, moved into the damp forest for several hundred yards and finally stopped in a large clearing. Around the edge of that clearing stood a series of roughly squared-off blocks of stone, each of them about twice the height of a tall man. The villagers spaced themselves among those stone blocks, forming a torchlit circle, and the blindfolded seers, perhaps a dozen or so of them, gathered in the center and joined hands to form another circle. Standing immediately behind each of the seers was a large, muscular man—their guides and protectors, Garion surmised. In the very center, enclosed within that inner ring of seers, stood the silver-haired Vard and the giant Toth.

Garion and Silk crept closer.

The only sound in the clearing was the guttering of torches; then, very quietly at first, but with growing strength, the people in the circle began to sing. In many ways, their song was similar to the discordant hymn of the Ulgos, yet there were subtle differences. Though he was not schooled in musicology or harmony, Garion perceived that this hymn was older and perhaps more pure than the one which had rung through the caves of Ulgo for five millennia. In a sudden flash of insight, he also understood how endless centuries of confusing echos had gradually corrupted the Ulgos' song. This hymn, moreover, was not raised to UL, but to a God unknown, and it was a plea to that unnamed God to manifest himself and to come forth to guide and protect the Dals, even as UL guided and protected the Ulgos.

Then he heard or felt another sound joining with that unbelievably ancient hymn. A peculiar sighing within his mind signaled that these people, gathered in their strange circles, were bringing their combined wills to bear in a mystic accompaniment to the song their voices raised to the starry sky.

There was a shimmering in the air in the very center of the clearing, and the glowing form of Cyradis appeared, robed and cowled in white linen and with her eyes covered by a strip of cloth.

"Where did she come from?" Silk breathed.

"She's not really there," Garion whispered. "It's a projection. Listen."

"Welcome, Holy Seeress," Vard greeted the glowing image. "We are grateful that thou hast responded to our summons."

"Thy gratitude is unnecessary, Vard," the clear voice of the blindfolded girl replied. "I respond out of the duty imposed upon me by my task. Have the seekers arrived, then?"

"They have, Holy Cyradis," Vard answered, "and the one called Belgarion hath found that which he sought here."

"The quest of the Child of Light hath but only begun," the image stated. "The Child of Dark hath reached the coast of far-off Mallorea and even now doth journey toward the House of Torak at Ashaba. The time hath come for the Eternal man to open the Book of Ages."

Vard's face grew troubled. "Is that wise, Cyradis?" he asked. "Can even Ancient Belgarath be trusted with what he may find in that volume? His entire life hath been devoted to but *one* of the two spirits which control all things."

"It must be so, Vard, else the meeting of the Child of Light and the Child of Dark will not come to pass at the appointed time, and *our* task will remain uncompleted." She sighed. "The time draws nigh," she told them. "That for which we have waited since the beginning of the First Age fast approaches, and all must be accomplished ere the moment in which I must perform that task which hath lain upon us throughout the weary centuries. Give the *Book of Ages* to Eternal Belgarath that he may lead the Child of Light to the place which is no more—where all will be decided forever." Then she turned to the towering mute standing impassively beside the white-robed Vard. "My heart is empty without thee," she told him in a voice very near to tears. "My steps falter, and I am alone. I pray thee, my dear companion, make haste in the completion of thy task, for I am made desolate by thine absence."

Quite clearly in the flickering torchlight Garion could see the tears in Toth's eyes and the anguish on his face. The giant reached out toward the glowing image, then let his hand fall helplessly.

Cyradis also raised her hand, it seemed almost involuntarily.

Then she vanished.

CHAPTER TWENTY-FOUR

"Are you sure she said Ashaba?" Belgarath asked intently.

"I heard her, too, Grandfather," Garion confirmed what Silk had just reported. "She said that the Child of Dark had reached Mallorea and was journeying to the House of Torak at Ashaba."

"But there's nothing there," Belgarath objected. "Beldin and I ransacked that place right after Vo Mimbre." He began to pace up and down, scowling darkly. "What could Zandramas possibly want there? It's just an empty house."

"Maybe you can find some answers in the *Book of Ages,*" Silk suggested.

Belgarath stopped and stared at him.

"Oh, I guess we hadn't got to that part yet," the little man said. "Cyradis told Vard that he was supposed to give you the book. He didn't like it very much, but she insisted."

Belgarath's hands began to tremble, and he controlled himself with an obvious effort.

"Is it important?" Silk asked curiously.

"So that's what this has all been about!" the old man burst out. "I knew there was a reason for bringing us here."

"What's the Book of Ages, Belgarath?" Ce'Nedra asked him.

"It's a part of *The Mallorean Gospels*—the holy book of the Seers at Kell. It looks as if we were led here specifically for the purpose of putting that book into my hands."

"This is all just a little obscure for me, old friend," Silk said, shivering. "Let's go get cleaned up, Garion. I'm soaked all the way through."

"How did you two get so wet?" Velvet asked.

"We were crawling around in the grass."

"That would account for it, I suppose."

"Do you really *have* to do that, Liselle?"

"Do what?"

"Never mind. Come on, Garion."

"What is it about her that irritates you so much?" Garion asked as the two of them went down the hall toward the back of the house.

"I'm not really sure," Silk replied. "I get the feeling that she's laughing at me all the time—and that she's got something on her mind that she isn't telling me. For some reason, she makes me very nervous."

After they had dried themselves and changed into clean clothing, they returned to the warm, firelit main room of the house to find that Toth had returned. He sat impassively on a bench near the door, with his huge hands folded on his knees. All traces of the anguish Garion had seen on his face in the clearing were gone now, and his expression was as enigmatic as ever.

Belgarath sat beside the fire holding a large leather-bound book tilted to catch the light, his eyes poring over it intently.

"Is that the book?" Silk asked.

"Yes," Polgara replied. "Toth brought it."

"I hope that it says something to make this trip worth all the trouble."

As Garion, Silk and Toth ate, Belgarath continued to read, turning the crackling pages of the *Book of Ages* impatiently. "Listen to this," he said. He cleared his throat and began to read aloud: "'Know ye, oh my people, that all adown the endless avenues of time hath division marred all that is—for there is division at the very heart of creation. But the stars and the spirits and the voices within the rocks speak of the day when the division will end and all will be made one again, for creation itself knows that the day will come. And two spirits contend with each other at the very center of time, and these spirits are the two sides of that which hath divided creation. Now the day must come when we must choose between them, and the choice we must make is the choice between absolute good and absolute evil, and that which *we* choose—good or evil—will prevail until the end of days. But how may we know which is good and which is evil?

"'Behold also this truth; the rocks of the world and of all other worlds murmur continually of the two stones which lie at the center of the division. Once these stones were one, and they stood at the very center of all of creation, but, like all else, they were divided, and in the instant of division were they rent apart with a force that destroyed whole suns. And where these stones are found together, there surely will be the last confrontation between the two spirits. Now the day will come when all division will end and all will be made as one again—*except* that the division between the two stones is so great that they can never be rejoined. And in the day when the division ends shall one of the stones cease forever to exist, and in that day also shall one of the spirits forever vanish.'"

"Are they trying to say that the Orb is only *half* of this original stone?" Garion asked incredulously.

"And the other half would be the Sardion," Belgarath agreed. "That would explain a great deal."

"I didn't know there was any connection between the two."

"Neither did I, but it does sort of fit together, doesn't it? Everything about this whole business has come in pairs from the very beginning—two Prophecies, two fates, a Child of Light and a Child of Dark—it only stands to reason that there'd have to be two stones, doesn't it?"

"And the Sardion would have the same power as the Orb," Polgara added gravely.

Belgarath nodded. "In the hands of the Child of Dark, it could do just about anything that Garion can do with the Orb—and we haven't even tested the limits of that yet."

"It gives us just a little more incentive to keep Zandramas from reaching the Sardion, doesn't it?" Silk said.

"I already have all the incentive in the world," Ce'Nedra said sadly.

Garion rose early the next morning. When he came out of the room he shared with Ce'Nedra, he found Belgarath seated at the table in the main room with the *Book of Ages* lying before him in the light of a guttering candle.

"Didn't you go to bed, Grandfather?"

"What? Oh—no. I wanted to read this all the way through without any interruptions."

"Did you find anything helpful?"

"A great deal, Garion. A very great deal. Now I know what Cyradis is doing."

"Is she really involved in this?"

"She believes that she is." He closed the book and leaned back, staring thoughtfully at the far wall. "You see, these people, and the ones at Kell in Dalasia, believe that it's their task to choose between the two Prophecies—the two forces that have divided the universe—and they believe that it's their choice that's going to settle the matter once and for all."

"A choice? That's all? You mean that all they have to do is pick one or the other, and that's the end of it?"

"Roughly, yes. They believe that the choice has to be made

during one of the meetings of the Child of Light and the Child of Dark—and both stones, the Orb and the Sardion, have to be present. Down through history, the task of making the choice has always been laid on just one of the seers. At every meeting between the Child of Light and the Child of Dark, that particular seer has been present. I expect that there was one lurking about somewhere at Cthol Mishrak when you met Torak. At any rate, the task has finally fallen to Cyradis. She knows where the Sardion is and she knows when this meeting is going to take place. She'll be there. If all the conditions have been met, she'll choose."

Garion sat down in a chair by the dying fire. "You don't actually believe all that, do you?"

"I don't know, Garion. We've spent our entire lives living out the pronouncements of the Prophecy, and it's gone to a great deal of trouble to get me here and put this book into my hands. I may not entirely believe all this mysticism, but I'm certainly not going to ignore it."

"Did it say anything at all about Geran? What's his part in all this?"

"I'm not sure. It could be as a sacrifice—the way Agachak believes. Or, it's possible that Zandramas abducted him just to force you to come after her and bring the Orb with you. Nothing is ever going to be settled until the Orb and the Sardion are brought together in the same place."

"The place which is no more," Garion added sourly.

Belgarath grunted. "There's something about that phrase that keeps nagging at me," he said. "Sometimes I can almost put my finger on it, but it keeps slipping away from me. I've seen it or heard it before, but I can't seem to remember where."

Polgara came into the room. "You're both up early," she said.

"Garion is," Belgarath replied. "I'm up late."

"Did you stay up all night, father?"

"It seems that way. I think that this was what I was waiting for." He laid his hand on the book in front of him. "As soon as the others get up, let's pack and get ready to leave. It's time for us to move on."

There was a light tap on the outer door. Garion rose, crossed the room, and opened it.

Vard stood outside in the pale gray light of the dawning day. "There's something I need to tell you," he said.

"Come in." Garion held the door open for him.

"Good morning, Vard," Belgarath greeted the white-robed man. "I didn't get the chance to thank you for this book."

"You must thank Cyradis for that. We gave it to you at her instruction. I think you and your friends should leave. There are soldiers coming."

"Malloreans?"

Vard nodded. "There's a column moving out from Rak Verkat. They'll probably reach our village before noon."

"Can you give us a ship of any kind?" Belgarath asked him. "We need to get to Mallorea."

"That wouldn't be wise just now. There are also Mallorean ships patrolling the coast."

"Do you think they're searching for us?" Polgara asked.

"It's possible, Lady Polgara," Vard admitted, "but the commander at Rak Verkat has ordered these sweeps through the countryside before—usually to round up any Murgos who still might be hidden on the Isle. They stir around for a few days and then return to their garrison in Rak Verkat. If this present excursion is merely one of those periodic searches, the troops won't be very thorough and they won't be in this vicinity for long. As soon as they're gone, you can come back here, and we'll provide you with a ship."

"Just how extensive is that forest out there?" Belgarath asked him.

"It's quite large, Ancient One."

"Good. Malloreans aren't comfortable in forests. Once we get back into the trees, it shouldn't be much of a problem to slip around them."

"You will need to avoid the hermit who dwells in the forest, however."

"The hermit?"

"A poor deranged fellow. He's not really an evil person, but he's mischievous and he likes to play tricks on travelers."

"We'll keep that in mind," Belgarath said. "Garion, go wake the others. Let's get ready to leave."

By the time everything was ready for their departure, the sun had risen over the low range of hills to the east. Sadi looked out the door at the bright sunlight streaming over the village and sparkling on the waves in the harbor. "Where's the fog when you need it?" he asked of no one in particular.

Belgarath looked around. "We've got about four hours until the Malloreans get here," he told them. "Let's use that time to put some distance between us and this place." He turned to Vard. "Thank you," he said simply, "for everything."

"May all of the Gods be with you," the silvery-haired man replied. "Now go—quickly."

They rode out of the village and up across the meadow to the edge of the dark forest.

"Any particular direction, old friend?" Silk asked Belgarath.

"I don't think it matters all that much," the old man replied. "Probably about all we're going to need is a thicket to hide in. Malloreans get nervous when they can't see for a mile or so in every direction, so they aren't very likely to search these woods too extensively."

"I'll see what I can find," the little man offered. He turned his horse toward the northeast, but suddenly reined in sharply as two figures stepped out from among the trees. One was robed and cowled, and the other was a large, watchful man.

"I greet thee, Ancient Belgarath," the hooded figure said in the clear voice of a woman. She lifted her face, and Garion saw that her eyes were bound with a dark strip of cloth. "I am Onatel," she continued, "and I am here to point out a safe path to thee."

"We're grateful for your aid, Onatel."

"Thy path lies southward, Belgarath. Some small way into this wood thou wilt discover an ancient track, much overgrown. It will lead thee to a place of concealment."

"And have you seen what is to come, Onatel?" Polgara asked. "Will the soldiers search this wood?"

"Thou and thy companions are the ones they seek, Polgara, and they will search in all parts of the island, but they will not find thee and thy friends—unless it come to pass that someone doth point thee out to them. Beware of the hermit who doth dwell in this wood, however. He will seek to test thee." She turned then with one hand outstretched. The large man standing in the shadows took that groping hand and gently led her back into the forest.

"How convenient," Velvet murmured. "Perhaps a little *too* convenient."

"She wouldn't lie, Liselle," Polgara said.

"But she's not obliged to tell the whole truth, is she?"

"You've got a very suspicious nature," Silk told her.

"Let's just say that I'm cautious. When a perfect stranger goes out of her way to help me, it always makes me a little nervous."

"Let's go ahead and find this path of hers," Belgarath said. "If we decide later on to change direction, we can do it some place private."

They pushed into the shadows beneath the spreading evergreens. The forest floor was damp and thickly covered with fallen needles from the limbs overhead. The sun streamed down in long, slanting shafts of golden light, and the shadows had that faint bluish tinge of morning. The thick loam muffled the sound of their passage, and they rode in a kind of hushed silence.

The track to which the seeress had directed them lay perhaps a mile back in the wood. It was deeply indented in the forest floor, as if at some time in the long-distant past it had been much traveled. Now, however, it lay unused, and weeds and grass had reclaimed it.

As the sun mounted in the sky, the blue cast to the shadows beneath the trees faded, and a myriad of tiny insects swirled and darted in the shafts of sunlight. Then, quite suddenly, Belgarath reined in his horse. "Listen!" he said sharply.

From far behind them, Garion heard a series of sharp yelps.

"Dogs?" Sadi asked, looking nervously back over his shoulder. "Did they bring dogs to sniff out our trail?"

"Those aren't dogs," Belgarath told him. "They're wolves."

"Wolves?" Sadi exclaimed. "We must flee!"

"Don't get excited, Sadi," the old man told him. "Wolves don't hunt people."

"I'd rather not chance that, Belgarath," the eunuch said. "I've heard some very alarming stories."

"That's all they were—stories. Believe me, I know wolves. No self-respecting wolf would even consider eating a human. Stay here, all of you. I'll go see what they want." He slid down out of his saddle.

"Not too close to the horses, father," Polgara warned. "You know how horses feel about wolves."

He grunted and went off into the forest.

"What's he doing?" Sadi asked nervously.

"You wouldn't believe it," Silk replied.

They waited in the cool dampness of the forest, listening to the faint yelping sounds and an occasional bell-like howl echoing among the trees.

When Belgarath returned some time later, he was swearing angrily.

"Whatever is the matter, father?" Polgara asked him.

"Somebody's playing games," he retorted angrily. "There aren't any wolves back there."

"Belgarath," Sadi said, "I can *hear* them. They've been yapping and howling on our trail for the past half-hour."

"And that's all there is back there—just the noise. There isn't a wolf within miles of here."

"What's making all the noise, then?"

"I told you. Somebody's playing games. Let's move on—and keep your eyes open."

They rode warily now, with the phantom baying filling the woods behind them. Then there came a sudden, high-pitched bellow from somewhere in front of them.

"What's that?" Durnik exclaimed, reaching for his axe.

"It's an absurdity," Belgarath snapped. "Ignore it. It's no more real than the wolves were."

But there was something swaying in the shadows beneath the spreading trees ahead—something gray and ponderously vast.

"There! What *is* that thing?" Ce'Nedra's voice was shrill.

"It's an elephant, dear," Polgara told her calmly. "They live in the jungles of Gandahar on the east coast of Mallorea."

"How did it get here, then?"

"It didn't. It's an apparition. Father was right. Someone in these woods has a very twisted sense of humor."

"And I'm going to show this comedian exactly what I think of his little jokes," Belgarath growled.

"No, father," Polgara disagreed. "I think that perhaps you should leave it to me. You're irritated, and that sometimes makes you go a little far with things. I'll take care of it."

"Polgara—" he started angrily.

"Yes, father?" Her look was cool and direct.

He controlled himself with some effort. "All right, Pol," he said. "Don't take any chances, though. This funny fellow might have some other tricks in his bag."

"I'm always careful, father," she replied. Then she moved her horse at a walk until she was several yards in advance of the rest of the party. "It's a very nice elephant," she called into the woods as she eyed the huge gray shape swaying menacingly in the shadows ahead of her. "Have you anything else you might like to show us?"

There was a long pause.

"You don't seem very impressed," a rusty-sounding voice growled from somewhere nearby.

"Well, you *did* make a few mistakes. The ears aren't big enough, for one thing, and the tail is much too long."

"The feet and tusks are about right, though," the voice in the woods snapped, "as you're about to find out."

The gray shape raised its huge snout and bellowed. Then it lumbered forward directly toward Polgara.

"How tiresome," she said, making a negligent-appearing gesture with one hand.

The elephant vanished in mid-stride.

"Well?" she asked.

A figure stepped out from behind a tree. It was a tall, gaunt man with wild hair and a very long beard, with twigs and straw clinging to it. He was dressed in a filthy smock, and his bare legs were as white as fish bellies, with knobby knees and broken veins. In one hand he carried a slender stick.

"I see that you have power, woman," he said to her, his voice filled with an unspoken threat.

"Some," she admitted calmly. "You must be the hermit I've heard about."

A look of cunning came into his eyes. "Perhaps," he replied. "And who are you?"

"Let's just say that I'm a visitor."

"I don't want any visitors. These woods are mine, and I prefer to be left alone."

"That's hardly civil. You must learn to control yourself."

His face suddenly twisted into an insane grimace. "Don't tell me what to do!" he screamed at her. "I am a God!"

"Hardly that," she disagreed.

"Feel the weight of my displeasure!" he roared. He raised the stick in his hand, and a glowing spark appeared at its tip. Suddenly, out of the insubstantial air, a monster leaped directly at her. It had scaly hide, a gaping muzzle filled with pointed fangs, and great paws tipped with needle-sharp claws.

Polgara lifted one hand, palm outward, and the thing suddenly stopped and hung motionless in midair. "A trifle better," she said critically. "This one even seems to have a bit of substance to it."

"Release it!" the hermit howled at her, jumping up and down in fury.

"Are you really sure you want me to?"

"Release it! Release it! Release it!" His voice rose to a shriek as he danced about wildly.

"If you insist," she replied. Slowly the slavering monster

turned about in midair and then dropped to the ground. With a roar, it charged the startled hermit.

The gaunt man recoiled, thrusting his wand out in front of him. The creature vanished.

"You always have to be careful with monsters," she advised. "You never know when one of them might turn on you."

His mad eyes narrowed, and he leveled his stick at her. A series of incandescent fireballs burst from its tip, sizzling through the air directly at her.

She held up her hand again, and the smoldering chunks of fire bounced off into the woods. Garion glanced at one and saw that it was actually burning, setting the damp needles on the forest floor to smoking. He put his heels to his horse's flanks, even as Durnik also spurred forward, brandishing his cudgel.

"Stay out of it, you two!" Belgarath barked. "Pol can take care of herself."

"But, Grandfather," Garion protested, "that was real fire."

"Just do as I say, Garion. You'll throw her off balance if you go blundering in there now."

"Why are you being so difficult," Polgara asked the madman who stood glaring at her. "All we're doing is traveling through these woods."

"The woods are mine!" he shrieked. "Mine! Mine! Mine!" Again he danced his insane caper of fury and shook both his fists at her.

"Now you're being ridiculous," she told him.

The hermit leaped backward with a startled exclamation as the ground directly in front of his feet erupted with a seething green fire and a boiling cloud of bright purple smoke.

"Did you like the colors?" she inquired. "I like a little variety now and then, don't you?"

"Pol," Belgarath said in exasperation, "will you stop playing?"

"This isn't play, father," she replied firmly. "It's education."

A tree some yards behind the hermit suddenly bent forward, enfolding him in its stout limbs and then straightening back up again, lifting him struggling into the air.

"Have you had enough of this yet?" she asked, looking up at the startled man, who was trying desperately to free himself from the branches wrapped about his waist. "Decide quickly, my friend. You're a long way from the ground, and I'm losing interest in keeping you up there."

With a curse, the hermit wrenched himself free and tumbled heavily to the loam beneath the tree.

"Did you hurt yourself?" she inquired solicitously.

Snarling, he cast a wave of absolute blackness at her.

Still sitting her horse with unruffled calm, she began to glow with an intensely blue light that pushed the blackness away.

Again the look of mad cunning came into his eyes. Garion felt a disjointed surge. Jerkily, one portion of his body at a time, the deranged hermit began to expand, growing larger and larger. His face was wholly insane now, and he lashed out with one huge fist, shattering a nearby tree. He bent, picked up a long branch, and broke it in two. He discarded the shorter end and advanced upon Polgara, swinging his great club.

"Pol!" Belgarath shouted in sudden alarm. "Be careful of him!"

"I can manage, father," she replied. Then she faced the ten-foot-tall madman. "I think this has gone quite far enough," she told him. "I hope you know how to run." She made a peculiar gesture.

The wolf that appeared between them was impossibly large—half again as big as a horse—and its snarl was thunderous.

"I do not fear your apparitions, woman," the towering hermit roared. "I am God, and I fear nothing."

The wolf bit him, its teeth sinking into his shoulder. He screamed and jerked back, dropping his cloth. "Get away!" he shouted at the snarling wolf.

The beast crouched, its fangs bared.

"Get away!" the hermit screamed again. He flopped his hands in the air, and Garion again felt that disorganized surge as the insane man tried with all his might to make the wolf vanish.

"I recommend immediate flight," Polgara suggested. "That wolf hasn't been fed for a thousand years and it's dreadfully hungry."

The hermit's nerve broke at that point. He spun and ran desperately back into the woods, his pale, skinny legs flashing and his hair and beard streaming behind him. The wolf gave chase at a leisurely lope, snapping at his heels and growling horribly.

"Have a pleasant day," Polgara called after him.

CHAPTER TWENTY-FIVE

Polgara's expression was unreadable as she looked after the fleeing hermit. At last she sighed. "Poor fellow," she murmured.

"Will the wolf catch him?" Ce'Nedra asked in a small voice.

"The wolf? Oh no, dear. The wolf was only an illusion."

"But it bit him. I saw the blood."

"Just a small refinement, Ce'Nedra."

"Then why did you say 'poor fellow'?"

"Because he's completely mad. His mind is filled with all kinds of shadows."

"That happens sometimes, Polgara," Belgarath told her. "Let's move along. I want to get deeper into these woods before the sun goes down."

Garion pulled his horse in beside Belgarath's as they rode on into the forest. "Do you think he might have been a Grolim at one time?" he asked.

"What makes you say that?"

"Well—I sort of thought—" Garion struggled to put it into words. "What I mean is, there are two groups of sorcerers in the world—the Grolims and us. He wasn't one of us, was he?"

"What a peculiar notion," Belgarath said. "The talent is latent in everybody. It can show up any place—and does. It takes different directions in different cultures, but it's all related—magic, witchcraft, sorcery, wizardry, and even the peculiar gift of the seers. It all comes from the same place, and it's all basically the same thing. It just shows up in different ways, that's all."

"I didn't know that."

"Then you've learned something today. No day in which you learn something is a complete loss."

The autumn sun was very bright, though it was low on the northern horizon. Winter was almost upon them. Once again Garion was reminded that they were in a strange part of the world where the seasons were reversed. Back at Faldor's farm it was nearly summer now. The fields had been ploughed and the crops planted, and the days were long and warm. Here at the bottom of the world, however, it was quite the opposite. With a start, he realized that, except for that brief time in the desert of Araga, he had entirely missed summer this year. For some reason, he found that thought profoundly depressing.

They had been climbing steadily for the past hour or more as they moved up into the low range of hills that formed the spine of the island. The land became more broken, with wooded gullies and ravines wrinkling the floor of the forest.

"I hate mountain country," Sadi complained, looking at a cliff that suddenly reared up out of the trees. "Broken terrain is always so inconvenient."

"It's going to be just as troublesome for the Malloreans," Silk pointed out.

"That's true, I suppose," Sadi admitted, "but I'm afraid I still don't like hills and valleys. They seem so unnatural for some reason. Give me a nice flat swamp anytime."

"Let me check that ravine just ahead," Durnik said. "It's getting on toward sunset, and we're going to need a safe place to spend the night." He cantered his horse to a narrow notch, splashed across the turbulent brook that issued from its mouth, and disappeared upstream.

"How far do you think we've come today?" Velvet asked.

"Six or eight leagues," Belgarath replied. "We should be deep enough into the forest to avoid being noticed—unless the Malloreans intend to take this search of theirs seriously."

"Or unless that seeress we met accidentally happens to mention the fact that we're here," she added.

"Why are you so suspicious about those people?" Ce'Nedra asked her.

"I'm not entirely sure," the blond girl replied, "but I get an uneasy feeling everytime one of them sends us off in some direction or other. If they're supposed to be so neutral, why are they going out of their way to help us?"

"It's her Academy training, Ce'Nedra," Silk said. "Scepticism is one of the major branches of study there."

"Do *you* trust her, Kheldar?" Velvet asked pointedly.

"Of course not—but then I graduated from the Academy, too."

Durnik came back out of the ravine with a satisfied look on his face. "It's a good place," he announced. "It's secure, sheltered, and well out of sight."

"Let's have a look," Belgarath said.

They followed the smith up the ravine, with the brook gurgling and splashing beside them. After a few hundred yards, the ravine angled sharply to the left; farther along, it twisted back to the right again and opened out into a wooded basin. The brook they had been following upstream spilled out over the edge of a steep limestone cliff above the basin to fall as a misty spray into a pond at the upper end of the little canyon.

"Very nice, Durnik," Polgara congratulated her husband. "And that pond really didn't have anything at all to do with your choice, did it?"

"Well—" he said.

She laughed a rich, warm laugh, leaned across, and kissed him lightly. "It's all right, Durnik," she said, "but first we'll need shelter. *Then* you can see if the pond is occupied."

"Oh, it is, Pol," he assured her. "I saw one jumping." He hesitated. "I mean—well, I just happened to notice it in passing, is all."

"Of course, dear."

He lowered his head slightly, much like an abashed schoolboy, but Garion could see the faint flicker of a smile playing about the smith's lips. It was almost with a shock that he realized that his plain, honest friend was far more devious than he sometimes appeared. Since Polgara enjoyed catching him in these little subterfuges so much, Durnik often arranged things so that she *could* catch him—just for the sake of the pleasure it gave her.

They set the tents back under the trees, not too far from the edge of the pond. As usual, the chore of gathering firewood fell to Garion and Eriond while Durnik and Toth put up the tents. Also, as usual, Silk and Belgarath disappeared until all the work was completed. Sadi sat chatting with Velvet and Ce'Nedra, and his contralto voice seemed somehow as feminine as theirs.

As Polgara began to busy herself with supper, Durnik looked critically around at the campsite. "I guess that's about it," he said.

"Yes, dear," Polgara agreed.

"Do you need anything else?"

"No, dear."

"Well, I suppose—" He glanced toward the pond.

"Go ahead, Durnik," she told him. "Just be sure to come back when supper's ready."

"Are you coming, Toth?" Durnik asked his friend.

As evening darkened their concealed basin, and the stars

came out in the velvety sky overhead, they gathered about the fire and ate a supper consisting of lightly grilled lamb, steamed vegetables, and dark bread, all drawn from the supplies Vard had pressed upon them before they had left the village near the beach.

"A meal fit for a king, Lady Polgara," Sadi said expansively, leaning back.

"Yes," Garion murmured.

Sadi laughed. "I keep forgetting," he said. "You're such an unassuming fellow, Belgarion. If you asserted yourself a bit, people might take more note of your royalty."

"I couldn't agree more, Sadi," Ce'Nedra said.

"I'm not sure that's such a good idea at the moment," Garion told them. "Just now, I don't really *want* that kind of recognition."

Silk rose from the place where he had been sitting.

"Where are you going, Kheldar?" Velvet asked him.

"I'm going to have a look around," he replied. "I'll give you a full report when I come back, so that you can make note of it in the document you're preparing for Javelin."

"You're not taking this situation well at all, Prince Kheldar."

"I just don't like being spied on."

"Try to look at it as a friendly concern for your welfare. It's not really spying, if you consider it in that light, is it?"

"It amounts to the same thing, Liselle."

"Of course, but it doesn't *seem* quite so unpleasant that way, now does it?"

"Very clever."

"I thought so myself. Try not to get lost out there."

He went off into the darkness muttering to himself.

"How long do you think the soldiers will keep searching, Grandfather?" Garion asked.

The old man scratched absently at his bearded chin. "It's hard to say," he replied. "Malloreans don't have the same kind of brainless tenacity that Murgos do; but if the orders came from someone with enough authority, they probably won't give up until they've at least gone through the motions of making a thorough search."

"Several days, then?"

"At least."

"And all the time Zandramas is getting farther and farther ahead of us with my son."

"I'm afraid that can't be helped."

"Don't you think the slavers' robes would deceive them, Belgarath?" Sadi asked.

"I don't believe I want to take the chance. Murgos have seen Nyissan slavers moving around down here for so many years that they don't give them a second glance. Malloreans are probably more alert—besides, we don't know exactly what they're looking for. For all we know, they could be specifically looking for a group of slavers."

Silk quietly came back to the fire. "We've got company," he said. "I saw several campfires out there." He gestured off to the northeast.

"How close?" Garion asked quickly.

"Probably several leagues or so. I was up on top of that ridge, and you can see for quite a distance. The fires are pretty well spread out."

"Malloreans?" Durnik asked him.

"Probably. I'd say that they're making a sweep through the woods."

"Well, father?" Polgara asked.

"I don't think we can make any decisions until daylight," the old man replied. "If they're just making a cursory pass, we can probably sit tight. If they're serious about it, we might have to think of something else. We'd all better get some sleep. Tomorrow might be hectic."

Silk was up the next morning before daylight. As the rest of them rose to gather about the fire in the growing light of the dawn, he came back down the ridge. "They're coming," he announced, "and they're combing the woods inch by inch. I think we can be fairly sure that some of them will come up this ravine."

Belgarath stood up. "One of you put that fire out," he said. "We don't want the smoke to lead them right to us."

As Durnik quickly shoveled dirt over their cook fire, Toth stood up and peered off across the basin. Then he tapped Belgarath on the shoulder and pointed.

"What did he say, Durnik?" the old man asked.

The smith and his huge friend exchanged a series of somewhat obscure gestures.

"He says that there's a bramble thicket on the other side of the pond," Durnik interpreted. "He thinks that if we go around to the back side where the cliff comes down behind it, we might be able to find a good place to hide."

"Go look," Belgarath said shortly, "while the rest of us brush out any traces to show we've been here."

It took about a quarter of an hour to break down their tents and to obliterate any footprints that might alert the soldiers to the fact that someone had spent the night in this secluded place. As Silk was giving the campsite a critical last scrutiny, Durnik and Toth returned. "It's adequate," the smith reported. "There's an open place in the center of the thicket. We won't leave any tracks, if we're careful getting in there with the horses."

"What about from up there?" Garion asked him, pointing at the top of the cliff.

"We can cover the open place over with brambles," Durnik replied. "It shouldn't take too long." He looked at Silk. "How much time do you think we have? How close are the soldiers?"

"Probably about an hour away."

"That's more than enough time."

"All right," Belgarath said, "let's do it. I'd rather hide than run, anyway."

It was necessary to push the brambles aside to lead the horses into the center of the thicket. As Garion and Silk carefully rearranged them to conceal the game trail that had given them access to the hiding place, Durnik and Toth cut enough of the long, thorny tendrils to roof over the opening in the center. In the very midst of the task, Toth stopped suddenly, and his eyes grew distant, as if he were listening to something. His expression became oddly reluctant, and then he sighed.

"What's the matter, Toth?" Durnik asked him.

The giant shrugged and went back to his work.

"Grandfather," Garion said, "if there are Grolims with the soldiers, won't they look for us with their minds?"

"It's not very likely that any Grolims would be along, Garion," Silk told him. "This is a fairly small expedition, and the church and the army don't get along very well in Mallorea."

"They're coming, Father," Polgara told him.

"How far are they?"

"A mile or so."

"Let's work our way out to the edge of the thicket," Silk suggested to Garion. "I'd sort of like to keep an eye on things." He dropped to the ground and began to worm his way among the roots of the prickly brambles.

After a few yards, Garion began to mutter a few choice curses. No matter which way he twisted, the sharp thorns managed to find any number of sensitive spots.

"I don't want to interrupt your devotions," Silk whispered, "but it might be a good time for a fair amount of silence."

"Can you see anything?" Garion whispered back.

"Not yet, but you can hear them crashing around at the mouth of the ravine. Stealth is not a Mallorean's strong point."

Faintly from far down the ravine, Garion could hear several men talking. The sound, distorted by echoes bouncing off the twisting rock walls, came in odd bursts. Then there was a clatter of hooves on the rocks beside the tumbling brook as the Malloreans began their search of the narrow course.

There were a dozen or so soldiers in the party. They wore the usual red tunics and they rode their horses stiffly, like men who were not at all comfortable in the saddle.

"Did anybody ever say why we're looking for these people?" one of them asked, sounding a bit surly about it.

"You've been in the army long enough to know better than that, Brek," one of his companions replied. "They never tell you why. When an officer tells you to jump, you don't ask why. You just say, 'How far?'"

"Officers." Brek spat. "They get all the best of everything and they never do any work. Someday the ordinary soldiers like you and me are going to get sick of it, and then all those fine generals and captains had better look out."

"You're talking mutiny, Brek," his companion said, looking around nervously. "If the captain hears you, he'll have you crucified on the spot."

Brek scowled darkly. "Well, they'd better look out, that's all," he muttered. "A man can take being pushed around for just so long."

The red-clad soldiers rode directly through the campsite Garion and his friends had carefully obliterated and rode along the edge of the pond.

"Sergeant," Brek said in his complaining voice to the heavy man in the lead, "isn't it about time to stop and rest?"

"Brek," the sergeant replied, "sometime not too far off, I'd like to get through a day without hearing you whine about everything that happens."

"You don't have any reason to talk to me like that," Brek objected. "I follow my orders, don't I?"

"But you complain, Brek. I'm so sick of hearing you snivel about everything that happens that, about the next time you open your mouth, I'm going to bash in your teeth."

"I'm going to tell the captain what you just said," Brek threatened. "You heard what he told you about hitting us."

"How do you plan to make him understand you, Brek?" the sergeant asked ominously. "A man mumbles when he doesn't have any teeth, you know. Now, water your horse and keep your mouth shut."

Then a stern-faced man with iron-gray hair astride a raw-boned horse came cantering up the ravine and into the basin. "Any signs?" he demanded curtly.

The sergeant saluted. "Nothing at all, Captain," he reported.

The officer glanced around. "Did you look into that

thicket?" he asked, pointing toward the place where Garion and the others were concealed.

"We were just about to, sir," the sergeant replied. "There aren't any tracks, though."

"Tracks can be brushed out. Have your men go look."

"Right away, Captain."

As the soldiers rode up to the thicket, the officer dismounted and led his horse to the pond to drink.

"Did the general say anything about why he wants these people captured, sir?" the sergeant asked, also dismounting.

"Nothing that concerns you, Sergeant."

The soldiers were riding around the thicket, making some show of peering through the brambles.

"Tell them to get off their horses, Sergeant," the captain said disgustedly. "I want that thicket thoroughly searched. That white-haired man back at the village said that the ones we're looking for would be in this part of the forest."

Garion muffled a sudden gasp. "Vard!" he whispered to Silk. "He told them exactly where to find us."

"So it would seem," Silk breathed back grimly. "Let's get back a little farther into the thicket. Those soldiers are likely to get a bit more serious about this now."

"The thicket's all thorn bushes, Captain," Brek shouted back his report. "We can't get in there at all."

"Use your spears," the captain ordered. "Poke around and see if you can flush anybody out."

The Mallorean troopers untied their spears from their saddles and began to stab them into the thicket.

"Keep down," Silk whispered.

Garion pressed himself closer to the ground, wincing as he found a fair number of thorns with his thighs.

"It's solid brambles, Captain," Brek shouted after several moments of probing. "Nobody could possibly be in there—not with horses."

"All right," the officer told him. "Mount up and come on back down here. We'll try the next ravine."

Garion carefully let out the breath he had been holding. "That was close," he breathed to Silk.

"Too close," Silk replied. "I think I'll have a talk with Vard about this."

"Why would he betray us like that?"

"That's one of the things we're going to talk about when I see him."

As the soldiers reached the pond, the captain swung back up into his saddle. "All right, Sergeant," he said, "form up your men, and let's move on."

Then, directly in front of him, there was a peculiar shimmering in the air, and Cyradis, robed and cowled, appeared.

The officer's startled horse reared, and the man kept his saddle only with difficulty. "Torak's teeth!" he swore. "Where did you come from?"

"That is of no moment," she replied. "I have come to aid thee in thy search."

"Look out, Captain!" Brek called warningly. "That's one of those Dalasian witches. She'll put a curse on you if you're not careful."

"Shut up, Brek," the sergeant snapped.

"Explain yourself, woman," the captain said imperiously. "Just what did you mean by that last remark?"

Cyradis turned until she was facing the bramble thicket. She raised her hand and pointed. "The ones you seek are concealed there," she said.

From somewhere behind him Garion heard Ce'Nedra gasp.

"We just searched there," Brek objected. "There's nobody in that thicket."

"Thy sight is faulty then," she told him.

The captain's face had grown cold. "You're wasting my time," he told her. "I watched my men make the search with my own eyes." He gave her a narrow glance. "What is a Seeress from Kell doing here in Cthol Murgos?" he demanded. "You people are neither wanted nor welcome here. Go home and fill your mind with the shadows of brain-sickly imagining. I have no time for the babblings of adolescent witches."

"Then I must prove to thee that my words are true," she replied. She lifted her face and stood quite still.

From somewhere behind where Garion and Silk lay concealed there came a crashing sound, and a moment later the huge Toth, responding to the silent summons of his mistress, burst out of the bramble thicket, carrying the struggling Ce'Nedra in his arms.

The captain stared at him.

"That's one of them, Captain!" Brek exclaimed. "That's the big one you told us to look for—and the red-haired wench!"

"It is as I told thee," Cyradis said. "Seek the others in the same place." Then she vanished.

"Take those two!" the sergeant commanded, and several of his men jumped down from their saddles and surrounded Toth and the still-struggling Ce'Nedra with drawn weapons.

"What are we going to do?" Garion whispered to Silk. "They've got Ce'Nedra."

"I can see that."

"Let's go, then." Garion reached for his sword.

"Use your head," the little man snapped. "You'll only put her in more danger if you go running down there."

"Garion—Silk," Belgarath's whispered voice came to them, "what's happening?"

Garion twisted around to look back over his shoulder and saw his grandfather peering through the brambles. "They've got Toth and Ce'Nedra," he reported softly. "It was Cyradis, Grandfather. She told them exactly where we are."

Belgarath's face went stony, and Garion could see his lips shaping a number of curses.

The Mallorean captain rode up to the thicket with the sergeant and the rest of his men closely behind him. "I think that the rest of you had better come out of there," he ordered crisply. "I have your two friends already and I know that you're in there."

No one answered.

"Oh, come now," he said, "be reasonable. If you don't come out, I'll just send for more soldiers and have them cut down the thicket with their swords. No one's been hurt yet, and I give you my word that none of you will be harmed in any way, if you come out now. I'll even let you keep your weapons—as a gesture of good faith."

Garion heard a brief whispered consultation back in the center of the thicket.

"All right, Captain," Belgarath called in a disgusted tone of voice. "Keep your men under control. We're coming out. Garion, you and Silk, too."

"Why did he do that?" Garion asked. "We could have stayed hidden and then worked out a way to get them all free again."

"The Malloreans know how many of us there are," Silk replied. "That captain's got the upper hand for the moment. Let's go." He started to worm his way out of the thicket.

Garion swore and then followed him.

The others emerged from the back of the thicket and began to walk toward the Mallorean officer. Durnik, however, pushed past them, his face livid with anger. He strode quickly down the slope to confront Toth. "Is this your idea of friendship?" he demanded. "Is this the way you repay all our kindness?"

Toth's face grew melancholy, but he made no gesture of reply or explanation.

"I was wrong about you, Toth," the smith continued in a dreadfully quiet voice. "You were never a friend. Your mistress just put you in a position where the two of you could betray us. Well, you won't get the chance again." He started to raise his hand, and Garion could feel the surge as he gathered in his will.

"Durnik!" Polgara cried. "No!"

"He betrayed us, Pol. I'm not going to let him get away with that."

The two of them stared at each other for a long moment,

their eyes locked. In that moment, something passed between them, and Durnik finally lowered his gaze. He turned back to the mute. "You and I are through, Toth. I'll never trust you again. I don't even want to see your face any more. Give me the princess. I don't want you touching her."

Wordlessly Toth held out Ce'Nedra's tiny form. Durnik took her and then deliberately turned his back on the huge mute.

"All right, Captain," Belgarath said, "what now?"

"My orders are to escort you all safely to Rak Verkat, Ancient Belgarath. The military governor there awaits your arrival. It will, of course, be necessary for me to separate certain of your companions from you—just as a precaution. Your power, and that of Lady Polgara, is well known. The well-being of your friends will depend upon your restraint. I'm sure you understand."

"Of course," Belgarath replied drily.

"And do the plans of your military governor involve dungeons and the like?" Silk asked him.

"You do his Excellency an injustice, Prince Kheldar," the captain told him. "He has been instructed to treat you all with the utmost respect."

"You seem remarkably well informed as to our identities, Captain," Polgara observed.

"The one who ordered you detained was most specific, my Lady," he answered with a curt, military bow.

"And just who might that have been?"

"Can there be any doubt in your mind, Lady Polgara? The orders come directly from his Imperial Majesty, Kal Zakath. He has been aware of the presence of your party in Cthol Murgos for some time now." He turned to his men. "Form up around the prisoners," he ordered sharply. Then he turned back to Polgara. "Forgive me, my Lady," he apologized. "I meant guests, of course. The military vocabulary is sometimes blunt. A ship awaits you at Rak Verkat. Immediately upon your arrival there, you will set sail. His Imperial Majesty awaits your arrival at Rak Hagga with the keenest anticipation."

Here ends Book II of *The Malloreon*.
Book III, *Demon Lord of Karanda*,
will reveal what the Emperor Zakath intends for the company
and lead us further into the dark designs of Zandramas
and the strange ways of demons.

About the Author

David Eddings was born in Spokane, Washington, in 1931 and was raised in the Puget Sound area north of Seattle. He received a Bachelor of Arts degree from Reed College in Portland, Oregon, in 1954 and a Master of Arts degree from the University of Washington in 1961. He has served in the United States Army, worked as a buyer for the Boeing Company, has been a grocery clerk, and has taught English. He has lived in many parts of the United States.

His first novel, *High Hunt* (published by Putnam in 1973), was a contemporary adventure story. The field of fantasy has always been of interest to him, however, and he turned to *The Belgariad* in an effort to develop certain technical and philosophical ideas concerning that genre.

Eddings currently resides with his wife, Leigh, in the southwest.